The Umite Imperative

By Jim Melanson

The Umite Imperative

© 2016 by James Melanson

Available from CreateSpace

ISBN: 978-0-9949203-3-1

More titles available at:

www.jimmelanson.ca

Editorial service provided by Dorathy Gass

www.metwritingservices.com

Cover photograph licensed from iStockPhoto.com.

Alien head glyph created by Jonathan Hunt

www.huntillustration.com

Disclaimer

This story is a work of fiction. Names, characters, businesses, places, events, and incidents are either the products of the author's imagination or used in a fictitious manner. Any resemblance to actual persons, living or dead, or actual events, is purely coincidental.

To my American readers, please remember that as I am a Canadian author, this book is written in the Queen's English. We tend to not only say, "Eh?" a lot, we also liberally apply the vowel "u" in the oddest of places. For example: colour, neighbour, etc.

As well, we tend to use the letter 'e' in a lot of places you are used to seeing the letter 'a'. For example: grey vs. gray.

Acknowledgement

First and foremost, I want to thank God for giving me the ability to write these stories.

While my mother, father, grandmother, and uncles have all passed on — all my stories are partly possible because of them. As a child, I spent many hours sitting in our country kitchen on the small island where I grew up, listening to the endless retelling of tales: some simple, some complex, some tall, and all very entertaining. I think that the experience of the tradition of oral storytelling is what gives me the drive to spin-a-yarn or two of my own. Those were comfortable times and from a period in my life when I felt safe, loved, and that the world was good.

Cobus Scheepers is not only a character in this book, he is a real person. Cobus was my first "fan". His encouragement and enjoyment of my writing drove home the reason I do this: to entertain. As a thank you for his support in this journey, I asked him if he would like to be a character in the book and he jumped at the chance. With a video interview and some email exchanges, I got a feel for who he is and I think I've brought him to life in a way that you will enjoy. Cobus is also a beta reader for this novel, and his feedback has helped me make the story better. Thank you my friend!

Preface

In my first trilogy *(On Mars: The Mike Lane Stories)*, I introduced the Umites through the Men in Black characters. They were terrifying and aloof; whenever they showed up, people got scared and usually died.

I've always been intrigued by the whole trope of Men in Black, men in black cars, black helicopters, etc., as they relate to UFO phenomena.

When I wrote *Vengeance Daughter* (book three of the trilogy), I explored them a bit more by introducing the character of Kalabot, as the Umite Manager. By the time I finished writing that book, I had already started asking myself questions about "who" the men in black actually were, why they were on Earth, and what their back story was. That was the breeding ground in my mind for *The Umite Imperative*.

I purposely made the Shovitic characters, the MIB, very complex emotionally. As to the character of Kalabot, who you will shortly read about, I have to quote Winston Churchill: Kalabot is, "a riddle, wrapped in a mystery, inside an enigma."

Near the beginning of the ancient Sanskrit poem Mahabharata, the character Vyasa says, "If you listen carefully, at the end you'll be someone else."

I hope that you can find something in this story of acceptance and respect to take away with you.

I also hope you simply enjoy reading this story as much as I enjoyed writing it.

Now go, read!

Jim Melanson
Cobourg, Ontario
July 2016

Part I
The Imperites

The Oath of the Imperite

I, Sepherin, late of the House of Tekin, do take this oath by life for me, and mine, and theirs. Never will I turn from the face of the great enemy of Umitia. Without succour, or quarter, they and theirs will perish by my hand. This pledge I give to save the lives that they might take. I pledge my life to follow the rule and the orders of the Imperite Guards who bring me closer to the completion of the Imperative, for theirs is the way to freedom from the great enemy. May the clans of Umitia, my House, my household, my blood-kin, and my love-kin, be honoured by my sacrifice. Go where I may, for this honour I take nothing in return.

Chapter 1

Sepherin pressed herself into her mother's embrace. Part of her declared resolutely she must never let go, but she knew that would come. She heard her mother's sob, though it was barely audible in the din of the clan's great hall. With a sob of her own, hidden from ears by the folds of her mother's ornate robe, Sepherin resolved that she would not cry on the day of her own funeral.

She felt her mother's head move against hers; she felt her mother's breath tickle her earlobes. "Be brave, child. You know you must die so you can live, and honour our House. Everyone here loves you."

Sepherin nodded her understanding. She spoke quietly while her tight voice fought back the sobs that would lead to tears, "I don't want to go, mother. I don't want to leave you and father and ... who's going to make briska cookies for me?"

Alabast Tekinson pulled her head back and looked at her daughter with a smile, "I taught you to make those when you were five seasons old. I'm sure the planet you are going to will have the things you need. But ... if I could come with you I'd make them every day, my dearest one."

The younger woman's tears won. They burned hot and heavy as she placed her head against her mother's bosom, now caring little if she was seen.

Sepherin's grandfather approached and embraced them both with his long arms. He kissed his favourite granddaughter on the forehead, and then kissed his beloved daughter-in-law on the cheek. He smiled down at both of them as he pulled a small white cloth from his pocket, handing it to Sepherin to dry her eyes.

"It is time." His quiet voice pierced Sepherin's heart, as it did her mother's. It was time for Sepherin to die, and then take the Oath of the Imperite.

Since her selection, Sepherin knew this day was coming. But after a full season of combat and flight training, she still wasn't ready. The tears burned behind her eyes again as her grandfather slowly moved to the front of the hall. Her breath hitched, fighting against the heavy weight on her chest.

Danik and Piotr stepped up beside her. One of her brothers whispered in her ear. Sepherin smiled, then she laughed, and then the tears stopped. She smiled at her youngest sibling and kissed him on the cheek. Sepherin wiped away the last of her tears while their mother took her place. Piotr pulled up the hood on Sepherin's beautiful robe, and then turned to face the front of the room.

Her brothers both nodded to their grandfather.

"Sepherin Tekindottir, *ka ah buset, Aba-u-wala.*" The Head of the House, her grandfather, Themedit Tekinson, called the young woman forward in the traditional way by summoning the blessed one. She was sitting near the back of the room, wearing a heavy brocade robe and an intricately hand-stitched hood over her head. At his call, Sepherin lifted her arms so her brothers could take her hands as she stood. She was perfectly capable of rising and walking on her own, even under the heavy brocade, but this was how the traditional ceremony began, and tradition is important. She was the first of seventeen selected from her House for this season, but she was the only Tekin to be going on the next transport.

The assembled House of Tekin parted like a biblical sea. All those present in the great hall were family members of the woman who was just twenty seasons old. Her brothers slowly led her forward to the First Priest. Passing through the assembly of almost a hundred and fifty people, she inhaled the competing scents of incense and dried flowers, breathing deeply to keep the tears at bay. Every few steps she would hear a bell tinkle, and then the hand of an older woman reached under the heavy hood and dabbed at Sepherin's cheeks with a hankie. While today was indeed a blessed day for the woman, and for her family, it simply wouldn't do for her to emerge from under the hood with tears on her cheeks. What these elder women of her family did for her, they did as the last act of love they would perform for one about to die.

Nearing the podium where the First-Priest waited, a family friend from the Ashvelyn cast of clerics, Sepherin's brothers stopped moving forward when the last bell tinkled. With her eyes cast downward, peering out from under the deep hood which hid her face, she could see the feet of her mother standing in front of her on the flagstone floor of the family hall.

Alabast Tekinson reached forward and slowly pushed the hood off Sepherin's head. The woman smiled at her youngest daughter, holding her child's face in her hands. She leaned in close and whispered the blessing for success, using the old tongue words of the ancient cleric Deygun of Sandalit. It never failed, Sepherin always felt a tingle of excitement at hearing the old tongue. History and linguistics had been her passion until she had been selected to complete the Imperative. She knew it was coming, she had just known she would be selected. But all Falwasz Umites are encouraged to pursue their interests until they *are* selected, because not all are.

With her mother's blessing completed, the woman that had raised Sepherin selflessly then smiled, winked, and kissed her on the nose. Sepherin wasn't the first of her twenty-three children selected for the Imperative, and she wouldn't be the last. Alabast reached inside the neckline of her robes and removed a thin, but wide, necklace from around her neck. She reached up and placed the jewelry on her daughter, securing the clasp behind her neck, making sure it didn't get caught in her long, light brown hair. It was the one she had worn since Sepherin was born. The small herringbone links of platinum, hematite, and palladium glinted and gleamed in the light of the massive candle chandeliers. Alabast knew Sepherin had an eye on the piece of jewelry since she was a toddler, coveting it in ways which were as much funny as obvious.

The necklace was a heartfelt gift on one of the last days she would ever see her daughter; one of the last days any of them would ever see Sepherin.

As her mother drew her hand away, a tear formed in the corner of Sepherin's eye. The older woman smiled again and kissed her daughter once more on each cheek. "Be strong." Alabast dabbed the tear away and took her daughter's hand. Alabast took three more steps forward with Sepherin at her side. The mother held her head high, her eyes filled with the fire of pride for her daughter, and the sadness of a child being taken away for eternity.

Stopping in front of the First Priest, both women bowed and then waited. The hunched old cleric took a small green, earthenware pot and held it reverently in his hands. He began chanting an old liturgy as he paced around the two women, first in one direction, and then in the other. The cleric stopped in front of Sepherin at the end of his recitation. The much younger Second-Priest approached and removed the lid from the pot. The First Priest then, ever-so-lightly, touched the pad of his finger to the blend of the expensive powder perfume. With only a few grains of the Samadhi on the pad of his finger, he reached out and drew the potent aromatic across Sepherin's left cheek. He then repeated the process on her right cheek.

Sepherin inhaled deeply. Her mother had a small jar of this powder perfume on her bureau and would, every once in a while, allow Sepherin to wear it. It was the girl's singular pleasure of things that were "girly" which she allowed herself, preferring to live her life as the tomboy her father had raised.

Her mother held her hand, squeezing it reassuringly, as Sepherin knelt down on a red and gold velour pillow. Grandfather Tekinson turned and strode to the carved wooden door at the side of the hall. He lifted his fist and banged on the door, slowly, three times.

The door opened to reveal a man standing there in a black robe and a black hood. Grandfather Tekinson took the man by the elbow and led him in front of Sepherin, who continued to kneel with her head bowed, having let go of her mother.

"Sepherin Tekindottir, I command you to answer me," the black-robed man's deep voice echoed off the stone walls.

"I will answer."

"Do you surrender your life, willingly?"

"This I do willingly."

"Do you accept the fate of the Imperite, willingly?"

"This I do willingly."

"Recite the Oath of the Imperite."

Sepherin did, having memorized it for this day. It was the second time she had to recite it for others.

"Sepherin Tekindottir, do you accept your destiny?"

"I accept my destiny."

"Daughter of the House of Tekin," Michalz's voice boomed, "child of the Falwasz clan, today you die."

The man dressed in black, her father, reached into the folds of his robe and withdrew an old, exquisite, jewelled dagger. Raising it high above his head, holding it with both hands, he slowly lowered the dagger until the point of it gently touched the crown of Sepherin's head.

At that moment she screamed, long and loud, and then she stopped. A heartbeat later, all those assembled, except for the priests, screamed as she had.

Allowing a moment of silence to settle the room, Sepherin spoke again, "I have died. I am dead. I am among you no more."

Alabast moved behind the man and removed his hood, and then his outer robe. Michalz Tekinson stood there wearing a colourful robe identical to the one Sepherin wore, the same robe worn by all those who had gone before her, for over five hundred seasons. Every House in the Falwasz clan had their own tradition for sending off the Imperites, those committed to completing the Imperative. This death ceremony was part of the Tekin tradition.

"Sepherin Tekindottir, look at your father," his deep voice boomed in the large wood and stone chamber.

Sepherin looked up at the man who had taught her so much and asked so little. She smiled at him, and he couldn't help but smile back. Her chest swelled with love as she fought against the hot burn of yet more tears. She wanted to throw her arms around him, never letting go, never leaving her world.

She had no idea that her father had begged and pleaded *the* Manager to choose another, to leave his little Sephy alone. The decision had been fairly made, and not honouring that choice was simply not something any Umite would even consider ... at least not out loud. The Manager refused to intercede.

Michalz leaned down and kissed both of his daughter's cheeks, then after a pause, the tip of her nose. He stepped to one side of his daughter and Sepherin raised her arms and placed her hands in her parents' hands.

Michalz and Alabast then spoke loudly at the same time, "Sepherin Tekindottir is dead. Arise, Sepherin Tekin, Imperite of the House of Tekin. May every step you take, lead you to success."

Sepherin stood. The three of them turned to face the assembled House.

"I, Sepherin Tekin, honour this House with my sacrifice. May my fulfillment of the Imperative atone for that which our ancestors have wrought."

The crowd responded as one, "We thank you, Sepherin Tekin."

The band struck its opening chords, and the party began.

Chapter 2

Alex Lehmann banged his fist on the steering wheel. It had taken him four days to drive this far from British Columbia. The salesman was almost home, almost back to his wife's arms and his warm, familiar, bed. *Why the hell does it have to stall now, I'm so close. It's just so ... unfair.*

Turning on his cell phone, the low battery icon appeared and winked at him, mocking him, and then the phone powered down on its own. Alex got out of the car and considered popping the hood, but he knew that was pointless. Filling the windshield washer fluid and checking the oil, those were the extent of his car smarts. He didn't even know why he bothered looking. *What? There'll be flashing neon sign that says: Look here, idiot?*

He glanced both ways on the long stretch of road. There were no headlights in either direction. All he had was the starlight to see the country road. Alex looked up at the waning moon, which was almost new, and provided little in the way of illumination.

Alex sighed. *It'll only take me an hour.* He zipped up his jacket, locked the car, thrust his hands deep in his pockets, and started walking. It took him a while to realize he should have changed into his runners, as his dress shoes were starting to hurt. He stopped and looked behind him, looking through the puffs of his breath in the chill night air. He was far enough away from the car that he couldn't see it. Alex shook his head and kept walking towards home, ignoring the discomfort.

He only took a few steps when he stopped again. He noticed that whatever night-time country sounds he had been hearing, had disappeared.

He felt a tingling at the base of his spine.

The Imperite looked up and then smiled.

There was a flash of blue light.

Chapter 3

The Imperite Guards, those of the clan Shovitic from the planet Umitia, could be found in the oddest of places across the three known inhabited galaxies. As was their way, they always tried to attire themselves in a style that would allow them to blend in to the local culture.

These two Umites from the clan Shovitic, who were members of the Imperite Guards, mimicked the appearance of the Pikayan Humanesh before them. They wore long black robes, with black cowls over their head, and darkened glasses over their eyes sockets. They stood before Grand Sceptre Horvuth and listened to his drivel with equanimity, listening as patiently as they could. They were having a variation of the same conversation that they had been having with him for years. Where the two Umites had long grown weary of it, the Grand Sceptre seemed to thrive on it.

Were he a simple Pikayan trader, they would have dealt with him and been on their way hours ago. However, dealing with the ruler of a world, even one as wrapped in archaic religious clap-trap as this one, meant a different level of interaction. As the leader of that planet's largest population, they couldn't simply whisper a few veiled threats to him. They were here merely as supplicants, as penitents to his ego.

"Again, Grand Sceptre," Yinil interrupted the pseudo-cleric, speaking with his sibilant drawl, "I will tell you that these raids must cease. The Trem have no deep space faring capability. You are unevenly matched, and you risk destroying their society as it is. There are more suitable traders you can war with, ones that have deep space faring ability, ones that can defend themselves fairly."

The Nordic-looking Grand Sceptre Horvuth shook his head and sauntered around the stone courtyard of his villa. Neither Yinil nor Bilirit, his partner, had ever gotten used to the double-jointed knees of this particular race of Humanesh. The way they walked gave Yinil the creeps. That's saying something for a Shovitic, an Imperite Guard, whose mere presence could stop the heart of a weak man.

Horvuth stood almost as tall as they did. He had no fear of the Umites, no fear of the *Men in Black Robes,* as they were called. He knew they were merely the errand boys of a busy-body race. The Grand Sceptre did not believe they would dare use force with him or his people. The septuagenarian ruler was as strong and robust as the day he took his Orders, when fresh out of the Monastic Academy at Trillium Lake. Physically, there were few equal to him, even at his age. If they wanted to challenge him, he knew that he would gladly accept their challenge and show them who they were dealing with.

The only reason Grand Sceptre Horvuth entertained the fools was because if their ire was provoked, he knew they might side with the Trem from the nearby star system. Were they to do that, then things might become a bit more difficult for his planet's fleet of aggressive merchant traders, who many referred to as pirates.

He had to stand his ground and make them see why his people were a *just people* in the eyes of the Creator. The Men in Black Robes needed to be shown how it was the Creator's will that the Pikayan were the ones who were entitled; that they were the *clenched fist* of His judgement. His people had enjoyed the blessing of the Creator's graceful gift for centuries. He just had to guide these unbelievers, these unfaithful, to see the truth that maddeningly hid in front of them.

He turned to look at the shorter of the two tall men, Yinil, and wondered if perhaps they were so obstinate and unyielding because the Creator was willing Horvath to end them. He was then struck by the thought that given the abomination which lay behind their darkened glasses, perhaps they were not of the creator to begin with. Perhaps they were truly from the Fires of Torment. He had never had that thought before, but now that it was in his mind it made perfect sense. They were not here, as

16

they said, to bring peace and prosperity; they must be here on the Unholy One's own errand.

Horvuth further engaged them in words as he slowly sauntered closer to them, turning this thought over in his mind. All the while, his hand rested firmly on the hilt of the sword inside the folds of the dark brown robe. The realization of the Creator's will emboldened him, and his prayers to the Creator raced through his mind as he imagined the glory that would be his for slaying the Men in Black Robes, the ones that many have said don't exist.

His smile and his words danced around the truth he wished the two could have come to accept. Yet, a portion of his mind was relegated to imagining the arc of his swords mighty swing that would end them both with one fatal blow.

Movement in the edge of his vision caught his attention. As Yinil stopped talking, he and the two Umites looked skyward. Horvuth, the Grand Sceptre of the Humanesh planet Pikaya, stood in awe of what he saw, and then he became frightened.

They were shining metal, and they were round. They looked like two dinner plates pressed face to face. They were just big enough for four of the Imperite Guards ... and a significant amount of weaponry. The sky was filled with them, there were thousands of them descending from the vastness of space.

As he turned in a circle, standing in the mountain-top courtyard, his gaze took in a sky that was filling with them, fast. For as far as he could see, they were there. Tens of thousands of them descended from high orbit, encircling the planet, *his* planet.

When he looked back down at the Imperite Guards from Umitia, at the Men in Black Robes, he intended to demand an accounting for this action, this insult. Instead, he found a third robe-clad man before him. Slightly taller than the two who he had been verbally sparing with moments before, this new arrival had to be the one he had heard whispers about for many years.

"You ... you are ... *Kalabot*?" the Grand Sceptre asked hesitantly.

The Manager of the Umites pushed back the cowl of his black robe. His gaunt features, pale skin, and dark hair made him look like the grim reaper in mundane form. The embodiment of death came closer to the Grand Sceptre, yet his feet never moved.

He slowly reached up to his face and removed his darkened glasses. His ocular stumps stared into the Grand Sceptre's eyes. Kalabot's eyeworms stood at attention, pointing directly out at the Pikayan leader.

"I have grown weary of you."

Kalabot put his darkened glasses back on, and held a communicator to his mouth. "Destroy everything."

The Grand Sceptre inhaled in surprise as the three Men in Black Robes disappeared. Duty frigate 306, in high orbit above the planet, had TransMat them aboard after the Manager's command to the Umite fleet.

Within a night and a day, the entire planet was rendered a smouldering coal. Dozens of triunes of the Imperite Guard's patrol craft, the round metal ships, folded in different directions in pursuit of the trading fleet of the Pikaya. Within a ten-sleep, the entire Humanesh race of the planet Pikaya had been wiped from existence. Peace and order was restored to their small section of Barnard's galaxy. Unfettered commerce and healthy competition were restored to the other space faring races of that region, and the races in pursuit of space flight.

While Kalabot's guards had attempted to achieve this result with negotiation and words, it had become evident that they were not going to succeed. It was a rare case when the Manager became involved, but when he did, he rarely left anything alive in his pursuit of that goal.

Chapter 4

The Umites have a saying: *a journey of a thousand leagues begins with a single step*. In Sepherin's case, a journey of a hundred light years starts at the Imperite Guards' Spaceport. The spaceport was a model of efficiency for even the most adept of space faring races. It should be, considering this particular location had been in operation for 2,742 seasons.

The five Umites from the House of Tekin stood in the cavernous departure hall #3. Surrounded by unbelievably tall windows, Sepherin looked out into the distance, her eyes drinking in the beauty of the cobalt blue and orange sky of approaching dusk. She squeezed the large hand of the man beside her and turned to him.

Sepherin's last three days on Umitia had been a whirlwind of parties, teas, and private auciences with the elder House members. Roguk had finally told her how he felt, after a lifetime of best friend status. However, since she was about to travel 170 light years (1,608,000,000,000,000 leagues), a long-distance romance simply wasn't in their future. It was just as well. Sepherin knew Roguk's wife would have an issue with it. Instead, the two friends settled for a day and a night of passionate exploration of the landscape of each other's desires; giving into a forbidden temptation which had taunted both of them for years, knowing it would lead to — *nothing*.

Their desire was shared, but there was another reason it had never been spoken of. Roguk is of the Hobonol clan, and Sepherin is of the Falwasz clan. Umite clans simply don't mix that way. It just isn't done — and it's against the law.

She had engaged in many things in the last few days that weren't exactly *proper* for a young lady. Since she was leaving for good, though, for these last few days her parents and the elders had turned a blind eye to the "wilding" as they called it. Alabast and Michalz had made the decision in favour of not having their daughter's last memories of them darkened with resentment.

"One hundred and twenty days," Roguk shook his head, "you'll have forgotten all about me by the time you get there."

"Who are you?" She pulled his surprised face close, tilting it upwards, giving him a long, slow kiss. Her mother looked away politely while her father knelt down and busied himself rechecking the clasps on Sepherin's travel case — *again.*

The embrace ended far too soon, for both young Umites. Roguk and Sepherin both sighed. She turned and looked down at her parents, "Father?"

"Yes?" he stood from fiddling with the suitcase, satisfied it was clasped, *for the fifth time.*

Sepherin gave him a look; she glanced at Roguk and back at her father. She could see her late-middle-aged father was trying to find the right words to say. A man of his stature rarely interacted with the Hobonol; he had people for that. He also knew that he couldn't be discourteous, not with his daughter standing there, minutes before she would leave forever. Michalz looked around, to see if any of the Imperite Guards were nearby. There had been a lot of growing dissension in the clans, in some of the clans at least, towards the guards. Michalz had to be here to say goodbye to his daughter, but that didn't mean he wanted any of those damn Shovitic freaks knowing his business.

Michalz turned back to his daughter and her friend. He smiled, swallowed his pride, and looked at the labourer. "Roguk Fozretson, it would indeed give me great pleasure to have you come and bid on the contract .. "

"*Father,*" Sepherin spoke sharply.

"Dear, we talked about this," Alabast said, putting her hand on her husband's arm. Seeing the look on his face, knowing he was having difficulty with this, she did as all good wives would do. She turned to Roguk and asked on her husband's behalf, "Roguk, would you please be so kind as to consider accepting our *offer* of the contract for the new villa we are building for Sepherin's eldest sister?"

Roguk knew what was going on. He was young, but not stupid. He knew who he was, and where he came from. He also knew that his presence in Sepherin's life, as a friend, had been tolerated by her family far more graciously than any other Falwasz family would have. With a smile and a bow worthy of a proper gentleman, he responded just as formally, "Madam Tekinson, it would be with the humblest honour that I should provide this service for your House. I assure you that my men and I will craft the most handsome and durable home for Fedina Tekindottir."

"Thank you, Roguk. I am so glad that we will still have your acquaintance even though Sepherin is leaving us," she turned to her husband, yanking his arm slightly, "aren't we, *dear*."

"Yes, yes, quite; very pleased, very pleased," Michalz half-smiled and nodded his head at the labourer.

Roguk smiled and bowed once more, then turned back to Sepherin. "Well, my dearest, *dearest* friend. I'm afraid that my life will be empty with your absence, but my heart swells with the love of your sacrifice." He lifted her hand and kissed the back of it, "May we meet again across the great river of time."

She pulled his hand close and kissed it, then looked into her recent lover's eyes for the last time, "What could have been."

"What could have been," he responded with unashamed love.

Then Sepherin pulled back her fist and walloped him in the middle of his muscular chest. Roguk stumbled backwards and fell on his ass. Alabast sucked in her breath in horror; Michalz just smiled and nodded approvingly. Sepherin could hear her brother, standing nearby, pretending to examine the mural of the Battle of Redemption, snickering at poor Roguk.

"Don't you *dare* forget the girl who can kick your ass from here to the Hyperion Garden and back!"

Sepherin and Roguk laughed as she helped the man, only slightly smaller than her, to stand up. They kissed once more and then as they had agreed the previous evening, both turned away from each other as he departed. Sepherin closed her eyes for a moment as she composed herself.

She suppressed the urge to scream at the unfairness. She despised that she was being forced to go to a *stupid* planet, and fight a *stupid* enemy, for the *stupid* sins of her *stupid* ancestors; sins committed thousands of *stupid* years ago. She was leaving everything she knew, everyone she loved, her home, her friends, her pets, her ... she was leaving *everything*. And worst of all, she was doing it *willingly*, because it was *their way*, it was what she was *raised for*, it was what the Falwasz clan *did*. It had been this way for so long, no one alive could even remember stories of before. Sepherin smoothed her hair and adjusted her collar, taking a deep breath before she faced her parents for the final time. *At least Eleniak will be glad I'm gone. I hope she never finds out about last night.*

As Sepherin opened her eyes and looked at her parents, they all heard the first of three boarding chimes. She lifted her arms and wrapped them around her shorter mother; all of her family was shorter than her, and stockier as well. They embraced a long, long time; whispering mother-daughter words of love, of admiration, of appreciation. They finally pulled apart from one another, their faces filled with rivers of tears. Sepherin brought her hand to her throat and touched the necklace her mother had given her on the blessing night, the night of her ceremonial funeral.

"You're sure you don't want this back, Mother?"

Alabast took a slow deep breath as she shook her head, "No, child. Take it with you to remember me by." Alabast's heart was breaking that her youngest daughter was leaving, yet she was thankful that neither Sepherin nor Michalz ever found out he wasn't the girl's father.

The older woman reminded herself that her actions, distasteful as they had been, had saved the House of Tekin from ruin. The entire

House had been on the verge of dissolution, a fate which would have scattered the extended family to the six winds. *Thankfully the bastard has never laid claim to her.* Alabast knew he could never do so. It would mean death for the both of them. If by some chance they weren't executed, given his position, it would have driven a wedge between the clans that could start a civil war. She kissed her daughter on the cheek and pulled away again.

Now it was time for Sepherin to bid her final farewell to her father. She reached for him as the second boarding chime sounded. Michalz Tekinson, to his surprise, was already crying and blubbering before his daughter locked her arms around him. He had so many things he wanted to say to her; so many things he wanted to remind her of; so much advice he wanted to impart, yet there was so little time. He settled for what his heart was saying, "I love you, Sephy. I will miss you every moment that I'm awake and every moment that I'm asleep. Forever and a day, you will walk my thoughts, and soften my dreams."

"And so will you: my dear, sweet, handsome, grumpy, father."

They both cried, then they laughed, and then they cried some more. Sepherin waved her mother in, and the three of them remained locked in a familial embrace until the third chime sounded.

Kimla, the gaunt and austere-looking Imperite Guard, who was the Tekin family's liaison, came over and picked up Sepherin's travel case. "Well?" she asked, speaking slowly in the sibilant manner of all Shovitics. "Are we ready? Final boarding for the shuttle has been sounded."

Michalz glared at Kimla with unsuppressed hatred. He almost spat his response to her, "We are not deaf, *Guard*."

The venom in his voice was understandable. His foundry had been given a stop-production order, *again*, because his profits were more than twenty percent higher than his closest competitor. He wasn't allowed to fire the furnaces until the next reporting period, three more ten-sleeps away, yet he still had to pay his employees to stay at home and do nothing profitable for him. Michalz' foundry wasn't the only one suffering the latest rules of commerce coming from Kalabot's Office in the palace.

Sepherin nodded to Kimla. Wiping the tears from her face, she smiled and looked at her parents one final time. "I'm so afraid, I'm so hopeful, and I'm so sad, all at the same time." She paused, then she turned one hand palm upwards and spoke her final words in the traditional way, "Now as then."

"Then as now," her parents responded with down-turned palms.

As with Roguk, she had made an agreement with her parents the night before: they would turn and leave the terminal before she boarded the shuttle. Piotr, only a season younger than her, stepped into the circle to lead his parents away. Sepherin had said her goodbyes to him and her other siblings before leaving their home. Now, he just winked at her, playfully punched her in the shoulder, and then turned to usher his crying parents out of the terminal.

Sepherin turned to Kimla and straightened her suit jacket, a jacket in the style of the planet to which she had been assigned.

"I'm ready."

Kimla led her to the shuttle. They both stopped at the hatch. Many of the Falwasz did this, and the Imperite Guards had come to expect it.

Sepherin looked over her shoulder to be sure that her parents and her brother had departed the terminal. She looked at Kimla, looking at the female's sunglasses, imagining the terrifying things, which passed for eyes, that were hidden behind them.

Kimla was more sensitive than most Shovitics. That rare quality of empathy was why she was a family liaison and had never had an assignment off-world. She recognized that the next step the young Falwasz was to take was monumental for the Falwasz. As soon as the young woman took her next step forward, as soon as she set her first foot on the shuttle, her oath would be officially sealed. The Umite, from the House of Tekin, of the Falwasz clan, would officially become an Imperite. She would be oath bound to kill any and all Voiya she encountered, at the cost of her own life. It was a hereditary oath which would pass from her to her children, and to her children's children, but no further.

Sepherin took a deep breath and let it out slowly. She pulled her shoulders back and lifted her chin. She put a smile on her face and stepped forward, never to set foot on Umitia ever again.

Or so she thought.

Kimla stowed the new Imperite's travel case beside her carry-on bag, and then made sure Sepherin was properly secured in her seat. The Imperite Guard didn't bid her goodbye; she just turned and went back up the passenger ramp. It was easier for her that way. Social by nature, it was a lesson that Kimla had taken a while to learn. *Don't get attached to the Imperites, they always go away.*

Kimla went up to the top deck of the guard's departure facility. She pushed her sunglasses up her nose as she watched the shuttle finally rise silently in the air. She had to hold her brimmed hat as she tilted her head back to watch the shuttle climb into orbit around Umitia, her eyeworms closing slightly against the brightness. She watched the shuttle rapidly climb towards the interstellar transport awaiting its final passengers. After the small craft was out of sight, Kimla checked her schedule. She had seven more Imperites due for the next shuttle in two hours, bound for a different transport. She stood at the edge of the tall building and took a moment to gaze out at the wonderful gardens surrounding the entrance to the facility.

She spent a few moments watching a clansman family strolling around, the children pointing at this flower and that flower. Kimla could almost imagine the excited voices of the children, a thought that brought a smile, and then brought a frown. She pushed back

25

from the railing and headed towards the stairwell, wondering once again if she would ever be blessed by motherhood and have children of her own. She had come close to that dream. She had been engaged to a wonderful guardsman. Her intended wanted a family as much as she did. Their dream came to an end with the explosive decompression of his patrol craft during a surprise attack by a Voiya marauder. In the years since, she simply hadn't the heart to become so close to anyone else, lest she suffer the same heartache once again.

She put the sadness out of her mind. She made her way down to the guards' cafeteria. *I have time for some supper before the next departure. I wonder if they'll have any bugworm stew left, or maybe some battered grass-blade hoppers.*

Chapter 5

David MacFeet was a simple man. He didn't get far in life, and he didn't have much to brag about. But he was a hard worker, and an honest man. He'd raised two well-adjusted kids, and he'd never cheated on his wife. They lived simply, and were content with their double-wide at the trailer park in Moose Jaw. Even so, stretching one paycheque to the next one was always a struggle.

He was a human, from Earth, and had never heard of Imperites or Umitia.

David's quiet and sedate life, however, was about to become very 'interesting' — in the Chinese curse sense of the word.

On the west side of Expanse, Saskatchewan, was the largest family-run farm in the area. At this time of year, the crops had been harvested but there was still a lot to do. Having attained organic certification a few years before, the farmer was going to try his first winter cover crop of tillage radish and hairy vetch. It was late August and he had to get the ground ready for the planting, as well as get the rest of the farm ready for the wind and snow of a Prairie winter.

Burt, the farmer, had broken his ankle jumping off the back of his pickup. The injury made him take on a couple of men for a few weeks of work, to supplement what his own teenage daughter and two younger sons were doing.

David was lucky enough to get one of these jobs to supplement his income from his evening job. He got hired by virtue of the fact that he and Burt were old hunting buddies, from back when times were better, financially.

He liked to get in and start early, as Burt paid him for every hour he was there. This morning, he was on his way from Moose Jaw before the sun had started to peek over the horizon. It was just shy of 5 a.m. when he turned onto the rural road which took him to the farm. No sooner did he make the turn: his headlights cut out, the radio shut off with a burst of static, and his truck stalled. David let the truck coast to a stop, put it in park, and tried the ignition. Nothing happened. The engine didn't turn over; he couldn't even hear the starter ticking.

With the key in the power position, he should still have had lights and radio. It was like his engine and battery died at the same time.

Then he noticed a tingling at the base of his spine.

There was a flash of blue light.

The truck cab was flooded with brilliant white light. He put his hand up to cover his eyes, the brightness bringing pain. As they adjusted to the glare, he realized his truck was ... *inside somewhere?*

With no warning, his truck door was yanked open. David turned his head, and looked into the most terrifying face he could ever have imagined.

He screamed like a little girl.

As the echo of his own scream faded from his ears, David blinked a couple of times at the sunlight shining in his eyes. He heard a car door slam and whipped his head to the left, expecting to see that ... *thing* ... again. But he was looking at a farm field.

He let out a yelp of surprise as Burt stuck his head in the open window.

"David? What the hell are you doing?"

"I ... uhhh ... I ..."

"What the hell are you playing at, boy? You got something on the side? You been drinking?"

"No, Burt, I was ... I ... was ..."

"Shit, David. I thought something had happened to you. I called your place and Kelly said you left at 4:30 this morning. I drove from my place to your place twice, *twice*. And here you are, just lollygagging in the middle of the road. What the hell are you playing at?"

"No, Burt, I ... my ... my truck stalled and ..."

"Stalled? David, it's half past eight. This is my *fourth time* down this road. Where the hell have you been?"

"Burt, really, shit, I don't know what happened. The ... the engine ... then there was this light and then ..."

Burt leaned in and turned the key in the ignition. The engine started.

David had read the books, he'd seen the movies, and he realized exactly what had happened to him. He moved his hips from side to side on the bench seat of the pickup.

His arse hurt.

The grown man, in his forties, locked at his friend and burst into tears.

Chapter 6

The basket of clean laundry sat upturned on the bed. It was a spill of clean clothes leading to two neat piles, the contents half-folded and forgotten. The lights were low; the dimness would suit her coming mood just fine.

Sepherin stood in front of the full-length mirror mounted to the back of the door of the small bathroom. Only wearing her undergarments, she looked at her reflection as her right hand drew lazy circles on her belly. It had been six ten-sleeps since she last menstruated. Looking at her profile in the mirror, she could see, or imagined she could see, an ever-so-slight bulge of her abdomen.

She smiled at her reflection, feeling not her hand, but his hand; the hand that had so lovingly stroked her and caressed her. The memory of him moving inside her body excited her; remembering the feeling of him coming to his fullness within her made her moan. She remembered her own strident, aching, pleading release beneath him. They were savoured, but taboo memories which had carried her to sleep many nights since. The safety promised while lying curled in his arms had been — cruel. But it was still his hand that she could feel, tenderly stroking the sensitive area just below her navel. Laying in the sweat and warmth of their passion, she had kissed him slowly. She had reached down and taken his hand with the intention of pushing it lower.

As she looked at the reflection of her eyes, realizing his seed was growing inside of her, she remembered why she withdrew her hand, and then withdrew from his arms. The cold of the metal had come between them. She had tried to twine her fingers tightly with his, but the metal jarred her to the reality of the moment. A testament to the oath he was breaking as he lay with her, the metal band wrapped around his finger in a complete circle, a circle that he could never wrap completely around her.

After withdrawing her hand, she had sat on the edge of the bed and hid her face from him. She tried to leave, but he put his arm around her and pulled her back against his body, holding her tightly as the tears burned against her eyes. She wanted to flee. She wanted to flee the knowledge of what they had done. She wanted to flee the aching, empty promise of his arms. But they were strong arms, they were warm arms, and most of all, they were *his* arms.

Lost in her fears of the future, lost in her regrets of her sin, lost in her shame, lost in the confusion of her desire to throw herself into his embrace again, she turned to face him.

"Tell me you love me, Roguk."

"I do, Sepherin, with all that I am and all of my heart, I love you like I have loved ..." it was just the barest hesitation, so brief you wouldn't have noticed it if you weren't listening for it, "... no other."

She had leaned into him then, resting against him, surrendering to the warmth of what she knew was wrong. She resisted the fear that her longing for him was not truly shared; the fear that their one night together was merely an opportunity for him. Yet, still, her chest ached with the sadness she felt, knowing that she would never be held by him again. She didn't know if he had spoken a lie, a truth, or a half-truth. She had realized in that starlit room that she didn't really care. They had the one night together that she had desired for so long.

She left him in the darkness, long after the moon had passed high overhead. She had resolved to cherish the memory, but to put her shame behind her, lest the man she could never truly have, destroy her from so far across the galaxy.

Now she stood in front of the mirror, while her fond memory grew cold in her heart. As she looked at the barest hint of a bulge in her tummy, she knew that Roguk Fozretson was indeed reaching across the vastness of space. It wasn't his loving caress she felt, it was a slap across the face, dealt in the fleeting images of her mind by Eleniak Fozretson. Sepherin looked in the mirror and saw her own weakness, she saw her own selfishness, and she saw her sin.

She turned away from the mirror and put her clothes back on. *At least I have the Earth classes to keep me occupied, for now.* The twice-a-day classes were teaching her everything she needed to know about living on an alien world, so she could fit in without standing out. She tried to recall the morning's lessons on the mechanics of personal finances on the planet she was heading to. But the pictorials from the lessons kept being occluded by images of him, of Roguk; of his smile, his eyes, of his naked body. Her mind kept returning to the passionate moments which now betrayed her, like the sweet promise of a junkie's fix.

Resuming her laundry folding, she felt more isolated standing in her small room than she had ever felt. Her mother would never be there again for her to turn to; her father would never be there to make her clouds turn into blue skies; her brothers would never sneak into her room at night to scare her; her friends would never smile when she came into a room; and the man she loved had given her a gift which keeps on taking.

As difficult as she knew her life was going to be, he had made it worse.

She had made it worse.

They had made it worse.

He had whispered in her ear, "For just one night, one night before you leave ..."

Yes, resolve setting firmly in place, *it's because of him.*

In nine more ten-sleeps she would be on an alien world, living an alien life, with a baby in her belly. She never thought that there would ever come a day in her life, when she would hate Roguk.

That day had arrived.

Chapter 7

Tommy Lehmann drained his coffee mug and set it on the upturned wooden box beside him. He pulled up the hood of his bunnyhug, seeking more warmth from the damp July night air. He continued to gaze upwards at the dancing greens in the distant northern sky, odd for this time of year. The front porch of his small two-storey house faced that way, so he was perfectly situated to sit comfortably in the old wicker chair as he watched the show.

He sighed deeply and was reaching for the deck of butts in his sweater's front pocket, stretched tightly over his moderately big belly, when his Android chimed. He pulled it out of his pocket, and opened his email. It was a message from his Earth-uncle, Jay.

The first line of the email related that there was still no word of Alex; it had been three months. The second line of the email said: 'New flare; X-13, 0236 UTC, 2463.'

Wow, that's big.

He smiled. That just *has* to be another Imperite. He looked up at the Aurora Borealis and whispered a prayer for forgiveness and quick passing, for whoever it was. It also meant there would be another show of the Aurora Borealis in a few more days, once the solar flare's charged particles reached Earth. As he stared at the dancing curtains of green light in the sky, Tommy hoped Alex had disappeared because he had completed his Imperative. Until Tommy heard otherwise, he was going to hold on to that hope as a belief.

Tommy knew tonight's auroral show was most likely, due to its intensity, another unknown member of the Falwasz clan. He watched the beauty of the lights in the sky and wondered for the umpteen millionth time if he would ever be lucky enough to complete the Imperative. Alex left behind a wife and two kids, but Tommy had nobody. Nobody close at least, not as close as a spouse and child. He sighed with the silent forlornness that accompanied the thought a kindred man completing his life's goal at such a cost when he, Tommy, had no one to miss him.

At fifty years old, on the lesser side of average, Tommy had no plan or desire to have either a child or a wife again. He had been married, a union which ended sourly when the Umite Guards relocated him.

That was seven years ago.

The memories of Karyn and the memory of the torment which accompanied her departure from his life were still there, just below the surface. Times like this tickled them, and woke them up, making them growl unpleasantly around his heart. The only part of their separation and eventual divorce that he was grateful for was that he had never shared with her who he truly was, and the fact he wasn't from Earth, technically.

He pulled his phone out again and logged into this bank account. He transferred $3,000 to his Earth-uncle with the message, "For Alex's wife."

Chapter 8

Cassie Scott leaned against the window of her apartment above the Rexall drug store. She had turned out the lights so she could see the Northern Lights without the glare of the lamp on the window pane.

Thump.

"*Aarrggghh ... Fuck.* Why are the lights out?" Ritchie was hopping on one foot, pressing the toes of his other foot on his calf, and swinging his arms in the air to keep his balance

"Come here, look at this," she beckoned him over to the window.

"I think I broke my little toe."

"Wuss."

Ritchie hobbled up behind Carrie, pressing against her, wrapping his arms around her waist. "What am I looking at?" he asked the woman he hoped to marry, while brushing away a tear from the pain of stubbing his little toe on the end table.

"Up there," she pointed to the distant northern sky, her finger pressing against the window, just above the smudged fog from her breath on the cooler glass.

After a moment's pause, Ritchie whispered, "Wow, they're really bright tonight. I haven't seen them this clearly since I was a kid."

"Mmmm, so beautiful. I wonder why you can see them sometimes, but most other nights you can't."

"Dunno, something to do with solar flares I think; particles from the sun exciting the magneto-something-or-other, or something like that."

Cassie smiled and pressed back slightly against her boyfriend of two years. "It feels like something's excited," she moaned seductively.

"Well, you know, this close to a ... heavenly body and all," he nibbled her earlobe.

The short-haired, petite black woman turned in his arms and reached up to his broad shoulders. She kissed him lightly on the lips as her hips pressed forward against his, beckoning his manly attention.

"How's the toe?" she almost moaned.

"What toe?" he murmured.

She pressed her body closer, yielding to the gentle caress of strong hands, and his throbbing desire.

Chapter 9

"Sepherin?"

"Sepherin?"

The instructor clapped his hands together, *"Sepherin."*

She came out of her daze with a start, looking around to see her classmates smiling at her.

"I'm sorry, I was ..." *thinking about my baby.*

"Earth class, Sepherin, colloquialisms, you're going to the northern part of their world, yes?"

"Yes?"

"And?"

She looked around again. Agravita was giving her a look.

"I'm sorry, Savag, what was the question?"

Savag Kolom, Earth instructor from the Treanda clan, sighed impatiently, "What's a bunnyhug?"

Sepherin paused, feeling lost, feeling singled out. She had the crawling sensation on her skin like everyone was about to laugh at her. "Umm, something you ... do with a ... favourite pet?"

They laughed.

Savag rolled his eyes and looked at Agravita, "You're going to the northern lands as well, Agravita, do you know?"

"It's a sweater with a hood and no zipper."

"Very good. I think we've had enough today. I guess we'll end the class before I lose any more of you to daydreams." He looked pointedly at Sepherin.

Instead of looking away, she stared back at him defiantly. The embarrassment didn't wither her, it enraged her; it was a response she didn't expect, something that wouldn't have

39

happened a few ten-sleeps ago. Sepherin crossed her arms, daring him to say something else with the look on her face.

As the students started to leave, Savag asked Sepherin to stay behind. Agravita turned in the doorway, looking from him to her, then waved at Sepherin and headed down the corridor.

Savag took a seat opposite her. He smiled pleasantly as he folded his hands in his lap. "Sepherin, I've noticed a change in you lately. You're a bit distracted, and you've been short with me a few times."

She inhaled and let the air out slowly, forcing herself to unfold her arms, forcing herself to relax. She folded her hands in her lap, mimicking his posture. "If I've been an impertinent Imperite, then I apologize."

Savag smiled weakly, "It's not the impertinence that concerns me, Sepherin. I'm concerned by how sudden this change has come on. Is there something wrong?"

She crossed her legs and folded her arms again. She stared at him, wondering what kind of back-birth idiot he was. "Do you mean what's wrong as in: you're leaving your entire life behind?"

"I see. What I mean ..."

"Do you mean," she carried on, talking over him, "what's wrong as in you'll *never see* your parents again?"

He was nodding, opening his mouth to speak.

"Do you mean, what's wrong as in you're leaving *everyone you love behind*?" her voice was rising. He just looked at her.

"Do you mean, *what's wrong in leaving the only man you've loved behind? A man that you don't know whether he was lying or not*?"

Savag just nodded. This was good. She was opening up.

"Do you mean, what's wrong in leaving your *entire support network,* all the people who *care about you*, the only people you can *rely on*, the only people you can *count on*, the ... the only ...

40

the only people you can turn to? You're leaving them behind? Is *that* what you mean?"

"Sepherin," he held out his hands, "please, I understand. You aren't the first Imperite to go through this. The farther we get away from home the more ..."

Sepherin stood so fast the chair tipped over behind her.

"I want to go home."

Savag stood as well, a worried lock on his face, "Sepherin, you've taken the Oath. You can't go home; you know you can't."

She put her hands on her hips, glaring at him, unsure how much to say.

"Look, Sepherin, this ... these jitters, this homesickness, many go through it. But it will pass, once you're on your new planet you'll ..."

"I'm pregnant."

Savag stopped talking. He looked even more worried now. He looked at the open door to the classroom, then went over and closed it.

"Who else knows?"

"Agravita and Bilka."

Savag paced around the side of the room, running his hand through his hair, then through his beard. After a moment, he turned to Sepherin and asked, "Do you want to get rid of it? They can do that in medical."

The look of shock on her face said more than any words could have.

Savag nodded, "I had to ask."

Sepherin felt a worm of worry creeping up her spine as resolve settled into her jaw. "They won't make me get rid of it? Will they?" She said the words as if they were a challenge.

"Goodness, no! Certainly not. You aren't the first one this has happened to. You certainly won't be the last."

With her arms folded, she restated her desire, "I want to go *home*."

Savag set his own expression to one of resolve, "That is simply not possible, Sepherin."

"When this ship drops off the last Imperite at Beta Hydri, it returns to Umitia. I can just stay onboard. You're dropping off seven people on Earth. What's one less? There's already, what, close to twelve thousand Umites on the planet?"

"It's not a matter of *how many* are there, it's a matter of you having taken *an oath*. You cannot break that Oath; they cannot allow you to break the Oath. If even one Imperite breaks the Oath, *just one*, then — they simply cannot allow it; they *will not* allow it."

"What if I ..."

Savag held up his hands to stop her. He had heard enough and was getting angry, "Young lady. You took an oath. It's as simple as that. Thousands and thousands of Falwasz have gone before you, and yes, some of them were pregnant when they went. None of them were returned. Yes, it's scary, *I get that.* You're going to a new world, but you *will* have a family there to help you. You aren't being thrown into a *sarlacc pit*, you aren't being cast off like refuse. There will be help for you ..."

He stopped as he saw the tears forming in Sepherin's eyes. He could tell they were tears of anger, but they were still tears, and he was a man.

She finally finished her question, her jaw clenched tight, "What if I go to the ship's Commander and *insist*?"

Savag had come to the end of his patience, "Look, Sepherin, stop being a snotty little *shit* and grow up. You're an adult. You're an Imperite. You have a job to do, a job you've *sworn* to do. If you don't do it — then you're no better than an unemployed Hobonol. So stop you're whining and *smarten up*."

"I'm going to the Commander," she tried to brush past him.

Savag reached out and grabbed her arm, yanking her backwards, close to him, "If you go to the Commander whining that you want to go home, he'll have you killed and he'll toss your body out an airlock — or he'll just toss you out the airlock."

Sepherin looked up at Savag; rage, frustration, and fear all competing for first place in her face. She tried to pull away from him, but he didn't let go, he pulled her back to him, putting his mouth close to her ear.

"And if he doesn't, *I will*."

She broke free from his grasp and fled, holding her sobs at bay, running along the corridor and down two decks to get back to her quarters. She burst in through the door, startling Agravita who was waiting for her. Sepherin's face was soaked with tears. She took in a ragged breath and then fell to her knees, the sobs now free to come loud and hard. She was almost doubled over as the cries of forlorn hopelessness expressed her fears of helplessness. The feeling of being lost to the currents of events shoving her along paths she didn't want to travel anymore came back on her, stronger than they ever had before.

Agravita knelt down and held her trembling friend.

Chapter 10

Tommy raked the wet green grass into small mounds. He hated mowing the lawn. He kept promising to get himself one of those self-mulching mowers, but he hated the idea of spending the money when he could just rake the damn stuff himself, even though he hated it.

He finished the last pile, looked around at the front yard dotted with small pyramids of fresh clippings, then trudged to his garage. With the rake slung over his shoulder, he picked up a bundle of paper yard waste bags. He turned to find Mitch stepping around the corner with two bottles of beer in his hand.

"Howdy, neighbour."

"Mitch, fine morning, eh?"

"Sure is," he handed one of the bottles to Tommy, smiling at the man.

"Little early, *wha*?"

"Hair of the dog, me son. Hair of the dog."

The two men clinked bottles and tipped up.

"You need some help with that?" Mitch asked, drawing his shirt sleeve across his lips.

"Wouldn't mind you holding the bags open for me a titch," Tommy looked at the bundle of bags in one hand, and the beer in the other. He tossed the bags on the floor and leaned back against the workbench. "Grass can wait."

They both had another long pull on their bottles.

"So, Martha wants me to invite you to dinner tonight," Mitch said while giving Tommy a knowing look.

"Oh, good thunderin' heavens. Who's it this time?"

Mitch smiled, "Her cousin, Wendy. She's coming for the weekend and Martha has decided you two are perfect for each other."

"Oh? And why is that? What makes us so perfect for each other?" Tommy tolerated Martha's matchmaking simply because she and Mitch invited him over for dinner so frequently. Since Karyn had left him, or more accurately, he had moved away from Karyn, he rarely cooked full meals for himself. The first night in his house when he moved here, Martha had brought him a casserole and some soup. She'd been tempting him gastronomically at least twice a week since then. He'd become fast friends with Martha and Mitch in a short amount of time.

"Well, I think this time ... *well* ... you're a man, and Wendy's a woman, and ... *hmm* ... you're both breathing. I really do think this *is* her last-ditch effort to find you a woman."

"Maybe it's her last-ditch effort to find Wendy a man."

They both chuckled. Tommy had known Wendy for almost as long as he had known Martha. Even if he were of the marrying mindset; the sweater-wearing, cross-stitching, cat-loving, CBC-listening, old battle-axe cousin of Mitch's wife wouldn't even be on his radar. He'd already had to fight off her squirrely-eye advances once this lifetime; surely he could handle it once more, if the temptation was right.

"So, I know this is bad form and all, before saying yes, but what's for dinner?"

"Pot roast with roasted potatoes, carrots, and mushy peas." Mitch waggled his eyebrows. He knew that meal was Tommy's weakness, and so did Martha.

"Damn — the ol' girl means business."

"Yep."

Tommy sighed, "Once more into the breach, my friend." They clinked bottles one more time, and then drained them.

Mitch set his empty on the workbench. "Grass won't put itself in the bag, old man. Let's give'r," he said to the man twenty years his junior.

Mitch picked up the bundle of paper bags, and the two friends headed out to the lawn. They stopped short as a black sedan pulled into Tommy's driveway.

"Ahh, *fuck*. Give me a minute," Tommy said quietly, handing the lawn rake to Mitch.

He moved towards the car as the two men in black suits and black fedoras, with perfectly trimmed crew-cut hair, very square jaws, and wearing Ray-Ban sunglasses got out of the car.

"Taffi, Minino," Tommy quietly acknowledged them.

Taffi tilted his head to the side to look at the man behind the Earth-born Imperite, and then looked back into Tommy's eyes. "*Toe-may*, you are free to talk?" he asked with the slow, sibilant speech of the Shovitic clan. Tommy marveled once again at how their drawl sounded like it had both a Cajun and an Afrikaans accent at the same time.

Tommy turned, nodded at Mitch and waved his hand towards the lawn. Mitch looked down at the ground and headed towards the nearest pile of clippings.

"I haven't seen you guys for quite a while. To what do I owe the pleasure?" he asked, not concealing the snide tone.

Taffi was casting an appraising eye around the house and the property. He spoke slowly as well, "You look like you have a comfortable life here."

"Does the job."

"You still have — employment?" Taffi had to pause a moment to think of the word. Tommy just nodded in response.

"Your house, it is big enough for two?"

The question gave Tommy a jolt. He paused only a moment before responding, "Could be. Why you asking?"

"A host family — died. We need a new host for a new arrival," Taffi said slowly.

The only thing Tommy wanted less than a wife was some newbie alien disturbing his peace and calm, even if the alien was the same race as him. But, his spare room was ready to go. All they would have to do was unpack, not that the noob's ever brought much with them.

Tommy sighed, "Are you asking me or telling me?"

"Ask," Minino smiled. "Always, we ask. But ..." he let his words hang there a moment.

"But what?"

"But," Minino smiled, and Tommy immediately wished he hadn't, "the Manager would consider this ... a personal favour."

Tommy's faced showed he was confused, "The Manager wants me to do this? *The* Manager?"

Minino shook his head, "Yes, Tommy. *The* Manager."

Tommy's blood almost froze in his veins at the mention of *the* Manager. Kalabot was in charge of all the Umites, wherever they were, from all seven clans. Tommy knew the scary bastard had been in power for ninety-three seasons, and there was no hint he had any plans to retire. He had never met him, or seen him; but the stories were well known. The Earth-born looked around and saw Mitch was on the third pile of clippings, not paying them any attention.

Looking back around at the two Umites, Tommy pursed his lips and nodded his head once. "Fine, if *he* wants me to do it, I can't really say no, can I? When's the noob arriving?"

"Three more ten-sleeps," Taffi said.

"Fine, you'll bring them here or ..."

Taffi was slowly shaking his head, "Logistics prevent us from meeting this one. We will send you coordinates, and the time."

There was a lengthy pause. Tommy had a thought forming, a scary thought. Umites were careful not to draw too much attention to themselves. The incidence of Umites involved in accidents off the homeworld was low.

Tommy looked Taffi squarely in the eye. "When, exactly, did the host family have their — *accident.*"

Taffi looked squarely back in Tommy's eyes, "This morning."

Tommy looked at his watch. It was barely half-nine. "This morning? And you're here already?"

"We were close by," Taffi responded after another pause.

"Yes," Minino was nodding, "it was a terrible accident. Just, terrible. The whole family."

"Yes," Taffi added without nodding, "a tragedy. Just terrible."

Tommy had heard of the true-born bigotry towards Earth-born Umites. There weren't a lot of Earth-born, like Tommy, but there were enough. The family of a new Imperite would have right of refusal on a host family before their child is sent on their way. He knew it was highly unlikely any Falwasz clan family would have approved him as a host. However, once the Imperite was on the way, if something necessitated a logistical change, the Manager had full authority to make that change. *The* Manager could do anything he bloody well wanted, and no one would dare even *think* boo, let alone say it. Looking at the two Imperite Guards, in their Earth attire, Tommy knew the host family had died in an unfortunate accident, but not accidentally. For whatever reason, Kalabot wanted this Imperite with Tommy. He just hoped there was a damn good reason to share his house with another man, noob or not.

"Fine. You'll get me the info the usual way? Will you be coming back?"

The two Imperite Guards just turned away from the hereditary Imperite, got back in their car, and drove away.

Tommy watched them until they were out of site. *Arrogant bastards*, he said in his head as he spit on the gravel driveway. He went over to Mitch, took the lawn rake, and started stuffing another pile of cuttings into the tall paper bag Mitch was holding open.

"Those guys trouble?"

Tommy shook his head and paused. He looked up at Mitch, squinting in the morning sun, "Jehovah's Witnesses."

Mitch gave a deep, throaty chuckle, "Sure, Tommy. Sure."

Mitch was ex-RCAF. He knew Fed's when he saw them. Whatever the hell his neighbour was involved in, he couldn't care less. Tommy had pulled Mitch's wife, unconscious, from their house the night it caught fire. Mitch had been in the next town at his brother's place, and Tommy was coming home from work late. The neighbours across the way told Mitch how Tommy leapt out of his truck and ran into the burning house, not even hesitating for a second. As far as Mitch was concerned, Tommy could be an alien from another planet, and he wouldn't give a single figgity-fuck.

Minino turned left on the highway, heading to a place where their car could be discretely TransMat onboard the duty frigate in orbit. They drove in silence for a few minutes.

"This whole thing smells, odd," Minino finally said.

Taffi nodded, "Yes, very odd."

"We killed an Imperite, a true-born."

"And her Earther husband," Taffi added.

They drove in silence a little more. Both of them had been sickened at the thought of retiring the children. They had almost refused the order, but they knew it came directly from the Manager. Neither one of them wanted to wake up with that scary bastard standing beside their beds.

The Shovitic clan considered children of all the clans to be the most precious part of the protective service they were devoted to providing. A Shovitic family revolved around the needs and care of their children. The thought of harming a child was a horror, killing the two children was an act that would have haunted and tormented both of the Imperite Guards for the rest of their lives.

This was why they killed the adults and made it look like an accident. But they didn't kill the children. They had dropped off the two toddlers at the front door of a police station, and then fled before they could be apprehended. Well, before anyone could *try* to apprehend them. That had been an act that Kalabot would never know about. The secret that they had defied that part the Manager's direct order was something both Shovitics would take to their graves.

"Why is Kalabot so involved with a new Imperite?" Taffi spoke rhetorically, "This is what I'm asking myself."

Minino slowed the car and gave a wide birth to a duck and her ducklings finishing their meander across the two-lane highway. "I think we will never know what his interest is."

"True, true." After a moment, Taffi continued in his slurring drawl, "I think I will talk to my brother, and inform him of what we were told to do, and about the Imperite being put with an Earth-born."

Minino glanced at his partner for a moment, and then turned his eyes back to the road. He said nothing. Something was afoot with the Tekin Imperite, and he was as curious as he was confused.

Chapter 11

On Monday after work, Tommy had to drop Cassie off at home. Her car wouldn't start that morning, so Tommy was her ride for the day. Tommy and Cassie got along well. They always traded pleasantries and smiles. Tommy always helped Cassie carry the heavier boxes from the stock room, and Cassie brought Tommy a container of *tourtière* whenever she had the time to make it. Cassie was the first black woman Tommy had ever gotten to know, and truth be told, he found her more than a little bit pleasing to the eye. *If only she wasn't so young*, he would lament to himself.

He pulled his pickup truck to the side of the road, opposite Cassie's place. She leaned over and gave him a thank you kiss on the cheek before bouncing out of the truck. As Tommy waited for her to cross the road, he glanced upwards and saw her boyfriend, Ritchie, glaring at him from the apartment window.

If looks were daggers …

Tommy smiled and waved up at him, ignoring the young man's jealous gaze.

Cassie waved and yelled thanks again. Tommy tooted his horn twice and drove off.

Ritchie, seething, turned away from the window.

Chapter 12

Tommy spent the next few hot summer weeks focussing on work and tracking UFO reports on the web rather than dwelling on the thought of his impending houseguest. The UFO activity was higher than it had been since the flap of four years ago. He was surprised he hadn't seen anything odd in his night-time sky watching, given the amount of activity. Of course, not all the sources he checked were publicly available, so maybe the Voiya were being a bit more circumspect.

Tommy had been moved to Kincardine, in Ontario, due to the prevalence of Voiya activity in the area over the previous decade. For a reason that the Umite brain trust had not been able to figure out, the Voiya were extremely interested in people who lived near nuclear power stations. Kincardine was only a few minutes south of The Bruce, the largest power-producing nuclear plant in the world. In fact, there were at least three others of the Falwasz clan within about fifteen minutes of where Tommy lived; three that he knew about. There had been four in the area until his Earth-cousin, Alex, had disappeared a few months ago.

Three weeks after Minino and Taffi's visit, Tommy decided to focus on more practical matters. He made a trip to the health food store in Sarnia. It's run by a couple of throw-back-hippy-Wiccan women who stocked the oddest selection of things, and who loved to assault Tommy with their latest Korean tea blends and a couple of hours of incessant chatter. A quiet man by nature, people just gravitated to him ... the oddest people. Weird as the women were, he enjoyed talking to them, and the tea wasn't bad.

Before he left Jenn & Siobhan's store, he picked up three tins of plain roasted crickets, plus one tin of the new sea salt and vinegar-flavoured crickets. The evening after the two Imperite Guards visited him; before dinner with Mitch, Martha, and Wendy; Tommy had gone online and ordered a 5 lb bag of freeze-dried mealworms. He saw they had flavoured ones as well; so, he bought a bag of cheese-flavoured dried mealworms, for variety. He made sure they would arrive in less than four weeks so the new arrival would, at least, have a taste of something reminiscent of home. Tommy's mother, her Earth-name had been Jackie, had tried many times to get him interested in the crackly-crunchy crickets. He had flatly refused to even try them after he saw her catching them and roasting them herself. The dried mealworms he loved, especially when they were used in his own concoction of tomato, mushroom, okra, and mealworm stew. Add a little filet powder, or a dark brown roux, and it was almost as good as gumbo.

Four days before the noob was due to arrive, Tommy made sure the guest room was shipshape. He changed the linens on the bed, and he also bought some new towels. Finally, he dusted, vacuumed, and cleaned the window.

Aside from those preparations, he'd have to go shopping the day before the houseguest arrived. He would have to lay in lots of fresh and frozen veggies for the Imperite, because no true-born was able to eat red meat, chicken, or pork. Earth-born seemed to have no problem with those foods. None of the Umite doctors, from the Silthit clan, had a clue why that was. Tommy figured if the houseguest complained about him eating his morning *eggs and backey*, he could go to hell.

Twenty-six days after Taffi and Minino had visited him, they showed up again, just before Tommy was going to turn in for the evening. They only stayed a few minutes. They just needed to tell Tommy where and when to pick up the arriving Imperite. They provided no other details, other than the arrival would be wearing a three-metal necklace. He asked them for more information, but they apologized and said they were told no more about the Imperite.

Tommy didn't invite Taffi and Minino in for coffee or offer any other hospitality, as he would have with any other visitor. The sooner they were gone, the happier he would be. Tommy didn't have any problem with the Falwasz aliens, his own clan. He didn't care if they were true-born or Earth-born. Like the rest of the Umites, he detested the Shovitic clan who were the Imperite Guards and the rulers.

The two Guards finally got in their black sedan and drove away. Tommy went in the house and went to bed. None of them saw Mitch on his front porch. He sat in his Adirondack chair, with the outside light turned off, gently drawing on the dying embers of his pipe as he watched them.

Chapter 13

Cassie opened one eye to see the faint twilight of the late August morning creeping into her bedroom. Ritchie gummed his dry lips in his sleep and then continued his open-mouth breathing. She sighed. She loved Ritchie, but wished he'd learn to sleep with his mouth closed. She reached down and rubbed her tummy. She felt a little off, thanks to the spicy hot Thai food she had tried last night, no doubt. The queasiness soon passed after she quietly eked out a dainty little fart under the covers. She tried to go back to sleep, but her mind was rapidly filling with checklists.

Her mother had volunteered her, as she had done many times, to organize her church's BBQ booth at the Highland Games. Today, Saturday, was the day of the games. People would be coming from as far as Toronto, Niagara Falls, Buffalo, Sarnia, and Detroit for the day's events. It was her church's single biggest fundraiser of the year, even bigger than the White Elephant Sale she had been volunteered to organize on the Saturday before Mother's Day.

Cassie sat on the edge of the bed and yawned so hard she thought she heard her jaw crack. Holding her chin, she gently worked her mandible to see if there was any lasting pain. She'd had suffered TMJ disorder when she was a kid and didn't want to go through that again. She felt Ritchie's hand brush against her bare buttocks.

"Mmmm, come back here."

She swatted his hand and stood up. She knew if she gave in it would be another hour before she got up, if she didn't fall asleep after the early morning workout he was hinting at.

"Nope, sorry, love. I gotta get crack-a-lackin'. You want French toast?"

"Mmmm, French toast."

"Good, me too. Don't burn mine." Then she headed for the shower to the sounds of his groans at having been so adeptly suckered into breakfast duty.

By the time she emerged, the apartment was full of the smell of bacon and coffee. She could hear the sizzle of the dipped bread in the frying pan. Ritchie was a far better cook than she was, and she was perfectly comfortable with that truth.

Dressed, powdered, and with her short coarse hair brushed straight, she arrived at the kitchen table just as Ritchie took the last of the breakfast fare off the stove. As she devoured the French toast, made with a hint of nutmeg and apple, and as she plowed through six pieces of maple-smoked bacon, Cassie prattled on ceaselessly about the day ahead. By the time she'd downed her second cup of coffee and all the food in front of her, Ritchie knew more about running today's BBQ booth than anyone but Cassie.

While one portion of his brain listened to his beloved go on annoyingly about all the things she had to do, the majority of his brain was rehearsing what he was going to say tonight when the fireworks lit up the sky. He smiled to himself, proud of his ability to have kept the secret so long, proud of the fact he had hidden the diamond ring so well, and grateful she hadn't stumbled across it. Living together for the last year, he knew it was high time to make an honest woman of her.

Cassie still had a slight limp when she went to the living room. She had twisted her ankle the day before, coming up the steep stairs without turning on the light. She came back to the table with her cell phone. She asked Ritchie to pour her a third cup of coffee as she made a call.

"Good morning, Tommy ... I didn't wake you, did I? ... Good. I'm sorry for calling so early ..." she laughed, "... well, it was on my mind ... no, no, were still on, there isn't a cloud in the sky ... yes, it's all here ... no, not that, Maggie's bringing all the meats. I've got the four BBQs and tables here ... yes, all that stuff too ... half an hour? Awesome. Thank you *so* much for helping, Tommy. There's no way I'd have gotten any of this in my hatchback ... yeah, sure. See you then."

"Tommy, he the fat white guy?" Ritchie asked when she hung up.

"They're all white guys at the hardware store, and he's stocky, not fat. He's also one of the quietest and nicest men I know, besides you." She winked at him.

"He's not stocky, he's fat." Ritchie mimicked her.

She gave her boyfriend a withering look.

"He's not working today either?"

She sighed, "The only places open today are the tourist traps on Queen Street; even Gilley's is closed."

"My ... girlfriend," he almost said wife, "the hardware store girl."

She got up and kissed him, "Have a shower, will you? You smell like bacon and sex. I'm going to pull the stuff out of the shed. Tommy will be here in a bit, and I'd like you to help us load his pickup truck."

"Mmmm, sex." He reached out, pulled her into his lap and squeezed her ass.

She giggled and swatted at him, then kissed him slowly, deeply. Before his hand could move to a more captivating area, she jumped off his lap and picked up her cell phone, limping to the door. "You - shower - right this minute ... or you'll suffer the Hawaiian disease tonight."

"What? The Hawaiian disease? What the hell's that?" he asked, both perplexed and disappointed she had so easily evaded his hands.

She looked back at him through the kitchen door, coyly hiding part of her face behind the door-jamb. In a throaty and husky voice, she responded, "Lack-a-nookie-nookie." Then she giggled

61

and limped out of the apartment, grabbing her canvas satchel holding all her paperwork for the day.

By the time Ritchie came outside, smelling clean and looking fine, Tommy was backing his pickup truck down the narrow lane next to the building. Ritchie had only met Tommy in passing when he picked up Cassie at the hardware store she had been working at since high school. Ritchie, from Toronto, was more race-sensitive than his country-raised girlfriend. To her, everyone was just folk; to Ritchie, everyone needed to be assessed and carefully watched before being trusted, especially the white ones.

The two strong men made short work of lifting the heavy equipment onto the back of the truck. When Cassie wanted to get up on the truck to tie things down, Tommy grabbed her by the waist and lifted her onto the tailgate. She squealed and laughed, Ritchie glared at Tommy and bit his tongue. He didn't like Tommy's familiarity with her, the way the old man so easily touched another man's woman, the way the old man laid hands on his girl's waist.

Ritchie's attitude must have been broadcasting on his face. Cassie had stopped her incessant chattering and was focussing, a little too intently, on the rope in her hands.

Tommy stepped closer to Ritchie and offered, "Sorry, Ritchie. That was a little forward of me."

"Yeah, it was. Whatever." Ritchie turned and went back to the shed for the two tables Cassie hadn't had time to pull out. In a few minutes, the truck was loaded, and Tommy was on his way to the fairgrounds.

"Why did you get so jealous?" Cassie turned and asked her boyfriend after Tommy had pulled away in this truck.

"Jealous? What do you mean?"

She gave him an exasperated look, "Ritchie, you looked like you wanted to hit Tommy after he lifted me up on the tailgate."

"He grabbed your waist and lifted you up, and you giggled, and ..."

"Ritchie, I *asked him* to lift me up. Didn't you hear me *ask him* to lift me up?"

"Well ... no. I didn't. Why do you need help to get up on a tailgate? You're not that short."

She slapped him on the chest in mock dismay, "Short? You think I asked him because I'm short?"

Smartly, Ritchie said nothing.

"You know I twisted my ankle last night, asshole. It's still sore. *That's* why I asked him to lift me up."

Ritchie's face was burning and he was frustrated. He was frustrated with Cassie's fixation on the old white guy, and he was frustrated that he was so worked up over what he knew was nothing. He didn't understand why he got this way sometimes. He just did.

"So why didn't you get me to do it?" he was helpless *not* to ask.

"Because he was standing *right next to me.* You have to stop being so insecure, Ritchie."

Ritchie stuck his hands in his pockets and looked down at the ground. He *had* forgotten about her ankle, and she was right about Tommy being right next to her. He realized what an ass he'd been. "Sorry," he mumbled.

Cassie sighed with exasperation again; this wasn't the first time Ritchie's jealous side had shown itself. It had been cute at first; now it was just damn maddening. She knew she had to make the lesson stick, though; the jealous outbursts were something she was growing tired of. She'd almost broken up with him because of it — *almost.* She turned on her heel and strode off towards the front of the building without giving him a goodbye kiss. She had moved her car onto the street to make room for Tommy's truck.

She spoke loud enough for Ritchie to hear her, without turning back to look at him, "Be there in an hour, I still want your help today. But *only* if you can do it without being a miserable prick to Tommy."

Ritchie nodded, realizing as he did so that she couldn't see him. He opened his mouth to acknowledge her, but was cut off by her parting words.

"And you owe *my friend* a damn good apology."

It was almost eight-thirty by the time Ritchie got to the fairgrounds. He had gone back inside and done the dishes, then had another cup of coffee as he sat and chastised himself for pissing off Cassie. He didn't want her to have any reason to say no when he popped the question tonight. Luckily, Cassie's storms of anger passed quickly. She never held anything in, but she never held on to much either.

Sauntering across the parking lot and onto the fairgrounds, he could see that Tommy and Pastor Jacobson were finished unloading the BBQs, and now they were hammering together the booth. He strolled towards them, but stopped before getting close enough for them to see him. Tommy was trying to steady one of the uprights against his end of the small roof. Cassie was standing right beside him, with her arm around the fat bastard's waist, smiling up at him. Ritchie flexed his hands and clenched his jaw; he felt his cheeks start burning again. He wanted to walk over and hit the man, right in the face. She was his; *Cassie was his,* not that asshole's. And yet there she was, sugar and spice and everything sexy, and she had her arm wrapped tight around the old bastard.

Ritchie wondered why the hell she would do that, knowing her boyfriend was coming ... unless she *wanted* him to see? Ritchie numbed at the thought that maybe that was it, maybe she was trying to tell him something, but she was just too chicken-shit to say it. *Yeah, nice, after how good I've been to you, you want to fuck around with that old piece of shit?* Ritchie wanted to hurt him. He wanted to walk over and grab the old bastard and pound him into the ground. With so many witnesses around, though, it wouldn't be a good idea. He glared at the two of them, but mostly he glared at Cassie.

He just didn't get it. What the hell did she see in a fat old white guy? Ritchie knew himself well enough to know that at the moment he wasn't going to be civil to anybody, he didn't *want* to be civil to anybody. He just wanted to yell and scream and ... *hit*. He wanted to break something, or *someone*. Ritchie felt betrayed, but it was even worse because it was such a public betrayal. There were so many people around who saw her, saw his woman touching the other guy while she was smiling and having a good time. Ritchie turned around, his black face darkened with rage. He trudged back to the apartment, opened a beer, and sat at the kitchen table.

Pity party, table for one.

The booths at the fairground were all set up. The Church of Christ's booth had been finished for a while. Maggie, Carol, and Carol's daughter Tabitha were cutting up onions, tomatoes, and pickles. Pastor Jacobson had gone to the local Foodland where the manager was waiting to transfer the cases of pop and the coolers they had donated for the church's booth. He took Tommy's pickup truck as Tommy was down for the count.

Cassie rinsed her hands after helping with the tomatoes and went over to Tommy, who was sitting in a lawn chair by the BBQs.

"How's your back feeling?"

"Still sore, but the spasms are gone."

"At least you said something, I'm glad you didn't drop the booth on yourself."

Tommy nodded, "If you hadn't been there to grab hold of me, I might have done just that."

Jack Carter strolled over, "Hiya. You Tommy?"

Tommy squinted up at the man who had approached from sunward, "Yes?"

The small farmer stuck out his hand, "I'm Jack, Carol's husband. She called and asked me to bring down some of the good stuff for you." The man held out a pill bottle. Tommy looked at the label, 'Percocet 10 mg'.

He handed it back to the man, "Thanks, Jack, but I can't take those, I had a problem with them a few years ago." It was an easier lie than trying to explain that most Umites were severely allergic to opioids. They only used those kinds of painkillers in the most extreme circumstances, like surgery.

"How about some Advil then?" the man fished in his pocket and pulled out a small blue and silver plastic bottle.

"Ahh, yes. That would be great. Thank you." Tommy shook three out of the bottle and closed it up. He was about to pop them in his mouth, but stopped and looked around.

"Oh!" Cassie exclaimed, "Wait a minute." She went to the other side of the booth and came back quickly with a bottle of water. "Here you go."

Within a half hour, the crowds started to thicken up, and the women at the booth started flipping burgers and hot dogs. Cassie was so busy she still hadn't realized that Ritchie hadn't shown up.

Jack stuck around for a little bit, and chitchatted with Tommy. Eventually, Carol had her husband were standing at the row of BBQs helping them cook up the beef, and roast the ears of sweet corn.

Tommy decided he needed to get up and moving, if he didn't, his back might seize up and then he'd be screwed. He looked at his watch. He still had eight hours until he had to pick up the noob. As he was leaning forward in the chair to push himself up, he heard a familiar voice from his past, a voice he hadn't heard in a *long* time.

"Tommy? Tommy Lehmann? Is that you?"

Tommy looked around at the voice, "Paula?"

Cassie carried the two plates of burgers and ears of corn; she had the cans of pop stuck in the crook of her arm. She set it all down on the picnic table as the woman whom Tommy had introduced as his step-sister, helped him walk across the lawn; he was still favouring his back. Settling him onto the bench, Paula sat across from him, smiling at the young black woman as she went back to the church booth.

"Dick, and the kids?" Tommy asked, "Are they here too?"

She shook her head; the tall woman's pixie cut blond hair reflecting the sunlight as she did so. "No, Dick and I divorced six years ago. The girls are in college and David's with his dad this weekend."

"David?"

"My son, he's twelve."

"Oh, I see, I'm sorry for your troubles." Tommy had been surprised as hell to find his step-sister standing there by his chair.

67

They hadn't spoken in twenty years. They ate in silence for a few moments.

"You're not wearing your wedding ring."

He shook his head, "No, Karyn and I parted ways a few years ago when I moved here."

The silence descended again as they slowly ate and looked everywhere, but at each other. Finally, Paula spoke, "I've missed you, Tommy."

He chewed quietly for a moment, wondering what to say. Before he could say anything, Paula spoke again.

"Why did you never call me?" She set her corn cob down and put her hands between her thighs, leaning forward slightly. "I could have used my big brother when — when life got weird."

"Paula, you — you made it abundantly clear after your father died that you blamed my mom for his suicide and you blamed me as well."

"Oh, Tommy — I'm — I was hurting. I was hurting a lot. When your mom disappeared, with no trace, and no word — my dad loved her so much, I loved her so much. But then he couldn't take it. He couldn't take the not knowing; he couldn't ..."

"And my mom didn't put the rifle under his chin; I didn't put the rifle under his chin. Paula, your dad made a choice. And as much as he hurt you, he hurt me too. I missed him — I still miss him. He was there from the time I was five. He was the only man I ever knew as a father. They were both part of our lives and ... and whatever happened to my mom ..." Tommy knew full well what happened to his mother; he'd seen her taken. He knew she had fulfilled her Imperative, but he couldn't tell Paula that. His Earther step-sister had no clue the woman who raised her, and the boy who was her step-brother, were aliens.

"Did you ever hear anything? About what happened to her? Did the police ever find her?"

Tommy shook his head.

"I'm sorry. But Tommy, why didn't you ever call me? I know I said some horrible things that day, but — if you'd called ..."

"I did call, Paula, about a month after the funeral. Dick answered; he asked if you wanted to talk to me and you said, 'not in this life or any other life', so — I honoured your request. I never called you again."

"So this is *my* fault?" she raised her voice, "You just abandoned your family? With no *fight*? Just like *that*? And it's *my* fault?"

"Whoa, Sis, calm down."

"Calm down? Are you telling me to calm down?" her voice was bordering on shrill, "I go through the hell of dealing with my father's death, my divorce, the death of a child ..."

"Wait a minute, what child? Who died?"

But she didn't even hear him, she was too wound up, "*And now you're blaming me*?" She was standing now, and people were looking, lots of people. Her voice wavered, and tears were flowing down her cheeks, the bad kind of tears, "I come here and see the only man who loved me, who's still alive, and instead of welcoming me *you attack me*? You're a pathetic bastard, Tommy Lehmann; *I hope you burn in hell.*"

With the parting shot hanging loudly in the air she stomped off towards the parking lot. Tommy sat there dumbfounded. He knew Paula was always high strung, but this — today she'd gone to a whole new level. She sounded more bi-polar than pissed off. That was a possibility; her dad had been bi-polar.

He could see people looking at him. Most of them quickly looked away, suppressing a smile at the impromptu daytime drama which had quickly unfolded, and just as quickly ended.

As Tommy sat there, exposed, feeling like the world was staring at him, wishing the ground would open up and swallow him, a shadow spread over the table. He looked up to see Cassie standing there with a worried look on her face. "I guess that didn't go so well."

"You heard?"

"Everyone heard."

After drowning his sorrows in a couple of bottles of Moosehead, Ritchie made some coffee and started talking himself down. He knew Cassie loved him, she had to love him; a woman just couldn't fake the way she was with him. She said she loved him every day, and she showed him so at night. What he had seen, her and that guy, Ritchie knew it had to be something innocent, it just *had* to be. He looked up at the clock on the stove and saw it was just after one in the afternoon.

Ritchie splashed some water on his face, chastised himself for the final time, and then headed out the door. It only took ten minutes to walk back to the fairgrounds. He cut through the big parking lot again as it was close to the church's booth.

Tommy sighed and started to stand up. The picnic table bench conspired with his sore back to keep him in place.

"Here, let me help." Cassie reached out and steadied him as he extricated his legs from the picnic bench. She walked with him, steadying him, as he went to his pickup truck. He gave her the nickel history of his family on the way. He told her how his mom had married Ivan Lehmann when Tommy was five. He told her that his mom had disappeared twenty years ago. He told her how

70

his step-father had, in his grief, put a hunting rifle under his chin and checked out from his own misery.

Tears had formed in Tommy's eyes. He wiped at them with the back of his hand. Cassie pulled a folded paper serviette out of her pocket and wiped his eyes for him. Then she put her arms around him and gave him a hug.

"You're a good man, Tommy Lehmann, and I'm glad to know you. Everyone in this town who knows you thinks the same thing. So you don't worry about what she said, and what people heard." She pulled back and looked up at him, giving him a sympathetic smile. Then she stood up on her tiptoes and kissed him on the cheek. "You go home and get some rest. If you need any help, you have my cell phone number. Okay?"

Tommy nodded, "Yeah, thanks, Cassie. Mitch, my neighbour, he'll be home. I can get him to help me if I need to."

They said goodbye after Cassie helped him into the cab of his truck, and then waved as he drove off. She stood there a moment, watching him go, feeling sad for him; sad for the fact he had no one in his life right now. She thought she was lucky to have such a great boyfriend, green-streak notwithstanding. She looked down at her watch. *And just where the hell is Mr. Wonderful?*

Mr. Wonderful was standing by Red Parker's beat up old Volkswagen van. He was angry, he was numb, he wanted to scream, he wanted to cry, he was shaking, he wanted to kill, and he wanted to run. He'd always been the one to dump the girls; he'd never, *ever*, been dumped by a girl. He had absolutely no roadmap for how to respond to what he had just seen. His girl, with her arms wrapped around an old man, an old *white* man, *again*; and then ... *she kissed him*. He had gotten control of the hyperventilating, but his body was still shaking with rage. After a few minutes, he finally was able to stand up straight again; the urge to vomit caused by the adrenaline surge had passed.

He trudged back to the apartment. All he could think of was what the boys back home in Toronto would say: they'd say to kick the old man's ass, or worse. Ritchie set his jaw. It sounded like a fine plan.

Yes indeed, a fine plan.

Chapter 14

Sepherin closed the clasp on her travel case and then sat on the bed to wait. She missed Tarleena. Her friend's departure had just made Sepherin's mood worse, because she knew she would soon have to part ways with Agravita, who had grown as close as her best friend back on Umitia.

Tarleena, the third in her circle with Agravita, had debarked five-sleeps ago at the Ousoon homeworld. The Ousoon are known for their involvement with the Voiya, but the Voiya rarely ever took an Ousoon. That was why only three Imperites onboard had been assigned there. The full complement of Imperites on the Ousoon homeworld was less than twenty. Tarleena had said that unless things were to change, she and the others would be the last placements there.

At least none of her new friends had been assigned to the Kuabatay world. Mianda, a girl Sepherin had been in school with back on Umitia, had been assigned to the Kuabatay. She had raged for hours at the misogynistic throw-backs who expected their women to behave like obedient and subservient chattels, rather than as real women. To make it worse, she was the only one on the transport assigned to the Kuabatay homeworld, as there were only six Umites on their planet. None of the Imperites on this trip were assigned to the one world everyone wanted to go to, Pi Mensae. It was a luxurious paradise, with a higher than average presence of Voiya interlopers, and an already excessive presence of Imperites, even more than on the seed planet, Earth.

Sepherin had told Tarleena and Agravita about the pregnancy. Now, because of her belly, everyone on board knew. The captain of the ship, an Imperite Guard Commander, had summoned her to his cabin. He merely wanted to inform her she would not be returned to Umitia regardless of the pregnancy. Even though she had resolved not to ask, his words and attitude still pissed her off.

Savag's words about a quick death and an airlock had the desired effect, though. She kept her tongue still.

The Commander also needlessly informed her she was expected to continue with the fulfillment of her Oath to the Imperative. He spoke to her as though she were a child who could not be trusted. Regardless of the fact that she wanted exactly what he was telling her she could not have, with her nerves so on edge, his tone, and even the timbre of his voice, infuriated her. It was the first time she'd ever wanted to hit a Shovitic.

Oddly, the Commander had to have seen the hatred flare in her eyes, but he didn't rise to it like a Shovitic normally would. Two of the Falwasz Imperites had already been "taught a lesson" on board for disrespecting the Imperite Guards. By all rights and accounts, the Commander should have handed her ass to her. Instead, he simply dismissed her and went back to reading whatever he had been reading when she came in.

Her Earth instructor had been by her quarters this morning to inform her of her debarkation time. He also let her know there had been a change in the host situation. Apparently the family she had been assigned to, who were going to take her in as a distant relative, had been killed in an accident of some kind. The instructor then handed over a sheet of paper and a picture of her new host.

As the debarkation time approached, she sat in her quarters rereading the précis of information about the new region she was going to live in, and the person with whom she was going to live. She studied the image of the man, thinking he was incredibly normal looking. Yet somehow, he seemed oddly familiar.

As per her training, the last few days had been low on protein and high on carbohydrates. She had her last meal with the rest of her clan who were going to Earth. She liked all of them, but none of them were hosted near her, not even Agravita. With so many Umites on Earth, however, she hoped she may eventually run into one or two of them again. However, the latest reports had indicated that since their transit had begun, three more Imperites had completed their Imperative on Earth. The news surprised her; she wondered why in the hell the Voiya kept taking Earthers when so many of them were killed by stealth Umites. The attrition rate of Voiya was usually only one or two per season on Earth and Pi Mensae, approximately 13 per season galaxy wide.

She took a last look around the quarters she had been in for the last dozen ten-sleeps, to make sure she hadn't forgotten anything. She also wanted to make sure she left everything as she had found it. Order and tidiness were something important in her home growing up. At the appropriate time, she left the room. Bilik, Setiana, and Agravita were walking up the corridor to her quarters. The three of them were also assigned to Earth. Totting their similar travel bags and carry-ons, they all went to the matter transporter room together.

Savag, their principal Earth instructor, met them and ran down the transport schedule. The soft-spoken and portly Savag, of the House of Kolom, of the Treanda clan, was almost emotional at their departures. All told, it would take about an hour to get everyone on-world. Once they were finished transporting the Imperites to the planet surface, the large ship would head towards the final destination for this trip, the star that the Earthers called Beta Hydri.

Sepherin was third in line to TransMat to the surface. She would get to see the transport location for about a half a minute on the view screen before she departed. She had never been through a TransMat before, nor had any of the Imperites on this trip. They were all feeling apprehensive about it. There was nothing natural about having the fabric of space warped and twisted around you, so that where you were standing, became someplace else. There had been stories about the process going horribly awry, though all the crew merely smiled and turned away if you asked them about it. The travellers learned quickly not to ask too many questions of the Imperite Guards; no one liked seeing a Shovitic smile.

75

Setiana was TransMat first, and then Bilik, and then it was her turn. Sepherin and Agravita embraced tightly, kissing each other on the cheek. There were no promises, no words, they both felt exactly the same - and words were unnecessary.

Savag gestured her forward. He took both of her hands, and wished her success. Then to her surprise, he kissed her on both of her cheeks as well. She wanted to hit him. Things had been cool between them since their *talk*, although he had tried to bridge the rift. Now, while he seemed genuine in his emotional goodbye, Sepherin still saw him as the final betrayal in a line of betrayals. She let go of his hands and stepped back from him, turning her face away from his.

She stood on the TransMat field enhancer and watched the view screen. She saw a forested area. Savag pointed to a spot in the forest, indicating the spot where she would be TransMat. He then traced his finger in a straight line, stopping his finger at what appeared to be a corner of two roads, where her host was going to meet her. It was still light on the planet, though it looked from the angle of the shadows that the sun was setting.

"Ready?" Savag asked, but didn't wait for a reply.

Sepherin was looking into his eyes as she felt a tingling at the base of her spine. She exhaled, as she had been instructed to, and then she was looking at a tree. There was no pop, no hiss, no warble, no flash of light, no warning. One moment she was standing on the transport ship, then three shakes of a lamb's tail later, she wasn't. The only thing physical that she noticed was her lungs suddenly deciding on their own to inhale, deeply.

Sepherin took another deep breath, through her nose this time. The smell was — familiar — but slightly different. She could breathe okay though. She set down her satchel and took off her sweater. It was warmer than she expected. She was grateful it wasn't winter. She looked around and oriented herself. As it happened, they had TransMat her facing the exact direction she had to walk. She slung her satchel and sweater over her shoulder, picked up her travel case and started walking towards the road. She heard a mechanical engine in the distance.

Chapter 15

Tommy didn't drive home from the fairground, even though he still had about five hours until it was time to meet his new houseguest. Instead, he drove over to Highway 21 and stopped at the Tim Hortons drive-thru. He got a large coffee. "One cream and no sugar, I'm sweet enough", he would often say to elicit a laugh from the fifty-something woman at the window, the woman with the tattoos. Pulling out onto the highway, he turned south and drove the 40 minutes to Goderich, then another few minutes to his Earth-uncle's place on Londesboro Road.

He pulled into the driveway as his Uncle Jay came out to greet him. Jay wasn't his birth uncle, but he was an Umite. He was an Earth-born Falwasz, a member of the family his mother had married into when she arrived fifty years ago, a family that already had two other Umites in their ranks. Without planning or forethought, Jay's mother happened to marry another Imperite, making Jay an Earth-born true-blood like Tommy, something rare. Jay was of an age and temperament that he had become a bit of a life coach/mentor for younger Imperites. Some stayed in the area their entire lives, some were moved in and out of the area; while some, luckily, disappeared without a trace. Uncle Jay was only slightly older than Tommy, but the family honourifics was useful to explain how you knew someone.

Uncle Jay had been living in the area since he left high school. His wife was an Earther. She knew full what he and Tommy were, and couldn't care less. She was a chiropractor with a practice in Wingham, near the hospital. She got a lot of business from a large number of farms in the area. Her patients swore she had magic hands. Those normally wary people didn't hesitate to see her when their backs started acting up after a few days' hard work with the heifers.

Jay called to Estelle and they helped Tommy, still suffering with the pain in his back, into the house. Estelle cleared off the dining room table, and they carefully lay him face down on it. Twenty minutes later, Tommy stood up by himself. Estelle told him to watch where he was going from now on, because once you hurt your back, you were prone to hurt it again. His payment for the service was to sit down, share some pie and iced tea, and fill them in on what had been happening with him.

There wasn't a lot to tell, other than that he was going to be a host. They were as perplexed by this as he was and they started to talk about it, but as soon as Tommy mentioned Kalabot, the Manager, his Uncle Jay remembered he had some work to do in the yard. Estelle didn't have a clue who Kalabot was, but she took her husband's cue and changed the subject. She filled Tommy in on what had been happening with Carol and the kids since Alex had disappeared.

An Earther, Carol didn't know her missing husband was an alien. After he had disappeared, without his income to pay the bills, she had decided a few days ago she was going to move back out West with the kids if he didn't show his face soon. Neither Estelle nor Jay was allowed to tell her he wouldn't be back, or why. There was simply too much risk of her going to the authorities, or worse, the tabloids.

The rest of the afternoon passed quickly, and as supper time approached, Tommy declined an invitation to stay. He had to get going if he was going to make the rendezvous. With the usual family goodbyes behind him, he made his way north again. The rendezvous coordinates weren't far, but he took the long way back through Goderich. His system was running low on caffeine, so he made a stop at the local Tim Hortons.

The sun was setting, but he still had a good thirty or forty minutes of light. Tommy turned off Highway 9 and north onto

Side Road 25. A minute later he saw the end of the road, where it turned right onto Concession 2. As he approached the corner, he went past it and stopped his truck on the run-out before the sod farm field. He got out of the truck carefully, not wanting to hurt his back again. Estelle had indeed worked magic, he was pain-free for the moment.

He stood in front of the truck and leaned back on the bumper. He didn't have to do anything. He knew the noob would find him. After a couple minutes, he heard a twig snap. He stood up and turned to face the direction of the noise. He got quite a surprise.

It's a woman.

It's a pregnant woman.

Up until this moment, he'd had it stuck in his head that the Imperite was a man. He realized that Taffi and Minino had never actually said which gender the Imperite was. Tommy was looking across the road at one of the plainest looking girls he had ever seen, yet she still glowed with a beauty he couldn't describe.

And she was *pregnant*.

She was young, slender, and tall ... *and pregnant*.

For a moment, he thought that it was a human runaway he stumbled upon by coincidence. No, he *hoped* it was a human runaway.

And she's pregnant.

"Tameht?" she said without any trace of an accent.

Tommy smiled, *Nope, not a human runaway. Only an Umite would know my Falwasz name.* He stepped forward and nodded. He lifted his right forearm and turned his palm upward, "Then as now."

She gave Tameht, Tommy, the most beguiling smile he had ever seen as she returned the gesture with her palm facing down, "Now as then."

81

There was a small gulley on her side of the road, and Tommy crossed the road to assist her, as a gentleman should. She, however, simply picked up her travel case and leapt across the gulley without falling backwards into the brackish water. The gravity of Earth is 18% less than Umitia.

When she stepped onto the road, she let him take the travel case and set it in the back of the truck. Tommy turned to her and stood there for a moment, awkwardly. He wasn't sure whether to shake her hand, embrace her, or dance a little jig.

The pale woman gave a halting smile, then folded her arms across her chest and looked around. "So, this is Earth. It reminds me of home a little. A bit warmer, though, isn't it?"

Tommy shrugged, "I'll take your word for it. I'm Earth-born."

Now she gave a real smile, "I'm sorry, Tameht, of course, you've never been to Umitia."

"No, and please, call me Tommy."

They stood there for another awkward moment.

"So, you're ... pregnant?"

She nodded. He saw her lower lip tremble, and a shiver pass across her shoulders, even though the evening was warm.

Men, most men, honourable and sensible men, have a default response to a woman in need, in danger, or vulnerable. That default response is based on an archetype of the valiant rescuer. When he saw her lip tremble, and her shoulders shiver, after asking if she was pregnant, the *valiant rescuer* reared on its giant steed of manly good intentions: the urge to protect, to provide, and to shelter.

Tommy smiled, "Well, then I guess we're going to have a full house soon."

She looked at him, waiting for him to say something else.

Tommy reached out and gently touched her arm, "My house is your house ... "

"Sepherin," she smiled for real this time.

"Pretty name. But I think that we'll call you — Stephanie, Stephy for short. Okay? Shall we get going?"

She nodded and turned. He watched her go around the front of the truck. She may be plain and skinny, but she had a hell of a body and a fine ass. *And she's pregnant.*

She opened the door and got in the cab of the truck, like she had every right in the world to be there, which she now did.

Tommy hopped in and started the engine. "Were you waiting long?" he asked politely.

"No, not at all. I only had to walk less than a league, and I heard your ground car's engine ..."

"Truck."

"Excuse me?"

"Truck, this is called a pickup truck, or just a truck. No one says ground car."

"Oh, I see. Thank you. I heard your truck approaching not long after I was TransMat to the surface."

"Okay, it won't take long to get home. Are you hungry?"

She nodded, "Yes, I am and it's a pleasure to meet you, *Tommy.* Thank you for being my host."

"I didn't have much choice in the matter," he had an edge to his voice.

"Oh, I see." The young girl looked away, out the window.

Tommy rolled his eyes at his own faux pas. He realized what an idiotic thing he had just said. The girl had travelled a hundred million light years, literally, only to find out the people she was going to live with were dead. What he had said, the way he said it, had probably made her think she was being foisted on someone.

"I'm sorry, Sepherin, please forgive me. It's been a long day, and I'm tired, I didn't mean to speak so roughly."

She didn't look at him or say anything, but he saw her swipe at her face and sniffle. She might have been able to make him feel worse if she had told him he kicked a puppy *and* that it had died. However, Tommy wasn't sure even that would make him feel worse than he did at the moment. She was a young lady, she was trusting him with her life, and he'd made her cry. *Nice, real fucking smooth, ex-lax*, he chided himself. He slowed the truck down and pulled over to the side of the road.

Sepherin was looking at him, alarmed. Her posture showed she was ready to defend herself. Tommy figured her training was far better than his had been, so long ago, and hers was recent. He had no doubt she'd kick his ass from there to Sarnia and back.

Tommy turned slightly and looked directly at her, then smiled in a nice way. "Sepherin, please forgive me. I want you to know that you're welcome to stay with me for as long as you want to. I've prepared my house for you, you have your own room, and I've even stocked up on roasted crickets and dried mealworms. You're ..." he gestured towards her belly, "... child will be as welcome as you are. I've just been ... I wasn't expecting this; I'm still adjusting to the idea of sharing my house again."

She looked like she wanted to say something, but she also looked like she was going to cry harder.

"Sepherin, I'm sorry we got off on the wrong foot. You have nothing to worry about with me. I'll look after you until you're ready to look after yourself. There's no need to ..."

She burst into tears.

Chapter 16

Tommy didn't go straight home. He drove down to the marina as it had a nice restaurant with a nice view over the lake. He wanted some time to sit with *Stephy* and let her get comfortable with him, so she would perhaps stop being mad at him. As soon as they entered the establishment, Sepherin spun around and ran outside. She barely made it before retching; luckily she only suffered the dry heaves. Tommy ran out behind her, wondering what in the hell had caused her reaction.

After a few dry heaves and some heavy breathing, Sepherin stood up, and he put his arm around her shoulders. She didn't resist. They stood in the shadows; the sun was down and night had fallen. It wouldn't be too long before the fireworks, Tommy realized. He thought he should get the girl home as they might freak her out. He had no idea if there were fireworks on Umitia.

Looking up at the man, she smiled weakly, "I apologize Tameht, I smelled ..." she bent over and wretched again, still producing nothing with her stomach's efforts. Finally, she could speak again, "Fish, I don't understand, the smell of it ..." she trailed off, but, this time, didn't heave. "Perhaps, if you don't mind, we could just go to your home? I'm not hungry right now, and I'd like to rest. My upset stomach isn't being helped by the lighter gravity here on your ..."

Tommy shushed her quietly as a couple were just walking out of the door. They were city folk by their dress; Tommy didn't recognize them. He led Sepherin back to the truck.

The booths in Victoria Park all closed at seven o'clock. The fireworks would begin at nine. Cassie checked her phone for the umpteenth time; still no response from Ritchie, text or voicemail.

She hurried through the cleanup with the others, packing away all the perishables. Carol and Maggie were loading it into Jack's pickup, but there wasn't much left. Tabitha had disappeared hours ago with her friends. The booth itself, as well as the BBQs, would remain overnight and be taken away the next morning. Cassie had the presence of mind to ask Jack to come back in the morning and help the pastor with the big stuff since Tommy had injured his back.

Cassie drove home, planning in her mind the amount of shit she was going to heap on Ritchie for not showing up. It only took five minutes to get to her apartment. By the time she got there she had worked herself into a lather of righteous indignation. But Ritchie wasn't there. She looked at the empty beer bottles on the table. It took her about five seconds to figure out where Ritchie went. She pulled her phone out and called Tommy, but there was no answer.

She ran back out to her car. It took four tries, and one heartfelt prayer, for the car to start. Cassie headed for Tommy's place, it was only a ten-minute drive, but there was a R.I.D.E spot check on the highway, and she got stuck in the lineup.

Tommy slowed down as he went around the bend on Blanche Lane. Sepherin had perked up a little and was looking at the houses and all the 'trucks', as she kept calling the cars.

His house was the second-to-last one on the south side of the dead-end lane. Before he got to his driveway, he saw Mitch coming off his porch waving his arms in the air. Mitch trotted out to the road as Tommy slowed to a stop and rolled down his window.

Mitch took a breath to speak, but stopped when he saw the young woman sitting in the cab of the pickup. He only hesitated a moment and then went on, "Tommy, that young black fella, he's been waiting out front of your house for a couple of hours. I asked him what-was-what, but he said he was here to discuss something with you. He seems pissed off, too. I asked if he wanted to wait at my place and he said no. I asked him if he wanted to maybe come back tomorrow, but he told me to mind my own flippin' business."

Tommy thought about it a moment. There weren't a lot of coloured people in the area. Given this morning's little faux pas, he knew who it had to be.

"Must be Ritchie, Cassie's beau."

Mitch thought for half a second, "The little girl from the hardware store?"

"Yeah, him and I had a little difference of opinion this morning. He probably just thought of something to finally say about it. It ain't no thing, Mitch. I'll listen to him and then send him on his way."

"You want some backup with that?"

"Nah, he's a good kid. He's just gotta feel he's been satisfied, is all."

Mitch waved and backed away from the truck. He went to the corner of his house where he could keep an easy eye on Tommy's front yard. He picked up a cut-off of spruce 2x4 as he stood there, just in case. The single row of evergreens between their properties hid him from view unless you were looking for him.

"Is there a problem?" Sepherin asked.

"No, we just ... he didn't like the way I was with his girlfriend this morning, he just needs to have his say is all."

"Oh? And how were you with her?"

Tommy looked at Sepherin as he slowed to a stop in his driveway, "I was a proper gentleman; I just didn't stop to think how her boyfriend would react."

Tommy shut off the truck and opened the door to get out. He saw Ritchie standing up from the edge of the porch and striding towards him. He looked angry ... and determined. *Fuck, this is the last thing I need right now*. He looked at Sepherin, "You stay here; I'll sort this out quickly."

Ritchie stopped short in his advance when he noticed the woman in the truck. He chugged a laugh and shook his head. "How many bitches you got up your sleeve, old man?"

"Excuse me?" Tommy was taken aback.

"You got mine, plus you got another one? Does Cassie know about this slut?"

"Hey, Ritchie, watch your fuckin' mouth. You don't know who this is; she's ..."

"I don't give a shit *who* your bitch is, old man, I just know you got your hands full of my girl's ass and I'm here to tell you back the hell off."

Now Tommy was mad *and* confused. "Got my hands ... what? Ritchie, what the fuck are you talking about?"

"I saw you, I saw the two of you," Ritchie was advancing, his finger pointing at Tommy as he gesticulated with his other arm. "I saw you hugging her, I saw you kissing her."

Now Tommy was really off balance, "Kissing who? Ritchie, I don't know how much you've had to drink, son, but I don't have a clue what you're talking about."

"Oh, yeah? I saw you in the parking lot. I saw her arms around you. I saw her kiss you. Do you deny it?"

"That? *That's* what this is about?" Tommy chuckled, "Ritchie, go home and sober up. You didn't see nothin' to worry about. I ain't got ..."

But Ritchie wasn't satisfied. He growled and lunged at Tommy, but then found himself face down on the ground, squealing in pain. Neither of the men had seen her get out of the truck, or seen her move.

When Ritchie lunged, Tommy stepped back. But instead of getting bowled over by the younger guy who was taller and stronger, he instead found himself looking at the noob, with the young guy in a hand lock.

Ritchie was squealing with pain, writhing face down on the ground. Sepherin stood beside him. She had his left arm pulled up in the air behind him; she had his wrist bent at an unnatural angle; her left foot was on his neck, and the heal of her boot was digging into his brachial plexus. Ritchie was trying to get away from her, trying to get away from the pain, squealing loudly in pain and fear as he did so, but he couldn't get away from her foot or her hand. Sepherin didn't look like she was struggling in the slightest.

"Uh, thanks," Tommy said, "but I think you should let him go before you hurt him too much."

Sepherin looked at Tommy, then back down at the man on the ground. She took her foot off his neck and let go of his hand. She took a couple of steps back to give him some room.

Ritchie quickly pushed himself up, and stood up, rubbing his neck. He looked at Tommy, "You got your sluts fighting for you now, old man?"

"*Hey!*" Sepherin barked.

Ritchie turned to look at the woman who was taller than him.

"Just who are you calling a slut?" Some dirty names are universal.

"You, the slut fighting battles for her old man," Ritchie sneered at her. "It's time you got taught a lesson."

"Hey, Ritchie, leave her alone, it's not what you think, she's not my ..." Tommy reached out to grab Ritchie, but Ritchie feinted to the side. Tommy decided it was unfortunate that the boy was going to have to die, but if he laid a hand on the girl, then he *was* going to die. Tommy glanced to his left and saw Mitch walking towards them. *Fuck*. Tommy cursed in his mind, *Can't kill him if Mitch is watching.*

Sepherin held up her hand, though, stopping Tommy who had started to step towards Ritchie. She was smiling. She was looking at Ritchie. She thought he was a strong and good-looking Humanesh, who was almost as big as Roguk. Almost.

"It's okay, Tommy," at least she remembered his Earth name, "I look forward to this Hobonol *'teaching me a lesson'* if he can."

"Hobo-what? The fuck did you just call me, *bitch*?" Ritchie lunged at the woman, his chin coming squarely into contact with the heel of her boot. As his head snapped back, he felt a pile driver land right in the epigastric region of his stomach. The force of her punch translated enough energy to his solar plexus to stop him cold. Ritchie fell to the ground clutching his chest, he was able to breathe in, but he couldn't exhale, he felt like his lungs were going to explode. He landed face first, not even noticing the pain of the cuts to his face from the stones. He gasped, and gasped again. He wasn't gasping *for* air; he was trying to get enough air in to force his lungs to exhale; yet he couldn't even remember in that moment how to exhale.

He felt the woman kneel beside him. One of her hands was gently massaging his neck, while the other hand was rubbing the middle of his back. "Think about water, don't think about breathing, think about floating in water ... just think about water ... you aren't going to die, you're going to breathe, you're going to be okay, just think about ..."

Ritchie gave a mighty exhale. His body went slack; he started taking in whopping lungsful of air and puffing them out; tremors passed through his hands and shoulders as he got his breathing under control again. He rolled over onto his back and looked up at the faces. His head was hurting, his face hurt, he felt dizzy, and his stomach felt like it was going to empty. His breathing finally slowed down. He realized Tommy was pressing something on his face. He skittered his upper body to the side and brought his hands up defensively.

"Whoa, Ritchie, you're bleeding. You're bleeding, son. Hold on, let me put some pressure on it."

Ritchie's face was a mess. He had several cuts on his face from the gravel driveway and was bleeding from all of them. He looked up through the tears in his eyes and saw Tommy dabbing at his face with a white cloth. The fight had gone out of Ritchie; he didn't want any more of what had been given to him. He saw the nosey neighbour leaning over Tommy, looking concerned, but also ... smirking? Ritchie shifted his head and looked at the girl, the woman, the ... whatever she was. She was kneeling there, looking impassively down at him. She didn't have any concern on her face, but she didn't have any malice either. He saw them all look up at the sound of a car door shutting.

"Oops," Mitch said. He was glad he'd dropped the 2x4 in the trees when he darted over to help Tommy. He smiled at the thought, *Helping Tommy, right. Whoever the little filly is, she could take on a whole army of these young fellas.*

"What the hell?" Cassie pushed the woman out of the way and knelt beside Ritchie. She looked up at Tommy, "What the hell did you do to him? Tommy? Why?"

She took the cloth from Tommy's hand and was dabbing at Ritchie's face, tears welling up in her eyes. Ritchie opened his mouth to speak, but realized he had a loose tooth, and that he could taste blood in the back of his throat. He turned his head and spat it out; just the blood, not the tooth.

91

"Baby, what did you do?" Cassie was looking at Ritchie. She figured out pretty quickly he'd gotten out of line, which was the thought that had brought her here. It obviously hadn't gone well for him, but, he looked so beat up; it was too much. She had never thought Tommy was violent, but sometimes you're just wrong about people.

Tommy reached down to help her lift Ritchie to a sitting position, but she pushed his hands away, "Haven't you done enough?"

Tommy was at a loss for words. There was so much to say, to explain, but there was nothing that was going to settle this down quickly. He didn't get a chance to speak though.

Cassie felt the woman's hand on her shoulder; she spun her head around to look at her.

"Tameht didn't do this, I did. Your friend," Sepherin looked down at Ritchie, "got out of line. He tried to attack my ..."

"Uncle," Tommy threw in quickly.

"Yes, my uncle. I needed to stop him. Then he tried to attack me. I needed to stop him again."

"But did you have to do *this* to him? Did you have to hurt him so badly?"

Now Sepherin smiled, "He's not hurt bad, he just has some cuts and bruises. If he had attacked me on my ..." she almost said homeworld, "... where I come from, I would have killed him." She just let that hang there, staring at Cassie, not flinching.

"*You* did this to him?" Cassie was incredulous. Ritchie was a former football player. The thought of such a slender woman doing this ... was inconceivable.

Mitch pulled on Tommy's shoulder, to move him away. He knelt down, "Miss Cassie, let me help you get him to the car." Mitch and Cassie picked Ritchie up and led him to the car. Ritchie tried to push them away, but he was still dizzy, so he finally let them help him. After she pulled out of the driveway and sped down the lane, Mitch turned to Tommy and then the young lady. He smiled and stuck out his hand, "Hi, I'm Mitch, Tommy's neighbour. And you are?"

Sepherin knew what the hand gesture was from her training, she took hold of the man's hand and pumped it three times, then let it go. She had practiced enough times onboard the transport that she made it feel almost natural.

"My name is Sephy."

"Stephy," Tommy corrected.

"Stephy," she said, then gave Mitch a big disarming smile. "I'm Tameht's niece."

"Tommy," her host said, feeling like an idiot.

"Tommy," she said, continuing the smile.

Mitch looked from one to the other, for an awkward moment, then sighed and said, "Well, nice to meet you Stephy. I'm Mitch; I live right next door."

"I'm pleased to meet you, Mr. Mitch." She was proud of herself; her Earth classes had covered formal and informal greetings. It was a nice little reprieve from the tense situation Tommy had dropped her into the middle of.

"No, just Mitch is fine."

She smiled and tried again, "I'm pleased to meet you, Just Mitch."

Tommy stopped this runaway train in its tracks, "Well, Mitch, since the excitement's over, Sephy's ... *Stephy's* travelled a long way, so if you don't mind, I'm going to get her inside and settled."

At that moment, they heard the loud whistle and bang of fireworks. All three looked up, towards the fairgrounds, as the sky lit up with the patterned bursts of colour. Tommy glanced towards Sepherin to see how she was reacting.

Her face held a big smile, and it looked like she was actually happy, as compared to her so recent upset.

"Pretty", was all Sepherin said.

The three stood there silently and watched the seven-minute long show. When it was over, the young woman grabbed her travel case from the back of the truck and picked up her carry-on satchel from the front seat. She went to the front door of the house and waited for her host.

Mitch slapped Tommy on the shoulder and leaned in close, "Did she call you ... *Tammy*?"

"Mitch ..."

"Hey," he put both of his hands up in front of him, in a halting gesture, "Whatever floats your boat, my friend."

"Mitch, she's my niece."

"Uh, huh. Then how come you've never mentioned her before? You've told me about everyone else in your family."

Tommy sighed, "Mitch, please. Let it go."

His neighbour and friend smiled, "Yeah, man, whatever you say. It's all good. You get her settled in, and we'll talk tomorrow." Mitch turned and went back to his place, waving to the young woman who was waiting patiently on the porch for her host.

Tommy walked up to the front door, pulling his keys out of his pocket.

"So, is it always this exciting around here?" she asked innocently.

"No."

She stood close to him as he put the key in the lock, "You called me Sephy. My dad used to call me Sephy."

"Your dad did?"

"Yes," she smiled, "you remind me of him."

94

"I do? I remind you of your ... dad?" he said to the plain, but fetching young woman.

She nodded.

Great, I remind her of her dad, Tommy thought as he pushed the door open, *why doesn't she just kick me in the nutsack, too.*

Chapter 17

"Well?"

Ritchie leaned forward on the kitchen table, pressing the bag of frozen peas against his face, trying to hide behind them. They had driven back to the apartment in silence, and then they went upstairs in silence. When Ritchie sat down, Cassie handed him the bag of frozen veggies to help with the swelling. The piper was now demanding payment ... for a whole lot of things.

"I should call the cops," Ritchie sulked. His head rocked back from the slap across the face, the side without the frozen peas pressed against it.

Cassie looked as stunned at what she had done as Ritchie did. She put her hand over her mouth and sobbed. She collapsed into the chair across from him.

After a few sobs, she got control of herself. "Why didn't you come to the fairgrounds this morning? I was counting on you to help."

"I did come ..."

"Bullshit!"

Ritchie gritted his teeth, "... and when I got there, you were standing next to him, putting up the booth. You had your arm wrapped around him, and you were smiling up at him, like a couple of lovebirds."

Cassie gasped with surprise, "Ritchie, *you asshole*, he hurt his back holding up the parts of the booth. I was helping him stand up until the pastor got the screws into the joints. The man spent the next four hours in a lawn chair, barely able to move. *I was helping him not drop the whole booth on top of himself.*"

"Yeah? Really? Just helping him?" Ritchie had tossed the bag of frozen veggies on the table. The urge to fight was coming back, "And what about later? Huh? *What about that?*"

Now Cassie was confused, "Later? What later?"

"I came back later after I cooled down and was willing to forgive you ..."

"Forgive *me*? You were willing to *forgive me*?"

Ritchie ploughed on, knowing he was being irrational again, but unable to stop himself, "... but I came back and saw you two; I saw the two of you in the parking lot."

Cassie screamed with frustration, finally realizing what he was talking about.

"I saw you with your arms around him, sticking your tongue down his throat!"

"I WAS NOT STICKING MY TONGUE DOWN HIS THROAT, YOU IDIOT. I KISSED HIM ON THE CHEEK!"

"THERE! YOU ADMIT IT! YOU KISSED HIM!" he screamed back at her.

Cassie got up from the table and went to the sink, having no idea why she did so, other than to put distance between her and the man she had trusted, who she had *thought* trusted her.

She turned to face him again, "Ritchie, let me explain this one time and one time only. Tommy's sister showed up. He hasn't seen her in 20 years, not since their dad died. She upset him, and she publicly humiliated him. I was helping him walk back to his truck because his back was still in pain. He was upset, he was angry, and he was hurting. Yes, Ritchie, I hugged him. Yes, Ritchie, I kissed him ... *on the cheek*. I did exactly what it was that Jesus teaches us to do; I was being *compassionate*."

Cassie watched Ritchie's face. She watched complex emotions moving across it; she watched him getting lost in his thoughts. Still standing against the counter with her arms folded, she asked him, "Do you think that if I was going to be silly enough to carry on with an older man, behind your back, that I would be so *damn stupid* as to do it *in public?* In front of the *whole town?* Do you really believe I'm *that much* of a *whore?*"

The word sunk in: whore. It made Ritchie realise exactly how much of an idiot he had been. Everything just snapped into place in his mind; he knew Cassie was one of the few people he trusted completely, wanted to trust completely. He knew everything that he had been feeling, and the things he had been thinking, had come from jealousy, nothing else. They had come from *his* insecurities, not from *her* actions. He slumped in the chair, defeated.

"Why don't you trust me, Ritchie? What have I ever done to make you think I'm a whore?"

"I don't," he said quietly, "I don't think that at all."

Now she was getting angry again, "You just sat there *and told me* I was fucking around behind your back with Tommy. Don't you *dare* think you can back out of this, mister. I *thought* you loved me, Ritchie Turner, I *thought* you trusted me."

"I do, I do trust you, I just ..."

"You just *what?*"

Ritchie had no comeback.

After a moment, Cassie spoke again, "Did you really try to attack that woman? At Tommy's?"

"She attacked me first."

"Why *was* that, Ritchie? Why did she attack you first?"

Ritchie said nothing; he just fiddled with the bag of peas, staring at the table in front of him.

"Was it because you tried to attack Tommy? Was that it? Ritchie? Is that why the skinny white girl beat your black ass?"

Ritchie clenched his hands into fists, took a deep breath, and then let it out slowly as he unclenched his fists. The room was silent for a long time.

Finally, Cassie broke the silence, "How do you expect me to trust *you*, ever again? Ritchie, this — jealous streak of yours — it was cute at first, but then — now — it's just too much. It's *too much*. You need help."

Ritchie got up from the table, "Wait here."

He went to the bedroom and reappeared a moment later. He stood in front of Cassie, holding the ring box. She looked at it, and then looked up into his face.

He tried to smile, but it faltered, "This is how you can trust me. I was going to — tonight, with the fireworks, I was going to ..."

Ritchie took a deep breath and then got down on one knee. He held the box up and opened it, revealing the small diamond ring.

"Cassie," he was finally able to smile at her, "will you marry me?"

She didn't say anything for a moment; she didn't even look at the ring. She just looked into Ritchie's eyes. She couldn't believe what he was saying, what she was hearing. It was the first time anyone had ever tried to buy her off. She had a horrible image in her mind: ten years from now, with him on his knees, apologizing *yet again* for something he would do; perhaps something far worse, something with his fists. She realized that what was happening right now, what had been happening, was only the opening act in a lifelong drama which she finally knew she wanted no part of.

Cassie took a deep breath, cupped Ritchie's face in her hands, and kissed him lightly on the lips. She pulled her hands back and stepped around him.

"I'm going to stay at my mom's tonight. When I get back tomorrow, I want you gone." She stopped and turned in the doorway, looking at the dumbstruck man still down on one knee, "I don't ever want to see you again."

Chapter 18

Shortly after midnight, Tommy heard movement downstairs. When they came in, Sepherin had sat on the couch and promptly fell sound asleep. He figured she may have trouble sleeping with the excitement of arriving at her new planet; he knew he would have. Tommy threw an afghan over her, left a small lamp on, and then went to bed.

Now that the sound had awakened him, he waited for a few minutes to see if she was going to sleep again. When he heard the toilet flush, he realized she didn't even know where the spare bedroom was. He got up, put on a housecoat, and went downstairs. He found her standing in the kitchen, arms wrapped around herself, just staring out the window. She turned at the sound of his approach.

"I realized I didn't even show you where your room was."

She smiled, "Thank you, Tommy, but I'm not tired right now. I was thirsty, but wanted to try something other than water." She looked around the kitchen, "Which of these things is the ... refa ... refritit ... refrigitatator?"

"Refrigerator, this one," he stepped over and opened the door. Sepherin peered in, seeing fresh vegetables, and a lot of other things she had no clue about. Tommy reached in and took out a can of Diet Pepsi. He popped the tab on it and handed it to her, "Here, this'll wet your whistle."

She tried it, and she smiled.

He opened a cupboard and pulled out one of the cans of roasted crickets. He pulled off the lid and held it out to her. She looked at the contents, sniffed them, and then took a hesitant bite of one. She moaned, and rolled her eyes.

"These are much better than roasted grass-blade hoppers."

101

Tommy grabbed a can of pop for himself, and they sat at the small kitchen table. She told him a little about the journey here, about the Earth classes and the topics they covered. She told him she just needed some time to start relating everything she had seen and heard to the new world around her. Eventually, she started talking about her family.

"My full name is Sepherin Alabast Contina Tekin."

"Tekin?" Tommy looked surprised, "You're from the House of Tekin?"

She nodded and Tommy smiled at her, "So am I."

Now she looked surprised, "Really? The House of Tekin? But I thought you were Earth-born?'

Tommy nodded, "I am, but my mom was of the House of Tekin. I guess that means we're related."

"What was her name?"

"Jackie."

"I mean her real name, her Umite name."

"Oh, Jakula. Jakula Kara Contina Tekin."

Sepherin's eyes went wide, "For real? Jakula Tekin?"

Tommy nodded.

"What do you know of your mom, of her life back on Umitia, before she came here?"

"Well, I know she was married young, and that she had a son. Then she was selected for the Imperite program."

Sepherin was smiling, "And her son, the one she had on Umitia, do you know what became of him?"

Tommy shook his head, "No, not really. Mom only talked to me about him once. I found her crying in her room when I was about ten years old. She said it was her other son's birthday, then she told me a little bit about him, but then I was sworn to secrecy."

"His name was Michalz."

"Yes," Tommy said, surprised. "That's right. How did you know?"

"Because Michalz Tekinson is the son of Jakula and Themedit Tekinson, and because he's my father. Themedit is my grandfather. He presided over my funeral ceremony. I grew up with a picture of your mom in my house."

Tommy's face showed the incredulous response to the news, "Really? Michalz is still alive? My brother? He's your father? Then this means ..."

"I really *am* your niece," she smiled and dabbed at a tear. Sepherin stood up and went to the living room. She came back with her satchel. She rooted around in it and brought out an envelope containing pictures. "Mom had these printed to bring with me."

She went through the pictures, showing Tommy the first pictures he had ever seen of Michalz, and his father Themedit. He reached over and took the picture of a young woman, no older than Sepherin was. He knew this one.

It was his mom, standing in a garden on an alien planet.

His finger touched her face, and traced it. There was no mistaking it was the face that had smiled at him, scolded him, laughed with him, cried for him, and loved him without condition. He heard her laugh, he heard her bedtime songs, and he remembered the feel of her hand holding his when he was sick. He also remembered the day she was taken from the house by the Voiya drones and the pod of five Vesna.

"May I ... keep this?" he looked at Sepherin, and she nodded.

Sepherin got up, sat in Tommy's lap and put her arms around him, "So you really *are* my uncle." She kissed him on the forehead.

Tommy embraced his young relative. "Quite the coincidence, eh?"

"Yeah," she said hoarsely. "Quite a coincidence."

Neither one of them thought it was a coincidence at all. But they were both at a loss to make any sense of it, or to come up with a reason for it.

Sepherin sobbed, but fought back the tears. "I'm so glad to find this out." She snuffled and wiped at her nose with the back of her hand. "I've been wondering what I was going to do. Having a host is one thing, but arriving at a host's place pregnant is ..."

"Is exactly ..." Tommy interrupted her, "... what happened to my mother. She was pregnant with me when she got onboard the transport, but she didn't know t." Tommy smiled at her, "So that means, my dear, you aren't going to have to go through anything alone. I'm going to be right here with you, through every step of it, blood-kin with blood-kin."

Sepherin stood up and walked around the kitchen, clutching her arms across her chest again. Tommy could see there was something still troubling her. She looked like she was trying to decide whether or not to say something. He knew that feeling: the need to share and unburden, counterpointed by the risk of exposing yourself. He waited patiently and let her come to her own decision. It didn't take too ong.

Sepherin stopped pacing and looked at her uncle, "I was going to ask them to take me back, back to Umitia."

Tommy's brow furled, "Really? They'll do that? They'll let you go back?"

She shook her head, "No. My instructor told me that if I asked, they'd kill me for being an Oath-breaker."

"Oh, I see."

"I just — I have a life inside me now. I'm — going to be a mom. I don't want to die. I don't want my child to be a hereditary Imperite either; I don't want — I don't want my child to die because of who I am." The tears were flowing freely now.

"I just — it's so damn unfair, Uncle Tameht. We're paying for the sins of our ancestors, for what happened a long time ago. When is it enough? Will there ever be a day we don't have to sacrifice ourselves anymore?"

"Stephy, you're asking questions far above my pay grade. I just am what I am. It's what I was raised to be. The odds of actually being taken by the Voiya are fairly slim. Most Imperites live their whole lives here without ..."

"And that's exactly my point. There are how many thousands of us on this planet? And what, they average two or three a year completing the Imperative?"

"But what else are we going to do? How else are we going to fight the Voiya?"

"*Exactly*. Why is it up to us to fight the Voiya? Who made us the galaxies' protectors? And if we're so fired up to fight the Voiya, why don't we *fight them* instead of *sneaking around* trying to pick them off? Why? *Why is that*, Uncle Tameht?

"Stephy, please, I don't know. I just ... I just know, that's why ..."

She put her hands up, "Never mind. I'm just — *angry* — for many reasons." There was no way she was going to get into a rant about Roguk and his wife. She'd cried enough for one day.

She sat down at the table again and took another sip of her pop.

Tommy was tired, and he was confused. He didn't know what she was looking for, or what she wanted him to say. He hadn't expected her outburst. He'd never, ever, heard an Imperite express the things she had. He wondered if he should talk to his Uncle Jay about it.

"I didn't mean to get agitated with you, Uncle Tommy. I just don't want to be here. I want to be home, with my mom and dad, where I can raise my little one safely."

Tommy nodded. "I get it, Stephy, I do. But you can't go home. You know that, right?"

Neither one knew Michalz wasn't Sepherin's birth father. That fact, however, is irrelevant — for the moment. Sepherin and Tommy had discovered they were bonded by family, which is often a far stronger and more durable bond than the bond of blood. Being blood-kin is a bond of happenstance, where love-kin is a bond of choice. The only unfortunate part of this whole conversation was that they had no idea how soon things were going to change.

They had no idea how far the bond of family would make one person go, or do the things they would do.

Chapter 19

Zekra got back in the dark sedan, with two cups of coffee in his bony hands and a stack of tabloids clutched under his arm. They had stopped for coffee in Indian Springs, Nevada, at the Chevron gas station's Food Mart. The tabloids were the latest editions and the two Imperite Guards needed some fresh intelligence. They had just finished dealing with a trainee drone pilot, from Creech Air Force Base, who had seen something he needed to forget he had seen.

Zekra handed the two hot cups of coffee to his partner, Shivinin, and slammed his door shut. He took one of the Styrofoam cups back from Shivinin and took his first sip. He was disappointed there was no Starbucks in Indian Springs, the coffee he held was swill compared to that nectar, but he had to admit he had tasted worse. He took off his fedora and tossed it in the back seat, then adjusted his Ray-Bans, which had started to slide down his long, thin nose. He settled into the seat for the hour-long drive back to their base, just south and west of the Yucca Airstrip.

As they drove in silence, Zekra sipped his coffee, and began flipping through the checkout stand papers he had picked up. He finished scanning one full-colour tabloid and then tossed it on the floor between his feet. The second one didn't prove to have anything more interesting than another Elvis sighting, although if it was Elvis, he'd be 85 years old and even Zekra doubted he'd recognize him, Umite or not.

The third tabloid was a black and white weekly that reported news from around the world. This one had a story which caught Zekra's interest.

He looked up to see where they were, to see how much longer he had for his research. Shivinin had turned north on Mercury highway from I-95 about ten minutes before. They were at about the halfway point of the drive. Zekra drained the last of the mediocre coffee, rolled down the window, and tossed out the empty cup. Shivinin reached over and poked him on the arm, sneering at him. They'd both had the lecture about environmental responsibility on their host's planet.

Zekra ignored his partner and turned back to the tabloid, reading the story about the "Farmer Who Got Butt Probed" more carefully. Most of these stories were bogus, coming from creative writers who needed to earn $10, or from some narcissist who needed fifteen minutes of fame. This story, however, surpassed the standard test of three "hits". This story had five hits. This meant there was a high degree of probability that it was true. Zekra tore out the page, folded it, and put it in his pocket.

"Got one?" asked Shivinin.

"Yes, it appears so," Zekra responded.

He finished the black and white tabloid, and then continued on with the next one lying beside him. He finished the last of the six papers as Shivinin turned west onto the approach road to the Nevada National Security Site. Quickly passing through the double security gate, Shivinin stopped the car near a small door on the southern end of the Device Assembly Facility. They went inside, down seven levels in the elevator, and then got into the electric golf cart which was reserved specifically for them. This time Zekra drove. Twenty minutes later, navigating three long cement tunnels, they were deep underneath the north-east slope of Black Ridge. As they stopped at the charging station, Shivinin finally let go of the safety bar attached to the dash of the electric cart. He looked at this partner and gave silent thanks, once again, that Zekra wasn't allowed to drive the gas-powered automobiles.

As the two Shovitics got out of the cart they stopped and sniffed the air, then looked at each other. They smelled ... an Eridani drone?

Shivinin unlocked their office door and turned on the light. He stopped and sniffed again, he could still smell the stench. He turned on the computer hooked up to the military network and checked his messages. Sure enough, an Eridani (Voiya) scout vessel had crashed in Kentucky the previous evening. All aboard were killed, but the body of the mostly intact drone was transported to the secure facility deeper under the mountain.

Zekra had already grabbed the can of Glade air freshener in the closet, and was spraying the room to mask the disgusting odour of the drone. Umites, specifically the Shovitic clan, could smell Voiya drones from further away than they could smell the Vesna, Trigla, or the Voiya themselves.

Zekra sat down at the desk opposite his partner, and logged into his workstation. He unfolded the paper he took out of his pocket, typed a few words into the computer, and then handed the story from the tabloid to Shivinin. The Imperite Guard read the story, twice, making note of the same five "hits".

"Who is in this area?" he asked in the slow, sibilant, Shovitic drawl.

After a moment Zekra replied telepathically, *Femi and Corvu. I will send a message to them. They are dealing with someone in ...* he looked closer at the screen again, *Vancouver.*

Shivinin stared at the wall for a moment, and then closed his eyes. He opened them after finding the memory that had stirred at the mention of Saskatchewan in the story. "Taffi recently went to Wyoming, so send your brother and Minino, they will be closer."

Chapter 20

Tommy eased the large propane-powered forklift forward, swaying from side to side like a metronome to make sure he was lined up properly. He stopped at just the right distance and lowered the large pallet of 2 x 6 x 12 pine onto the one below it. Once it was in place, he withdrew the forklift and drove back towards the shed where the machine was stored. He could finally go back inside and take it easy for a few minutes. While Estelle's chiropractic magic had done wonders, when he got up this morning his back was aching; but not as bad as it was two days ago. He'd already had four Advil and it was still early in the day.

Walking from the shed, he saw Cassie standing outside the back doors of the hardware store. She was having a smoke and sipping coffee. That surprised Tommy, as he had never seen Cassie with a cigarette in her hand. He hadn't seen her when he arrived for work, and he'd been in the wood lot for the last hour unloading a string of transports. Tommy steeled himself and moved towards the doors, watching Cassie, to see how she was going to react.

Cassie didn't see him until he was almost at the doors. She set her coffee on the window ledge and crushed the remainder of the smoke under her foot.

"Tommy," she said.

He stopped, "Good morning, Cassie."

"Tommy, I ... I'm sorry. I'm sorry for Saturday, for what Ritchie did, what he tried to do."

Tommy was nodding slightly, "Yeah, well, we can't control other people's actions."

"I know, but I feel — I'm sorry he took out on you what was business between him and me. He gets powerful jealous sometimes and ..."

"Cassie, you don't have to apologize to me. We're good, so long as you're good with us. I'm sorry we had to hurt him but — it was either him or me."

She smiled, "Thanks, Tommy. I like having you as a friend. I didn't want Ritchie's behaviour to get between us."

Tommy nodded again, "Fair enough, Cassie. It won't."

"Good, I'm glad."

"Has he calmed down? Or is he still wound up?"

"I don't know."

"Oh?"

"I stayed at my mom's Saturday night. I told Ritchie to pack his stuff up and leave. I told him I never wanted to see him again."

"Oh, Cassie, really? I hope you didn't do that because of me, because of what happened Saturday."

"No, I did it because I'm sick of Ritchie's jealousy. I did it because he tried to attack that woman with you. I did it because I need to be trusted, and he doesn't trust me. I did it because he thought he could buy me off with a diamond ring."

"A diamond — *ring*? He proposed?"

"Yeah, after we got home, we got into it. Once he was backed in the corner and saw no way out, instead of respecting me enough to try and earn my trust back, he pulled out a diamond ring to buy me off with a marriage proposal. Like I was supposed to go all girly and forget everything that happened, everything that he had said to me. *Fuck* — men. I'll never understand you assholes."

"Boys are stupid, throw rocks.' That made her laugh. "I'm sorry for you, Cassie ... or happy for you? Whichever you prefer."

"I'll let you know, I'm not sure yet myself." She turned to open the door for them, "So who was the woman anyways? She kicked ass."

"My niece, she's come to stay with me for a while. She'll be here all winter."

"That's good to hear. I've always thought it was a shame that someone as nice as you was alone all the time. I'm glad you have some family with you, especially over the holidays."

She didn't know that Tommy wouldn't live to see the coming weekend.

Chapter 21

The Umite duty frigate had to TransMat Taffi and Minino, along with their sedan, from Casper, Wyoming. Ten minutes later it TransMat them again to the outskirts of Moose Jaw, Saskatchewan. The two Imperite Guards then acquired a local map, and found the mobile home park where their target lived. They drove by the trailer a couple of times, and then went in search of some palatable food.

A recommendation from another gas station attendant, a nervous and mousy young man, led them to the Chrysalis on Main Street North, at the corner of High Street. There they enjoyed a nice vegan lunch, something they found increasingly hard to come by. Of course, after ordering the vegan meals, the waiter stammered at their request for dried mealworms on the side. Alas, it was not an option. Minino thought of how the nervous young man would look if he shoved him out of an airlock.

Taffi and Minino had that effect on the Humanesh of Earth, giving them the heebie-jeebies. All of the Imperite Guards serving on the planet had the same effect. They made people nervous merely by being around them. It had been suggested that perhaps this was a response to their peculiar pheromones. The people they visited on business — they made them feel much worse.

The two Umites waited until the sun was just starting to set before returning to the white, run down mobile home. They found their persuasion visits were more effective at both sunset and sunrise, for whatever strange reason. At least this was Canada, so it was unlikely the target would greet them with a loaded gun.

Parking the sedan on the paved laneway at the front of the trailer, both Imperite Guards exited the car and took a careful look around. The backside of the trailer had a rusted swing set standing in the overgrown grass. It was kept company by an armoire and overstuffed chair, both of which looked like they were in the final stages of decay, and probably inhabited by more than one type of varmint.

There was an old pickup truck in the driveway, as well as an even older Honda Civic. That meant the target was most likely home, another good reason for dusk and dawn visits.

Seeing no one out and about, they took long, lanky strides up to the front door. They climbed the steps and stood on the small landing for a moment, just listening and scanning the area. Satisfied there was no one watching, Minino reached out and rapped on the door three times, slowly.

They heard movement inside, and a middle aged woman opened the door only a crack, trying to hide herself behind it while eyeing them apprehensively.

"Yes?"

Taffi smiled without parting his lips, "David MacFeet, please?"

She hesitated only a second, then called over her shoulder, "David, there are some men here to see you."

The man from the picture in the tabloid appeared behind the woman, and stepped around her to the door. His face blanched as he saw who was standing there.

"Yes? Can I help you?" he asked, guardedly.

"We have come to discuss recent events."

"Excuse me? To what?"

Minino took over, "We need to speak with you about what you have been telling the papers. May we come inside?"

"Ahhh, no thanks. No, thank you, I don't want to talk about it." David started to close the door, but Minino was faster. He reached out with both hands and shoved the door inward, forcing David backwards.

The two men in black suits and black fedoras, with perfectly trimmed crew-cut hair, very square jaws, and wearing Ray-Ban sunglasses stepped into the mobile home as David bumped into his wife and knocked her to the floor.

Kelly squealed and David recovered quickly, "Hey! What the hell do you think you're doing? Get the hell out of ..." He stopped as the first one who had spoken pulled a large handgun from under his jacket.

"It would be in ..." Taffi paused, and looked at Kelly, "... her best interest, if you were to remain calm and listen to us."

Kelly had quickly regained her feet. She grabbed David's arm, whimpering, "Listen to them, David. Just listen to them. Hear what they have to say. Then make them leave."

Taffi stepped to the side so he had a better angle on both of them. He had no intention of shooting them, which would have gone against everything that they stood for. Shooting these two Humanesh would have made him no better than a Voiya. The Imperite Guards only killed Earthers in the most extreme of circumstances, like a reporter running with a story with classified information which they refused to let go of, or when they were in the pursuit of honourable justice. Regardless, the effect that brandishing the Desert Eagle had on people was extremely productive. The Desert Eagle handgun was a lousy combat weapon, but up close it captured people's attention.

Minino ran the 'interview', for lack of a better term. His creepy, slow, sibilant, Shovitic drawl was almost as terrifying for the two Humanesh Earthers as was the way his pale skin looked in the dark clothing, standing there in the darkening light of early evening.

"You have been telling people about certain things that you say have happened to you. This will stop, right now. You will not mention these things anymore. Do you understand?"

David looked at him, dumbfounded. He had wondered if any MIB's would show up, and here they were ... and they were as terrifying as he had fantasized they might be. He had also, foolishly, fantasized about standing up to them.

"No, I won't stop telling anyone anything."

"David," Kelly almost screamed, still clutching his arm, "what the hell are you doing?"

He glanced around at her and then back at the two MIB, "You can't stop me from saying anything I want to. Your friends ... they took me and did things to me and I want the world to know about it. You can't hide behind your secrecy and your threats when you're doing this to people."

Minino was shaking his head. He decided to speak to them both telepathically. He knew he was much easier to understand that way, *No, David MacFeet, you are wrong. We did not do that to you. We are not with those ones, the ones who did this.*

"Bullshit," David hadn't even realized they were speaking directly into his mind. "If you aren't with them, why are you here? And what are you going to do? Shoot us? Are you going to shoot us if I don't agree? Is that what you're going to do?"

Kelly was still whimpering, her tears had turned her makeup into a river of black, blue, and rouge on her cheeks. There was a distinctive smell of fear — and urine — coming from where she was standing.

Minino stepped closer to David, but David didn't back up this time. Minino looked at Taffi and nodded.

Taffi put the gun away.

Minino smiled at David. The human whimpered at the ghastly site of the Shovitic's mouth. The Shovitic's gums emit two different gasses, and when they combine, what passes as teeth for them are caused to look like a psychedelic acid trip from hell. Once a person has seen a Shovitic smile, they never want to see it again.

118

David MacFeet, this is Kelly, your wife? Yes?

David nodded.

Your parents, they are Sam and Doris. They live here in Moose Jaw, yes?

David nodded.

Minino looked at Kelly, *Your father lives in this community of trailer homes, yes?*

She just whimpered and put her face closer to David's shoulder.

David MacFeet, if you speak anymore to anyone about what happened to you, we will come back. If we come back, I will reach down through your throat, and pull your lungs out through your mouth. Do you understand?

David had, if it was possible, gone paler. His hands pushed Kelly further behind him.

Minino shifted his gaze, *Kelly MacFeet, if your husband speaks to anyone else about what happened to him, then we will come back to see you. I will shove my arm so far up your anus that I will be able to take hold of your heart, and rip it from your quivering body. Do you understand?*

Kelly just squealed, panting, trying to get rid of the buzzing sound in her ears which meant she was close to fainting.

Minino looked at David again and stepped closer to him. He used his outside voice, knowing the sound of it would increase the fear, "David MacFeet, if you tell anyone else about what happened to you, I will take your parents," he turned his head slightly, "... and your father, Kelly MacFeet; I will take them to a planet where Humanesh are considered ..." Minino smiled again, for effect, "... where they are considered — a delicacy."

Kelly fainted. David turned to grab her, but tried to keep an eye on the two MIB who had just threatened him and his wife with a heinous death.

Taffi knelt beside the woman. David tried to push him away, but Minino pulled him back.

"Stop! Don't hurt her."

Taffi looked up at him, but then turned his attention back to the woman. He pulled a small gray box out of his pocket and set it on the woman's forehead. David saw colours, subdued colours, start dancing across the top of the box. After a few seconds Taffi retrieved the box and stood. *She is okay. She just fainted. She will wake in a few minutes.*

Minino let go of David and the human moved forward on his knees to his wife. He made sure she was breathing, and then turned to face the two terrifying men, still on his knees.

"Just tell me why. Why do you do this? Why do you take people?"

Minino answered him, *As I said, we don't do this. We are not part of those who do.*

"THEN WHY ARE YOU HERE PROTECTING THEM?"

We are not here protecting them, Taffi responded this time, *We are here to protect you Earthers.*

David was lost, "I don't understand. How can you say you are here to protect us when you just threatened to kill us, and eat our parents?"

This was a sore spot between Taffi and Minino. Minino didn't think the Earthers needed any explanation. He believed they just needed to do what they were told. Taffi, on the other hand, thought the Earthers would be more likely to cooperate if they knew the stakes.

Minino just stood there patiently while Taffi responded, *We are here so that our people can kill those who did this to you. They are our bitter enemies. However, we can only entrap and kill them if our people can get to them, without those aliens knowing who they are. If too many people start talking about the things that happen, about being taken by the — enemy — then an outcry will begin and the governments will have to do something. If your governments have to do something, it will lead quickly to a war. It will lead to an interplanetary war that your pitiful race is not able to win. If your planet goes to war against the Voiya, then everything on this planet would be destroyed. It would become a lifeless rock, floating in space.*

David stared at him, trying to process everything he just heard. Finally he asked, "Then why don't you just go and kill them? Why don't you just fight them yourselves? Out there, in space?"

Taffi was shaking his head. *We are a small race. We can be very effective, but only by stealth. If we declared war, then the Voiya would destroy us quickly, and then there would be no hope for any of the Humanesh worlds.*

"Worlds? Plural?" David asked, his eyes wide.

Taffi and Minino both nodded.

This region, Taffi continued, *is a region of much activity. There is far more in your sky, in your — space, than even your governments know about. On your moon, on Mars, on Venus, there are many who have an interest in your world, for its riches, and most of them are not friendly. It is surprising that your planet has lasted this long. Your world must not do anything that will hasten the attention of things even scarier than the Voiya.*

David just looked at him, finally realizing their mouths weren't moving as they talked. He was about to ask if they were in his head when Kelly moaned. He turned to the sound of her voice, she was starting to come around. Taffi took the small box out of his pocket and looked at David.

David looked at the box, and paused only a few seconds before nodding.

Taffi placed the box on Kelly's forehead again, and she stopped moaning, falling back into a deep sleep. Taffi put the box back in his pocket.

"David MacFeet, what I have said to you, do you understand?" Taffi continued out loud.

"Yes, I understand. But couldn't you have just explained it to us? Did you have to threaten us? Did you have to scare her so bad she pissed herself and fainted?"

Taffi pulled on David's arm so that the Earther was looking right at him. Taffi removed his sunglasses and watched David recoil in horror.

"David MacFeet, what I have said to you, is not a threat. It is a promise. If you speak any further of being taken, or if she speaks to anyone of you being taken, then we *will* come back — and you *will* regret that, very, very much."

David knelt there, shaking with fear, rage, and frustration — but mostly with fear. Finally, he nodded. "I understand. I won't say anything about it again to anyone, ever. Neither will she."

Taffi put his sunglasses back on. He smiled, but kept his mouth closed. "Good. That is very good David MacFeet."

From her other side, Minino knelt down and slid his long skinny arms under Kelly's legs and back. He easily lifted her, like he was lifting air itself, and stood up. He turned to the front of the mobile home and went into the living room, gently laying the woman on the sofa.

Taffi stood up straight and held out a hand, helping David stand up. *She will sleep for a few hours. When she awakes, she will not remember our visit.* He turned to look at Minino laying her on the sofa. *She will not remember anything from one hour before we arrived. It is up to you to convince her that nothing else must be said about what happened to you.*

David nodded and the two men just turned for the door.

122

"Wait, please," David called out to them.

The Imperite Guards stopped and turned, waiting for him to speak.

"I remember them taking me, but I don't remember anything they did to me. Why did they take me? What did they do to me?"

"Experiments," Minino said.

"What — what kind of *experiments*?" David was shaking, he wasn't sure he wanted to know, but this was the only chance he would ever have to find out.

Taffi responded with one word, "Invasive."

The two Imperite Guards got in their car and drove away. David never saw them again, and never discussed his experience ever again. Neither did Kelly.

Chapter 22

A half hour north of the nuclear research facility at Chalk River, Ontario, is a small town on an island in the middle of the Ottawa River. Not any bigger than a hamlet, the town is called Rapides-des-Jaochims and is technically on the Quebec side of the border. There are two hydroelectric dams, one on each end of the island. The only road off the small island town goes into Ontario, passing over the southern hydroelectric dam.

Gilles Boisbriand had worked at the hydroelectric dam for fifteen years. He'd been moved there by the Umite planetary coordinator, who used an Umite contact to get Gilles the job. Coming to the area with a big savings account, he soon bought into a seasonal retreat called The Northern Lodge. As part owner of the facility, he claimed one of the cabin's as his personal residence. After adding some upgraded plumbing and a wood stove, he had lived there year round for the last twelve years.

A loner, who had never been married, he shared his small cabin with a cat named Marquis-du-Sod. It was a playful bilingual name referring to the cat's love of digging up the flower bed that Gilles kept trying to plant every spring. For purposes of expedience, Gilles simply called his feline roommate: Sod.

On the Monday after the highland games in Kincardine, an event which Gilles was not aware of, he had to go downriver. There had been some Ministry of Natural Resources concerns about erosion effects since the two hydroelectric power plants, one on each end of the island, had to increase the outflow pressure of water due to the recent spring and summer's higher-than-usual inflow level. Ontario's Ministry of Natural Resources (MNR), had responsibility for both sides of the river, even though the side with the erosion was technically in the Province of Quebec.

Gilles said goodbye to Sod, leaving a bowl full of dry food and a bowl of water for him on the floor. He trailered his small outboard motorboat down to the church camp, opposite the uninhabited

Fraser Landing and Deep River Depot, where the MNR had their concerns.

Launching the boat with the help of one of the camp guests, Gilles also had a picnic cooler and a good book with him. The sandy beaches on the unoccupied shore were pristine and beautiful. The sunny late-August day had simply screamed at him to use the time for a little relaxation. With the given amount of increased Voiya activity in the area, Gilles had spent most evenings out wandering around the hydroelectric dams, something that was almost of as much interest to the UFOs, the Voiya, as the Chalk River nuclear research facility much further downriver.

With the boat in the water by 9 a.m., it took Gilles about three hours to examine the shoreline and take the pictures he needed to take. There were indeed some erosion patterns evident, more so than usual, but there wasn't enough for the MNR to get their boxers in a twist about. When he got back he would file his report, submit his pictures, and then everyone would forget about it until some other local decided to complain again.

With the official part of the trip done, Gilles had a big smile on his face as he swung around the point and moved into the leeward side of Deep Water Bay, a secluded area which the residents couldn't see from the far side of the river. He beached his twelve-foot aluminum boat on a stretch of sand which looked like no one had ever set foot on it.

He enjoyed his lunch, and his book. He went for a skinny dip in the water, then toweled himself off and lay in the sun. He applied a liberal amount of sunscreen to keep his skin from burning. He eventually finished off the thermos of coffee, but despite the effects of the caffeine, while reading his book, Gilles dozed off. The sun was at an angle that soon put it on the other side of some trees, but it was warm enough that he fell into a deep, peaceful, and relaxing sleep.

Several hours later, Gilles came to with a start. He opened his eyes to the darkness and had a moment of panic, until he remembered where he was. He checked his watch, barely able to see it in the moonlight. It was just past 9:30 p.m. He quickly got dressed and started gathering his things.

It dawned on him that he didn't hear anything. He'd been listening to birds and cicadas through the day. He was instantly on guard. Birds and cicadas would go quiet if there was a predator around. He scanned his eyes along the banks of the water, looking at the forest, cursing himself for falling asleep and being so exposed. There hadn't been any black bear reports in the area lately, but the area was known for them. He knew there was something else the birds and cicadas might detect the presence of: another kind of predator.

Gilles looked up in the sky. The air was clear, the sun was down, and the sky was filled with stars. With so little light pollution in the area, the Milky Way stood out clearly — except for one patch. There was one small oblong patch of darkness where he couldn't see the Milky Way — and the small patch of darkness was moving. It was moving towards him. Gilles smiled, after a lifetime of waiting he was looking at his first Voiya craft. It couldn't be anything else.

He stepped closer to the edge of the water, away from the trees, making himself more visible. He knew they tracked movement easier, so he moved quickly along the beach, then turned and went the other way when he couldn't go any further. His excitement was building, his breathing was heavier. The purpose of his existence was about to be realized. That which he had trained and waited for, was upon him. The reason he had travelled a hundred light years, leaving all he knew behind him, was about to be realized; but only if they took him. It would only happen if they noticed him and transported him aboard the ship. The small patch of black was almost overhead. *What if they don't? What if they just pass me by.* He started breathing faster; he was gritting his teeth; his body was tensing with desire and fear; he was clenching his fists. *Please, please, please, please ...*

127

As the patch of darkness came directly overhead, Gilles felt a tingle at the base of his spine.

There was a flash of blue light.

After the flash of blue light came a brilliance which took him by surprise. His hands instinctively flew up in front of his face to shield his eyes. The white light of the room he was in was so strong it seared into his eyes, making them hurt. It was coming from the walls, the ceiling, and the floor.

In the almost blinding haze of light, he saw a figure move. It moved right in front of him. He was staring down into the hideous face of a Voiya Master. It stood there, dressed in its garish floor-length robes, and Gilles felt the creature telepathically forcing its way into his mind. He looked up and saw five Vesna, the quintessential "grays" of popular UFO culture, approaching from behind the Voiya.

True to his training, Gilles tried to scream in fear. He stepped back, trying to get away from them. He started thinking of every terrifying scene of every horror movie he had ever watched. He needed to put images of fear and irrational beliefs in his mind for them to find. He needed them to take him out of the matter transmission chamber; otherwise they might be able to get him off the ship before he carried out the Imperative.

Thankfully, the Voiya and their servants couldn't tell a Falwasz Umite from an Earther without a blood test.

After ten seconds, Gilles slumped to the floor, playing possum. He was chanting the Mantra of Freedom in his mind while focussing on the images of horror.

The tonal rhythms of the Mantra of Freedom blocked the neuro-pathways that allowed the Voiya and Vesna to exert their mind control. To them, the sounds he was making in his head were nonsensical gibberish which they ignored. The mantra allowed his mind to be engaged in the active pursuit of a goal, rather than reacting to the fear of the situation, which was considerable, even for an Imperite.

His subconscious was, more pointedly, not retreating within itself. That's what gives the Vesna, and the Voiya, the ability to control a person's autonomic and physical functions. If he didn't give them an "in", then they couldn't control him. However, if he responded as they expected, they wouldn't actually know that. There was no biofeedback component to their mental control; they had to rely on observation of their target.

He kept up the litany of the Mantra of Freedom in his head — not out loud, not yet.

Om shay om pu tam lay om pu scm par um tah nom.

The training was precise. He kept repeating the words in his head, focussing on the rhythm and the words themselves. Reciting this pattern in his head meant that he could retain consciousness, retain control. He also had to make the effort to be physically limp. If there was tension in his limbs, it would make him suspect.

The first thing the Vesna (the scientists) do with abductees is to give them a simple blood test. There is a particular protein in Umite blood that was three times higher than in the blood of any other Humanesh race. It was the only way you could positively identify an Umite. If the marker was present, the Voiya's standing order was to kill the subject, and that came directly from the Regentship on the Voiya homeworld of Eridani Prime.

Unfortunately for the Voiya and the Vesna, they always waited until they got back to the examination room to do the blood test. In most cases where they unsuspectingly took an Umite, they never got that far. They did, however, get out of the matter transfer chamber.

The Voiya were not only vicious, they were paranoid. Their ships were designed so that the TransMat would not, *could not*, operate anywhere inside the ship except for the matter transfer chamber. This was so that they didn't have to worry about one of their crew-servants deciding to space them in their sleep. This also meant that when the Imperites were moved out of the matter transfer chamber, they couldn't be spaced by the Voiya either. Once outside of the matter transfer chamber, the only thing the Voiya, Vesna, Trigla, or drones could do was to fight for their lives. Luckily for the Imperites, none of the Voiya or their crew-servants are adept to close-quarters combat.

Gilles felt himself being picked up and carried. Though his eyes were closed, he was able to tell he passed through a doorway. The light on his eyelids changed, the smell of the air changed.

It was time to act.

Gilles flexed his arms and legs, breaking the hold of the Vesna's small hands. He landed on his side and as he stood he opened his mouth and the Mantra of Freedom became the Song of Freedom, the tonal rhythms being sung at the top of his lungs. The words not only prevented their mind control, the guttural-toned words sung loudly would disorient the Vesna. He would keep this up until the last of them were dead.

"OM SHAY OM PU TAM LAY OM PU SOM PAR UM TAH NOM."

His actions and those rhythms were the most terrifying thing a Voiya Master could encounter. This particular master, Nuursan of Jesnok, spun on his heels, starring at the Humanesh that was more than twice as tall as he was. His tiny hands flew up to cover his auditory orifices and the Voiya Master screamed in fear. He watched in horror as the Mahal of the Vesna pod, the leader of the pod, had both of its arms ripped from its body by the Humanesh. He saw another of the Vesna punched so hard in the head that the hand of the Humanesh went right through the Vesna's skull.

The Voiya turned and fled as he sent out a telepathic alert. As the petite alien reached the end of the short corridor, ten vicious little misanthropic drones came around the corner at full speed, charging towards the Humanesh. As the Master rounded the corner, he stopped to look back at the carnage. The other three Vesna were all dead, one with its head ripped right off of its torso. The Humanesh was using the body of that one as a club, beating and flailing at the drones. The Master smiled as he heard the man scream when one of the drones sunk its teeth into his leg, and then another one did the same to the other leg.

The Master headed for the bridge of the relatively small spaceship. It was the safest place on board. The contingent of six Trigla guards would protect him there. He had already given the order for them to fall back to the bridge in case the Humanesh got past the drones.

Paul, his wife, and their four pre-teen children sat around the campfire. Paul Jr. was telling the others about the nature hike he'd gone on with his dad that afternoon. The family did this each evening when they camped by the Ottawa River, sitting around the fire and sharing their experiences, or at least their perspectives on the adventures of the day. Paul and Jane raised their kids in a communicative home, encouraging open sharing.

This was why Jane, listening to the children, found it odd that her husband's attention seemed to be far away. He was sitting in this campfire chair, a can of Diet Pepsi in his hand, staring across the river and up at the sky. He happened to turn his head to look right at her. His face said something was wrong, but he just turned back and looked off into the night-time sky.

Jane turned her head, still murmuring in the right places to her son's tales of the dragon flies they had seen cavorting in the late afternoon sun. She cast her glance where Paul was looking, and after a few seconds, she saw the patch of darkness that seemed to be moving in front of the stars. It slowed to a stop a little ways down river, and then it started moving east, rapidly. In no time flat, it disappeared.

She turned back to Paul, who was staring at her again, his face pale.

"Come on kids," she said, standing up and interrupting Paul Jr., "time to go inside."

After the chorus of complaints and dragging of heels, all the kids were inside. Paul spent the whole time watching the sky. Once the fire was out, he joined her at the door to the large camper trailer.

"I want to leave tomorrow," she said quietly.

Paul just nodded. They would never return to that campground.

By the time the drones were all dead, Gilles was in agony. He leaned against the wall to gather himself. The wounds left by the chunks of missing flesh, and muscle, on his arms and legs were on fire. He had no choice but to keep moving. He was here on the Voiya ship. If he didn't succeed, he would die trying. There was no going back.

He stood up straight, screaming with the fire and pain of the wounds. He was bleeding heavily, but he was also pumped full of adrenalin. At the first doorway, he stopped and pressed the small square button. The double doors slid open and Gilles recognized a medical theatre. He went in and looked around, searching for anything he could use as a weapon. He found a dozen small round things, like marbles, in a clear plastic box. Gilles rolled them around in his hand, realizing these were the tracking devices they sometimes placed inside Earther's nasal cavities. He put them in his pocket. He picked up what looked like a bone saw.

He only had to go down three relatively short corridors before he found the bridge.

⬤

The drone pushed itself up on its one remaining arm, shaking its head. It felt heavy, too heavy. It shook its body and another dead drone rolled off of it. The drone looked up just in time to see the Humanesh disappearing around the corner towards the place where they made the ship go.

There was a pain, an indescribable pain. It looked to the pain, to the arm where the pain was coming from, only there was no arm. It looked at the stump where the appendage had been ripped from its body. The black ichor of life dripped from the stump, the coagulants quickly slowing down the flow as soon as they were exposed to air. The genetic engineering would shortly stop the flow of black blood altogether.

The drone looked towards the corridor ahead. It pushed itself up and regained its feet. As it tried to move it stumbled, crashing back to its knees. The drone chattered its teeth and looked around. All of the other drones from its hive were dead. There were none left to help him, none to aid him in protecting the Master. The Master must be up ahead, where the Humanesh had gone, in the place where they made the ship go.

The drone struggled to its feet again, staying up this time. It moved forward, stumbling into the wall, but staying on its feet, moving towards its prey. A great swatch of black ichor was painted on the wall as it moved, as the stump of its arm dragged behind it. The minimal pain receptors irritated the drone, enlivened it, and helped it focus its mind through the haze of disorientation from blood loss.

It stopped and poked its head around the first corner, using caution because it knew it might be the Master's only salvation. The next corridor was clear.

Gilles knew the bridge was where the Voiya would retreat. He made it there quickly. The layout of corridors and rooms were exactly the same as he had been taught so many years ago. Outside the door to the bridge were six armed Trigla. The seven-foot plus, brown leather-skinned creatures were crouched down, pointing weapons towards him. The first one fired and Gilles ducked back around the corner just in time. The energy charge left a big enough scorch mark on the wall to make Gilles wary of getting struck by one.

Luckily for him, the Trigla are incredibly curious creatures.

He took out two of the dozen marble-sized round trackers and rolled one into their hallway, and a couple of heartbeats later he rolled the other one. He waited until he heard the movement. He backed up and then rolled a third one along the floor. When he saw the brown head, with feathers and baubles hanging from the ridge line running behind its brow, Gilles snapped his hand out, grabbed the creature's throat and pulled it forward around the corner, right onto the sharp blade of the saw, cutting his own hand deeply in the process. The creature fell, clutching its cut throat. It made a horrible, raspy squealing sound as it quickly bled to death. Gilles tossed the bone saw out of the Trigla's reach and picked up the weapon it had been carrying.

He looked at his bleeding hand, so damaged he thought his thumb was in danger of falling off. There was no pain; he still had too much adrenalin in his system.

The drone peered around the next corner, breathing heavily, but keeping its jaw still so the chattering of its teeth would not give it away. The drone saw the Humanesh; the threat to the Master. The drone saw the Humanesh kill one of the foolish Trigla. The drone zeroed in on the cutting tool the Vesna used, tossed so carelessly on the floor. The drone shut its eyes, focussing on its own body, summoning all of its strength for the sake of the Master.

The Master was all. The Master was everything. The Master's love was what drove and enlivened the drone. The life of the Master was sacrosanct above all things, even the drone's own life. The Master must come first. The Master must survive.

The drone opened its eyes. The Humanesh was firing the gun towards the room where the Master had to be — the room where they made the ship go. The drone started moving up the hallway, making no noise, moving with single mind and single purpose towards the cutting implement on the floor.

Get the weapon.

Kill the Humanesh.

Save the Master. Save the Master. Save the Master. Save the …

Gilles fished the other nine round trackers out of his pocket. He heard the feet pounding in the hallway. He counted to three and then tossed the handful of marble-sized objects around the corner. He heard the squeals of surprise as those charging his position wound up going *ass over tea kettle* when their running feet skidded on the small objects and toppled into each other.

That was the moment of disorientation he needed.

Gilles stepped around the corner and shot all five of them, taking a round of energy in his own shoulder.

He screamed. The pain was blinding. It was like a blow torch had opened his skin and then a box of salt had been poured in the wound. He thrashed around, wildly, banging into the walls, clutching at his shoulder, the pain wouldn't go away. He fell to his knees and kept screaming for what seemed like an eternity, his vision watered and was occluded by the tears.

Finally, the pain started to abate. He panted and wheezed through his teeth. He wanted death at that moment. He wanted it to overtake him and end the agony. But he knew, a part of him knew, that he wasn't done. The Imperative wasn't just an oath. On his way to the planet, during the Earth classes and continued training, at some point he had been hypnotized and subconscious instructions were given to him. The Imperative would push him forward when he wanted to run away. This was done exactly for this type of situation.

Gilles pushed himself to his feet, his breath ragged.

He pushed off towards the door to the bridge of the ship. There was a blur in the corner of his eye. He turned to see a drone, a drone missing an arm. Gilles was surprised — he thought they were all dead. It had the bone saw in its remaining arm and was swinging it. Gilles put up his arm to block the attack, but the force of the swing carried the sharp blade right through his arm, severing it just below his elbow. Gilles screamed and lashed out, killing the drone with one punch.

He looked at the stump of his arm spurting blood. He knew he only had seconds before the darkness, and failure, would overtake him. He quickly undid his belt and pulled it out of his pant loops. He wrapped it around the stump and pulled it tight, as tight as he could, while being blinded by his tears again. The pain was incredible. He swooned and fell back against the wall, but he didn't let go of the belt. The grayness danced at the edge of his vision, but he forced it back as he pulled the belt even tighter. He wrapped the remaining length around the stump two more times and then tucked it in. He knew he had to move, to act now, while he still could.

The Imperite stood, picked up a Trigla weapon, and then moved forward. He heard a cat meow right behind him. He spun on his heels, "Sod? C'est toi la?"

There was nothing there.

"You're a bad little boy. You should kill yourself." He spun again at the sound of his mother's voice, his Umite mother. But there was no one there.

He sniffed the air: he smelled fresh briska cookies.

He sniffed again: he smelled urine and feces.

His mother's voice taunted him again to end his life.

He heard his father's voice telling him he was a failure.

He heard his own voice screaming at him to run.

Gilles closed his eyes and resumed the Mantra of Freedom in his mind.

That damn Voiya is in your head.

Seconds later, he staggered forward, carefully stepping over the Trigla.

One of them moved.

It weakly reached out and grabbed Gilles ankle, almost pulling him off balance. With his one good arm, he brought the shoulder stock of the weapon down on its head. He had to do it several times before the Trigla finally stopped gripping his ankle — and stopped breathing.

It was only a few more steps to reach the door to the bridge. He took a moment to gather himself. The little Voiya bastard was still in there, and it wasn't injured. The Voiya never fought any battles themselves, unless they were backed into a corner and had no choice. At least, Gilles had the little shit's cowardice in his favour.

He looked down and saw blood trickling from the stump of his arm. He retightened the belt.

He felt woozy.

He didn't have long.

He picked up the weapon and used the muzzle to press the black button by the door. As the door slid open the Voiya Master jumped out of the flight couch and turned to face the Humanesh. Its beady, bloodshot eyes shifted from side to side. Gilles heard its voice in his head.

You are going to die human, you have failed.

Gilles pointed the weapon at it and fired.

Nuursan of Jesnok fell to the floor, dead.

"Huh," Gilles said to no one. It had been *that* easy.

Gilles stepped forward and looked down at the Voiya. He spat on the creature and gave its final benediction, "*Brûle en enfer.*" Burn in hell.

Gilles sat down heavily on one of the three acceleration couches. He was woozy, his head was spinning, his ears were buzzing, and his respiration was slowing. He looked at his arms and legs, at the chunks of flesh missing. He looked at the stump of his arm, which oddly enough, he no longer felt any pain from.

Now, there was only one thing left to do. But he was so tired, he needed to close his eyes, for a moment, for just a moment. He just needed to gather his strength. Selila cupped his face, turning it up to her. He looked into her brown eyes, feeling his heart fluttering with anticipation. He could smell the spices from her morning bath, and the soap she used to wash her hair. She was wearing the silky green dress he had helped her pick out for their first formal clan party. "I love you," he heard her whisper, as her lips … Gilles snapped his head back. He looked around wildly to find her, to see where she had gone. But she wasn't there, she hadn't been there. He felt the pain begin and looked down at the stump of his arm, seeing the body of the Voiya Master lying on the floor.

There was no time to rest, no time to gather his strength. He had to act now.

Right now.

Act now and the pain will be gone.

Gilles turned in the acceleration couch and put his remaining hand on the control interface. He was able to manipulate the touch controls to bring up the coordinate map for the solar system, Earth's solar system. His lessons from so many years ago were coming back fresh and vivid in his mind, thanks to the buried hypnotic suggestions. He activated the command to lock his current location, and then he moved the targeting reticule over the sun. Two more entries locked the location to 1.5 million metres inside the sun's chromosphere.

He paused before executing the fold. With his last breaths, he thought of his parents, and the day they saw him off on his journey towards this moment.

He smiled at the memory of his mother's cheek against his, the memory of her voice speaking her final words of love for him. "I honour you," he said to the memory of her face, and imagined her smiling at him.

He reached towards the control that would activate the folding engine, instantly transporting the ship between the two selected points. He hesitated a final moment, remembering the girl he had left behind on Umitia a lifetime ago. He smiled again at the thought of Selila's final embrace, her scent, and the passion of her final kiss.

"Now as then."

Gilles Boisbriand, Imperite of the House of Kudon, closed his eyes and smiled; he exhaled his last breath as he initiated the fold into the star.

On board the Imperite Guard's duty frigate known simply as 802, high above Earth, the on duty sensor technician raised his hand for the watch commander's attention.

"Gravitational anomaly," he said in the slow Shovitic way. "There is minimal transition wake, it appears to be outbound."

The watch commander said nothing. He stood there with his hands at his side, waiting.

Forty-five seconds later the sensor tech turned in his seat and looked at the watch commander, "Massive solar prominence, the energy output is consistent with the detonation of a Class-V micro-singularity engine."

Chapter 23

Tommy sat in the break room with Val, the other woodlot representative working outdoors today. It was just after lunchtime, and they were almost ready to head back outside. As Val filled both of their travel mugs with coffee, Tommy saw an image of the sun on the news. He turned up the sound.

"... lacking explanation. Here is our science correspondent, Trish Negala."

The image of a slender Eurasian woman with long brown hair replaced the news anchor.

"Thank you, Gord. NASA reports that another massive flare was detected less than twelve hours ago now. They classify it as an X-14, with anything over X-9 being considered abnormal. They tell us that these larger flares, sometimes much larger than this, are not unheard of, but they are also not common. They detect these several times a year and they occur, it seems, for no apparent reason. We've reported on sunspots and solar flares before, and how they run in eleven-year cycles. Today we're on the down slope of that activity curve, so we should be seeing less of them. The only reason this one has captured the public's attention, is because it's the fourth one in the last two weeks. Typically, there are only three or four of these, "rogue flares", as they call them, each year. So what does this mean for us on planet Earth? Well you can expect to see some amazing Aurora Borealis if you are in the north, in about five or six days. Other than the lightshow, if you operate ham radio, you might experience some interference about the same time. These solar flares pose no danger to those on Earth unless they are shooting right at the planet. Even then, the only real danger is to those in airplanes or on board the International Space Station. This rogue flare we're reporting on isn't going to hit us directly, but we are going to pass through a sizeable amount of the charged particles it's carrying with it from the surface of the sun. So for this flare, there's no need to worry. It

was pointed in a direction that won't directly intersect with Earth. This is Trish Negala, reporting for CBC News, Toronto."

Tommy turned down the sound on the television again. He smiled to himself because he knew full well what caused the rogue flares — most of them. It meant someone had completed their Imperative.

He took the travel mug from Carl and headed outside when he heard the whiskey and cigarette voice of the manager yelling for him from down the corridor.

"Tommy, my office, now."

Tommy groaned inwardly, hastily playing back everything that had happened since he arrived. He knew it couldn't be anything he had done, but whenever the boss called him to her office, his stomach always turned and twisted; and he couldn't help wondering what he was about to catch hell for.

"Yes, Michelle?" he stuck his head in the office, but stayed leaning against the door. The frumpy woman ten years his senior, with too much rouge and a Dolly Parton wig, turned in her chair to look at him.

"How's your truck running, any fuckin' problems with it?"

"It's running fine, why?"

"There's a conference for employees I was ignoring, but some little shite at head office just called and ripped me a new fuckin' arsehole. I need to get Cassie and Lenora's ass to Toronto on Thursday morning. They need to be there by 9 a.m., and I don't need them to get fuckin' lost. If they aren't there on time, my ass is grass."

"Oh, yeah? Is that crabby grass?"

"Shut up, fuckhead. Will you do it? Will you drive them?"

"Sure thing, you covering the gas?"

"Of course, don't be silly. I'll pay you a full day's wage, cover the gas, cover two meals, and throw in an extra $40 spending money. Might as well, *monsieur le dickhead* at head office is picking up the tab. You're going to have to entertain yourself while they're at the fuckin' conference, so take a book."

"What's it about? The conference I mean?"

"Fuck if I know, *'how to keep people fuckin' happy and not fucking up in the workplace'* or some touchy-feely shit like that. I figure they'll sit around in a circle all day, holding hands and singing Kumbaya until everyone feels all fuckin' warm and squishy inside."

"Michelle, you're such a charmer," Tommy allowed a grin, "you ever think about selling Bibles?"

"Fuck off, Tommy."

"Do they know they're going?"

"Nope, I need you to tell them when you make arrangements to pick them up." She handed him two sheets of paper with hastily scrawled information.

"Okay, boss, I'm on it. I'll have them meet me here at 5 a.m., they can leave their cars in the lot out front."

"Whatever, now get the fuck back to work will ya? I'm not paying you to stand around jawin' me to death." The older woman turned back to her computer and dismissed Tommy with a wave of her hand.

She could turn a straight man gay with that mouth, he thought as he walked away from Michelle's office. Tommy read the information and then went in search of the two women.

Chapter 24

Zekra sat at his desk reading dispatches from the palace while Shivinin dozed in the chair at his desk. His mouth was open and he was snoring. Zekra couldn't focus on the reading with the horrible racket going on. He looked at his partner who was leaning back in his chair, his feet up on the desk, and his hands folded across his stomach. The dozing Shovitic looked peaceful — *too peaceful.*

Zekra started tearing off small pieces of paper and squishing them into tight little rounds. He tossed one at Shivinin; it bounced off his cheek. He tossed another one; it bounced off his eyeworms, closed tightly over his mostly empty eye socket. The third one found its mark, going right into Shivinin's mouth. The Umite gagged, hacked and sat up, huffing and spitting. Zekra laughed at his partner.

"Asshole."

As Shivinin tried to lean back in the chair again, this time putting his fedora over his face, the three-tone chime made them both look at the locked cabinet that the sound came from. Shivinin was closest; he pushed his chair over to it, entered the six-digit code, and opened the door.

The ERB device was lit up, indicating an incoming call. He picked up the handset and waited for the miniscule wormhole to stabilize the transmission. After a moment he heard the connection tone.

"Station twelve," Shivinin stated without any pleasantries.

He listened for a moment, and then hung up after saying, "It shall be done."

He locked up the communication device and turned to look at Zekra, with a perplexed look on his face.

"Well?"

A status check on an Imperite has been requested, he responded telepathically.

145

Which one?

Sepherin Tekin. She arrived recently, didn't she?

Zekra opened a folder on his computer, found her file, and started reading it.

She's the one that was reassigned, her original host family died in a car accident. She's only been here a few days. Why are we checking on her? Is there a problem with her new host?

I was just told to have the status check performed.

Zekra held up a long skinny finger, squinting with concentration at the computer monitor, *Did you know that her new host is an Earth-born?*

Shivinin sat back in his chair; it was his turn to be surprised. *No, I did not know that. They put her with an Earth-born?*

Why would Command be interested in her? Zekra was confused.

It's not Command who is interested in her. Shivinin was leaning forward and looking pointedly at his partner, *I was speaking with Kalabot.*

The two aliens stared at each other for a moment, wondering why *the* Manager of the Umites had any interest in an individual Imperite, especially since it was only a few days after she had arrived. An Earth-born host was rare, but not unheard of. That, in and of itself, wasn't a reason for a status check.

Zekra looked back at the woman's file and then sighed, accepting that such knowledge was far above his station to consider.

I will call Taffi and Minino. They are back from the west and working the central region of that country.

Zekra had no idea what he was sending his brother to face.

146

Chapter 25

On his way home, Tommy thought about taking Sepherin to Toronto, but he realized that a three-hour drive with four people in the cab of the truck would be too much. He waved to Mitch and Martha, who were sitting out front of their place, as he pulled in his driveway. The front door and the windows were open, which gave him a bit of a start. He still wasn't used to having a houseguest.

Sepherin wasn't in the living room or the kitchen, so he went upstairs to see if she had fallen asleep. He had promised to teach her how to make his mushroom, okra, and mealworm stew. He lightly knocked on the door to her room, but there was no answer. *Must have fallen asleep*, he thought as he turned away. He'd only taken two steps when he heard a sob coming from her room.

He turned back and listened close to the door, he heard another sob. He knocked again, "Stephy? Are you okay, dear?"

"No."

"What's wrong, Stephy? Can I come in?"

There was no response. He didn't like just going in, in case she wasn't decent, but he was concerned she was sick. There had been rare reported cases of new arrivals contracting serious infections, sometimes life threatening. He sighed and opened the door slightly, enough to see if she was dressed or not. The tall young woman was sitting on the edge of the bed, in front of the window, with her elbows on her knees and her face buried in her hands.

"Stephy? Can I come in?"

She just nodded and sobbed harder.

Tommy sat beside her on the bed and put his arm around her in a fatherly way. It seemed to be a cue for the floodgates to open. He pulled her closer. She reached up with one hand, holding on to the front of his shirt, turning her face into his chest. He listened to the keening of her trying to hold back the wails, but unable to stop crying. This went on for several minutes. Tommy just sat there, holding her, letting her get the poison of distress out of her system, covering the front of his shirt with tears and snot.

Finally she leaned away from him, looking around for something to wipe her hands and face with. Tommy fetched a box of Kleenex from the dresser.

She wiped her face and her hands, blew her nose, and then looked up at him. Her cheeks were red, her eyes were bloodshot; she looked small, weak, and vulnerable.

"So what's this all about? Did something happen?"

"Roguk," was all she could say, biting her lip to fight back the tears again.

"Row ... what? What's a row-goo?"

She smiled, and then bit her lip again. Finally she was able to say, "Roguk Fozretson, he's the father of my baby. I'm just ... I ... miss him, and I hate him, and I'm having his ..." It took a few moments for her to compose herself again. "I'm having his child and he doesn't even know it. I can't even get word to him. The guards never take information home. Besides ..." she trailed off.

Tommy waited a moment for her to continue, but she didn't. "Besides, what?" he finally asked.

He could see she was tormented. He could see on her face that something was deeply disturbing her, something that had to be more than just the pregnancy and the distance from home. Those things you just cry out, this was something eating at her.

Tommy knew from his own experience, after his Earth-father died, a person could blame themselves for all sorts of things which weren't their fault. He had carried the blame for Ivan's suicide for many years before he was able to move beyond it. He could see there had to be an unsettled equation in this pregnancy, something making it worse for her. Perhaps the boy was from another clan. That would definitely be a problem for her. Such unions, he knew, simply weren't permitted. But then he realized, no one here on Earth would know, or care.

She finally took a deep breath and let it out, "Even if I could tell Roguk, I can't tell him. He's married."

Tommy nodded his head slowly, "I see. That's — quite the little twist in the story. But, like you said, you can't tell him. He'll never know, no one will ever know. The only one who knows he's the father is you, and me. And Stephy, I'm not going to say anything about it."

"But, do you think less of me? Do you ..."

Tommy chuckled, "Stephy, I couldn't care less who the father is or what the circumstances are. You're here with me, I'm your blood-kin, and you need me. That's all I need to know. So don't even think anything like that, there's no judgement here. None of us are perfect."

She nodded and sniffed, picking at the balled up tissue in her hand. She looked at him, her face covered in tear tracks.

"Uncle Tameht, I have a bad feeling."

"Of course you do, sweetie. The way you've been crying, you've got yourself all twisted in knots."

"No, it's not that. It's — ever since I got here, with you. I have a feeling that something bad is going to happen, something — horrible. It's like the baby is telling me to run, if that makes any sense. It's telling me to get away. It doesn't want to be here."

Great, she's losing her fucking mind. Tommy put his arm around her and squeezed her shoulders. "It's just the hormones talking, Stephy. You know the baby can't talk to you. It's not even fully formed yet. It's ..."

"I know, I know. It sounds crazy."

She leaned against him, holding his arm, letting the urge to cry diminish. Tommy just sat there without saying anything else man-stupid and let his niece draw whatever strength she needed from his presence.

"I'm scared," she said eventually. "I can't stay with you forever; I'm going to have to build a life for myself. I thought I was ready for this, I thought I was prepared, but now — I'm not usually this weepy, but the last few ten-sleeps have been horrible. I mean, the last few — weeks? Is that the word?"

Tommy nodded, "Yes, weeks, they're seven sleeps long."

"I'm sick and tired of crying. 'm a strong woman. I'm a trained killer. I travelled over 50 parsecs to get here. I left everything I know and love behind to complete a ridiculous oath based on the sins of our ancestors, and ... and ... *these hormonal tidal waves are making me crazy.*" The tears started again.

Tommy was starting to feel out of his depth. A pregnant woman was something he had never had to deal with.

"I have an idea. You stay here, I'll be back in a few minutes."

As he stood up, Stephy flopped down on her side on the bed. He turned and looked at her again before leaving the room. She looked so vulnerable lying there, even though he knew she could half kill a man without breaking a sweat. Still, every long-buried fatherly instinct that he had never needed started to wake up.

Tommy went next door and found his neighbours still out on the porch.

"Martha, Mitch."

They both greeted him.

"Martha," Tommy got right to the point, "Mitch told you about my niece that has come to stay with me?"

Martha nodded, "Yes, he did. 'm looking forward to meeting her.

I wanted to give her some time to settle in first, though. Would you two like to come to dinner?"

"Martha," Tommy hesitated a moment, "well, you see, I think I need your help with her."

"Oh?" Martha set down her glass of iced tea and leaned forward in the chair. "Is the child alright? Is she ill?"

"She's — she's in the family way, Martha, and she's going through some powerful emotional ups and downs. She can't — the father's not in the picture anymore and her family isn't available for her, and ..." He shrugged, "I want to help her, Martha, but this is something I have no clue about. I just don't know how to help her."

Martha stood, "Here, Tommy. You sit with Mitch and let the women folk handle the women stuff." She stepped down off the porch, marched straight over to his house and in the front door.

"Beer?" Mitch asked.

An hour and a half later, Mitch was checking the foil wrapped potatoes on the BBQ in the backyard. A plate of steaks was waiting on the side. He had made the executive decision that Tommy and his niece would be dining at their place this evening.

Tommy sat with him, quietly jawing about this, that, and the other. Mitch didn't ask any questions about the girl, the pregnancy, the father, or the circumstances. Tommy kept looking over towards the house, and a couple of times had got up to go see how things were going. Each time he did, Mitch made him sit back down. All he had to do was tell him there was a good chance Martha and Stephy might be talking about menstruation or child birth. That was all Tommy needed to plank his ass back down in the chair. He shuddered at the thought of walking in on one of *those* conversations.

As Mitch closed the lid on the BBQ and turned the heat down, they heard the screen door on the front of Mitch's house open and close. They both looked at the back door: no one came out, but they could hear the women's voices inside. Hearing them helped Tommy relax — Stephy was talking, not crying.

Finally, they heard Martha call from inside, "Mitch? The potatoes done yet?"

"A little more than that, maybe," he hollered back through the open window.

"Well put the steaks on, dear, we'll bring everything else out," there was a pause, "just three though, Stephy's one of those vegetarians. I'll cut up some to grill for her."

"Fair enough!" Mitch yelled back.

Ten minutes later, the back door opened and the two women came out, laden with plates and fixings for the table. Sepherin unburdened her arms and then came and sat beside Tommy. She had changed her clothes, and her hair was brushed. She looked like she was wearing makeup too, which was odd, because Tommy's mother had told him there was no such thing as makeup on Umitia. That must have been Martha's doing.

Sepherin reached out and took Tommy's hand, giving it a squeeze as she looked at him, appearing to be a lot calmer than she had been, perhaps even content.

"Thank you, Uncle Tommy. Some woman-chat was just what I needed." She kissed him on the cheek.

Chapter 26

Two days later, Thursday morning, Tommy was up at 4:00 a.m. He left one of his two credit cards on the table, along with a stack of cash. Martha was taking Sepherin to do some shopping later in the day. She needed maternity clothes, and other feminine things he didn't want to think about. His Uncle Jay and Aunt Estelle were coming on the weekend, so Sepherin wanted Martha to help her pick out makeup and teach her how to apply it before then. He scribbled a quick note with his cell phone number and left it on the table as well.

Tommy had agreed to pick the two co-workers up at their homes, rather than have them leave their cars at the hardware store. He picked up the tall, lanky Lenora at 5:00 a.m. She was dressed nicely, smelled pretty, and was snoring quietly less than a minute after getting in the truck. That only lasted the five minutes it took to drive to Cassie's.

After Cassie climbed in the pickup, he stopped at the Tim Hortons so they could load up on Timbits (doughnut holes) and coffee. He had expected the trip to be a non-stop litany of girly topics between the two women, but Cassie was quiet, subdued. Lenora filled the void by talking enough for *both* of the women. Tommy was growing more concerned though, as his little friend was usually a chatterbox. Three hours later, they arrived in Toronto. Another half hour of city navigation and they were pulling up out front of the hardware chain's head office. Halfway to Toronto, Tommy realized he never brought his cell phone with him, he had left it in his other jacket. They agreed where and when to meet at the end of the conference since they couldn't call Tommy, then he went off to amuse himself.

He found a coffee shop next to a convenience store, and picked up some tabloids to peruse as he sipped his quad grande Americano. A tabloid that enquires about many things had an interesting story. A man from Alabama reported that aliens took his wife, and the woman who came back wasn't her. He claimed she was a duplicate. Tommy knew that was nonsense, at least he thought it was nonsense. There had been no reports of the Voiya putting clones in place of the ones they took, but hey, they were Voiya, anything was possible. Tommy read the story again and starting counting the hits: They took the woman at night (hit); there was a bluish white light (hit); the man reported he was paralyzed while his wife was abducted (hit), though he was fully conscious (hit); during the abduction the air smelled like a hot electrical wire, like ozone (hit); when she came back, there was a mark on her shoulder blade, three small red dots in the shape of a triangle (hit).

As Tommy finished, he wasn't snickering any more, he was worried by what he had read. The story had six hits, so either the guy writing it was lucky, or there was a fair amount of truth to the story. He still doubted she had been replaced by a clone, but he decided he'd ask the Imperite Guards the next time he saw them. Regardless, Tommy knew that the man the story was about would, if he hadn't already, be getting an unsettling visit from two assholes dressed in black.

After his coffee and tabloid were finished, Tommy did some shopping, and then wandered around aimlessly, looking at the downtown sights. By late afternoon he was parked near the chain's head office again, slouched in the cab of his truck with a cup of coffee and his book. It was a book about Dr. Jekyll and Mr. Hyde, but it was from Hyde's perspective.

The conference ran a bit late, and when the women found him, they were all starved. Some of the attendees, all from out of town, decided to go to the Keg Mansion for a nice dinner. Tommy joined them, as Cassie seemed like she wanted to go, though she still wasn't saying much. Lenora bailed on them after dinner. She had called some old friends and decided to stay in town overnight. She was going to get the Greyhound back to Kincardine the next day since she wasn't working again until Saturday.

After dinner, Tommy and Cassie drove off into the sunset, literally, on their way back home. Cassie still wasn't saying much, and Tommy kept getting one-word answers to his questions about the conference. He decided to just let it be. She was probably upset about the stuff that had happened with Ritchie. Tommy thought it best not to push her about it.

Chapter 27

Mitch went out on the porch, using his hand to close the screen door quietly behind him. It was just after 10 p.m., Martha had dozed off in front of the television and he didn't want to startle her awake. Young Stephy had worn her out with their day-long shopping trip in Sarnia. He packed his pipe carefully, struck the match, and puffed quickly to get the tobacco lit. He let the pipe rest for a minute, and then struck a second match to get the pipe lit properly.

As he slowly enjoyed the flavours, he stepped down off the porch to have a look up at the sky. There had been a lot of Northern Lights recently, which was odd for this time of year, and he wanted to see if they were on display again. The corner of his eye caught some movement and he looked over towards Tommy's place. His neighbour's niece was standing out on the front lawn. It sounded like she had sobbed, so Mitch turned and headed over to see if she was okay.

He stopped for a moment in the row of trees between their properties. He saw her wipe at her face, and heard her sob again. Mitch knew Tommy was going to be home late, and he didn't want the young woman to be alone if she was upset, but now he was hesitant about intruding. Then he heard her start talking, to no one, just staring up at the stars.

"I'm so sorry, Roguk. We're having a baby and you'll never know, you can never know. They won't tell you. They won't let me send word to you, not that I would. Something like that would destroy the life you have and I can't do that — and yes, I really hate you right now, but I miss you too, I miss you so much. And I miss my mom and dad and — everyone. You're so far, far away. I wish you were closer. I wish — I wish you weren't ... this planet is nice, Roguk, it's a nice planet. I found an uncle here, my real uncle, my father's brother, and he's going to take care of me ..."

She stopped and gasped. Mitch's pipe had gone out from the lack of draw. He'd heard everything she said. He saw her put her hand up in front of her mouth, moving her head slowly like she was watching something. Mitch looked up and quickly saw it, a point of light in the night sky that was moving. It was small, but brilliant green. Being an ex-Air Force pilot, Mitch could tell the light source had to be at least 50 km away and the speed it was moving, was unreal.

"Is that us or them?" he heard Stephy wondering out loud.

And then his jaw dropped. The light did a ninety degree turn at speed, it didn't slow down. Then it did it again. The light zigzagged 60 and 90 degree turns, about eight in a row and then it took off, faster than what was humanly possible. During his entire career at the Canadian Air Force, he'd never seen a UFO, though they were sometimes talked about. Standing there with his mouth wide open, he knew that was exactly what he had just seen.

Mitch had a flashback to the Saturday morning about a month ago, when those two men dressed in black came to see Tommy, and Tommy said they were Jehovah's Witnesses. That wasn't the first time he'd seen them around Tommy's place either, and Mitch knew Feds when he saw them. He thought about all the evenings he'd seen Tommy sitting out on his porch, just watching the sky. He thought about how quiet Tommy was, how he never drew any attention to himself. He thought about how he kept correcting Stephy's words the first night they met. He thought about how Stephy just appeared in Tommy's life, someone he had never mentioned before. Mitch felt the need to urinate.

He dropped his gaze back to the young woman. She was looking directly at him, arms folded across her chest; she was standing there motionless, just staring. Finally she came over to him, slowly. Mitch took a step backwards, but then stopped. He was uncertain about what to do, what he was going to say, and what she was going to say — or do. But Mitch was also man enough to know he couldn't run from what he had just seen, what he had just heard, or the tough little filly in front of him.

Sepherin stopped only an arm's length in front of Mitch. A full head taller than him, she just looked down into his eyes. Finally she broke the silence, her voice soft, but strong, "Did you hear me talking?"

Mitch just nodded.

She chewed the corner of her lip for a moment.

"Are we going to have a problem?"

It took Mitch about one second to make an executive decision. Tommy brought this girl home, and was protective of her. Tommy had also saved Martha's life. He shook his head, "No, Stephy. There's no problem here."

Sepherin smiled and stepped closer to Mitch. She put her hands on his arms, leaned forward and kissed him on the cheek. Then she looked him right in the eyes again, "We're here to save your race, not harm you. You don't have anything to fear from us." She looked over her shoulder in the direction the light had disappeared, then she looked back at Mitch, "Them, on the other hand, they're a problem. They're why we're here."

Then she turned and went back in the house without another word.

Mitch let out a breath he had been holding too long. He leaned against the maple tree, and rested his hands on his knees. His head was spinning, his ears were buzzing, and his breathing was deep and heavy. It took a couple of minutes to get himself under control.

His neighbour was an alien. His neighbour's niece was an alien. She was a — *pregnant* alien. He was living next to aliens from another planet. *They're from another planet*, he kept thinking.

Finally he got hold of himself; the truth of what he had heard was sinking in. The man he had been friends with for seven years, the man who had dined at their table hundreds of times, the man who had saved his wife from a fire, the man who's niece was alone and pregnant, the man who lived next door to him was from another planet. He was an alien, an honest-to-goodness alien from outer space.

Mitch looked at Tommy's house. He could see Sepherin standing in the window watching him. Mitch stood tall and waved to her, then turned back to his place after tapping out the bowl of his pipe on the tree.

"If they're what aliens are like," he said quietly, "I'll take a dozen of 'em."

He went in the house and gently woke his wife. "Martha, we have to talk."

Chapter 28

Cassie hadn't spoken in over an hour. Tommy was starting to think it was him, that she was pissed at him, that maybe she blamed him for the problems between her and Ritchie. He wanted to say something, but he didn't want to be trapped in the truck with her for another hour if she turned ugly. She wasn't usually that sort, but you never can tell what's going to happen when a woman is pissed off with you. He also figured if she was pissed with him, then the kindest thing he could do, given the situation, was to just shut the hell up.

As Tommy made the left turn on Highway 9, just south of Walkerton, Cassie tried making a call on her cell phone, but it died on her and she burst into tears.

"Cassie? What's wrong?" he ventured, deciding that if she was pissed with him, maybe they should talk it out.

She cried harder. Tommy pulled the truck over to the side of the road and turned in his seat to face her, "Tell me what's going on Cassie. You've been quiet all day. Are you mad at me?"

She looked at him, an incredulous look on her tear-covered face, "You? Mad at you? Why would I be mad at you?"

"I don't know, maybe because of Richie, maybe because ..."

He had to stop because she started crying again, harder. Finally, amid the chugs and sobs, she said, "I can't get hold of him, I'm trying to get hold of him, he's not taking my calls, and my phone's dead."

"Oh, I'm sorry Cassie, I didn't know you two were back together."

"We're not back together and I don't want to be back together, I don't want him in my life, but I — I found out last night I'm pregnant."

That took Tommy by surprise. He had *another* pregnant woman in his life.

"If you don't want him in your life, why are you trying to call him?"

"Because he's going to be a father and he has a right to know, and we'll have to work out how we're going to — what we're going to ..."

Tommy didn't want her to start crying again. He reached for his own cell phone, but then remembered he didn't have it. He looked at her and was about to speak, but the truck stalled.

Then the headlights went out.

Then the radio went out, with a burst of static.

Then he felt a tingling in the base of his spine.

Then there was a flash of blue light.

Then the cab of the truck was filled with a brilliant white light.

Tommy and Cassie both threw their hands up over their eyes because of the light. Tommy heard the door of the truck open behind him. He turned in his seat.

Then Cassie started screaming

Tommy kept true to his training, the training which had been ingrained in him from childhood.

First it had been games, then it was the stories, and then it was the truth. His mother and Earth-grandparents (the Umites that hosted his mother) were all involved in the training. Tommy was handicapped only by the fact he did not have the subconscious programming a true-born Imperite is given. However, that handicap was easily made up for by his commitment, and his incredibly good memory. The training was relatively simple in purpose, though not so simple in execution:

Step one: Get out of the matter transmitter room.

Step two: Kill everything.

Step three: Destroy the ship.

Step one was what occupied his present thoughts.

When the Voiya and the Vesna appeared around the truck, he made a show of screaming (it was actually easy, given how fast it happened and how surprised he was) and tried to push them away, weakly. It would take the Voiya and Vesna several seconds to establish a strong enough telepathic link to immobilize a human. During that time, while they were still in the matter transmitter room, he had to make it look good, to make it look like he was an average Earther.

Once outside of the truck, he started repeating the Mantra of Freedom in his head. As it wasn't words, it was only a tonal rhythm, it wasn't something the telepathic Voiya or Vesna were able to discern, to them it was just Humanesh terror-gibberish. When you think of a word in your mind, there is an image associated to it. With the tonal rhythm, they were sounds, not words. Tommy had no images directly associated with those sounds. His mind just imagined horrible, despicable creatures from schlocky horror films he had watched.

It was something all the Imperites were trained to do. Watching horror films was something they started doing after arriving on Earth. He had no idea if there were horror films on other planets, or what those Imperites did. To the Vesna who were forcing their way into his mind, they were simply catching glimpses of a terror-reaction, just like any other Earther would have.

The purpose of the Mantra of Freedom was proactive. Tommy's mind was actively engaged in the pursuit of a goal, and he was not simply reacting to fear, he was not trying to disengage from what he was seeing. He wasn't going to give the hideous bastards an "in" to his mind.

As Tommy pretended to recoil and react in fear, he watched as Cassie struggled against the Vesna and then collapsed. They had made the connection and taken over her ability to control herself. That was the cue for Tommy. He slumped to the floor as well.

163

Om shay om pu tam lay om pu som par um tah nom.

As Tommy felt himself being picked up and moved, he could also feel the pressure of their thoughts. It was like someone pressing on the bridge of his nose, on his forehead, and on the base of his skull, all at the same time.

Om shay om pu tam lay om pu som par um tah nom.

He knew what to expect, but expecting it and actually feeling it were two different things. It was disconcerting to say the least, but he had to concentrate on the words in his head.

Om shay om pu tam lay om pu som par um tah nom.

He felt them moving him. The light changed, as did the feel of the air. One of the Vesna must have been distracted for a moment, though, as he heard Cassie whimper, and then go quiet.

Cassie.

In the excitement at being on the verge of completing the hereditary Imperative, he had completely forgotten about Cassie.

Cassie, his friend.

Cassie, his co-worker.

Cassie, the Earther.

Cassie, the *pregnant* Earther.

Om shay om pu tam lay om pu som par um tah nom.

He didn't want Cassie to die, not the way he was going to die. He didn't want his pregnant little friend subjected to what they were going to do to her, and quite possibly, to her foetus. He had to decide, and he had to do it fast. Let it happen and let her live, or kill them all.

Om shay om pu tam lay om pu som par um tah nom.

He felt himself being turned in a new direction. The light on his eyelids changed again. He felt himself being lowered onto a table. If they got the straps on him ...

He heard Cassie groan.

He almost gasped with surprise as it struck him that there *was* a third option.

Om shay om pu tam lay om pu som par um tah nom.

Tommy's eyes flew open. One of the almond-eyed, ovoid-skulled Vesna was right above him, looking into his face.

Chapter 29

Zekra was pacing in the office. Shivinin was in the bathroom. When Zekra called Taffi, his brother informed him that he and his partner would need to come see him before performing the status check. Zekra knew enough not to question him any further on the communications device, regardless of how secure it was.

Zekra continued pacing as he heard the toilet flush, the water in the sink run, and then the air freshener being sprayed. The partners had pizza for dinner. The cheese always upset Shivinin's digestive system.

As Shivinin emerged, there was a flash of blue light. Zekra looked up to see Taffi and Minino standing in the office.

"Now as then," Taffi and Minino both said, each holding a hand palm facing up.

"Then as now," Zekra and Shivinin both replied, each holding a palm facing down.

The four Imperite Guards took their seats and without preamble, they got into it, telepathically, just in case there was anyone listening.

So, brother, why did you have to come see us? Zekra began.

Taffi responded, *It seems that there is much interest in this particular Imperite, and we are — concerned.*

Indeed? There has been no other communications regarding her, other than the assignment of her new host.

Taffi fidgeted, which was a peculiar act for a member of the Shovitic clan. It dawned on Zekra that there must be something dangerous that Taffi knew. However, Zekra was an impatient man.

Well? Brother? What is it?

"Tell them," Minino said out loud.

Taffi nodded, *Minino and I were contacted about this Tekin Imperite and her host family.*

Zekra and Shivinin shared a quick glance. Both men leaned forward, though it wouldn't make any difference in a telepathic communication. It was still one of those gestures unconsciously common to all races.

Taffi continued. *We were instructed to re-assign her to the Earth-born Tekin, but we were instructed to kill her original host family first.*

The senior partners both looked like they had been slapped. The eyeworms around their mostly empty eye sockets were moving in a frenzy.

Shivinin was the first to speak-think, *You — killed the original host family? You killed an Imperite?*

Taffi nodded, *Yes. The Imperite, her Earther husband, and two hereditaries.*

Zekra and Shivinin knew that meant two children.

That those two children still lived, in defiance of Kalabot, was a secret Taffi dared not even share with his own blood-brother and his partner.

They were all silent for a moment.

Shivinin finally asked the obvious question, *Who told you to do this?* He already knew the answer. Such a decision could only come from one person, but he needed to hear them say it.

Taffi spoke out loud, the word hanging in the air, "Kalabot."

Zekra stood, pacing again.

Shivinin asked the next question. *Did you say the Earth-born is a Tekin as well?*

Taffi nodded.

So Kalabot had you kill the Imperite's host family, and then had her placed with an Earth-born, from her own House? Why?

I do not know, Taffi answered, *but the coincidence does not stop there. The Earth-born's mother was Jakula Tekin, mother of Michalz Tekinson, who is the father of Sepherin Tekin.*

Zekra spun around, *Kalabot had you place her with a blood-kin?*

What is so special about this Imperite? Shivinin asked the two Imperite Guards sitting in his office.

We have no idea.

Chapter 30

When Tommy's eyes flew open, one of the almond-eyed, ovoid-skulled Vesna was right above him, looking into his face. The Vesna recoiled in its own horror as Tommy opened his mouth and turned the Mantra of Freedom into the Song of Freedom, practically screaming it at the top of his lungs, over and over.

"OM SHAY OM PU TAM LAY OM PUS SOM PAR UM TAH NOM."

Tommy's right hand shot up and grabbed the Vesna that had been leaning over him. With his hand gripping the Vesna around the throat, he used the leverage to pull himself up and swing his legs over the edge of the table. Then he squeezed the Vesna's throat and pumped his arm once, hard enough to snap the creature's neck.

He dropped the corpse to the floor and leapt off the table, swinging around fast, his lower back squealing a warning to take it easy. Two of the Vesna were holding Cassie on the table. Their attention was broken, and she was now trying to kick and flail her arms — and she was screaming. The Vesna *hate* screaming. It disorients them, and makes them act rashly.

A Vesna was on the other side of the table Tommy had been on. It was moving towards him rapidly, holding a metal tube which had a blue light on the end. Tommy had been told many times he would not be able to overcome the effects of that device; he couldn't let the blue light touch anywhere near his head. Tommy kept chanting the words loudly as he leapt back over the table, directly at the Vesna with the device. His unexpected move had the desired effect.

In every instance of experience with the Humanesh, the Vesna knew the Humanesh would recoil and do anything to get away from them. The inherent terror of the abduction and experimentations worked in their favour. In this instance, however, the Vesna was so shocked and surprised at Tommy's advance, it lost focus for a moment. The woman's screaming wasn't helping.

Tommy not only grabbed the metal cylinder out of the Vesna's hand, he drove it deep into the middle of the its skull as Tommy's body impacted against it, forcing it down onto the floor. Vesna number two died with only a weak squeak of protest.

Movement on Tommy's right caused him to snap his head in that direction. He saw the back of the Voiya Master as it fled the room, the doors closing behind it.

Tommy didn't even have to look, he knew another Vesna was coming at him. There was a tool armature above the table Tommy had been laying on, the one he had just leapt across. He reached up and grabbed it, then lifted both legs and launched them at the third Vesna that he could now see. The mass of a full-grown Vesna is only about 30 kg, and Tommy had strong legs. The Vesna went flying backwards, ass over tea kettle, but quickly regained its feet.

Tommy let go of the medical armature hanging from the ceiling and spun around. He glanced at the two Vesna holding Cassie to the table. The third one, the one he had just kicked, was moving towards the door to escape the room. Tommy was faster. He lunged and grabbed the Vesna just as it was approaching the door. Tommy grabbed it by the arm, and took one step backwards. With all his might, he swung the Vesna's body around so that it slammed into the table Tommy had been on. The force of the impact caused the arm Tommy was holding to rip clean off the Vesna's body at the shoulder. The creature fell to the floor, screaming the most hideous scream he had ever heard. Tommy stepped up to the creature, as it back pedaled to get away from him. The Earth-born Umite began swinging, bludgeoning the Vesna to unconsciousness with its own arm. It didn't take long.

When Tommy looked up at the two remaining Vesna, they were still trying to hold Cassie down, but she was still struggling and screaming. Her screams and Tommy's unceasing Song of Freedom filled the room like a cacophonous maelstrom. He could tell the

Vesna were thinking of bolting, to get away from him, to get away from the sound. They kept looking at the door; he could see the terror on their faces. He was singing the words too loudly to receive any thought transmission they may try to send to him. As he started to move towards them, he wondered if it was indeed escape they were anticipating, or had they perhaps called the cavalry?

The door opened. There were four drones standing on the other side of it.

Definitely the cavalry then, Tommy thought.

Per his training, there could be no hesitation. The easiest way to lose a fight against the Voiya's casts of servants, especially the hideous little drones, was to hesitate in your assault. As soon as the door opened and Tommy saw the drones, he charged them, swinging the Vesna's arm above his head. He tossed the arm behind them, causing the drone at the back of the pack to follow its prey reflex and chase the escaping appendage. Tommy pulled back his fist and hit the first drone hard enough in the forehead to kill it instantly. Even though their skulls were much thicker than the Vesna's, the drones were still no match, individually, for a full-grown Humanesh male. Their effectiveness came from acting as a pack.

The second drone leapt at him and Tommy caught it at arm's length, while bringing his right foot up hard, connecting with the third drone under the chin. He killed it by the force of the blow from his foot snapping its neck. Tommy struggled with the drone in his hands. The three-foot tall, gray, vicious little misanthrope, with an enlarged head, had a large mouth full of sharp teeth. It was trying to bite Tommy's arms and his face. Its claws were digging at Tommy's arms, gouging his skin, trying to pull its face closer to Tommy's. The Imperite was bleeding from the wounds. The fourth drone, the one who had gone chasing the arm, came back in the room with the arm stuck in its mouth like a dog retrieving a stick.

173

At that moment, there was a blood-curdling scream behind Tommy, and it wasn't Cassie. Both of the drones looked, which was exactly what he needed. He quickly put one hand around the neck of the drone struggling with him, pushing it away from his face. His attention turned to the remaining drone. Tommy rammed his hand, with his finger and thumb stuck out, right into both of the large eyes of the drone standing there with the Vesna's arm in its mouth. Tommy clamped his fingers around the bridge bone between the eyes. The drone made a horrible noise, a horrible roar of pain. The drone dropped the arm and its mouth was snapping its sharp teeth, trying to bite the air in front of it where the pain was coming from. Tommy tossed the blinded drone on top of the one-armed Vesna who was awake again, writhing on the floor. Without the ability to see what it landed on, the blinded drone attacked the one-armed Vesna. The drone was in too much pain and too frenzied to recognize or respond to the Vesna's telepathic commands.

With the last drone still struggling, his hand wrapped around its throat, his forearm pushing up its chin so it couldn't bite him, Tommy managed to grab both of its clawed hands. He held its neck to high up to snap it one handed, and it was too thick with muscle to strangle it. Tommy looked over at Cassie.

One of the Vesna who had been holding her down was lying on the floor, appearing to have been eviscerated. She had hold of the other Vesna around the neck with both hands. She was slamming its head down on the table over and over, shrieking, "DIE YOU BASTARD, DIE!"

Tommy was shocked. He'd never heard Cassie swear before.

Finally she stopped, the lifeless body of the Vesna sliding to the floor and plopping into a pool of the black ichor which had come from the wounds of the first one she killed. Tommy never did find out for sure what she did to the first one, but from the look of her hands, he had the thought that she had actually ripped the Vesna open with her fingers.

174

As the ship's complement of Vesna were now all dead, Tommy stopped yelling the Song of Freedom. The drone in his hand was getting heavy, and getting annoying. The drones aren't telepathic. Tommy looked at it, wincing at the pain in his arm where the thing was still gouging him. He let go of the hands, grabbed a leg, and then let go of the neck. Grabbing the other foot, Tommy swung the chittering drone in an arc and slammed its neck against the edge of the nearest table. It died instantly. He tossed its body in the corner and turned back to Cassie.

She was hyperventilating. She was looking at her hands, looking at the bodies, looking around the room they were in, and then she looked at Tommy.

Wide eyed and terrified, she screamed at the top of her lungs.

It was a scream of more than fear; it was the scream of her entire view of reality coming unglued. It was a scream that acknowledged everything she thought was true had just been turned upside down. She'd always thought aliens and UFOs were a bunch of malarkey. She'd always thought that the people who claimed they saw UFOs needed some help, or some attention, or maybe both. Yet here she was, in an alien spaceship, with dead aliens around her, some of whom she had killed herself.

She screamed again.

And then again.

And then some more.

Chapter 31

Sepherin was bug eyed in front of the television. They had nothing at all like this back on Umitia. After coming inside and watching Mitch go back to his place, she spent a few minutes rooting through Tommy's stash of horror movies, finally deciding to watch *Alien*. The creature had just burst out of Kane's stomach when she heard three heavy, slow knocks on the door. The sound startled her, she squealed in surprise, and then laughed. The Imperite paused the movie and went to the door.

She ducked her head down to look through the peep hole. Stephy groaned inwardly. Standing on the porch, with the screen door open, were two men in black suits and black fedoras, with perfectly trimmed crew-cut hair, very square jaws, and wearing Ray-Ban sunglasses — at 11:10 p.m.

Shovitics, just what I need.

She opened the door; both of the men looked up at her.

She was, quite surprisingly, taller than them. The two Imperite guards shared a look. They had never heard of a Falwasz being taller than a Shovitic — ever.

"What do you want?" she asked without any pleasantries.

"Sepherin Tekin?" one of them asked.

"Yes, but they call me Stephy. Now I'll ask again, what do you want?"

They both gave a slight bow of their head. "May we come in?"

"No, tell me what you ..."

She didn't finish her sentence. They pushed her backwards and stepped into the house.

"Hey, just what the ..."

The Imperite Guard that had spoken reached out and slapped her across the face. "Show respect, Falwasz."

They stepped around her. She put the back of her hand up to her face, touching the spot which stung from the slap. She was both scared and angry. She could take one of them easily. She'd put her combat instructor in the infirmary three times. She wasn't sure about taking two of them at once though. Assaulting an Imperite Guard, however, was punishable by death. She knew she had no choice but to put up with them.

Taffi looked at the frozen image of the paused movie, he approved of her choice. It was a good movie, one of his favourites. He turned to face her.

"Your host? Is he here?"

"No, he's not."

"When will he return?"

"I don't know."

The two Imperite Guards looked at each other.

"Where has he gone?"

"None of your …" she stopped as Taffi took a step towards her. "He's gone to the city. He had to drive some people there and back, for his work."

Taffi stared at her, for an uncomfortable amount of time. Sepherin refused to bow under the gaze. She stared back at him, defiantly. She hated the Shovitics. She hated the Shovitic's that were Imperite Guards even worse. They were why she was so miserable. They were the ones who selected her. They were the ones who brought her here. They were the ones who could take her home, but would rather kill her if she asked.

"How often? Leaving you alone at night, I mean."

"Only this once."

Minino turned away and started going through the house. He checked every room and closet; for what, Sepherin had no idea.

After clearing the ground floor, he went up the stairs. She could hear him going in each room.

"Tell me, Stephy?"

She nodded.

"Tell me, Stephy, is the host good to you? Is there any problem with him?"

"No. We get along like two callot pups."

Taffi smiled, much to her revulsion, though she didn't show it. He had a callot pup of his own when he was a child. The fury little sabre-toothed pup had been his constant companion for years, until it finally died in his arms from old age, not much bigger than when it was first born.

"And arrangements for you? You have your own room?"

"Yes, of course I do."

Taffi nodded, looking at her belly. She was wearing one of Tommy's large sweatshirts. It was doing a good job of covering her pregnant bulge, until she rested her hand on top of it.

Taffi lost the smile on his face. "Minino!"

His partner came down the stairs, one hand inside his jacket, swivelling his head from side to side.

Taffi looked at his partner. *The Imperite is pregnant.*

Minino looked like you could have knocked him over with a feather. He stood beside his partner and looked at Sepherin. This discovery made the whole situation even stranger, more confusing.

She sighed deeply, and then lifted her sweater. They could see her bare pregnant belly.

How far along are you? Minino asked her.

"Almost thirteen ten-sleeps."

They both quickly did the math. It meant the father was back on Umitia. Taffi realized why she was being less than pleasant.

This is, unfortunate for you. Did you know the foetus could have been disposed of on the …

Taffi didn't get a chance to finish. Sepherin stepped forward and grabbed him by the shirt and necktie, death sentence be damned; she wasn't in the mood for any more threats about her baby. Her fist pushed up against his chin as she pulled him in close to her, but then pushed him away from her as she turned to face the real threat. Minino had pulled his handgun and pointed it right at her head.

Minino knew the training and was expecting her next move, but it came so fast he still didn't have time to pull the trigger. One of her hands slapped against his forearm as the other hand slapped viciously against the back of his hand holding the gun, forcing his wrist into a position that overrode his brains signals to his fingers. No sooner did he feel her hands hitting his, he was staring down the barrel of his own handgun —and the safety was off.

She moved the gun from him to Taffi who had staggered back a couple steps, and was reaching inside his jacket.

"If any of you bastards think for one *second* you're going to harm my child …"

"Please, no …" Taffi turned his head to look at his partner, slowly removing his hand from his jacket. *She is distraught and emotional. We will forgive her for this.*

"No, we will not forgive this," Minino growled.

Sepherin's other hand shot out and punched Minino in the face, making him stumble backwards and trip over a footstool.

The gun moved back to Taffi. She didn't flinch. Her eyes were boring into Taffi's sunglasses.

"With all that Kalabot has done for this one, do you think he will congratulate us for killing her? We must forgive her, Minino."

Minino thought about it for a moment. He knew Taffi was right. This one was special, for whatever reason. And if Kalabot was willing to kill an Imperite and her entire family just to put this one with a blood-kin — he shuddered to think of what Kalabot would do to them if they executed her, as they would be fully justified to do so based on her actions.

Minino slowly stood, "Very well, we will forgive this — if she returns the weapon."

Sepherin held out her empty hand to Taffi, "Gun, now. You can have them back when you leave.'

Taffi and Minino looked at each other. *This one is indeed — different.*

Yes, very different. She's almost — like us.

Sepherin took Taffi's handgun and put it in the front pocket of her sweatshirt. She closed the door behind her with her foot and then motioned for the two Imperite Guards to sit on the couch.

"Now, just what did you mean by, '*all that Kalabot has done for her?*'"

Chapter 32

Tommy let Cassie scream; it was a stress response, he knew that. He let her get it out of her system. He wrapped his arms around her. She let him, still screaming. Tommy watched the door, ready to react. He had to figure out how to get Cassie off the ship. He wasn't going to let her die, but now that he was onboard he couldn't leave. His need to complete the Imperative was too strong. It was genetic. To not complete it, would dishonour his mother, his father, his whole House, and his whole clan; even though he had never met any of them.

But even more powerful was the need to protect Cassie. Protecting Earthers was, after all, why the Imperites so willingly sacrificed their lives.

After thirty seconds of holding her, her screams finally stopped.

Coming back to a sense of where she was and who she was with, Cassie pushed back from Tommy, scrambling to get away from him. There was a piece of metal on a tray, something which looked like it went someplace the sun didn't shine. She held it up in front of her, defensively, looking at Tommy with wide eyes, her whole body trembling.

"You don't look scared," she said through her ragged breath.

Tommy just shook his head.

"How do you — what was that screaming thing you were doing?"

"Song of Freedom," there was no sense lying to her.

The door opened and Tommy moved, fast. A Trigla guard came in the room with its weapon pointed at the wrong corner. Tommy grabbed the weapon, pulling the Trigla towards him. The two of them started struggling; the weapon fell to the floor. The Trigla, with its brown leathery skin, being almost eight feet tall, had a distinct advantage over Tommy and was making the most of it. Before Tommy got bested by it, he saw Cassie moving out of the corner of his eye. She climbed up on the nearest table, took two steps and jumped high on the back of the Trigla. She wrapped her legs around it, clamping one hand over its mouth and one hand over its nose, and then she held on for dear life. Now, instead of pushing against the Trigla, Tommy started pulling its arms, pulling them towards him, holding the Trigla in place so that it couldn't rid itself of Cassie. It only took a couple minutes for the Trigla to fall unconscious. As it went down, Cassie jumped clear. She picked up the weapon on the floor and pointed it at Tommy.

The weapon was a gun, of alien design. The barrel was four feet long, and had a mushroom opening on it like an old blunderbuss. The stock, trigger, and magazine looked similar to an Earth weapon. It operated the same as an Earth weapon too. They found that out when the door opened and another Trigla appeared. Cassie swung the weapon around and shot it, point blank. The creature fell back into the hallway and the doors closed again. She turned to point the weapon at Tommy again, but he was already moving. He grabbed the barrel and grabbed her hand, pulling it off the gun and her finger off the trigger. Cassie moved backwards, fast, tripping on a body and falling hard. Then she pushed her way back on the floor, away from Tommy, glaring at him. She quickly found herself in a pool of black ichor and without traction to get any further away from him.

The Trigla on the floor, courtesy of Cassie, started to groan and move. Tommy shot it in the head.

"Who the hell are you?" she finally asked him as he moved to stand over her.

"I'm your friend," Tommy said and held out his hand.

She looked around quickly and then back at him, "Where the hell are we?"

Tommy sighed, *Might as well get his over with*. More of them would be coming soon and he figured it would go easier with her help, rather than having to watch her as well.

"You're on board an alien spaceship. We were kidnapped — taken — whatever you want to call it. They want to perform medical experiments on us. I stopped them — *we* stopped them. Now I have to get you off this ship."

"How? How did you stop them? What was that awful noise you were making?"

"It was the noise that — it's called the Song of Freedom. I'd love to talk some more, Cassie, but more of them will be coming soon and I really need to get moving."

She was breathing heavily, looking at his still outstretched hand.

"Tell me who you are, really. Are you an alien?"

Tommy dropped his hand; this wasn't going how he wanted.

"My name is Tameht Tekin. I'm an Umite from a planet a hundred light years from here, at least my mother was. She was pregnant with me when she came here and I was born on Earth, but I'm still, technically, an Umite; so, yes, I'm an alien. My people have been coming here for over 500 years, for just this reason: to kill these bastards. And that's what I'm going to do. I'm going to kill them all and then destroy the ship, but only if I stop yammering and start doing."

Tommy held out his hand again, "And somewhere in all this, I have to get you off the ship."

He turned at the sound of the slithering and snapping teeth. The blind drone had finished gnawing on the corpse of the now-dead, one-armed Vesna. Tommy stomped on the drone's head, repeatedly, until it finally stopped moving. He turned back to face Cassie, who looked like she was about to come unglued again.

"So, you're telling me you're an alien? That you're from outer space? From another planet? You expect me to believe that?"

Tommy sighed in exasperation, "Cassie, take a look around you."

185

She did. She looked back at him, "So, you're not going to eat me then?"

"Not unless you cook me dinner first."

There was a pause, then the chuckling started, then the laughing, then the laughing became hysterical gibbering. Then it turned into screams. It only lasted a few seconds till she got control of herself again.

She pushed his offered hand away and stood up on her own, carefully wiping the bottom of her sneakers on the nearest corpse.

"You're really an alien?"

He nodded.

"And you're going to destroy this ship of theirs?"

He nodded.

"And you're going to get me off this ship, get me home?"

He nodded.

She surprised Tommy by walking over to a cart against the wall and picking up the three sharpest objects she could find. She handed one of them to Tommy, "Here, take this, and you use the gun. I guess we aren't going to get far if you have to carry me so I might as well help, right?"

Tommy reached out and took one of the sharp objects from her hand; he handed her the gun. "Just don't shoot me. I'll be more effective with these. When the door opens, they'll charge in, maybe a lot of them. Just start shooting anything that moves and keep shooting till they stop, *but don't shoot me.*"

"No promises, spaceman."

He snorted a laugh, she was starting to sound more like her old self. Maybe the shock was wearing off, or maybe it was just getting worse. "We need to get out of here and turn right, and then we keep following corridors as far forward as we can. Once we take the bridge, I can get you home. Just keep moving, don't stop. Don't slow down, don't pause, just keep shooting, keep swinging, keep kicking, and keep moving."

"Were closer to that first room we were in, aren't we? The room they ... beamed us up to?"

"Yes, why?"

"Can't you just beam me down? Now? Before we have to fight our way to the — wherever you said? Can't we both go?"

Tommy shook his head, "I have no idea where we are. They don't usually break atmosphere when they take someone, because they always return them. But we could be anywhere over the planet right now."

"I'll walk."

"Cassie ..."

"Tommy, I'm scared, I think I pee'd myself, and I have alien blood and guts all over me. I want to get off and I want to get off now, not after ..." she gave an exasperated huff. "This may be your thing, Tommy, but it's not mine. I just want to get out of here."

Tommy rubbed his chin. He quickly recalled the training on how to use the TransMat equipment. It was a fairly simple process. The shipboard systems handled all the details; it was a point-and-click type of thing, at least to TransMat someone outside. He knew he didn't have the skills or training to attempt a TransMat inside a structure.

"Fine, we'll go there first, and I'll get you off."

"But I haven't cooked you dinner yet."

Now it was Tommy's turn to laugh. Her humour was still a stress response, like the screaming. Tommy knew that, but he didn't care. If she was laughing, at least she wasn't crying.

"Cassie, when you get home, I need you to go see Stephy and tell her what happened. See her, don't call her. And Cassie, for heaven's sake, do not, and I mean *do not tell anyone* what's happened, or what you've seen. If you do — things will start getting interesting for you again, and not in the good way."

"Is she an alien too?"

Tommy just nodded his head.

It took her a few seconds to process that, or to decide how to respond to it. Finally, she just said, "Okay."

"Alright, get ready to move. Remember, if we face resistance, keep shooting and moving; don't stop. And sing, too. Loud, at the top of your lungs, or even just scream. The screaming disorients the Voiya and the Trigla."

"The what?"

"The tall brown ones, the ones with the guns, they're the Trigla. Those," he pointed to the corpse of one she had killed, "are the Vesna, but they're all dead, I think. These ships typically only have five on board."

"And those," she pointed to a drone corpse.

"Those? They're vermin, and the screaming doesn't bother them. They're used to it. Just try and keep away from their teeth. They're vicious, their teeth are sharp," Tommy held up his injured arm, "and they'll rip chunks of flesh out of you. But, at least, they die easily. Just go for the head and the throat. Going after their arms and legs won't slow them down."

"Okay, if you say ..."

The door opened.

Four drones rushed into the room; they were all arms, legs, and snapping teeth. They charged at Tommy who was in front of Cassie. A Trigla came in behind them and Tommy heard the gun fire. The Trigla ducked as Tommy grabbed a drone and slammed it

188

down on the floor. Another one latched onto his leg as Cassie fired again, this time she got the Trigla in the face. It fell with a thud, dead.

Tommy screamed and reached for the drone on his leg as another drone landed on his back, winding upside down when Tommy stood. Cassie got a two-fer on the drones with her next shot, and then he felt the one on his back being pulled off as he pulled the one from his leg.

Cassie screamed and the gun discharged, the electrical pulse of energy passing close enough to Tommy's head that he felt his hair stand on end. He reached down and grabbed the last drone, then spun around with it still in his hand. Cassie had dropped the gun and was struggling with a drone that had wrapped itself around her head. Tommy swung the drone in his hand, knocking the drone off of her, but knocking Cassie to the floor as well. He broke the neck of the drone in his hand and turned to grab the one behind Cassie. Only Cassie was sitting up, holding the gun again, and pointing it right at him.

She jerked her head to the side.

Tommy dove out of the way.

She fired.

There was a yelp of pain and the clatter of another gun falling to the deck, the doors were still open.

Cassie hopped to her feet, bleeding from a wound to her cheek, and her arm. The drone's claws were sharp and had cut her fairly deeply.

The last drone lunged at her again, but she must have heard it. She ducked as it was almost on her. It went sailing over her hunched form and connected with Tommy's swinging foot. Tommy smiled, *Gotta love steel-toed work boots.* The drone's skull all but exploded.

"Let's go," he held out his hand.

Cassie put the gun up in a posit on ready to fire. She stepped past Tommy, and looked out in the hallway. She looked over her shoulder to see him standing there, looking at her with his jaw hanging open. "What? You said you were going to get me off this thing, let's move … and pick up that other gun will you? Don't expect me to fight *your* way out of this."

Tommy smiled, picked up the gun, and they turned left. Cassie flinched as Tommy fired to their rear. Another Trigla had appeared, but ducked back just in time. It was only a few more feet to the matter transmission room.

Just as they reached the door, it opened and two more drones came out. Cassie screamed and fired blindly, missing both of them. The first one landed on her, sinking its teeth into her shoulder. She screamed again. The upper half of its head disappeared with the energy blast from Tommy's weapon, leaving her ear ringing. She shrugged off the corpse, pulling its claws out of her arm, as she saw Tommy hook the curved end of the gun barrel in the mouth of the other drone and pull the trigger.

Tommy grabbed the back of her bloodied sweater and pulled her into the matter transmission room. He hit the black button on the door to close it. "You okay? You good?"

She nodded. He handed her the gun in his hand since hers was laying in the corridor. He turned to find the control panel and stopped cold. Then he started screaming the Song of Freedom.

Cassie spun around and saw the Voiya standing on the other side of the room, pressed back up against the wall, looking left and right, its face filled with competing flashes of fear and rage. She raised the weapon and pointed it at the pint-sized villain.

"Don't kill it," Tommy stopped to whisper, "yet."

Tommy lunged, dashing around the end of his pickup truck, which was still in the room. He moved fast, while resuming his vocalization of the tonal rhythms. The creature's eyes flew wide open and he screamed like a little boy as he ran. The small, hideous-looking Master, the size of an eight-year-old child, had nowhere to go in the round room, but it ran anyway. It took Tommy all of five seconds to grab first its arm, and then put a hand around its skinny neck.

Tommy stopped the Song of Freedom and screamed at the creature, "IF YOU TRY TO CONTROL ME, SHE KILLS YOU. DO YOU UNDERSTAND, VOIYA?"

Tommy went silent, waiting for a response. The Voiya looked from one to the other. It finally nodded.

"Who are you?" Tommy asked.

Tommy and Cassie heard its voice in their minds.

I am your better, human scum.

"What is your *name*?" Tommy's hand around its neck shook the little creature.

Tommy watched the little bastard's face, seeing it thinking of what its options were. The creature finally slumped his shoulders.

I am Raznick of Chernasai.

"I need you to show me where we are, where the ship is right now."

The Voiya tried to move, but Tommy held it firm.

The Master pointed to the wall near the door where they came in. *Over there is the control interface. I need to be close to it to operate it.*

Tommy pulled him over to the wall. "Remember, Voiya, any tricks and she shoots you in the head."

Tommy looked at Cassie. She was crying silently, but pointing the weapon. The adrenalin had to be wearing off because the gun was shaking so bad he doubted she could hit the wall opposite her. *Great, just don't fucking shoot me.*

The Voiya sneered and made a noise that sounded like a laugh.

191

Tommy smacked it in the head with his open palm. "Fucking telepaths."

Standing where the Voiya indicated, the little creature waved his hand. A holographic display appeared, floating in the air in front of them. The creature quickly displayed an aerial image.

Tommy didn't recognize the landscape.

"Zoom out," Tommy said.

The Voiya Master complied.

"Further."

"Further."

"Shit, show me how to do it."

The Voiya, still with his neck in Tommy's grip, showed him the hand motions and where to make them. Once Tommy got the hang of it, it was almost like a Google map, only his hand was the mouse.

Tommy made a pinching gesture to zoom the image out further and further, finally realizing they were over Texas. He swiped his open palm over the aerial view to move it around until he found Ontario. He reversed the pinching gesture to zoom in, swiping his hand a few times, and he finally found Kincardine. He wanted to get Cassie close to home, without showing the Voiya where home specifically was. He didn't care about his truck, he wasn't going to need it anymore. He kept manipulating the display, zooming down to a street-level view. He indicated a point two blocks from his house.

"Take us there."

No.

Tommy tightened his grip, looking into the freak-show face of his adversary, "I told you, *take us there*. Do it now!"

No, you're going to kill me. Why would I do this for you?

"I won't kill you if you take us there."

You lie.

Tommy sighed, "Yeah, you're right. I'm lying. I am going to kill you."

He spun the Voiya around, slamming it back against the wall. He knelt down on one knee, painfully, and leaned in close to the disgusting creature's ugly head. He put his mouth near its auditory orifice on one side.

"But you get the option of dying quickly if you take us there. If you don't ..." Tommy paused to look in its eyes. He reached for his waistband and removed one of the sharp objects. Holding it up in front of the Voiya's face, almost touching its eyeball with the sharp point, Tommy put his mouth next to its head again and whispered, "If you don't take us there, then I'll take my time and kill you slowly ... piece by piece."

Then for effect, Tommy opened his eyes wide and stared into the Voiya's eyes, and laughed maniacally. He knew that the Voiya would be even more terrified by a crazy Umite with a weapon, than just an Umite with a weapon.

Tommy heard Cassie whimper. He turned his head and saw her starring at him wide eyes, moving the gun back and forth between him and the Voiya. *Nothing I can do about it right now.* He turned back to the Voiya. He could feel it trembling under his hand. Tommy was about to say something, but then smelled a familiar odour. He heard a trickling sound too. He looked down, as did the Voiya. Tommy saw the yellow puddle slowly expanding from under the Voiya's robes.

The double door slid open.

Cassie screamed and turned around; she fired the gun, hitting one of the three Trigla in the knee. He fell to the floor and the two Keystone Trigla behind him tripped, piling on top of him.

STOP.

They all heard the Master's voice in their heads.

LEAVE —NOW. The Master was communicating with the Trigla.

"Tell them to leave their weapons," Tommy growled.

The Voiya nodded once, but was no longer broadcasting to Tommy or Cassie. The two uninjured creatures stood and helped their compatriot up. They moved out of the room and the doors slid shut again, their weapons remained on the floor.

Ten minutes later, the Voiya ship was moving into position over Kincardine. Cassie was standing in the middle of the room, no longer shaking. She looked at Tommy, pleading with her eyes.

"Please, Tommy, please come with me. Please."

"No, Cassie. You know I can't. I need to honour my mother's House."

Tommy turned back to the holographic view screen, pointing one of the weapons right at the Voiya's head. He reached out and indicated the spot again, "Right there, put her right there."

As the Voiya made the final adjustments, Tommy lowered the muzzle of the weapon to point at the Voiya's groin. "You monkey around with her and you die slowly, as promised."

The Master, glaring at Tommy from the corner of his eye, nodded once. He reached up and input some final commands then turned his head. *It is ready to execute, shall I return your female now, Umite scum?*

Tommy looked at Cassie. She was trembling again, but at least she wasn't crying. He didn't see the Voiya modify the command on the holo-screen.

"Thank you, Tommy," was all Cassie could say.

Tommy looked back at the Voiya, "Do it now."

To Tommy's surprise, the Voiya smiled. Then Tommy was looking at the side of a white house.

"DAMN IT!"

Tommy spun around. Cassie was standing a few feet behind him. She swooned to her knees. Tommy looked up. He could just make out the oblong patch of darkness in the night sky, and watched it moving away slowly.

"Son of a bitch." He muttered, slinging the weapon over his shoulder.

He went over to Cassie and helped her stand. "Come on, come with me. We need to treat your wounds and get some disinfectant in them."

"No. I'm going home. I'll get my own treatment." She turned and started walking away.

Tommy leapt forward and grabbed her shoulder, spinning her around. "Cassie, if you head out on your own right now, they might come back and take you again — out of spite towards me. You need to come with me. They won't touch you if you're with me. You're protected if you're with me."

She yanked her shoulder out of his grip, the pain from the wounds making her wince. Her voice of concern for him had turned to a voice filled with venom. "Go to hell, Tommy the alien."

Then as she took a step backwards, with no warning, her eyes rolled up in her head and she fainted.

Chapter 33

Minino glared at Sepherin as she spoke with Taffi. He knew there would be no repercussion for killing an Imperite who had attacked them; in fact, it was standard procedure. But for killing someone who Kalabot was personally interested in was a different story; it required careful consideration before acting. Unfortunately, Minino's patience was growing thin.

Sepherin asked only a few questions, but listened closely to the things Taffi told her. He decided to tell her everything, to see if she would give a clue as to why she was so important to Kalabot. She disappointed him, however, when she just shook her head and told him she had no idea why there was so much interest in her. She told them that she had never met Kalabot other than at the address he gave her class when they were first inducted to the Imperite program, although she thought conscripted would be a more accurate term.

Three tears had run down her face when Taffi told her about killing the original host family, on Kalabot's orders. But then the tears stopped, resolve seeming to settle over her oddly shaped features, oddly shaped for a Falwasz.

Minino couldn't help but notice how narrow her face was. It was long and thin, like her nose was. She was exceptionally tall, and her complexion was fair; far lighter and softer than the swarthy Falwasz.

Minino felt a jolt when the idea formed that she looked like a cross between the Falwasz and Shovitic clans.

That's — impossible.

Tommy looked at this watch, it was 11:30 p.m. He looked

around the street he was on, only two blocks from home. There was no sign of his pickup truck: it was still on the Voiya spaceship.

Shit.

Thankfully, there was no one out and about this late. The house where the little bastard had TransMat him was in darkness, and no lights had come on to the sound of their voices. The house was only steps from the highway, and there were cars passing by every minute or so. If he picked Cassie up and tried to carry her home, he would never be able to get her over all of the backyard fences between here and there. He'd have to carry her along the highway for two blocks and someone would see them for sure.

Tommy reached down and felt Cassie's pockets. It was there, on her right side. She'd put it there while in the truck. He pulled out the phone, thumbed the power button and waited, *Please, please, please ...* The phone came on, booted up and had bars, and a bit of juice left. *Thank you.* He dialed a number.

"Mitch, it's Tommy. I need your help."

Sepherin was pissed off. Not only had she almost killed herself by attacking the two Imperite Guards, they were so scared of her they were willing to overlook it. *Why are these Shovitics scared of me? Why am I so special? It can't be just because I'm pregnant.*

Regardless of the questions she had, Sepherin was fed up with their overbearing bullshit. She had lived with Shovitics for 120 days on the way to Earth; now she had these two back-births threatening to kill her, and then deciding she would be allowed to live as though they were conveying a gift. She was frustrated as well because they had no answer to the question about why Kalabot was so interested in her. For her, Kalabot was this mysterious figure on-high, the leader of the Umites, a mysterious presence about whom rumours abounded.

She held the gun on them, it didn't waver even the slightest. The safety was off. They sat in silence, though she could see the two of them were having a telepathic conversation that she was excluded from.

Mitch stood by the open car door as Tommy got in the back seat, holding Cassie in his arms.

"Tommy, what the hell happened to you two? You look ... what the hell happened?"

"I'll tell you when we get home, Mitch."

"Home? Hell, I'm taking you to the hospital."

"*No!* Mitch, no, we can't go to the hospital, we have to go home. We can heal this, we can fix this, but we can't go to the hospital. They'll ask questions I'm not going to answer."

Mitch stood there looking at Tommy. *Are those claw marks on them? And what's the black stuff? Is it blood?* In the end, Mitch knew Tommy was a good man. He also knew, now, that Tommy was an alien. He didn't know about little Cassie but ...

Mitch just shook his head, shut the car door, got in the driver's seat and started the car.

There was a chirping sound, Sepherin's gaze and the gun trained on Minino.

"Is my communicator," his hand moved towards his outer pocket.

"Don't answer it. You're out of reach for now."

He folded his hands again.

There was a sweep of light on the wall behind him and they heard an engine shutting off in the driveway.

"That will be my host." Sepherin stood and let her gaze linger on them a moment longer. "Don't move."

She went to the door, surprised to see Mitch standing there holding the screen door open. Tommy was rushing up the steps with the unconscious black girl in his arms. They both looked like they had been to hell and back.

Sepherin stepped out of the way, but bumped into something solid. She was spun around and thrown back against the wall. Minino ripped the gun from her grip. He grabbed her hair and bent her forward, pulling her head down. Grabbing her sweater, he stepped away from her, forcing the sweater over her head. It was much easier than trying to dig the other gun out of her pocket.

"What the hell's going on here?" Tommy yelled. Mitch lunged through the door and went for the Man in Black holding the gun. Taffi stepped forward, grabbed Mitch by the arm and used his momentum to send him crashing to the floor.

"STOP!" Minino yelled, pointing both guns at Sepherin and Tommy.

Sepherin had lost her balance, but was steady on her feet again. Standing there in a sports bra, she looked at Tommy. "I'm sorry, I didn't know what to do. They came and ..."

Minino pointed the gun at Sepherin's head, "You, Sepherin Tekin, attacked us and that is punishable by death."

They all screamed in pain and clutched their ears, except for Cassie whose limp body fell to the floor when Tommy reacted to the painful noise. However, reaching for their ears did nothing. The screaming was in their heads, it was in their minds.

Only it wasn't screaming.

It was shrill.

It was shrill wailing.

It was the shrill wailing of an angry child.

It was the shrill wailing of an angry ... *baby*.

The sound stopped in Sepherin's head, but the others were still squealing with the pain, clutching their ears, stumbling around. She put her hands down on her bare belly, looking at the slight bulge. She knew that her unborn child was ... *saving me*?

She felt the heat of love emanating from her belly. She felt the child's love for her as though it were a furnace, warming her from the inside out. She was sure her face would be pink if she could look in the mirror, pink from the heat of love. She smiled, and thought about images of love from her own childhood.

After feeling a small kick in her tummy, Sepherin looked around the room. She felt more at peace, more calm, more sure of herself than she had in many ten-sleeps. She saw the two handguns on the floor. She reached down and picked them up, just as Cassie was coming to and looking around her.

Tommy, Mitch, and the two Shovitics stopped swaying around, stopped screaming, and stopped clutching their heads.

Taffi and Minino looked at Sepherin: she was pointing both guns at them — again.

Sepherin smiled.

"What in the hell was that?" Mitch asked, shaking his head, and reaching down to help Cassie stand up.

"Was that ..." Tommy hesitated a moment, "Was that the ... *baby*?"

Taffi sniffed the air, Minino along with him.

They both looked at Tommy.

"Oath-breaker!" Taffi said.

Minino pointed at him, "You were on a Voiya ship!"

"Yes, we were. But I had to get her off, she's not one of us." Tommy was pointing at Cassie.

"YOU WERE ON A VOIYA SHIP AND YET YOU LIVE?" Minino yelled.

"YOU HAD A DUTY! YOU WERE TO KILL THEM AND DESTROY THE SHIP!" Taffi was yelling as well.

"I had to get her off the ship!" Tommy said forcefully, through gritted teeth. His fists were balled up and ready to strike, to defend himself. He also knew that assaulting an Imperite Guard was punishable by death. It struck him how a bad night had just become a much worse night. He could taste more death in the air.

"YOU HAVE NO EXCUSE! YOU ARE AN OATH-BREAKER! YOU WILL BE EXECUTED!"

"No, he won't," Sepherin said softly.

Sepherin was staring at Minino. "You're going to walk out of here and forget about this, forget about us. You'll report to Kalabot that I'm doing fine, just fine, and he has no reason to worry about me. Then you'll never come back here again, ever."

The two Guards were both breathing heavily, almost vibrating with rage. This was too much for either of them. Forgiving the Imperite for her forwardness, for assaulting them, that was one thing; but to forgive an *Oath-breaker?* That was simply not possible. And now, this piece of dirt Falwasz dared, *dared* to give them orders?

Taffi and Minino looked at each other and nodded. It was time for these things to learn who was in charge, be damned with the consequences back on Umitia.

Taffi spoke out loud, "Inform the frigate to prepare the holding cell for this ..." he lunged at Sepherin as Minino lunged at Tommy.

There was no hesitation. Sepherin shot Taffi through the heart.

Cassie screamed.

Mitch jumped back.

Minino hit Tommy high and knocked him down, landing on top of him. He drew his fist back, and then Sepherin shot him through the side of the chest. The bullet tore his lungs open and ripped a hole along the outer edge of his heart. Minino rolled off Tommy, trying to scream. No sound came out of his mouth, only foaming blood bubbles. He was too far from any other Imperite Guard to communicate telepathically; he couldn't warn anyone about the oath-breakers. Thirty agonizing seconds later, while staring at his pregnant executioner standing above him, the last draw of life's breath left him.

Cassie was clutching Mitch's arm, hyperventilating. She mewled loudly as sanity threatened to slip away from her again. As Minino's life slipped away from him, Cassie fled out the door and into the darkness.

Sepherin watched her go, knowing that she was going to be a complication that would have to be dealt with.

The young Imperite turned to her uncle.

"Are you still mobile? Do you need to see a doctor?"

Tommy looked at her, his eyes reflecting the frustration and misery he was feeling inside. He looked at Mitch, who just stood there saying nothing. Tommy looked back at Sepherin, "We have to do something about these bodies, quickly."

Mitch knelt down by the closest alien and felt his pants pockets. He reached in one and pulled out a set of car keys. He turned and headed for the door, "I'll open the trunk."

Chapter 34

Mitch went through the trees between the houses. He grabbed a big can of gasoline for his snow blower, and an armful of hardwood for the fireplace. He went back to Tommy's and dropped everything on top of the bodies in the trunk.

Tommy drove the Guards' car, following Mitch for thirty minutes to the abandoned Schmidt Lake quarry. It had become a defacto dumping ground in the area for old cars. It was also a place where the local teenagers liked to party on the weekends. They drove around for a few minutes to make sure there was no one in the open pit to witness what they were about to do.

The two men put the wood under the Shovitics' bodies in the trunk of their own sedan. Then Tommy doused it all with gasoline. Mitch lit a wooden match and tossed it in the car. The *whump* sound was loud, but not too loud. The flames shot up from the impromptu pyre, as did the thick column of smoke. It quickly died down to a steady burn. The gravel pit was deep enough and far enough off the main road they doubted that anyone would come to investigate. This late at night, both men also doubted the column of smoke would be seen at all. They only waited a few minutes, deciding to leave after the smell of burning flesh reached their nostrils. They didn't speak a single word to each other the entire time.

Had they waited, they may have seen, in the cooling remains, the dull blue light of the subcutaneous locator beacon that both of the Shovitics' bodies contained.

Chapter 35

Tommy and Mitch drove back in silence. Mitch had questions, but he needed Tommy to be settled and not feel backed into a corner before he asked them. He waited until they got back to the house.

Sepherin had finished cleaning up the blood by the time they got back. She had put all the furniture back to rights, and it looked like she had even dusted. The throw rug that had been on the floor of her bedroom was now on the living room carpet, covering the black blood stain from Taffi. At least Minino's black blood had been on the hardwood floor, much easier to clean up.

When Tommy and Mitch came in the front door, she was sitting on the couch, sipping a Diet Pepsi, and watching the movie she had started earlier.

She stood up when they entered. "Come with me," she held her hand out to Tommy. They went to the kitchen and he sat down, slumping forward on the table on his elbows. Sepherin got the first aid kit from the bathroom, something she had explored days before, and opened it up. She didn't know exactly what everything was, but she had emergency medical training back on Umitia when she was a teenager, so with Mitch's quick explanation of the bottles' contents, she was able to muddle through cleaning his wounds and put bandages on him. The bites on his leg were deep; she knew he was going to have to see someone about them. However, butterfly patches and lots of gauze tape would do the trick for now.

"So," Mitch began, leaning against the kitchen door, "who were those men that you killed, and why did you kill them?"

"Imperite Guards," Tommy said.

"Shovitic scum," Sepherin added.

"Impa ... what?"

"He knows," Sepherin said quietly, "I wasn't careful earlier. He heard me talking to myself."

"Yeah, yeah, you're aliens, both of you, I get that," Mitch was nodding his head. "But I'll ask again, who were they and why are they dead?"

While she was placing medical tape on one of Tommy's dressings, Sepherin answered him. "They're the ones in charge of my planet. They bring us here and dump us here for the rest of our lives. Our purpose is to kill the Voiya, the bad aliens, the ones who did this to Tommy. It's our job to complete the Umite Imperative, so they call us Imperites, and they are the Imperite Guards."

Tommy turned to look at Mitch. "And I was abducted by the bad aliens earlier tonight, with Cassie. But we were able to escape. When I came in, they smelled the bad aliens on me and because I was alive, that means I didn't kill them and destroy the ship, so that means I broke the oath that my mother took before she came here."

"Your mother?"

Tommy nodded, "I'm an Umite, but I was born on Earth. My oath is hereditary; still just as binding."

"Uh-huh. I see."

"Really?" Sepherin asked.

Mitch shook his head, "No, not really. But, they were aliens, right? The guys you killed?"

Sepherin and Tommy both nodded.

"Is little Cassie an alien?"

Tommy shook his head.

"Okay, so that's that then."

"You're good with this?" Tommy squinted up at his friend.

Mitch was silent for a moment, deciding how to answer.

"Listen, Tommy, you're okay in my books. I like you. And Stephy, I quite like you as well, so does Martha. As for those two guys, well, far as I know there ain't any laws about killing aliens from another planet, so, whatever. I'm going to go home and ..."

They heard another car pulling in the driveway. Sepherin looked out the window. "It looks like an official car, it has writing on it and lights on the top of it."

"Great, cops." Tommy looked at Mitch, "Go out the back, leave the light off, get to your place and make like you've been there the whole time."

"No, Tommy, I'm part of this ..."

Tommy pushed the first aid kit into his hands and shoved him towards the back door, "If you're here ... if you're not here ... just go, *go!*"

What Tommy said made sense. Mitch went out the back door quietly.

Tommy grabbed Stephy's arm, "Just play it cool. I just got home. We'll make it up as we go along," then he raced upstairs.

By the time the officers knocked at the door, he was coming down in track pants and a housecoat to cover the bandages, brushing his teeth, reeking of some gawd-awful cologne to cover the lingering smell of the gasoline.

Tommy nodded at Sepherin and she answered the door.

"Yes, may I help you?"

"Evening ma'am, I'm Constable Thompson and this is Constable Blair from the Ontario Provincial Police, mind if we come in?"

"May I ask what this is about?" she asked as sweetly as possible.

"Stephy," Tommy said from behind her, "let the men in, it's okay."

The two police officers entered without hesitation and stood in the living room looking around

The one who had spoken first continued, "Mr. Lehmann, Tommy, yes?"

Tommy just nodded, toothbrush still in his mouth.

"We've had a report of a disturbance here earlier, a strange report. A young lady says that " he looked at Sepherin, "that you shot and killed two men, here in the living room."

Sepherin felt the baby kick, once. She put her hand on her belly and rubbed gently, soothing it *Not yet,* she thought-spoke to her unborn child.

Tommy went to the kitchen and spit out his toothpaste. He came back in the room and said seriously, "Officers, you can see everything's fine here. There are no bodies lying around. Who told you that?"

Constable Blair was toeing the throw rug. "Do you always have this here?"

Sepherin sighed and smiled, "They found you out Uncle Tommy."

Tommy looked at her, a numb feeling spreading across his face and chest. He felt the urge to pee.

She turned back to the officers, still smiling. "Go ahead, pull it back."

Constable Blair reached down and picked up the edge, walking backwards on the throw rug to peel it back. There was a black stain on the carpet underneath.

Tommy's breath had slowed, he felt a pain in his intestines and his bowels felt like they were going to release. He felt a bead of sweat on his temple. He saw the first cop had a hand resting on his gun.

Sepherin turned around to the book case behind her as the constable put his fingers on the dark spot and lifted them up. He swirled his fingers around and sniffed at them.

"It feels oily."

"Yes," Sepherin turned back to them, holding out one of Tommy's DVD's, "Uncle Tommy here decided to do some fixing on the mow lawner, but he needed to watch this disc about small engine repair while he was doing it." She handed them a Popular Mechanics DVD on maintaining a two-stroke gas engine.

Tommy refrained from giving a deep sigh, he also refrained from fainting. Instead he jumped in, "Yes, you found me out. I'm an idiot. I put some plastic down, but it had a hole in it and as you can see, the oil leaked through."

"He even got some here on the wood floor," she looked down where she was standing and pointed, "There, you can see some traces of it in the cracks."

"When did you do this?" Constable Blair looked up at them.

"Today," they both responded.

The cop stood up and put the carpet back in place, seemingly satisfied.

"Who's Mitch?" Constable Thompson asked.

Tommy and Sepherin looked at each other. Tommy responded, "Mitch? He's our neighbour. Why?"

"Was he here this evening?"

"No, he wasn't, not that I know of anyways. I was in Toronto all day. I just got back about twenty minutes ago."

"I thought you were changing the oil in your lawn mower, today, in your living room?" Constable Thompson asked quickly.

"No," Sepherin spoke up quickly, only the barest hint of tremor in her voice. "I put the throw rug down on it today. He made the mess *yesterday*."

Tommy smiled and just nodded his head sheepishly, feeling like his bladder was going to explode.

After a pause, obviously evaluating what they were saying, Constable Thompson prompted, "And Mitch? Was he here today or was he in Toronto, too?"

Sepherin was shaking her head, "I saw him outside earlier, but he hasn't been here. Why, do you think he killed someone too?" She nailed facetiousness in one.

Constable Thompson ignored her jibe, "You got back twenty minutes ago? Not an hour ago?"

"No, I don't think so, doesn't seem like that long ago. Did you notice the time when I got in, Stephy?"

"No, sorry, I was asleep on the couch when he got home. I just woke up a few minutes before you got here."

"How did you get back from Toronto?" the police officer asked.

Shit, the truck isn't here.

"Well, that was an adventure in itself. We were on the way back when it broke down south of Walkerton. I'm going to get my neighbour to drive me back in the morning to see if we can get it going."

Tommy looked at Sepherin, she smiled back at him, arms folded across her chest, a look of absolute serenity on her face. He looked back at the officers.

"Anyways, we had to head out on foot. A few minutes later this guy stops and picks us up."

"Us? You were with him, miss?"

"No," Sepherin shook her head, "I've been here all day."

Tommy was nodding, "It was Cassie, from the hardware store. Her and Lenora went to a conference in the city. It was a last minute thing, the boss asked me to drive them."

"So the three of you had to hitchhike from Walkerton?" Constable Thompson asked.

"No, just Cassie and me. Lenora stayed in Toronto."

The constable was writing notes in his book as Tommy spoke. He flipped back a couple of pages, and then looked at his partner. Finally he asked, "Mr. Lehmann, when you last saw Cassie tonight, where was that?"

"The guy dropped her at her place, and then he dropped me off. I insisted he drop her off first, I wanted to make sure she got home okay, she's been a bit off lately."

"Who was this guy that gave you a ride?"

"Michael something."

"You don't know his last name?"

"Nope, we just traded first names is all."

"And how did she appear when you left her, did she have any injuries?"

"What? Injuries? Hell, no! She was perfectly fine when she got out of the car, physically anyways. Why? Has something happened to her?"

The constable wrote down Tommy's comments then took a deep breath and let it out slowly. He looked up at Tommy, searching his eyes for an uncomfortably long time. Then he looked at Sepherin, searching her eyes as well. He continued, ignoring Tommy's question.

"You said Cassie has been 'off' lately, what exactly did you mean by that?"

Tommy hated himself for what he was about to do, but it was the only option he had at the moment. He certainly didn't want to test Mitch's theory that there was no law about killing aliens, when the only proof they were aliens was some barbecue meat in the back of a car that would just be a burned out hulk by now.

Tommy hesitated; he didn't want to say what he was going to say, but he had to. "Cassie and her boyfriend broke up a few days ago, and she's been taking it hard. She feels ... I don't know ... she feels all alone, even when she's surrounded by people. She's all quiet, and brooding, and thinks people are talking about her. I think it's worse because she just found out yesterday that she's pregnant ..."

"Pregnant?" the look of shock on Sepherin's face was an honest response.

Tommy nodded, "Yeah, she just told me on the way back, just before we broke down actually. She was trying to get hold of her ex to tell him, to figure out what they were going to do, but her phone died and ... she lost it in the car. She broke down and started crying, and carrying on. I was really concerned for her, but after a little while she seemed to pull herself together again. Her folks are real churchy types; I imagine they aren't going to be too happy with her when they find out. I know they gave her a real hard time when her boyfriend moved in with her last year." At least that part was true.

The constable was making more notes. Finally he closed the book and looked at his partner, "Well, Gord? Anything else?"

Constable Blair just shook his head.

Constable Thompson turned back to Tommy, "One more question and then we'll go. And I apologize in advance if it seems strange, but, were you and Cassie abducted by aliens tonight?"

Tommy and Sepherin looked at each other and then burst out laughing.

"Aliens?" they both said, as if they had rehearsed it.

The constable hooked his thumbs in his utility belt, "Sorry, I had to ask. Cassie gave us quite a tale about aliens and spaceships. She said that you killed a bunch of them before getting the midget alien to beam you back to Earth. She said you," he looked at Sepherin, "killed two Men in Black here in your house."

Tommy stopped smiling, "Man, she's really fucked up over this Ritchie thing. Such a shame. You said something about her being injured?"

The constable nodded, "Truthfully, with the wounds she has and the story she told, we think they're self-inflicted. We took her to the on-call doctor in town. He cleaned her up and we dropped her off someplace safe for the night. She'll be fine, but we're going to follow up with her and see if we can get her in for a psychiatric assessment. We'd have done it tonight, but, you know, country hospitals and all. They don't have psychiatric residents available this late."

Tommy looked sad and nodded slowly, "Well, I hope she gets the help she needs. She's a fine girl."

The two constables said good evening and then left.

As they went to the car, Blair nudged Thompson, "You honestly think he's her uncle?"

"I wouldn't mind being her *uncle* for the night."

The two men chuckled.

As they opened the car doors, Blair looked across the roof at Thompson and asked, "What's a mow lawner, anyways?"

His partner looked back at him thoughtfully. "It sounds like something an alien would call a lawn mower."

Neither of them laughed.

After a lingering look at the house, they finally got in the car and drove away.

215

Chapter 36

Shivinin considered himself a gourmand, a chef with exceptional skill. He sighed deeply and watched as Zekra covered the breakfast frittata with first ketchup, then Frank's Red Hot sauce, and then a dollop of horseradish. *Why do I even bother? I should send him to the cafeteria for breakfast.*

Zekra tucked into the food, smacking his lips, and cramming buttered toast into his mouth with the frittata. He looked up at Shivinin who was just sitting there.

"Are you not going to eat?"

"I've lost my appetite."

Zekra shrugged, grabbed Shivinin's plate, and used his fork to push its contents onto what was left on his own plate.

And then he added more ketchup.

And then he added more hot sauce.

And then he added more horseradish.

And then he grabbed two more pieces of toast.

Twenty minutes later the two Guards walked the six metres from their living accommodations, and through the back door of their office.

Shivinin picked up the envelope that had been shoved under the front door sometime during the night. He sat at his desk and started going through the small sheaf of reports. As he did this, he pulled open the bottom drawer on one side of the desk, pulled out a three-pack of Twinkies, and sated the hunger he felt from the breakfast he didn't eat. He knew the smell of them would drive Zekra up the wall with want, but having had a two-helping breakfast, he knew Zekra wouldn't have anything else until lunchtime.

Zekra was doing his best to ignore the smell of the delicious little creamy-filled golden logs. He booted up his computer, connected to the military network, and checked his overnight messages. He was looking for word from his brother and Minino. There were only six messages in his inbox and none of them were from Taffi.

Out of the corner of his eye, he saw Shivinin lean forward at this desk, focussed on what he was reading.

"Zekra, look at what came off the police computer in the area near the Imperite."

He handed the paper over and Zekra scanned it once, and then read it slowly. As he read, Shivinin saw his partner's hands start trembling slightly. He was reading the constable's report about a fantastic tale from a mentally unbalanced woman who claimed she had been abducted by aliens, rescued by another alien, and that an alien had killed two other aliens, two Men in Black.

Zekra looked up at him, "The Earther claims the Imperite killed them?"

"Try to make contact with them." Shivinin prompted.

Zekra reached over to the small cabinet by his desk and picked up the encrypted radio from the charger. He called in his native Shovitic tongue, "One-two calling eight-oh-two."

"Eight-oh-two."

"One-five, they are aboard?"

"Negative."

Shivinin stared at Zekra, Twinkie crumbs lining his lower lip.

"You are tracking them?"

"Affirmative."

"Are they still at the target's residence?"

Now there was a slight pause. "No, they have moved off several leagues. It does not appear they have moved in some time."

"Are you able to get a visual on them?"

"Stand by."

Three minutes later they heard the orbiting duty frigate communications officer call them again, "One-two, we need you on board, right now."

The orbiting frigate had TransMat them aboard, showed them the image, and then TransMat them down to the location of the beacons belonging to Taffi and Minino. Ten minutes after the frigate saw there was a problem, Zekra and Shivinin were standing in the quarry west of Walkerton.

They approached the burned out hulk of the car; it looked like one of the military sedans assigned to the Imperite Guards. The two men peered inside, and then Shivinin lifted the trunk hood.

At the first glance, he knew exactly what had happened to Taffi and Minino. Zekra stepped up to the trunk and looked inside. He started to reach towards the beacons, which were giving off a faint blue glow. Shivinin stopped him, and looked at his partner's face. He shook his head and made Zekra step back.

It only took a minute for Shivinin to dig the two beacons out of the charred meat, and confirm the ident numbers on them as belonging to Taffi Dinhiz and Minino Yuetya.

Fortunately for the Shovitic clan, they don't have tear ducts. This is odd because Humanesh all over the three known inhabited galaxies *do* have tear ducts. What is not commonly known, however, is that the Shovitic clan of Umitia aren't actually Humanesh. Of course, only the Shovitic's know that, and they don't share that tidbit of information. If the other six clans knew that the Shovitic masters of their world were not of the same race, things would get very interesting.

While they don't have tear ducts, Shovitics can still grieve. Shivinin stood beside Zekra, with his arm around his shoulders, and waited patiently for his partner to suffer the first waves of grief for the loss of his twin brother.

Chapter 37

She had been up all night waiting for more of the Shovitic bastards to show up. Tommy had slept for a few hours, then got up with the sunrise to cook breakfast for them. He was still in discomfort from the bites, but the bleeding had stopped with the bandages and the cooking helped him focus and relax.

Sepherin sat at the table with her arms crossed. She looked at her uncle as he tucked into his eggs, sliced animal, and browned potatoes. He ate more of the toasted bread slices than she imagined was possible. She chewed on the corner of her lower lip, wondering how he could eat so casually after what had happened. She turned away from the sight of him ravenously shoving food into this mouth and contemplated the bowl of oatmeal in front of her. It was all her upset stomach could handle right now.

Sepherin may have appeared calm on the outside, but she felt like she was coming apart on the inside. She kept looking up at Tommy, expecting him to say something — but he didn't. They had crossed a big line last night — *she* had crossed a big line last night. She had killed the two Imperite Guards, a crime punishable by death no matter what world it occurred on.

But she didn't know if that was worse than being an oath-breaker, which, she finally realized, she and Tommy both were: he for not killing the Voiya; her for striking, and then killing the Guards.

Her hands absentmindedly stroked her small baby bulge, wondering if she would live long enough to hold her child in her arms. Sepherin knew that she had done the right thing, protecting her unborn and protecting her uncle. She knew that in the court of people's perception, Falwasz people, they would understand. If Earthers knew the truth, as evidenced by Mitch's reaction, they would understand as well. The only ones who wouldn't understand would be the other Imperite Guards — and Kalabot. Unfortunately, they were the ones with the power.

As she watched Tommy finish eating, using the last of the toast to sop up the yellow-cooked yolk from the unborn chicken, she knew there was only one thing they could do.

"We have to leave."

Tommy looked up at her, chewing on the last of the breakfast.

Finally, he nodded. "You're sure about that? You think they'll trace it back to us?"

"They will. I'm sure of it."

He took a large sip of coffee, swallowing it slowly, staring at her.

"But they don't know where the bodies are. We drove a fair piece and put them in a place where lots of cars are dumped and ..." he didn't say burnt out. He thought it better that she didn't know all the details, though he realized she wasn't stupid either. He'd come home smelling of gas and smoke, it had to have been obvious.

Sepherin then remembered something, something that had been a rumour during her time at the Imperite Academy. "Uncle Tommy, did you notice a locator beacon in their bodies?"

"Locator beacon?" he looked alarmed.

"It was a rumour, one we heard a few times. The Guards all have locator beacons," she pointed low on her abdomen, "just under the lowest rib on the left side."

"Inside the body?"

She nodded.

Tommy looked around, rubbing his hands together, then rubbing them on his pant legs. She could see the alarm on his face.

"I have to go back then."

"It was just a rumour, I don't know for sure if it's true, but ..." she trailed off.

Tommy stood, leaving his dirty dishes on the table. "I'll get Mitch to drive me. We'll have to go back. If they do track them and find the bodies, they'll certainly come hunting for us next."

Sepherin said nothing. She knew it might be a wild callot chase, but if they could do anything to head off the inevitable, they had to try.

She stood and hugged her uncle, then watched as he grabbed his coat and headed out the back door. Sepherin, ignoring the mess on the table, went upstairs to start packing for both of them. She looked out the window of her room as Mitch's car pulled out of the driveway. Tommy was looking at the house.

Their eyes met.

He waved at her as they sped off.

The baby kicked and Sepherin cried out loud.

She knew that she would never see her uncle again.

Chapter 38

Though they appear drab and monochromatic, the Shovitic clan has a deep appreciation for colour, form, and texture. To the surprise of those who are lucky enough, or unlucky in some cases, to visit the Imperite Palace: they are surprised to find some of the most colourful and lavish gardens on the planet. The grounds of the Imperite Palace are even, many of those visitors say, more beautiful than the Hyperion Gardens outside Kilkestand City.

The appearance of these gardens is due, in no small part, to the work of Cobus Scheepers. The retired propulsion researcher, of the Silthit clan, is the chief groundskeeper at the Palace, the Imperite Academy, and the spaceport. He's one of the few clansmen allowed to come and go as he pleases around the institutions run by the Shovitic clan. What he loves most of all about his job is not the grand planning and coordination of many beds of flowers; what he loves most is being on his hands and knees with his gloveless fingers running through the rich dirt, as he tends to individual plants. For him, a single bloom, an individual blossom, is the microcosm of the macrocosm. He sometimes fancied that all of life could be found in the cycles of the perennials that he cared for.

Looking up from his work, he was not at all surprised to see the creepiest man alive watching him from a few feet away.

"Kalabot, fair morning to you," Cobus said with a smile.

The leader of the Umite race just looked at the gardener of gardeners. It was not his way to communicate pleasantries, only necessities. He lifted his hand and presented a glass bowl with an amount of water in it.

"What will it be today then? What are you in the mood for?" Cobus asked.

"I need to think deeply on a matter of significance. It is something that is ..." the Shovitic leader trailed off, appearing to be lost in thought. After a pause he raised his other hand, with one finger pointed in the air, "It is something that is of conceptual importance to me, a matter of fundamental definition."

Cobus squinted as the sun broke the corner of the palace proper, brushing the dirt off his hands with his apron. He was thankful the brim of Kalabot's hat kept his mouth in shadow, so he didn't have to see what lurked behind his lips when the man spoke. Cobus took the bowl from Kalabot and led the way to another garden bed. Glancing over his shoulder, he was still amazed after all these years that Kalabot could move without actually looking like he was walking. The man who was a mystery, even to those close to him, looked as if he was simply gliding along the grass.

Stopping near a patch of darker hued plants, Cobus set down the bowl, put on his gloves and picked up his small pruning shears. A moment later he handed the glass bowl back to Kalabot. Floating in the water was a blossom with five vibrant, pointed, purple petals; a ring of small, fuzzy, pea-shaped, green anthers; and a long yellow pistil and stamen.

As he offered the bowl, the gardener warned him, "When you're done with that, Kalabot, dispose of it carefully and without touching the yellow or the green parts. This plant contains a deadly poison, and even the slightest touch will debilitate you if it doesn't outright kill you."

The leader of the Umites took the bowl and held it contemplatively. He lifted it to his nose and gently inhaled the bold scent, made bolder by his incredible sense of smell. Finally his pale, gaunt face cracked the barest hint of a smile. He slid his darkened glasses down his patrician nose and looked at the gardener.

"You have selected well, old friend." Kalabot inclined his head and put his darkened glasses back on. "With gratitude," he said, as he turned and went back to the Palace.

The gardener smiled. It had been many, many seasons since he had first seen a Shovitic without any coverings over their eyes. It was a sight that could induce nightmares in adults, and screams of horror in children. People avoided looking at the mostly empty eye socket, with the ocular stump and its glassy iris. More disconcerting than that, was the two-dozen moving eyeworms (for want of a better term) that rimmed the cavity. Cobus was so used to the sight that he no longer shuddered because of it. The gardener watched the Manager move without moving, as Kalabot returned to his dark office in the Palace with no windows.

Cobus looked down at the grass, still damp with the morning dew. There was only one set of footprints. There was no track and no trail; there was no indication at all that Kalabot had stood before him only seconds before. The gardener shook his head and went back to tending the plants he loved so dearly.

The double doors closed behind Kalabot as he moved across his spacious, high-ceiling office. He easily moved around the body of the Imperite Guard who had brought the news of the two who had been killed on Earth. It was the Guard's unfortunate slip of the tongue to suggest that Sepherin Tekin or her host may have been involved. Kalabot had looked up at the mention of the girl's name, and the Guard had collapsed in a heap on the floor; he had simply ceased to be alive. Kalabot had realised that his response was rash, but it was what it was. He had the power to deal death, but he did not possess the gift of dealing life. Of course, he could have moved back a few minutes in time and stopped himself, but the dead Imperite Guard was annoying anyways, so he didn't bother. Kalabot would deal with the body later.

Moving behind the desk, he turned on a small lamp and set the bowl with the blossom in the middle of the pool of warm light it cast.

Behind his chair, covering the entire wall was row upon row of books, from floor to ceiling. Printed books were a passion of his, though they were rare to find anywhere else on the planet. Many of the tombs he collected were from other worlds, in other languages. He loved the look of them, the feel of them, and even the smell of them. He moved the ladder on its rollers to the right place, and then climbed several rungs. His fingers traced the spines of different materials until he found the one he was looking for. He tipped it out then held it against his chest as he climbed back down and pushed the ladder out of the way.

Sitting at the desk, he reached forward to slightly adjust the bowl, centering it perfectly in the soft yellow light. Taking a deep breath, aligning himself, he opened the book of *Talidich Meditations*, written by Kovulian the Lesser. He quickly found the meditation he was looking for and read it slowly, translating it in his head as he went along:

Secrets of the Two Ka

A secret has a blade with two edges. It is a trust rendered, and it is a deception embraced. Which is worse: coddling the quiet scream of a lie or the warming embrace of another's suffering? When one accepts a secret to be kept, one keeps fresh a wound in two ka. When one rejects the keeping of a secret, only one ka is healed. Ask yourself with brave truthfulness: what price would you find worthy of another's ka? What price would you find worthy of your own ka?

Kalabot closed the small book and then folded his long fingers over top of it. He was quite taken with the word, 'ka'. The word's intent in the mediation was similar to the Shovitic word '*koum*', which referred to the vital spark of life.

He breathed deeply a few times as he lifted his gaze to the beautiful colours in the glass bowl. They were different under the yellow light of the incandescent bulb. They were muted, yet vibrant in a new way. Though the water was perfectly still, the blossom began turning slowly under Kalabot's gaze. He looked deeply into the blossom, deeply into the colours, deeply into himself. He allowed his ears to ignore the distant sounds of administration. His peripheral vision narrowed, casting aside the gloomy reflections in the room with no windows. His nostrils flared slightly with each breath as he moved deeper into his own thoughts, the swirling colours filling his vision.

He saw only the blossom in the bowl in the light.

He saw only the blossom in the light.

He saw only the blossom.

Time stilled.

The matter he needed to meditate upon was Sepherin Tekin, his illegitimate daughter. When he saw that she had been selected for the Imperite program, he was relieved. The older she had gotten, the more worried he became that her paternal lineage may be discovered. With her going off-world, the risk was nonexistent. Alabast Tekindottir would not reveal a secret which would be a death sentence for herself and for him.

When he learned from the transport watch commander that Sepherin was with child, he had, in a fit of rare paternal consideration, arranged for her to be housed with a blood-kin. It was all he could do, all he *would* do, for the offspring he had never acknowledged. The inherent cost of the arrangement, retiring an Imperite and her family, meant nothing to him. Once an Imperite was off-world, they were pawns, beneath consideration for one as important as he was.

But thinking of Sepherin Tekin led his thoughts to the night she had been conceived. He could feel his heart beat faster in his chest as he remembered the night of Alabast's entreaty. His breath quickened at the thought of the taboo gift she offered him.

Kalabot knew he would kill any Shovitic that took such a moment of pleasure, the law demanded t. But he is — *the* Shovitic — he is *the* arbiter of the Umite law, he is *the* Manager.

The old Shovitic remembered the olive-skinned beauty of the Falwasz woman as she stood before him. He remembered the startled surprise he felt as she reached for the strap on her gown, and pushed it off of her shoulder. He remembered the way his chest tightened with the sudden need to breathe heavily, to pant, to drink in the moment of time and fill his senses with her essence at his most base level. He had known he was going against all that he demanded, yet he still reached forward, unable to resist the temptation. He remembered the tremor in his hand as he pulled the edge of her gown, revealing her full, firm breast. He remembered the look of sadness in her eyes as her nipple swelled under the touch and caress of his palm. He remembered how that look of defeat, of despair, of a final attrition of her soul had filled him with lust.

"For all to be restored to my House, I will give you anything that you ask. But only this time. Only this one time."

Her words had echoed in his ears, competing with the buzzing of the pulse that had started pounding through his head. His body, ancient even then, responded as she pushed the gown down to the floor, revealing her Falwasz hips; hips which were made to bear children and cradle men.

She had stepped forward, closer to him, pressing her breast harder into the palm of his hard, her nipple growing firmer. She reached up and took off his darkened glasses. She didn't frown. Her lips did not curl in revulsion.

She faltered only once, but then succeeded in forcing a smile.

With her gown on the floor, she had then taken his other hand and led it to feel her readiness.

He reflected on the pleasures her body had given him that night. She had brought him to ecstasy in a way that no Shovitic woman was capable of. He wondered why those who lived so long ago had established the edict that the clans should not interbreed. He asked himself, laying there on the floor of his office as her heaving body rolled off of him, *Why is this particular pleasure worthy of death?*

He remembered lying there, lost in the heaving afterglow of his own pleasures as she stood and dressed.

He wanted to beckon her back to him, but he knew she would not return to his embrace.

He wanted to touch her again, in that way.

He wanted to hear her moaning as she had when he brought her to her fullness, again and again.

He wanted to return to the feeling of her warm, moist, softness wrapped around his hard, yearning desire until he had completed his rhythmic presence in her.

He wanted every muscle in his body to clench tightly again, while he moaned long and low with the release of his pleasure.

He remembered the look on her face as he came to his feet. His prone body simply tilting upwards until he was standing, looking like a macabre, naked living doll. She had a look of nervousness in her eyes at that moment, but she still found her voice as she tucked loose strands of hair back into the bun high on her head.

"It will be as promised?"

Kalabot nodded once, his ocular stump fixed on her face, his eyeworms undulating slowly in the host's own sea of endorphins.

"The House of Tekin is without fault."

He remembered the feeling of emptiness that filled him as she had turned without another word. She was a graceful vision of temptation, striding from his office, without even another glance.

The blossom in the bowl of water was spinning faster, causing ripples against the glass. The green anthers spread further out with the centrifugal force. The yellow stamen seemed to stand more erect, mocking the empty yearning framed by his memories.

It was many ten-sleeps later during an inspection of Kilkestand City that he had seen her. She was walking along the sidewalk, on the other side of the street. He stopped and stared, his entourage stopping with him, but not knowing what he was staring at. His face would have reflected shock had he not been a master of self-control, when not in her embrace.

Her belly bulged with child. He quickly calculated the time since their encounter. It was too much of a coincidence. In the following ten-sleeps, a trusted Imperite Guard kept an eye on the *Mater* of the House of Tekin. When it was reported that she had given birth, the agent collected a sample of the child's blood from the hospital, swearing the doctor to secrecy under the penalty of a heinous disfigurement.

Kalabot had run the blood tests himself, the potential results being a death sentence.

Staring at the spinning blossom, he remembered the shock of the molecular level tests which confirmed without a doubt, the child was a hybrid of Shovitic and Falwasz DNA. For centuries, the knowledge that Shovitics could not breed with any of the clans had been an absolute certainty. Kalabot knew at that moment, as he looked at the test results, that it had been an absolute lie. He had sighed deeply as he finally understood why the penalty of cross-clan mating was punishable by death. The Shovitic blood strain needed to be kept pure, for reasons no clansman other than the Shovitics knew about. With the child in Alabast Tekindottir's belly, a dangerous situation had risen.

To say that Kalabot had been upset by this discovery would be a drastic understatement.

The trusted agent had died under the hand of Kalabot's boiling wrath, because the Umites have a well-known axiom that 'dead clansmen tell no tales.' Kalabot then made sure the doctor and his innocent wife would tell no tales, either. The innocent wife didn't know nothing-from-nothing about the baby or the Manager's interest; Kalabot was just having a bad day.

Were the truth about this child to be known, were it to be revealed that Kalabot had sired a Falwasz bastard, let alone mated with a Falwasz, the law was clear on that matter. Both Alabast and he would be publicly executed, if they could catch him. But such a self-saving move would require abandoning all that he knew, all that he was.

The easiest solution was to kill the child. Once the child was dead, there would be no trace and no link between him and the Falwasz woman.

After he had reached that conclusion, Kalabot had closed his eyes and moved himself through space and time to stand in the nursery of the bastard child, late at night. He reached down and picked up the infant, intent on snapping its neck before it could cry. But as he moved the pink swaddling cloth aside, the baby opened its eyes and looked up at him.

Then she cooed.

Then she yawned.

Then she closed her eyes and went back to sleep.

Kalabot, the leader of all Umitia — was moved. Kalabot, the butcher of more *koum* than any other Shovitic, stood transfixed. Kalabot, the arbiter of terminal judgements, had been unable to complete the simple task at hand.

He just had to reach forward.

He just had to squeeze and twist.

He had felt a great weight upon his wrist, preventing his hand from moving, as though a presence larger and more powerful than he was interceding. As he stood there, Kalabot clearly remembered wondering if the little girl in his arms was the child that had been foretold of in the ancient legends. If so, it was even more of a reason to kill her, yet he still had not been able to move his hand any closer to her neck.

Lost in thoughts which he had not been expecting, he had lifted the infant closer and sniffed, then drew in a second deep breath. He drank in her smell; he drank in her scent. His heart was pounding at the smell of her newborn skin, powdered and perfumed as only a Falwasz baby would be.

He remembered how he had heard the quiet gasp when the door opened. Without moving his feet, he had turned to look at the terrified face of Alabast Tekindottir. She was trying to hold her breathe, but she kept heaving great gulps of air, her eyes wide, her body trembling.

He remembered how her voice had hoarsely whispered, "Please, no."

He knew at that moment he could not harm the child. He also knew at that moment, that no one knew the truth about the child except for him and the child's mother. He could see in her face that there was fear for the life of the child, but there was also a fear of the truth becoming known.

They were bound forever in the secret they shared: the wounds to both of their *ka* would be forever raw.

He had looked down upon the child a final time, the weight gone from his wrist. His long finger had reached forward and touched the infant on the nose. Still sleeping, the baby's lips had puckered at the object in front of her face, as though to suckle on the tip of it. He quickly pulled his finger back, his eyes going wide. The child had responded to him, *his child* had responded to him.

He had then looked up at Alabast, who was holding her hands out for the baby. He gently passed his daughter to her mother. Alabast had clutched the child close to her bosom, and then she whispered to Kalabot once more.

"Please, for all that's merciful, don't harm her."

He remembered how he had looked into Alabast's eyes, seeing the underlying terror. He remembered looking down at the child, who was awake again, quietly fussing, her small eyes moving over his face.

Kalabot nodded once. He then commanded in a whisper, "Her name?"

"Sepherin *Tekindottir*." He had heard Alabast's fear, or perhaps her anger, rising closer to the surface.

Kalabot had then just closed his eyes and moved himself through time and space again. He arrived in the small hours of the night's darkness, standing at the crossroads of four flower beds. He had sunk to his knees, and yearned for tear ducts to release the surging emotions thrust upon him.

Sitting at his desk so many seasons later, through the meditation upon the spinning blossom, he found what it was he had sought. He had found the answer to the question which troubled him.

He had found the price of his own *ka*.

His daughter would finally have to die.

Chapter 39

Zekra and Shivinin called for another unit to help them. Femi and Corvu were completing a visit to an abductee with a big mouth, and then the duty frigate would TransMat them across the country. They would be at least an hour before they arrived.

The two Imperite Guards from station 12 had come so fast at the frigate's request, that they hadn't had their wheels TransMat on board. This meant they were going to have to wait for the other two. Shivinin thought it was a good idea, the waiting. It would give Zekra some time, to hopefully cool the blood-rage he felt. That was why he never made the request for the frigate to go get their vehicle.

They walked around the abandoned quarry, filled with hulks of cars, trucks, and long-abandoned equipment. Zekra was too wrapped up in his grief to have detected the scent, but Shivinin had caught a whiff of something familiar. Where Zekra's gaze was focused on the ground in front of him, Shivinin was testing the air periodically. As he moved away from the burned out hulk, he lost the scent.

Zekra leaned back against the bumper of an old Ford which had given up the ghost many years before. Shivinin stood nearby, giving his partner and friend time to process. The report about the Earther had said that the Imperite, the new arrival, had killed Taffi and Minino. Shivinin hadn't really believed it, at first, not until he saw the bodies. The Earther had also said they had been on a spaceship, and that the other Imperite, the host, had killed many aliens; but not all of them, not the Voiya Master.

The human's words meant there were *two* oath-breakers to deal with.

Shivinin and Zekra looked up at the sound of an engine approaching in the distance. The two Imperite Guards took cover behind a large rusted-out tanker truck. They watched the reddish-brown car drive down into the quarry. They said nothing as they watched it slowly drive around with the occupants apparently checking for anyone that might be watching. The two Umites ducked down as the car passed within a few feet of them. They both sniffed the air at the same time, and then looked at each other.

As soon as the car passed out of sight, they hurried through the rusted-out hulks, keeping out of sight. They knew that whoever was in the car had been on a Voiya ship, but they needed to see who it was to decide how to proceed.

They saw the car pull to a stop near the back of the burnt-out sedan. The passenger got out and approached the final resting place of the two dead Guards. The scent was unmistakable. Not only could they smell drone, they could smell dead drone. The man's cologne, soap, and shampoo had removed all trace of the scent of Vesna. However, the drones' viscera dried on the bottom of his boots was a pungent and offensive odour which was unmistakable. They knew that the man, though they didn't recognize him, was an Imperite — and that he was an oath-breaker. He could only be the host to the new arrival.

Bent over the trunk, it was obvious the man was going through the charred meat. Shivinin realized he was looking for the locator beacons. As Shivinin was about to suggest a stealth approach, he heard Zekra growl, deep in his throat. Before he could stop his partner, Zekra leapt over the rusted-out car they were behind, while pulling his Desert Eagle handgun out of his shoulder holster.

Shivinin didn't hesitate; he followed his partner with his own handgun in his hand. Both Imperite Guards ran towards the car and the gruesome operation going on.

Zekra screamed in rage and began shooting.

The man at the trunk ducked behind the car as the driver of the reddish-brown car reversed, then sped forward behind a stack of old mining equipment. Zekra and Shivinin kept running towards the burned-out sedan.

"OATH-BREAKER! SHOW YOURSELF!"

Shivinin went around the rear of the sedan as Zekra leapt over it in one bound. He landed hard, but didn't fall. Both Guards looked at the empty place behind the car.

Shivinin saw the man stand up from the front of the car holding a metal bar in his hand. Before he could warn Zekra or shoot the man, the attacker swung hard and Zekra went down with a yell of surprise and pain. Shivinin shot at the Imperite, but the man dodged fast and ran behind more refuse. Shivinin saw Zekra getting up, so he ran to the left, to come around the other side of the stack of old equipment the man had disappeared behind. At the moment he rounded the corner, the reddish-brown car was right there, coming right at him. He didn't have time to move.

He tried to jump above it, but it was too fast to get enough height. He landed on the hood of the car then bounced off the windshield. He hit the ground and rolled; his glasses came off and his gun went flying out of this hand. He tried to scramble to his feet as he saw the Imperite running towards him, but he wasn't fast enough: a solid boot hoofed him right in the middle of the gut.

Shivinin screamed with the pain and rolled away from the blow. He was scrambling backwards on his hands and feet, looking at the Imperite coming towards him with another piece of metal held high over his head, ready to beat Shivinin with it. Even his inordinately strong Shovitic physique wouldn't be able to stop such a blow.

He saw his handgun, only three feet away, but before he could get to it the Imperite was on him. His heavy boots, with the stink of drone on them, landed on each side of Shivinin's body. The Humanesh had his lips pulled back in a grimace of rage, his teeth exposed. His eyes were wild and focussed only on his target.

Shivinin could see the Humaresh's chest rising and falling with adrenalin and exertion. From the corner of his eye he saw the white reverse lights on the car which had struck him. He saw it starting to move towards him as the Imperite's arms began the downward swing of the metal bar in his hand. Shivinin's handgun was still out of reach.

The Imperite's head exploded in a red spray of gore.

Shivinin scrambled out of the way of the car as Tommy's corpse fell to the ground, the stump of his neck shooting out arcs of red blood. The metal bar in his hands had missed Shivinin and fell harmlessly to the ground.

Zekra was running towards his partner while trying to fire his handgun, but nothing happened. It was empty.

The car stopped only momentarily; the backup lights went out and the driver took off, the rear wheels causing a spray of gravel that both Guards had to turn away from to protect their face. Even with the speed loader, by the time Zekra had reloaded and Shivinin had picked up his sunglasses and handgun, the car had gone around a corner. Both Guards ran after it, trying to get a clear shot, but the driver zigged and zagged, quickly putting the junkyard-like contents of the old quarry between him and his pursuers. Three bullets had hit the trunk of the car, but none had found their mark on the driver.

Both Guards were breathing heavily. They slowly walked back to the body as they caught their breath. Shivinin watched Zekra unzip his fly and urinate on the corpse of the Imperite. It was something so disrespectful and disgusting that he should have been shocked and offended. But he understood what Zekra was going through. Having found his brother's dead body, then finding the oath-breaker rooting through the Umite's mortal remains, Zekra's actions were understandable.

When he was finished, they each grabbed a foot of the dead Imperite and dragged his corpse to a stack of rusted refuse. They

240

tossed the slack body into the middle of the pile. A suitable resting place for a piece of scum Humanesh involved in the killing of Taffi and Minino. He had to be involved, how else would he have known where the bodies were?

As Zekra scuffed the gravel over the blood stain while reloading his handgun again, Shivinin pulled out his communicator and called the duty frigate.

"Send me the most recent image of Tameht Tekin."

A few moments later Shivinin stared at the image on the communicator's small screen. The picture was a few years old, but it was definitely the man that had stood over him, trying to kill him. He held out the device to his partner. Zekra looked at the image and nodded.

"We need to get moving. I do not think we can wait for Femi and Corvu. Sepherin Tekin may well be trying to flee."

Nodding, Zekra walked back towards the burnt-out sedan as he spoke, "Yes, the little Falwasz *bitch* needs to be taken to face her precious Kalabot. But I cannot leave my brother and Minino here, not like this."

"We will bury him. I will have the frigate send down shovels."

Zekra looked around at the setting, his face clearly showing what he thought of the idea, "Here? You would bury two Imperite Guards — *here?*"

Shivinin nodded, "You are right, friend. Here is not ..."

They both heard the siren in the distance. It was getting louder.

"Come with me," Shivinin said, pulling Zekra's arm. They walked over to the burnt-out sedan and Shivinin thumbed the communicator.

A few minutes later the Ontario Provincial Police cruiser sped into the quarry. The constable drove around the entire site. He didn't find any body, he didn't find any blood stains, and he didn't find any burnt-out car with charred corpses in the trunk. The constable shook his head, wondering why he had taken the crazy old fool so seriously. He looked at his notebook where he had written down the man's license plate. Running the marker on his mobile work station, the constable decided he'd drive to the man's house and see if he was crazy or just an asshole. But before he did that, he realized after checking his watch, he had to go to traffic court and defend three speeding citations. He'd go see the nut-job later.

Mitch rested his head on his hands on the steering wheel as the cop car sped off towards the quarry. The tears finally came. They were tears of relief for getting away with his own life, and tears of grief for the loss of his friend. He had been turned around in the seat, with the car in reverse, looking right at Tommy when his friend's head disappeared in an explosion of gore.

A career military man who had been responsible for many deaths, his actions had always been from the cockpit of a fighter plane. He had never been up close and personal to the act of a violent death before. As he looked in the rear-view mirror at the cop car speeding away, while the tears flowed freely, his body started shivering, then shaking uncontrollably. From the spread of warmth between his thighs, Mitch thought it was odd he had no shame that he had just pissed in his pants.

He finally got the shaking, sobs, and tears under control. He looked down at the passenger seat beside him, at the bullet holes. Whatever kind of guns they had, the bullets had gone through the trunk, the back seat, and through the front seat. He reached over and fingered the three holes in the dash, sure that he would find the slugs in there if he pulled it apart.

Mitch took a deep breath and let it out slowly; he headed home. He did nothing about the wet seat or pants; they were the least of his worries. He needed to get home and get Martha to safety, to get Sepherin to safety. With Tommy gone, and since he was present at his death, Mitch felt responsible for the young woman.

An icy hand gripped his heart. *What if they get there before me? What if they find Martha before they find me?*

He pressed his foot down on the accelerator.

Chapter 40

Martha sipped at her tea. She had been up early with half her housework done when Tommy came banging on their door. He and Mitch had taken off in the car without as much as a 'by-your-leave'. She stood at the kitchen window looking out at the backyard, watching the shadow of the house retreat ever so slowly as the morning sun moved in the sky. She stood there for a long time, just sipping her tea.

Aliens. Really. I can't believe that old fool would take to believing such nonsense. Martha sighed deeply. *There's no getting around it. We're getting older. We're at an age where — I think I need to make an appointment with Dr. Cottle. If Mitch is going daffy on me, we need to get a handle on it soon.*

She heard the car skidding to a halt on the gravel driveway.

"Land sakes," she said to herself as she set down her teacup. A moment later Mitch burst through the front door looking like a wild man.

"Good heavens! Mitch! What happened to you!" She had taken in the look on his face and the wet stain on his crotch, all at the same time.

"Get your jacket and purse, Martha, we have to leave, *right now!*"

"What on Earth are you talking about, Mitch?"

"There were more of them, Martha. I took Tommy to the ..." he hadn't told her about Sepherin killing the aliens. "Martha..." he sighed with exasperation. "Please, Martha, get your coat and purse, we need to leave, *now!*"

She wasn't having any of it. She folded her arms and gave him the look he knew all too well. She started tapping her foot and waiting.

"Martha ... Tommy's dead."

"What?" she was shocked. She unfolded her arms and stepped over to her husband, putting her hands on his shoulders as he started crying again. She pulled her husband of forty years closer to her, hugging his quivering body while he got the tears under control again.

"They killed him," he whispered.

"Who? Who killed him?"

"The aliens, more of them."

Martha shut her eyes and breathed deeply, then pushed back from Mitch.

"I think we need to go see Dr. Cottle."

"No, Martha, no. I'm not crazy. I told you last night, what Sepherin said, and Tommy *confirmed it* when he got home. They ... they're ..."

"But why, Mitch? If they're aliens, why would aliens kill other aliens?"

"Because ... *because!*" he shouted.

"*Because why*?" she shouted back at him. "*Mitch, this is crazy talk! There's no such things as aliens!*"

"Yes, there are," Sepherin's quiet voice came from the back door.

Mitch and Martha both turned to look at her. She opened the screen door and stepped into the kitchen with her travel case.

"Whatever Mitch told you, it's true."

"He said your Uncle Tommy was dead."

Sepherin's eyes welled up with tears, but she bit back the sob. She set down the case and then sat in a chair at their table. "I figured as much, when I saw Mitch come back alone. I knew when they left — I just knew it."

"There were two more, like them, in black," Mitch said to her, still holding his wife's shoulders.

Sepherin stood again, "I have to leave. They'll be here soon. Did they see you?"

Mitch nodded, finally letting go of Martha, "I hit one of them with my car, but he got back up again. The trunk has bullet holes in it," he looked at Martha, "if you still don't believe me." Then after a moment he added, "So does the front seat."

Martha went outside, leaving Sepherin and Mitch alone. They said nothing; they just looked at each other. Martha came back in, grabbed her purse and jacket, and then yelled at them, "Come on! What are you waiting for?"

Sepherin picked up the suitcase and looked at Mitch again, "Go change your pants. We need to leave before the fire trucks get here."

"Fire trucks?" Mitch asked.

"I set a fire in Tommy's basement; it should be going quite strong by now."

"What? Why? In God's name, why did you do that?" Mitch was angry, scared, confused, and filled with grief.

"The house is full of alien DNA, Mitch. I can't risk leaving any questions behind and having Earthers start poking around and finding out too much."

With that, she went out to the car with Martha. They waited only two minutes before Mitch came out in fresh clothes. He got in the car and started the engine, "Where to, Stephy?"

Sepherin shook her head, "I don't know. But we have to go find the black girl first."

"Cassie?" he said, confused, "Why? She ratted you guys out."

"Yes, and her name and information is on the report. If the Guards don't have her information by now, they will shortly. She's in as much danger as I am — as you are."

"But why?" he asked as he pulled out of the driveway.

"If they catch me, they won't kill me right away. They'll take me back to Umitia, and they'll need to take her as a witness to what I did. Then they'll execute me. Then they'll execute her, so she won't be able to tell anyone."

"Can't they just ... erase her memory, or something?"

"Engram modification is still an inexact science. For something like this, it would be too risky. It would be easier just to kill her."

Martha said nothing. She stared straight ahead wondering if perhaps she was the one that needed the appointment with Dr. Cottle.

The fire trucks sped by them after they turned onto the highway into town.

Chapter 41

Femi and Corvu arrived on board just after the extraction of the remains.

The frigate had a full medical suite which was rarely used, as was the medical team. The ship's primary medic and medical technician took half an hour to carefully remove the bodies from the trunk. They took another fifteen minutes to separate the two bodies as best as they could. They promised Zekra the two corpses were not mingled, but everyone who witnessed the procedure knew it was a lie. The damage to the bodies from the fire had been too extensive to be that exacting with the equipment at hand.

The remains were carefully, reverently, placed in two different airtight containers. The Watch Commander of the duty frigate promised Zekra the remains would be returned to Umitia for proper burial. The frigate was due to return to Umitia for a refit at the end of its tour, only a few ten-sleeps from now.

The burned out hulk of the sedan was then TransMat into space. The ship's energy weapon made quick work of vaporising the steel chassis.

After a quick briefing, Zekra and Shivinin got in the backseat of Femi and Corvu's sedan. It was TransMat to the planet, not far outside of Kincardine.

A few minutes later they stopped on the dead end street, watching the firemen go about their duties at a fully involved house fire. Corvu looked down at the map on his communicator, and then looked around at the two in the back seat.

"That is the house of the Imperites."

Zekra spoke quietly, "Smart girl. She leaves no trace."

Shivinin reached into the pocket inside his suit jacket and pulled out a piece of paper. After looking at the copy of the police report he had been reading that morning, he handed it to Femi who was behind the steering wheel.

"Find that address. Perhaps the Earther will know where we can find Sepherin Tekin."

Sepherin Tekin was standing in Cassie's kitchen.

Cassie wiped at the tears in her eyes, "But I don't *want* to leave. I don't want to go anywhere. I sure as hell don't want to go anywhere *with you*."

"Cassie, please," Sepherin stepped towards the young woman.

Cassie stepped back, and then went around the kitchen table, putting it between them.

Sepherin stopped and glared at Cassie.

Cassie's voice was wavering as she spoke, "You come in here and tell me Tommy's dead and that aliens are going to come for me and ..."

"You were on a spaceship last night, Cassie! What's the leap here? Why are you resisting the truth when you know it's the truth! Tommy told you who we are!"

"I don't know what happened last night. I know I hit my head. I know I fainted. I know ..." she burst into tears.

Sepherin tried to step around the table to comfort her, but Cassie shoved the table so that it was between them again.

"Leave, Stephy, or whatever the hell your name is, *just leave*."

Mitch's finger was tapping the steering wheel. He was watching the door beside the Rexall Drug Store that Stephy had gone through. He had tried to speak to Martha, but she just sat there, staring straight ahead, saying nothing.

His finger stopped tapping as he saw the black sedan stop a few doors down from the drug store. He squinted, peering intently at the occupants. He could see they were all in black and all wore sunglasses. The front doors opened and two got out, putting fedoras on top of their heads, keeping the sun off their pale, gaunt faces. They moved slowly up the street, looking at a sheet of paper and looking at the numbers on the buildings.

As they did this, he saw the two in the back seat get out. They were far enough away they didn't notice Mitch right away, but he certainly recognized them from the quarry. He wasn't afraid for himself this time, he was just angry. One of them was the bastard that shot Tommy. But Mitch had more to think about than just himself. His wife was beside him, and the young pregnant girl, *TWO young pregnant girls*, he corrected himself, were in the building the first two stood looking at from the sidewalk.

"Martha," he turned to his wife, "I want you to get out of the car and go to Jenny's place."

She said nothing, she just kept staring out the window.

Sepherin pursed her lips. This little Earther just didn't get it. She didn't understand what they were up against, what she was going to be up against if the Imperite Guards found her. She didn't understand that her life truly was in danger. Sepherin knew the clock was ticking and she didn't have time for this nonsense. She reached out, grabbed the table, and flicked it to the side like it was a dishrag, then advanced on Cassie.

Cassie screamed and tried to step back, but she was standing against the kitchen counter. She squealed and put her hands up as the much taller woman grabbed her shoulders and looked down at her.

"Do you have any idea how grotesque a death you'll have if they find you?"

Cassie wanted to fight, wanted to scream, but with the tall woman standing over her, her body had lost all its strength. She couldn't even speak.

Sepherin leaned down, put her lips next to Cassie's ear, and whispered to her some of the more inventive ways the Shovitic pricks killed Humanesh.

Cassie began crying again in earnest, unbridled fear washing over her. She felt absolutely helpless. She hadn't asked for any of this. She was pregnant, she was alone, Ritchie wouldn't take her calls, and her whole world was standing on end. She was the target of aliens who wanted to capture her and maybe kill her, yet right now she had an alien standing in her kitchen who wanted to save her.

Looking up at Stephy's face, she saw no malice, and no hatred. The woman was scared, like Cassie was. The alien put her hand on her own baby belly, gently caressing herself. Cassie reached up and touched her own belly.

She looked back up at Stephy, 'What's you real name?"

"Sepherin. Sepherin Tekin."

"What was Tommy's real name?"

"Tameht Tekin."

"So, you really are related?"

Sepherin nodded. "He's my father's brother. He's my — *was*, my uncle"

Cassie wiped at her face and took a deep breath. "You aren't going to hurt me, are you?"

Sepherin shook her head, "No, Cassie. I want to save you. Tommy thought highly of you, and I can't in good conscience run away and leave you here to face the Shovitics' wrath."

"I'm scared. I don't know what to do."

"Pack a bag and come with me, we'll get through this together. If we put enough time and distance between us and ..."

The kitchen door opened. Both women looked at the two men standing in the hallway.

As he pulled his gun, Femi growled, "Sepherin Tekin ..."

Sepherin didn't hesitate a tic, she moved as fast as lightning. Before the gun was fully pointed at the two women, she had crossed the short distance across the kitchen, grabbed Femi's wrist, bent his arm behind him and shoved him back towards the door, right into Corvu's arms. She wrenched the big handgun out of his hand and then pushed both Imperite Guards backwards so they fell down the stairs leading to the front door.

Great, another death sentence.

"Martha!" Mitch grabbed her arm. She finally turned to face him. "See those men over there?" He pointed to the two MIB outside, the other two had gone into the building. "Those are the aliens we've been talking about, Martha. One of them, the one at the back, he's the one that killed Tommy. I saw him do it."

He could feel she was starting to tremble under his hand. She looked at him, her mouth opening to say something, but she clamped it shut.

"Martha, please, go now, before they see you. They don't know who I am, but when they see me, if they see you with me, they'll come after you too. For the love of God woman, please get out of the car and go to Jenny's! I'll take the girls someplace safe and then I'll come get you."

Martha looked into his eyes, searching for any sign of deception, any sign of wild-eyed crazy, but she found none. He was her Mitch. He was angry, and he was serious. She had never caught him in a lie in their forty years of marriage, ever. He was the most competent, and rational person she knew. She finally believed him. She finally believed everything he said about Tommy, about Stephy, and about the aliens.

She leaned forward and kissed him on the lips, touching his cheek as she did so. The she turned and got out of the car without saying a word.

Mitch looked up in the rear-view mirror and watched her stride away confidently, not looking back even once. When she turned the corner towards Jenny's place, he started the car and looked across the street. The one he had struck earlier was looking right at him. Mitch glanced to the left and saw Stephy and Cassie running down the short driveway at the side of the building.

Sepherin slammed the door shut and locked it, knowing the lock wouldn't stop them. She could hear one of them yell in pain as they tumbled down the stairs. Stepping into the kitchen, Cassie was still crying, standing against the counter. Sepherin grabbed one of the high back chairs, turned, and wedged it under the door knob on the apartment's main door.

When she turned around, Cassie was standing right behind her.

"What do we do?" she was terrified.

"So now you believe me?"

Cassie just wiped at the tears while nodding her head.

Sepherin looked around quickly. "Is there another way out of here?"

Cassie nodded, took Sepherin by the hand and led her into the bedroom. Sepherin tossed the handgun in the garbage can on her way by it. Cassie led her to the w ndow at the back of the bedroom. There was a sloped roof for a small shed about three feet below.

Sepherin grabbed the window and lifted, then used her foot to kick out the screen. She stepped out onto the roof and turned back to Cassie, "Come on! What are you waiting for?"

Cassie was looking back at the room, "I don't have anything packed, I don't ..." she stopped as she heard something heavy hit the apartment door. She forgot about her stuff.

Sepherin helped her out the window, and then they went down the sloped roof a little faster than they should have. They wound up going off the low end of it without stopping. Luckily it was only four feet to the ground at the shallow end. Both girls landed on their feet and without stopping to look up at the window, they ran down the side of the building.

As they approached the sidewalk, Sepherin saw Mitch's car coming up the street, speeding towards them. He was coming fast, too fast. As she stopped running, she saw a man in black run from the sidewalk and out into the middle of the street, pointing a gun. Mitch accelerated. This time the Imperite Guard jumped out of the way, jumping back towards the sidewalk.

Sepherin was waiting for him.

She wrapped one arm around his neck from behind, and struggled to get control of the arm with the gun. She heard someone on the street scream and then felt a cold bun barrel against the back of her neck. She turned her head to see Zekra standing behind her.

Zekra sneered at the Imperite, "You killed my ..."

The man with the gun at her neck screamed in agony and went down to the ground, hard. Cassie had stepped forward from the driveway, unseen by Zekra, and she swung her foot as hard as she could, nailing him right in the nut-sack.

Ritchie had been a fan of the Saturday morning wrestling shows, and had made Cassie watch too many of them. With Zekra prone, she jumped in the air and came down hard, executing a WWE perfect elbow drop onto the side of Zekra's head. His screams of testicular agony stopped as he went unconscious.

She got up quick and looked at Sepherin, who was still struggling with the other one. He had a gun in his hand as well. Cassie was beyond terrified now. She was so scared that something in her had shut down, she'd stopped feeling anything. She was about to grab the man's gun hand and bite his wrist, but Mitch was out of the car, moving towards the man, swinging a tire iron.

The piece of steel came down on the alien's wrist. It struck hard enough that they all heard the bones break.

Shivinin screamed, and then dropped the gun. Sepherin let go of his neck, grabbed his shoulder, pulled back her other arm, and donkey-punched him in the back of the head. His sunglasses flying off, Shivinin fell to the ground, knocked out cold.

"COME ON!" Mitch yelled, grabbing Cassie by the arm. Cassie was standing there, just looking down at Shivinin's face; her complexion had turned ashen. His glasses had come off and she was looking at the limp eyeworms, unconscious as well, and the mostly empty eye sockets. Mitch pulled her again, but she bent over and threw up, all over Shivinin's shirt.

Sepherin stepped behind her, grabbed her under the arms, and propelled her to the open door of Mitch's car. She shoved Cassie in, got in behind her, and Mitch slammed the door. He looked up and saw the other two MIB running down the short driveway. Mitch jumped in the car, threw it in gear and tromped on the accelerator, letting the car's sudden acceleration close his door for him. He sped to the end of the block, turned left, and then gunned the engine again. Three minutes and six more turns later, he was on the highway headed south.

"Any idea where we're going to go?" he asked Sepherin without looking at her.

Sepherin was still holding onto Cassie. The young black woman had stopped crying, but she was still in an emotional state. When Sepherin had found out Cassie had told the authorities everything, she hated her. But now, seeing how scared and vulnerable she was, yet seeing that she was still able to summon the courage to attack Zekra when he pointed the gun, Sepherin was thankful Cassie had been there. *Perhaps this Earther isn't so bad after all.*

Sepherin looked up at Mitch, "I don't have any — wait, there was — someone was supposed to be coming this weekend. Tommy's Uncle Jay and Aunt Estelle. They live in — Goodrich?"

"Goderich, you mean?"

"Yes, that's it. She's a doctor of backs and he runs a repair shop for electrical things."

Mitch thought for a moment. He knew Jay and Estelle, he had met them several times when they had visited Tommy. It took a couple minutes, but he finally recalled something in one of their late night chin-wags about Londesboro Road.

"Okay, I think I know where they live, or at least the area. It won't be too hard to find them."

An hour later they pulled into Jay's driveway.

Chapter 42

Shivinin opened his eyeworms slowly, raising his arm to shield his vision from the light. He tried to move his other arm, but it was strapped to what he was lying on.

A Shovitic medical technician leaned over him. "Good, you are awake finally. Do you have any pain?"

Taking stock of his body for a moment, Shivinin finally replied, "I feel like I've been kicked in the head." He turned and looked at his arm tied to the bed, "And I cannot feel below the elbow of this arm."

Now adjusted to the light, he used his free arm to push himself up slightly, wincing at the pounding sensation in his head. He looked at his bound arm. The hand, wrist and part of the forearm were encased in a portable molecular modification unit. He lay back down slowly.

"Your wrist was shattered and you have a concussion. There is little I can do for the concussion except give you pain killers, but you know the risks associated with those. Your wrist will be repaired soon. For now, you just need rest. Several days' rest, in fact, to heal the concussion."

"Zekra? He is here?"

"He is still unconscious. He, too, has a concussion, but it appears to be more severe. We are considering engaging our Earther allies to perform a surgery if he does not wake soon."

"It's that serious?"

The medic just nodded, holding his hand towards the far side of Shivinin's bed.

Shivinin slowly turned his head, wincing as he did so, and saw his partner lying on another bed, hooked up to monitoring equipment. A holographic representation of Zekra's brain floated in the air above his head. Shivinin could see where the impact to the brain had caused the slight amount of damage which was keeping Zekra unconscious. Shivinin pursed his lips and closed his eyeworms.

"I will leave you to rest." The medic turned away from the bed.

"Wait, I need access to the ERB. I must report to the palace."

The medic stood by the doorway to the small room. "If you want to prepare a brief report, I can have it transmitted for you."

Zekra lifted his head and looked at the medic. "I need to report directly to the Manager."

The medic's gaunt and pale features seemed gaunter, and paler. "I will summon the Commander."

A few minutes later the duty frigate's Watch Commander came into the room. "I have been told you need to speak with Kalabot? Is this true?"

Shivinin nodded, "Yes. An Imperite killed two Guards, and attacked two more."

"Four more," the Watch Commander said, "she also attacked Femi and Corvu."

"They are here as well?"

"They are on board, but their injuries were inconsequential."

Shivinin gritted his teeth, "I would take great pleasure in executing the Falwasz oath-breaker, but she is of special interest to the Manager. Why she is, I know not. I need to report to him what has happened to find out how to proceed."

"The medical technician has said you need a great deal of rest, perhaps two full ten-sleeps, to recover from your injury. You partner will need at least that much time, and probably more."

They both turned their heads at the sound of the deep sigh. Zekra was moving on the bed, reaching up to touch his head.

"Shivinin?"

"Yes, Zekra, I am here. How do you feel?"

They watched him, waiting for his response. His eyeworms had opened, but they were lethargically undulating, not probing the air as they normally would. Finally Zekra spoke.

"I can't see."

Under the advice of the medical technician, the Watch Commander made Shivinin wait one full revolution of the planet beneath the ship before allowing him to leave his bed. When he did, Shivinin went straight to the Commander's duty office to use the ERB.

He dialed the three-symbol code on the ERB and held the handset to his ear. The internal mechanisms, using a power source that would run a whole city for a year, established an Einstein-Rosen bridge which was only six micrometers wide at the event horizon. The three-digit code indicated the unique magnetic wave signature was incorporated into the shape of the energy burst which created the tiny wormhole, and thus defined where the other end of it would appear. In this case, the three-symbol code of *Ott-Ehk-Fee* caused the other end to appear in the Manager's own ERB set.

Shivinin gave him a full report, including a summary of what was taken from the police report. As was expected, Kalabot ordered that the Imperite be returned to Umitia and that the witness to the murders be brought with her. What was unexpected was his order for Femi and Corvu to take the lead. He was reassigning Zekra and Shivinin to a more relaxing and less stressful posting.

Shivinin protested on the grounds he had seen the woman himself and he should be part of the search, which was going to take quite some effort. Kalabot informed him the decision was final. Shivinin returned to the infirmary to let Zekra know.

When Shivinin entered the room, Zekra turned his head. "Who's there?"

"Your partner, Zekra. I've spoken with Kalabot."

"And?"

"As expected, he ordered the Imperite and the witness brought to Umitia."

"This will not cause a problem, taking the Earther?"

"No, he has already informed General Rosewood. She is unhappy about this, but she will not protest due to the circumstances."

"I regret that I cannot join the search."

"You won't be alone. Femi and Corvu are to be the lead on this search. He has ordered us both to a new assignment."

Zekra pushed himself up to a sitting position, and then swung his legs over the edge of the bed. He held out one arm, "Help me stand, please. I would like to walk."

Shivinin took his arm and helped him stand. Still unable to see, Zekra held his partner's arm and shuffled alongside him, walking up and down the corridor outside the room.

"So what is our new posting to be? Please don't let it be the dessert."

Shivinin sighed, "Unfortunately, it is. We are going to Lake Walker as soon as you have regained your vision."

"That's not much of an incentive. Did you protest?" Zekra asked.

"Yes, I did. However, I was informed that the decision had been made."

Zekra paused his shuffling walk and turned his head towards his partner, though he still couldn't see him, "Your father is not my favourite person right now."

Chapter 43

Kalabot hung up the ERB handset and placed his hands flat on the table. He stared at the backs of his fingers for several minutes, breathing deeply and slowly to get his thoughts and emotions under control. Deciding she had to die was one thing, knowing she was going to die was something altogether different. To make it worse, the law demanded, *a law which he had written*, that the oath-breakers be brought back to Umitia for public execution.

Killing an Imperite Guard was simply unacceptable behaviour for anyone, except him, of course. He knew this must be the rule and that the execution must happen. At this moment, however, he found his nose was filled with the memory of the scent of the new born baby girl he had held only once, so many seasons ago.

Kalabot put on his hat and dark glasses, and then went outside. He stood on the steps of the Palace for a few minutes, letting the sun warm him. Where most Shovitics couldn't stand the heat of the sun, Kalabot secretly enjoyed the warmth it gave his body, which was often chilled from the inside with the secrets and sins that were his alone.

Casting his gaze around the grounds, he saw the head gardener working in one of the far garden beds near the lake. Kalabot moved in that direction, staying close to the more fragrant garden beds as he did so. He inhaled deeply, enjoying the scents and colours, trying to drown out the memory of the smell of the infant.

"Old friend," Kalabot startled the gardener, "what is the most pungent aroma in your care?"

"You're in luck," Cobus replied, "I have a rare specimen which smells like a rotting corpse. It only blooms for about four ten-sleeps per season. It's almost near the end of its cycle; it only has a few days left."

"Show me."

The two men proceeded along the edge of the lake in silence, heading to the larger of the greenhouses on the Palace grounds. When they entered the special room at the back of the greenhouse, the smell was overpowering. Kalabot looked at the plant with appreciation for its unique beauty. It stood taller than he. It was deep green on the outside of the massive petals, and deep burgundy on the inside. A massive dull-yellow stalk stood proud from the centre, looking almost like a loaf of homemade bread. The smell was almost exactly like a rotting corpse. Kalabot made to move forward, but Cobus put out his hand and stopped him, then pointed at the ground. There were dozens of dung beetles moving to and from the plant; some were just lazily moving in circles.

Kalabot just stared at the plant, his hands hanging loosely at his side. He inhaled deeply many times, his powerful sense of smell overwhelmed and repulsed by the odour. Finally smelling nothing but the hideous aroma of the plant which attracted pollinators with the smell of rotting meat, he turned and left the room. No sooner did he step outdoors, the smell of the infant returned. He stopped moving and just stood there, looking off into the distance.

The door opened and closed again behind him. Kalabot sensed the gardener standing nearby.

Cobus could see that Kalabot was troubled by something. It wasn't in the expression of his face, or his body language. It was something deeper: a feeling, a sensation, an empathic response. He took a few steps closer to the Manager and asked, "Would you care to tour the garden beds with me?"

Like all Umitians, Cobus spoke a dialect of English which was not different enough to be noticed as alien by Earthers. However, like all Umitians, he spoke with an accent that to Earther ears sounded like a combination of Afrikaans and Cajun. Unlike the Shovitics, there were no sibilants in his speech, no hissing "sh" sounds on the letter 's'.

Kalabot turned to look at him, and nodded once. Cobus led the way. As they moved along the many garden beds, the head gardener spoke at length about the new acquisitions, some cuttings that had been brought from a distant world. He talked about a problem they were having with the automatic watering system controls. He talked about his youngest granddaughter's latest antics in the school she attended.

Eventually they came to a grove of Kayam trees, imported long ago from the planet Sapro. The grove was a place where Cobus knew the Manager sometimes went to sit when things were heavy on his mind. The gardener sat down on a marble bench and indicated the space beside him. After a moment, Kalabot sat down, placing his hands flat on his thighs, staring straight ahead.

The late afternoon sun was reflecting off the surface of the calm lake. Kalabot stared at the brilliant mirrored light without really noticing it. The buzzing of small insects was lost to his ears. The tingling scent of the succulent plant bed near the Kayam grove was lost in the remembered scent of newborn baby.

Kalabot saw and heard none of this because his mind was many other places. Images of the Govin, the Dellasigian, and the Pikayan came to mind. He had personally been responsible for the entire eradication of these three races of Humanesh, the Humanesh of the planet Pikaya being the most recent. He had lost count of the number of kings, presidents, supreme dictators, ministers, first-men, khans, and barbarian leaders whom had died under his own hand. He had over 5,000 two-man teams of Imperite Guards, on seventy-two of the eighty-nine Humanesh worlds in the three known inhabited galaxies. Nine of those worlds had approached him to hire his teams to assist with control of their own populations in matters pertaining to government secrets. Kalabot was routinely exposed to intelligence, information on materials, progress of scientific and agricultural developments, as well as the latest in spiritual and esoteric teachings. He gathered all of these things, as well as individual secrets about the powerful players on all these worlds. He kept all of that information readily available in his eidetic memory.

Knowledge may be power, but for Kalabot, information was currency. It was how he was paid to assign the guards to the many worlds. He bartered secrets, exchanged facts, and revealed truths in ways and manners that brought benefit to himself, and to Umitia. *Beautiful Umitia*, he thought as he took a deep breath, *you are the jewel of a thousand systems and a dozen, dozen races.* It was all for Umitia, it was all for the Umites. Everything he did was for them. But Kalabot knew he was one of the few who held the beliefs of the old order from a time beyond people's memories. He was one of the few who knew that success meant sacrifice, and that planetary success came from rule by thumb, not by committee.

He turned to look at Cobus, the closest thing he had to a friend. The head gardener, from the Silthit clan, had also professed a belief in the old ways on a few occasions. He had also backed up his words by actions on not one, but two occasions. He had revealed information that led to the arrest, and eventual execution, of those who were plotting against the Shovitic rule, and Kalabot in particular.

Both men knew that the old order, established 5,000 seasons ago, had ruled Umitia with an iron fist. The strength of leadership and law in the old order had brought Umitia prosperity and growth. It was a society emerging from the chaos that had reigned after the war which had almost destroyed the Umite race. Had they not finally beaten back the Eben warships when they did, the entire Umite presence would have been lost from the galaxy. Since that time, the lawless, mercenary, and homicidal Umite race had turned itself around and become a peaceful race on a world which invited contemplation and expressions of beauty. The six clans had, that is, but not the Shovitics. The Shovitic clan retained the warrior mentality and armaments, but they moved forward with a real mission in life, instead of a mission of conquest for gain.

After the war, the Umite race became the galaxy's policemen, the galaxy's peacekeepers, the galaxy's watchmen. In more recent history, their actions had raised the ire of the Voiya Masters, the tantaloids in charge of the Eridani Dominion. The Eridani were the race that had attacked Umitia nearly seven hundred seasons ago. It was a brief war, but the Imperite Guards' fleet had been assisting the Eben with a matter in the Govi system and not been able to fold back as quickly as they wanted to. The result was another 10% of the Umite population lost to the weapons and Trigla warriors from the Eridani Dominion. Eventually, however, the clansmen themselves made the final push of resistance that drove the Eridani from the planet. Of course, the late arrival of a significant portion of the Imperite Guards' fleet helped.

As the warrior cast, the Shovitic clan carried the burden of revenge against the Voiya, but as they soon found out, they could not do it by might alone. The Eridan were widespread and secretive, making it difficult to mount a decisive campaign against them. Destroying their homeworld wasn't an option for the Shovitic warriors, because the Eridani planet was the ancestral home of the Trigla, who were, effectively, Voiya slaves.

Over 95% of the Umite race had been lost to the war centuries ago with the Eben, who had now become something more akin to tolerated neighbours and occasional partners, instead of enemies. The Shovitics, the Manager in particular, knew the might and power of the Imperite Guards' fleet was still no match for the firepower and sheer tonnage of warships that the Eben could bring to bear, should they choose to.

However, as genocidal as the old war had been, it was the relatively recent Voiya attack which stung more in the hearts of the Umites. The Imperite Guards finally turned to the clansmen for assistance in the vengeance.

The Umite manager of that time was named Tellarem. He had spoken widely and convincingly to the clans. Through his forceful eloquence, a convincing plan, and a planet-wide desire for vengeance, the Falwasz clan had committed it's progeny to the completion of what Tellarem had dubbed, the 'Imperative.' It was an honour the entire Falwasz clan was only too eager to accept. The one thing the clan of farmers and land owners had in abundance, was people. They were the largest of the clans. It was the abundance of walking cannon fodder that made the plan viable.

With moderate success over the following one hundred seasons, the Imperative simply became their way, and continues to this day, almost six hundred seasons later.

As all societies seem to have a dark period in their history, the Umites seem to have had more than their share. Aside from the disastrous and almost genocidal war with the Eben, and the brief war with the Voiya: there was also the clan's rebellion. Around 2,300 seasons ago, the six clans rebelled against the Shovitic rulers.

The iron fisted rule after the war with the Eben had become a machine of oppression. It resulted in moves of desperation by those under that mailed glove of governance and legislation. In a bloody revolt which lasted almost a ten-sleep, Umitia came to peace again with a new manager in charge. He was a Shovitic who understood the power of honey's attraction over that of vinegar. While there were growing pains during his period of rule, the Umite society which emerged again was one of true peace, respect, and was beneficial to all of its citizenry.

For the 2,300 seasons since then, the Shovitic race had quietly tolerated the touchy-feely nonsense. They simply didn't have a desire to engage in another blood bath amongst the clans who had been almost wiped out by the war with the Eben.

It was this iron fisted rule which Kalabot had been slowly working to bring Umitia back to during his lengthy tenure. It was the reason he was so hated by the six clans.

Kalabot was the fifty-third manager since Tellarem, the twenty-seventh since the establishment of the new order. He had risen to the post one hundred and three seasons ago, when he was in his forty-second season. He had outlasted and outlived every other manger since the old order had fallen at the end of the rebellion. Kalabot's only distraction since his appointment had been Sheata, his wife. She had been a defective birth, and therefore had not been able to pursue the normal Shovitic vocations in military roles or in commerce. She had come out of the womb with misshapen features, poor eyesight, one leg shorter than the other, and an inability to speak.

When she was thirty seasons of age, she met Kalabot during his inspection of a new Shovitic housing facility which she had decorated with her artwork. He had taken pity on her, and then he had taken an interest in her. Her lack of ability to speak was made up for by her ability to produce the most stunning works of visual art, even more stunning, it was said, than those produced by the Silthit clan. Learning to speak the complicated sign language, Kalabot had learned how to talk to her and for the first time in his life, Kalabot had felt love.

Already in his sixtieth year as manager of Umitia, they were married and had two children, both perfectly formed and healthy Shovitic children: Morik and Shivinin. A few short years later, Sheata died in an accident. The scaffolding she was working on to create a large mural, several stories high, had collapsed, crushing her under the metal structure when it toppled over.

Kalabot had shut down completely. Through Sheata's love and patience, he had started to come out of his natural shell and open up, just a little bit, to those around him. When she died, he turned off all of his feelings, shipped his children off to be raised by strangers, and focussed every ounce of his lifeblood into the work of the Imperite Guards.

His one and only confidant, his one and only friend, had been taken from him. He grieved not only the loss of her presence in his

271

life; he also grieved for the loss of the trusted advisor and confidant she had become.

As he sat on the marble bench, in the shade of the Kayam trees, listening to the gardener prattle on about inconsequential matters, he thought that maybe it was time for a change. Maybe, with his present difficulties, he needed to be able to share the burden, and thus halve the load that bore down upon him.

He looked at Cobus, remembering how the retired Silthit gardener had saved their world from turmoil, and perhaps saved the Manager's own life by revealing the information about the radicals. The gardener was paid a lowly stipend which supplemented his meagre retirement income, yet he never complained, and never professed problems with his finances as other Silthit were prone to do. In fact, the only thing he had ever asked for was creative control over the gardens that he cared for so lovingly, and the ability to choose his own staff from amongst all the clans. He truly was a gifted Silthit. His ability to create lavish, flourishing, and beautiful gardens sometimes reminded Kalabot of his own wife's abilities with a brush and paints.

Cobus finally ran out of things to distract the Manager with and settled into quiet contemplation of the beauty around them. He had observed Kalabot's eyesworms gyrating and wrestling with each other behind the darkened glasses, dancing feverishly around the Shovitic's eye sockets. The only time Cobus had ever seen the Manager this agitated was on the anniversary of his wife's death.

While Cobus had spoken of inconsequential distractions, Kalabot had said nothing; but to Cobus, the Manager had the look of a man who needed to speak. Taking a deep breath, wondering if years of planning, preparation, and sacrifice were about to pay off, he finally spoke directly to the Shovitic's apparent turmoil.

"You seem troubled, old friend."

Chapter 44

The black sedan pulled into the gravel driveway. The two men in black suits and black fedoras, with perfectly trimmed crew-cut hair, very square jaws, and wearing Ray-Ban sunglasses got out of the car. They both glanced briefly at the burned out shell of the house next door, then got on with their business.

The man who opened the door must have been approaching seventy, yet he still commanded a strong and robust presence.

"Are you Mitch?" Femi asked.

"Who's asking?"

Femi looked confused, "Why, I am."

Mitch grinned at the look on the alien's face, "I might be, I might not be — dumbass. It depends on who you are and what you want?"

Femi looked around to see if there were any neighbours watching. Corvu was standing rigid, with his hands hanging at his sides, staring at the Earther.

Looking back at Mitch, pulling down his dark glasses, taking note of the fact that Mitch did not react to the sight of what passed for his eyes. Femi said in his sibilant way, "Perhaps we could come inside, to discuss the matter of my associate whom you struck with your car?"

Mitch closed the door slightly, "I think you should fuck off, buddy."

"Mitch?" Martha called from behind him, "Who is it? What to do they want?"

"They're looking for a wild goose, and they're just leaving."

Femi smiled. He lashed out with both hands, planting one on the door and one in the middle of Mitch's chest, pushing him back into the room. Femi and Corvu both rushed forward through the door, slamming it behind them.

Mitch flew backwards, landing four feet from where he had been standing. He was wincing and clutching his chest. It only took a couple of breaths to realize he had a few broken ribs from the impact of the MIB's hands.

Femi had intended to grab the man and lift him to his feet, but much to his surprise he found Mitch's wife wasn't cowering or screaming. She was standing in the door to the kitchen holding a shotgun in her hands, pointing it at them, the barrel shaking with her fear.

"Leave, right now, leave my house," she said, her voice close to cracking. She had seen enough to know that something wasn't right in Kincardine, but she still wasn't a hundred percent convinced it was aliens. The two men, forcing their way into her home and attacking her husband was another matter altogether, aliens or not. Since Mitch had returned from delivering Stephy and the black girl to wherever he had taken them, he had kept his hunting shotgun loaded and on the top of the hutch in the kitchen so it could be reached easily and quickly. It had made her nervous having it there, but now she was glad for it. When she had heard the venom in Mitch's voice while confronting the men at the door, she had taken the gun down to be ready to pass it to him. When he went flying backwards from the assault, she only needed to raise it to point it at the men who came in the house.

"It would not be in your interest to pursue such a course of action," Corvu spoke in his odd way.

"Shoot them," Mitch said hoarsely from the floor.

Femi and Corvu exchanged a few words telepathically. With a nod, Femi rushed forward as Corvu reached inside his jacket. Martha screamed, closed her eyes and pulled the trigger.

Nothing happened.

The man dressed in black was on her in an instant. He pulled the gun from her hands and punched her in the face. The sixty-eight-year-old woman fell backwards with a scream, landing on the kitchen floor, clutching her nose.

Corvu pulled his Desert Eagle out of his shoulder holster and held it on Mitch.

"NO!" Mitch yelled. The old man turned and pushed himself up from the floor and reached towards his wife, despite the pain in his side and chest. He was reaching for Femi and the shotgun, but Corvu stepped forward and kicked him in his already broken ribs. It was preferable to shooting him before they got the information they came for.

Mitch yelled and collapsed with the agony of the strike. He felt like something had been driven through him. His breath came in gasping rasps, each one shooting fire into his body. Within a few moments, he was having a hard time getting a breath, he could feel the sweat on his forehead, and his breathing had an odd crackling sound on top of the raspy sound. He could tell one of the ribs had punctured a lung, and from the amount of pain he was in, he knew the other lung had probably collapsed. Mitch looked up at Martha. She was sitting up on the floor of the kitchen, her hands to her face, blood streaming down her chin.

"Leave us alone, we don't have her."

Femi squatted down beside Mitch. After looking deeply into his eyes, he pulled out a small box from his pocket. The device had coloured lights along one edge when he activated it.

"Lay back down," Femi said, gently pushing against Mitch's shoulder.

Mitch was in no position to do anything about it, so he complied. Femi placed the device on Mitch's chest and he activated it. Mitch could see the lights moving faster and faster on the box. The faster they moved, the easier his breathing got. Finally, the pain was gone and he could breathe without the odd noises, though he couldn't breathe deeply.

"Am I healed?" he asked, unsure of why they would do that.

"No, but your nervous system has been sedated. It will hold for a few hours."

"What about her?" Mitch tossed his head towards his wife.

Femi turned off the device and put it back in his pocket. "I am not so generous to the one who held a weapon on me."

"Please," Mitch finally said, "she is innocent in this. She had nothing to do with it. She was just protecting me."

Still squatting beside him, Femi looked at Mitch and asked, "Where is the Imperite?"

Mitch said nothing; he just looked at his wife, then back at Femi. "Make her better; then we'll talk."

They both heard Corvu sigh deeply, then curse in an old Shovitic dialect, though Mitch didn't know what he said. Corvu stepped over Mitch and into the kitchen. He grabbed Martha by the hair, and yanked her head back.

She screamed in surprise and pain.

Corvu put the large calibre handgun against the side of head. "Earthman, I saw you attack Shivinin. I saw the Imperite get in your car. Tell me where she is, or I will end your mate's suffering, permanently."

"No, please, no!"

"TELL THEM! TELL THEM MITCH! JUST TELL THEM!" Martha screamed.

Femi grabbed Mitch's shirt collar and pulled him closer. "He will not hesitate to end your mate's life, Earthman. *Now tell me, where is the Imperite?"*

Martha screamed again as Corvu pulled harder on her hair, her hands were slapping at his arm; her legs were kicking uselessly on the linoleum. She was crying hysterically, *"Mitch, tell them, please tell them, please make it stop, make him stop hurting me!"*

"FINE! I'LL TELL YOU! LET HER GO AND I'LL TELL YOU, YOU BASTARD!"

He told them. Femi and Corvu looked at each other and nodded, they knew who Jay was and where he lived.

Corvu shot Martha through the heart. Then he shot Mitch in the head.

After wiping off the blood spatter, Femi went down into the basement. Crouching by the furnace, he cut the yellow natural gas line, and then went back upstairs, shutting the door to the basement behind him. Corvu had already lit a candle he saw on the living room coffee table.

The two Imperite Guards drove towards the highway, and turned south. Less than five minutes later, just leaving the township of Kincardine, they heard the explosion in the distance.

Chapter 45

Cassie had stopped crying by the time Mitch got her and Sepherin to Jay's place. They were on their way again within five minutes, both Jay and Estelle taking the two young women to Toronto. They figured the easiest way to hide was to do so in plain sight, in a city of millions. They were less likely to stand out in a place where they could blend in. A tall pregnant white woman with a short pregnant black woman: who would notice them?

Jay and Estelle kept a stash of cash around the house, just in case, and they gave four thousand dollars to Sepherin and Cassie. A half hour into the four-hour trip, Cassie closed her eyes and finally slept, more from emotional exhaustion than physical fatigue. Sepherin didn't say much to her shepherds, this was the first and only time she would meet them.

The Earth-born Imperite and his wife dropped them off at one of the less seedy motels on Kingston Road, in Scarborough. They told them to call if they needed help, but they both knew Sepherin never would. They also knew she would not let her young friend call any of her family either. Sepherin and Cassie had been marked by the Imperite Guards. They had become two of the most wanted people in, literally, the galaxy.

The girls got a motel room, and then Cassie ordered pizza, using a fake name and paying in cash. They talked quietly about what their next move was going to be. Cassie knew what it needed to be, though she dreaded it. Sepherin spent ninety minutes telling her about Umitia, the Imperite Guards, the Eridani Dominion, the Umite Imperative, and how the Imperites achieved that goal.

The room had two double beds, one for each. They drew the blinds and went to bed early, both of them finally admitting they were exhausted. Sleep didn't come easily for Sepherin, though. As soon as she lay down, she started thinking about her Uncle Tommy. They had only a few days together, but he had become important to her. Her attachment to him was far deeper than she had suspected. As she tried to shut out the thoughts, and the feelings, she felt the warm trickle of tears pooling on the side of her nose. Then much to her own surprise, she sobbed.

As the tears started to come in earnest, she felt Cassie slip under the blanket next to her. Pressing her body against Sepherin, Cassie reached around and pulled the woman close to her. The tiny woman held her close, saying nothing. She was just there for her.

The comfort Cassie brought with her embrace, gave Sepherin the freedom to finally grieve. She cried, as quietly as she could, yet without shame. After some time, Sepherin finally drifted off to a disturbed sleep, waking often, leaving Cassie with her eyes wide open and her own fears painting macabre images in her mind.

The next morning they partook of the continental breakfast in the motel lobby: small packs of cereal and day-old muffins, with watered-down juice, skim milk, and weak coffee. Following the directions of the desk clerk, they took the city bus up to Lawrence Avenue and then transferred to another bus for an hour long ride to Varna Drive. They waited 20 minutes for one more bus which would eventually drop them at Leila Lane in Lawrence Heights.

They were greeted by several police scout cars, a dozen officers, and a covered body lying on the ground. The yellow police tape kept everyone back as a man in a uniform was taking pictures. Sepherin was surprised. Such a public murder would never have happened on Umitia. The occasional murder that did take place was something which was always made to look like an accident, so as not to draw the attention of the Imperite Guards. Justice on Umitia was swift, and severe. She was also not used to seeing men in uniforms working to *protect* the public, as the relationship with the guards back home was very different.

Hurrying to get away from the media's cameras which were still recording, Cassie quickly led Sepherin down the street and around the corner. Luckily for them, they dodged the cameras and thus avoided the notice of the facial recognition algorithms working overtime at the NSA, thanks to General Rosewood, the Imperite Guards' official contact in the U.S. Air Force.

The two women walked along the sound barrier that lined the highway beside Leila Lane. It only took two minutes to get to the last of three low rise apartment buildings. Ritchie's grandmother lived in a second floor, two-bedroom government housing apartment which looked out over Flemington Park and its small ball diamond.

The girls late night conversation had included plans to get Ritchie to take them in and help them hide, at least until Sepherin's baby was born. Then she'd be on her own. Cassie, however, had still not spoken to Ritchie. He'd left a message on her phone to forward his mail to his grandmother's place. If he wasn't here, at least it would be a start to finding him. She knew there was a hard conversation coming, but the women didn't see any other option. As well, Cassie knew she had to tell Ritchie about the baby. He was the father; it was the right thing to do.

A creepy-looking old guy held the door for the pair of them, leering at them and sucking his teeth as they squeezed by him. Both women ignored the feeling of being undressed by his old man's eyes. They went up the cement stairs to the second floor and found the apartment.

Cassie was freaking out inside. She was afraid that Ritchie was going to reject her and the baby; she was even more terrified he'd want her back and want her to stay in Toronto. She wanted, more than anything, to go home. She wanted to walk in her parent's front door, wrap her arms around her mother and father, and never let go of them. She wanted to not be pregnant. She wanted to not be chased by aliens. She wanted to not have seen the things she had seen in the last three days. She wanted to not have impending death hanging over her head. She wanted them to make it all better, because that's what parents are supposed to do, even if their kids are gown up: they're supposed to make everything better.

As they stood in front of the apartment door, Cassie took a deep breath and let it out slowly. She raised her hand to knock, but hesitated. She felt Sepherin take hold of her other hand and give it a slight squeeze. Cassie had stopped hating Sepherin by the time they arrived in the city. She had stopped being afraid of her. The alien had risked everything to come and save her. She doubted they'd ever be BFFs, but at least they were complicit in their pursuit of safety from, in her own words, "the Shovi-freaks, or whatever the hell they're called."

With another deep breath, Cassie knocked lightly on the door. Her head soon started pouncing and her chest tightened. She realized she had been holding her breath waiting for the door to open. Her shoulders slumped as she let out her breath. Both women tilted their heads as they heard a shuffling sound inside.

An old lady's voice could be heard on the other side of the door, "Who is it?"

"Nana Kelvin, its Cassie, from Kincardine. Is Ritchie home?"

"Who?"

"Ritchie, your grandson."

"Yes, I know he's my grandson. Who did you say you were?"

Cassie smiled. Doris Kelvin was hard of hearing, but she knew perfectly well who Cassie was. She was stalling.

Cassie raised her voice, "Nana Kelvin, I'm here to see your grandson. He got me pregnant and we need to ..."

There was the sound of three locks clicking and the door practically flew open. The wizened little old black woman, with her gray hair pulled back in a bun, was wearing a faded floral dress about twenty years old. She stood looking at Cassie over her glasses, her mouth open.

With a weak smile, Cassie shrugged her shoulders and said, for want of something better to say, "Surprise!"

Finally the woman was able to speak. "Pregnant? You're pregnant?" she asked, in a hushed voice. She finally looked at Sepherin. "Oh good heavens, don't tell me he knocked you up too?"

The girls both chuckled, more from relief than anything. "No," Cassie said, "just me. I'm sorry to tell you this way ..."

The little old woman seemed to not hear her. She turned around and shuffled into the apartment, leaving the girls to come in if they chose to. Both Sepherin and Cassie jumped in surprise as the little old lady roared like a lion, "RITCHIE! *RITCHIE!* GET YOUR DUMB BLACK ASS OUT HERE YOU SON-OF-A-BITCH!"

Ritchie popped his head out of a doorway in the apartment's long hall. "Gran, what the heck's ..." he looked up and saw Cassie and Sepherin standing inside the apartment door. Then his grandmother was on him. She reached up and grabbed a fold of skin on his neck with one hand and started slapping him in the head with the other. He tried to block the blows, but it was his gran, he was powerless to do anything that might hurt her.

"STUPID! STUPID! STUPID! HOW MANY TIMES HAVE I TOLD YOU TO BAG THAT THING SO YOU WOULDN'T DO THIS? AND WHY THE DICKENS DIDN'T YOU TELL ME I'M GOING TO BE A GREAT-GRANDMOTHER? WHY DIDN'T YOU ..."

Richie finally broke free form her, "*Whoa! Whoa! Whoa! Gran! What the hell are you ...*"

She renewed the slapping, "DON'T YOU *DARE* SWEAR AT ME YOUNG MAN! DON'T YOU *DARE* USE THAT THUG TONGUE IN YOUR HEAD TO DISRESPECT YOUR GRANNIE, BOY!"

"*Gran! Wait!*" he finally backed away from her, "What are you talking about? Great-grandmother?" Then it finally dawned on him. He reached out and wrapped his arms around his grannie and held her close so she would stop hitting him. He looked up at Cassie. "You're *pregnant?*"

Cassie had come into the apartment hallway; Sepherin followed her and closed the door behind them. Cassie's face was wet with tears. Her breath was fast and shallow. She nodded her head. The tears started flowing faster.

"Who's is it? That old bastard's?"

"Ritchie!" Cassie cried out with shock, *"How can you say that?"*

"I *saw* you with him, Cassie. I know you were with him."

"You saw nothing of the sort!' She looked from Ritchie to his grandmother and back to Ritchie again. She stepped closer to him, but he held up his stand to stop her.

"Yeah, I know what's going on. You're on your own now, paying for everything yourself, and you can't afford it. You couldn't get that apartment till I was with you, and now you need money. So you're going to hit up the guy you think's a soft touch. *Well screw you, bitch!"*

"Ritchie!" his grannie scolded, pulling back from him. At least she didn't hit him this time.

Cassie was crying harder. She was more terrified that his grandmother was going to think she was a slut than she was upset about his rejection. "You know perfectly well that's not true, you know Tommy and I are — were — just co-workers, just friends. There was nothing between us, Ritchie, you're just *so damn jealous all the time!"*

"Mmm-hmmm," his gran said, glaring at him. "Green streak a mile wide in this one."

"Jealous?" He asked. *"Jealous?* I see you kissing him and hugging him and then you come home and tell me to pack my shit and leave, and you're telling me I'm just *jealous?"* He started advancing again, his hand stuck out and his finger pointing at Cassie, "Get your ass out of here right now, and take your …"

Sepherin moved so fast she was just a blur. She stood between Cassie and Ritchie. He stopped short, his face growing dark, baring his teeth.

"*Please* tell me that you want to do this again," she said in a low, menacing voice, looking down at him. She was smiling. It wasn't a pleasant smile.

The muscles in his jaw were working; his eyes were moving back and forth, looking in each of her eyes, trying to judge his chances.

"Ritchie," Cassie said quietly from behind Sepherin. "We're in trouble. There are some — someone's chasing us. We need ..."

"The fuck should I care? Why don't you get your ol' man to help you out? Why don't you go shack up with him?"

"Because he's dead."

Everyone was silent for a moment. Ritchie looked back and forth between Sepherin and Cassie, trying to figure out if she was telling the truth or playing a game.

Finally, Mrs. Kelvin spoke, "Dear? Who's dead?"

"Her boyfriend," Ritchie muttered. He opened his mouth to say something else, but Sepherin took a small step forward, her grin had disappeared.

"Tommy, my *friend*. He's the one your dipshit grandson thinks I was screwing, *but I wasn't!*"

Ritchie snorted and looked over his shoulder at his gran, "You gonna let her talk to you baby boy that way, Gran?"

The old women folder her arms and looked over her glasses at him, "Handsome *is* as handsome *does*."

He turned back to face Cassie, "I don't give a flying fuck what your problem is."

"Ritchie, they want to kills us — kill her — and kill me, and that means kill your baby."

Ritchie folded his arms, "I don't believe you. I don't believe it's mine either. You're just here for money. I'm not letting you ride my coattails anymore."

"Coattails?" his gran said incredulously, then shook her head. "Mayhap if you had a job."

"Gran ..."

The old woman went to brush past as she said, "You girls come on in and sit down a spell. We'll figure out ..."

"No!" Ritchie gently grabbed his grandmother by the shoulder and stopped her. "No, they aren't coming in here."

"This is my house, boy, and I'll invite in whoever ..."

"The whore that ruined my life? You want to bring that ..."

Cassie started crying again.

Sepherin grabbed Ritchie by the front of his shirt, pulling him so close his head had to tilt upwards and their noses were almost touching.

"Enough of that!" Mrs. Kelvin reached up and put her hands between her grandson and the giant white woman. He'd told her about what had happened the night he confronted Tommy, trying to get some sympathy. Looking at the woman standing there holding his shirt, Mrs. Kelvin had not doubt in her mind she could open another can of whoop-ass on her grandson and serve it cold.

Sepherin looked down and saw nothing but kindness and concern in the old woman's face. She locked back at Ritchie, then let go of him and stepped back. "Come on, Cassie. We've said all we can say here."

"Yeah," Ritchie chimed in looking at Cassie. "Take your pit bull here and get the fuck out of here, *baby-momma*."

"Ritchie! Language! Please, stop!" his gran pleaded.

The two young women turned without saying anything else and left the apartment. Walking down the hall, Cassie even stopped crying long enough to giggle at the sound of the hell Ritchie was catching.

Standing out front of the building, Cassie looked up at the blue sky and let the warmth of the sun start to soak into her, to relax her, to calm her. With some distance from Ritchie and his spiteful words, she wasn't sure if she was upset or relieved that he wasn't going to help them. More than being worried about the immediate future, she was pissed at what he'd said, and how he'd said it.

"The money that Jay and Estelle gave us," Sepherin asked quietly, "is it enough to take care of our immediate needs?"

Cassie looked up at the pale woman, "It'll get us started. It'll get us a small place at least, if we can find someplace furnished. We'll have to get jobs soon."

"Okay, how do we find a place? That should be first."

"We'll need to …"

"Cassie?"

Both women turned to the sound of Mrs. Kelvin's voice, speaking quietly again. She was coming out of the building entrance, clutching her purse and a sweater.

"Nana, I'm so sorry for …"

"Now, now, dear, don't you fret. My grandson's an asshole despite how his mother raised him, God rest her. I never knew what you saw in him in the first place. I always thought you were too good for him." She looked at Sepherin, "I'm sorry, dear, in all the excitement we weren't properly introduced. I'm Doris Kelvin, but you can call me Nana, if you'd like."

Sepherin smiled and held out her hand as she had been instructed on the trip to Earth, pumping the woman's hand exactly three times. "I'm pleased to meet you, Nana Kelvin. My name is Stephy."

The slight old woman had a fierce grip, she pulled the tall women down to her height, and kissed her on the cheek. Looking down at Sepherin's belly, she asked, "How far along are you?"

"A little over …" she quickly did the conversion from ten-sleeps to the Earth calendar, "… four months."

"And the father?"

Sepherin just shook her head.

"Well, that's the way nowadays, I suppose. Will you girls walk me up to the bus stop? Some damn fool got in the way of a bullet last night and them weirdos with cameras are all over the place today."

Cassie and Sepherin looked at each other. Sepherin asked, "Could we maybe walk through the park behind your building? Would that get us to the buses? We don't want to walk past the cameras again."

The old woman was quiet for a moment, looking at Sepherin, then Cassie. "Someone's really after you girls?"

"Yes," Cassie said, shooting Sepherin a quick glance, "her ex-boyfriend is — he used to hit her."

Sepherin was surprised, but followed what Cassie was saying. When the old woman looked up at her again, Sepherin frowned and looked away. "Yes," she said quietly, not meeting the woman's eyes, "he used to hit me — and other things."

Mrs. Kelvin stood a little taller and put a disapproving look on her face. "Well, Ritchie may be a little shit sometimes, but at least he ain't no wife-beater. You girls come with me. No one will bother you if we're together."

The three women walked slowly; Sepherin and Cassie helped Mrs. Kelvin across rough spots on the ground. Instead of heading back to the bus, hearing they needed a computer to find a place to live, Nana Kelvin changed direction and lead them down to the Community Centre on Replin Road. Nana Kelvin argued with the woman at the desk for a few minutes, and then they were led to a public computer to use. The old woman went and got Styrofoam cups of tea while the girls started looking online for someplace to live.

Nana Kelvin sat and talked quietly to Cassie about her family, eager to learn more about the other half of her future great-grandchild's kinfolk. She wasn't entirely sure about what happened with Cassie and her grandson, but she figured Ritchie was likely the one at fault. She had already decided that Cassie was a good girl from what she knew about her, and that the baby in her belly was indeed her grandson's. She hoped her grandson would come around to accepting the child in time. Regardless of what he might or might not do, Nana Kelvin was determined to part on good terms with the young woman, hoping she would be part of the child's future.

While the two women talked, with some prompting from Cassie, Sepherin quickly got the hang of using a browser and Googling. She struggled with some spellings, however, and Cassie needed to help her. Even though they spoke the same language, Umitian script was phonemic, where the Earther English alphabet was a grapheme. She'd studied it on the way to Earth, but it wasn't her strongest subject.

She looked for two-bedroom apartments that were furnished. The ones she found were far too expensive. After some digging for an hour, she found a Craigslist add for a one bedroom apartment, furnished, and the person who posted the advertisement was willing to cut the rent in exchange for some help around the house.

Mrs. Kelvin looked at the advertisement with the girls and smiled. "You two could blend in there quite nicely, two young women living together in a one bedroom apartment."

"Why is that?" asked Sepherin.

"Because it's in the Village, dear," Nana Kelvin winked.

Cassie almost choked on her tea.

Chapter 46

Cobus watched the Manager walk across the lawns. No, glide across the lawns would be a more appropriate statement. The Shovitic was heading back to the windowless Palace.

The gardener was still stunned. He just wasn't sure what he was more amazed at: that Kalabot had confided in him, or *what* Kalabot had confided in him. Revealing the fact that Kalabot had bred with a Falwasz was something which displayed the Manager's level of trust in Cobus. Such information, revealed, would mean the man's execution, as well as Alabast's. The fact that the offspring was an Imperite who was being sought for apprehension, to be returned and executed as an oath-breaker, was even more shocking.

As Kalabot entered the Palace, Cobus Scheepers finally was able to take a breath. He went to the closest garden bed and knelt down, pulling weeds without paying much attention to them. He was trying to figure out what he was going to do with the information. If he were to reveal what Kalabot had told him about the mating, it would mean the death of Cobus' half-sister. But the fact his niece was going to be executed, that was something he had to act on.

Cobus cursed his own luck. After so many years in place, after the sacrifices of the agents of the Cabal of the clans to get him there, he had the mother of all bombshells, but could not tell anyone. But no matter what the cost would be, he could not let his niece, Alabast's daughter, die; even if it meant his own life.

He sat back on his feet and sighed, adjusting his wide-brimmed hat. The illegitimate son of an itinerant merchant, his own father and mother had risked the death penalty. A Falwasz and a Silthit mating, and worse, breeding, was just as bad as the union of a Falwasz and a Shovitic. Obviously, the planetary administration had never become aware of the fact that Cobus was Alabast's half-brother. Were it so, Kalabot would never have shared any of his story with him, and would have ordered his still-living mother executed. It was almost laughable that the broker of information who controlled worlds did not know something that would become so pivotal in the events to follow.

No, he decided, *I can reveal nothing about their despicable union. I can never even mention it to Michalz. But I'll be cast in the eternal fires if I let him kill little Sephy.*

Michalz and Alabast liked to take a walk after the evening meal. It helped them both with the digestion, and to clear the cobwebs of their day so the evening could be enjoyed more fully. When the weather was nice, as it was this early evening, they strode along the path next to the river behind their estate house.

Technically, as the head of the House of Tekin, the estate belonged to Themedit, Michalz' father. However, he only occupied a small wing of the estate, allowing his son and heir, along with his wife and children, to call the estate their home.

This evening Michalz and Alabast walked slowly, arm in arm, discussing the austerity measures they were implementing to get through to the next reporting quarter when the foundry could open again. Michalz already had enough contracts lined up for his light-weight, incredibly strong castings, that he could find himself in the same position within a few ten-sleeps of the next quarter opening. He had, only today, turned down a lucrative contract because of this.

The Shovitic rulers were ruthlessly enforcing the anti-monopoly provisions of the commerce laws which prevented any one company gaining a significant advantage over another, regardless of the size of the company. The Tekins were not the only family being affected by a stupid law that set an industry's maximum profits based on the poorest performer in the industry. The Shovitic rulers claimed this would breed a commercial system based on helping one another, and sharing of technologies and profits, for the betterment of Umitia. If the lowest performers bottom line was assisted in rising, so too would the maximum profit line of all the company's betters. The Shovitics claimed this was good for everyone, and it was, unless your company got shut down because you were *too* good at what you did. The end of a quarter found many businesses closed, at risk of the dissolution of their House and seizure of their assets if they failed to comply with the new rules. This law applied not only to heavy industry, but to every classification of business from spaceship manufacturers down to mom and pop grocery stores.

Michalz was on another one of his rants about the Shovitics and their lack of understanding of a free marketplace. He could speak freely to his wife on their evening walks. The house staff knew they were to be left alone and never disturbed, so he had no fear of one of them overhearing him and reporting his treasonous words to curry favour.

A little over a league into their sojourn, the couple came to the small clearing where the natural water spring was found. A wooden trough had been placed at the hillside water source when Michalz was a young boy, to bring the water to the clearing where it could be enjoyed. The crisp, clear, cold water was a favourite destination of the children and the adults in the hot weather. This evening, Alabast cupped her hands under the water trickling from the end of the trough. As her gaze rose with her hands cupping water, she saw a face through the trees, smiling at her, and she froze.

Noticing her reaction, Michalz looked to the woods as well, and then smiled.

"Cobus, what on Umitia are you doing hiding in ..." he trailed off as his half-brother-in-law raised a finger to his lips. The man approached the edge of the tree line, but would not step into the clearing. Instead, he beckoned the Tekins to come closer.

Alabast swooned when he informed them that their daughter had been deemed an oath-breaker. Learning Sepherin was responsible for the murder of two Imperite Guards, and was being sought for return to Umitia for execution, Alabast voice croaked an exclamation of despair.

"Those damn bastards!" Michalz dark complexion had gone darker, painted with broad strokes of reds and purples. "They take her from us, force her on this *damn stupid* quest of theirs, send her alone to another planet, and then when she defends herself they want to kill her?"

"But she wasn't defending herself, Michalz, she was defending her kin, your brother."

Michalz looked like he had been slapped. "My brother? *What in the Holy One's name are you talking about, old man*?"

"Her host family died, she was reassigned to Tameht Tekin."

Michalz didn't recognize the name. "Who is he? What do you mean he's my brother?"

"He was the son of Jakula Tekin. She was pregnant when she left on her journey. He's the son of Themedit, he's your younger brother — *was* your brother."

"Was?"

"The Imperite Guards murdered him in revenge for the deaths of their own."

This was the first word Michalz had of anything to do with his mother since she had left Umitia, when he was a child, barely able to walk. He was overcome with emotion at Cobus' words. Alabast wrapped her arms around her husband and held him tight as he started to slump. She and Cobus led him to a deadfall a few metres away and the three sat down.

After a few moments Michalz asked, "And my mother? Is she still alive, do you know?"

"I asked the Manager as he related his burden to me, apparently your mother completed her Imperative over thirty seasons ago."

A brief moment of tears for a woman he barely had any memory of, plus the warmth of his wife's embrace, quickly helped Michalz regain his composure. Then the realization he had a brother struck him again, making him dizzy with the punch of unfairness life had brought him. He had no knowledge of the man who was his blood-kin, no understanding of who and what he was, and he never would. He would never know the man, or raise a mug of ale with him, or anything with him, because of the damn Shovitics. Because they had taken his mother when he was so young, because they had kept all knowledge of her new life from them, he would never understand the joy of a blood-kin brother. And within a few heartbeats of learning the man existed, Michalz learned the Shovitics had executed him for something someone else had done, that someone being his own daughter.

Cobus and Alabast kept their silence. They understood what Michalz had to be going through, and they knew there were no words which would bring any comfort, any respite to the torrent of emotions painted on his face and revealed in his posture.

"Why is the Manager so *burdened* by the fate of an Imperite?" Michalz finally asked.

Cobus looked at Alabast, holding her gaze for a moment. He saw her eyes flare briefly, he saw her lips purse. She knew that he knew, and he could tell she was terrified at what his next words may be.

"Apparently," her half-brother began, "one of the dead guards is a distant relation of Kalabot's and for some reason this has greatly troubled him. Not only this, he is deeply concerned about the effect that a public execution will have on the Shovitic relationship with the clans."

"Humph," Michalz snorted, "like that relationship could get any worse."

Alabast spoke up, deflecting the course of conversation away from Kalabot's 'burden'. "My dearest," she turned to Michalz, "we simply cannot let this happen. If they find Sepherin and bring her home, we — we must be prepared."

Michalz nodded as Cobus spoke again, "Yes, I agree with you most heartily dear sister. We must call the leaders of the Cabal together ..."

"Accch!" Michalz waved his hands in the air, "The Cabal! What have we done lately? Nothing! We have done nothing except hold *secret meetings* and *drink kimsa*. What good will it do? None, I tell you, *none*! We should be called the Silent Cabal for all the good we do."

"Michalz, please, I know you are upset, but the network is vast. It's full of people waiting for the right time. We have been working for years laying the proper foundations. Look how long it took for them to get me into the Palace. Look at how many people were sacrificed to make that happen. I know you are upset old man, but it's time for a plodding response, not a knee jerk reaction."

Michalz turned away from Cobus, not wanting to say something insulting to a man he loved and respected.

Cobus continued, "I will most certainly know when she is captured and when she arrives. But we must have a plan in place. Even if she were caught today, it would still give us many ten-sleeps to prepare, but we must not waste time. I do fear that if a child's mother is executed, it will indeed bring us to a civil war, a bloody civil war."

"A child's *mother*?" Alabast looked at Cobus, her face going pale. Michalz also spun back around to look at him.

Cobus looked at her, then his eyes and mouth went wide with realization, "Alabast, Michalz, my dearest ones. I'm so sorry. I forgot to tell you — Sepherin is with child."

Michalz and Alabast looked at each other, not voicing the recrimination of allowing Sepherin her time of 'wilding' before departing. It only took them half a breath to figure out who the father was; a fact which could have far reaching ripples in their community, not to mention the death of her lover.

Michalz nodded as Alabast spoke, "We must speak to Roguk."

Chapter 47

Femi and Corvu had been waiting at Jay's place when he and Estelle returned. Tommy had been very dear to them, and they were both upset at learning of his death. However, Jay was an Earth-born and Estelle was an Earther. When Corvu pulled his gun and put it to Estelle's head, Jay didn't hesitate in telling them where he had taken the girls, but he told them he dropped them off at the train station in the city instead of where he really dropped them off.

Because they were only accessories after the fact, and not directly involved in the death of the guards, Femi and Corvu let them live. Jay knew what would happen if he opened his mouth to anyone about the recent events.

The two Imperite Guards drove straight to Toronto and went to the train station. It took only a little bit of convincing, and a flash of their eyes, to get the guards on duty to review the video tapes from the security cameras. Knowing the approximate time the women were dropped off, backed up by the travel time and the time that Jay and his wife had returned, the two Guards were fairly certain Sepherin and Cassie had never gone into the train station.

This meant they were somewhere in the city. Considering that the spread of the city let it blend without interruption into the surrounding municipalities, they were looking for the two women in a population of over six million Earthers. They certainly had their work cut out for them. They weren't concerned that the women would have moved on to some place smaller. The two Guards knew the Imperite's best chance for survival was to get lost in a large metropolitan setting.

Femi called the Watch Commander in the duty frigate and requested additional teams. Three hours later, in an unused warehouse on Unwin Avenue, Femi and Corvu briefed the five additional teams of Imperite Guards on the target, and the witness. Looking for an oath-breaker who had killed two of their own had them all on edge and thirsting for Falwasz blood.

They divided the city into six sectors; the teams would switch sectors every five days. They decided to stick to the city proper, knowing that the denser core of the city would provide her more cover, and more opportunity to hide. The teams' only course of action for the first few days would be for each team to drive around in their black sedan, in their assigned sector, and smell the air. If they were within half a block of where the Falwasz had recently been, their super-sensitive noses would smell her. Unfortunately, given the smells and climate, it was only a five minute window they had to work with. After that approach, if she was still not found, they would take more aggressive measures.

On the off chance of some blind luck, the team on loan from Russia, Fitid and Senji (the only female Imperite Guard on remote posting, on any planet) went to the police. They posed as concerned relatives reporting her missing. The Police Constable wasn't stupid, he knew something was up. He said nothing directly to them, but when they departed, he copied down their license plate number and checked it on the Canadian Police Information Centre (CPIC) computer. Twenty minutes later the Chief of Police got a call from the Prime Minister's office. Ten minutes later, the Police Constable who took the report decided to take some annual leave, and forget all about the man and woman dressed in black suits, thankful that the Chief hadn't suspended him.

On his way home, he smiled at the fact his sometimes selectively dodgy memory had caused him *not* to enter the missing person information on the computer. When he got to his house, he went out in the backyard and burned the hardcopy report he had filled out with the two odd-ball characters sitting across the desk from him. Then he went inside, turned on Netflix, opened a bottle of rum, and got shit-faced while binge-watching *Breaking Bad*, season three.

Chapter 48

"Pizza Town, how may I help you? ... Yes, sir, we still have the special ... certainly, a medium is enough for three people ... do you just want the one-topping special or ... of course, bacon, mushrooms, and extra cheese it is, would you like anything to drink with that? ... Will there be anything else with your order? ... Okay, then, the total with tax is $19.47, and it's free if the driver isn't there in 45 minutes, the time is 2:33 ... have a wonderful day, sir, goodbye."

Sepherin disconnected the caller. After removing her headset, she went to get some pop from the kitchen of their apartment.

The landlady, Carlota, had been an absolute sweetheart since they moved in to the second-floor apartment, and gone out of her way to make them comfortable. After Carlota heard the contrived story of Cassie's abusive and controlling ex-boyfriend who wanted to kill her for getting pregnant and leaving him; and hearing about the orphaned Sepherin, whose fiancé had been killed in a car accident; Carlota's mothering instinct emerged.

One of the things she had done for the girls was to give them the computer she had before buying a new one. It was perfectly serviceable with Windows Vista on it, and it allowed Sepherin to get a job working from home. The only expense had been a special phone line that was set up for the company's phone switcher to route inbound calls directly to her apartment. She took the orders, entered them in the computer, and didn't have to go out every day. It was just safer that way.

The apartment was one bedroom, but was spacious and bright. The bedroom was on the third floor, the stairs leading to it were at the back of the kitchen. The whole flat had recently been redecorated, and had all new appliances. The house had been Carlota's pet project since purchasing it two years ago. She still had to finish the basement, but she was working at saving the funds for that venture.

The only thing Sepherin hated was that she had to keep the windows closed all the time, so the rafts of her dead skin cells would not be picked up and carried out through them on the wind. That was the easiest thing for a Shovitic to smell, from a distance. Up close, within thirty or forty metres, they can differentiate the smell of a person's sebum to determine their race. But it's still the shed skin cells which let them hone in on an individual. Unfortunately, the smell of Umites, especially the Falwasz clan, was distinct from Earthers' scent. The Imperite Guard's sense of smell is four thousand times more powerful than any other Humanesh race, almost as good as an Earther canine.

Cassie would often sit out on the front balcony, bundled up in a jacket and blankets, but Sepherin never joined her. It was too risky.

Back at her desk, sipping Diet Pepsi, Sepherin looked up at the apartment door when she heard the key in the lock. She reached beside the computer for the chef's knife she always kept close at hand.

"Hey, you," Cassie said, shutting the door behind her.

Sepherin got up, "Here, let me take those."

Cassie handed her one of the grocery bags. "We're both getting big girl, you don't have to take all of them."

Sepherin took the bag in the kitchen and started putting the items away. Cassie quickly joined her, setting a box on the counter.

"So, you still mad at me?" Sepherin asked.

"Nah, you were asleep. I know that. I should be used to your tossing and turning by now."

"Yeah, but ..."

"Maybe I'll get a football helmet; then I won't have to worry about getting an elbow in the face again." She reached up and wiggled the tip of her nose. "You're lucky you didn't break it."

Sepherin came up behind Cassie and put her arms around her, laying her head down on the top of Cassie's head. "I really am sorry."

Cassie pushed her away with a smile and reached in the bag she was unpacking. She pulled out the cellophane package with a flourish, "Look what I found."

Sepherin gasped with surprise and grabbed the bag, "Cheese-flavoured dried mealworms! Where did you find these?"

"A store in Carrot Common has them. They have plain, ranch, and BBQ flavoured as well."

Sepherin tore open the corner of the bag, tipped a few in her hand, and tossed them in her mouth. She was smiling pleasantly as she slowly savoured the flavour and chewy texture.

"I still don't get it, Stephy. You won't eat any meat products, but yet you still go all fat-kid-on-a-chocolate-bar, for bugs, *ewww*." She crinkled her nose.

"I'm from outer space. It's complicated."

They both laughed.

"Just don't go forgetting the rules about the pregnant Earther girl."

"I know, I know: no avocado, no fish, no bugs of any kind, no matter how delicious they are."

"And why is that?"

"Because you're a chicken."

"No, it's so I don't throw up all over the dinner table."

"No, it's because you're a *chicken*."

They were silent for a moment. Cassie turned away to put the rest of the groceries and quietly said, *"Buck-awwwk."*

Sepherin was about to say something else, but stopped as they heard a voice outside the door, at the top of the stairs, "*Yoo hoo! Girls? Are you home?*"

Sepherin and Cassie smiled. Carlota knew full well they were home. The house may have been redone, but you could still hear everything going on, from any room in the building.

Cassie opened the door and invited her in.

"I won't stay long," she said in a voice which was still a touch manly, despite the hormone treatments. "I made some brisket, would you two like to come for dinner? Stephy, I made vegetarian cabbage rolls for you, dear." Carlota's big smile under her hawk nose was always infectious.

"*Mmm*, I love your cabbage rolls," Sepherin looked at Cassie, nodding enthusiastically.

"Sure, Lota, we'll be down in …" she looked at Sepherin just as the phone rang. Sepherin dashed to pick up her headset, "I've got another forty-five minutes … Pizza Town, how may I help you?"

"Can we bring anything?" Cassie asked her landlady.

"No, dear, just bring your effervescent selves."

"I just bought a coconut cream pie," Cassie pointed at the box on the kitchen counter, "you sure?"

"Coconut," Carlota said slowly, "makes me think of piña coladas and that …" she rolled her eyes and clutched her large knuckled hand to her chest, "… sweet, sweet boy who served them in Fort Lauderdale."

"Oooh, sounds like sexy a story, *dish!*"

"Bring the pie, sweetie, I'll dish with the dish after dinner." Carlota gave Cassie's arm a quick squeeze and went back out through the door.

The Shovitics would never stand for behaviour like this, Sepherin thought as Carlota regaled them with the tale of Davy, the pool-bar server from her vacation two years ago. Same-sex relationships were strictly forbidden on Umitia, under penalty of death. A lot of things were forbidden under the penalty of death back there. Sepherin smiled as Carlota expertly spun the tale. Initially, the thought of a woman in a man's body, or a man becoming a woman, had been something incomprehensible to Sepherin. Over the last three months, getting to know their landlady and friend better, she found herself liking 'Lota' as they called her, more and more. If she closed her eyes, and not minding the voice, the person talking was all woman. She still had some electrolysis work to be done, and her hormone treatment hadn't completely changed her voice, but Sepherin soon decided she didn't care. Carlota's mother hen approach had won her as much as her amazing cooking had.

The bond developed early between the three of them. Two weeks after they moved in, Cassie woke Sepherin up in the middle of the night. They heard Carlota crying. Pregnant belly notwithstanding, Sepherin was out of the bed, down the stairs, and had kicked in Carlota's front door. She sprinted through the flat with the chef's knife in her hand, looking to end the bastard that had made her new friend cry.

Sepherin was surprised to find Carlota sitting on the kitchen floor, a bottle of rum in her hand, and makeup running down her face from the tears. Sepherin quickly made sure no one was in the flat and then called Cassie down.

305

Cassie put the booze away, while Sepherin lifted Carlota to a chair at the kitchen table. Dampening the end of the dish towel, Sepherin cleaned up Carlota's face, while Cassie made some instant coffee. Carlota told them she had been thinking about how alone the girls were, and how alone she had been when she first came out. She had still been serving in the Royal Canadian Navy as a Chief Petty Officer, 2nd class, when her name was Karl. The years that had passed since then had been extremely difficult for her. After deciding to transition, her family had been somewhat supportive, but distant. She had found it easier to just move to Toronto and go it on her own, away from the small town ridicule and derision.

Her own story had made her realize how difficult it was going to be for Stephy and Cassie, which led to the rum, which led to more bad memories, which led to more rum, which led to the wailing and tears as she sat on the kitchen floor.

In the midst of her coming back to soberness, she made Sepherin's blood freeze.

"I saw one of those cars today."

"What cars?" Cassie asked, as Sepherin was refilling the coffee cup.

"One of those black cars you talked about, with the men wearing dark suits."

The baby kicked in Sepherin's stomach. Cassie and Carlota both turned as the mug crashed to the floor.

Sepherin was staring at them. "Lota, where did you see it at?"

"Uptown. I was coming from my doctor's office on Eglinton Avenue."

An image of Sepherin and Cassie, running down the street, hand in hand, flashed in front Sepherin's mind. She felt the sense of urgency emanating from her womb.

Sepherin ignored the image, knowing it was intended for her only, though she put one hand on her stomach to comfort the child. Sepherin had paper towels in her hand, cleaning up the broken mug. "What were they doing?" She wasn't looking at Carlota; she didn't want her face to betray the nervousness she felt.

"Oh, nothing. It was just a dark car, with two men in dark suits. I remembered Cassie had said to watch for them, they might be her ex's people."

As Sepherin finished cleaning up, Cassie reached out and took the older woman's hand. "Lota, were they pale looking?"

"Why … yes, they were. It was odd. I thought at first they were albinos, but they had dark hair."

Sepherin got the flash of an image of two Imperite Guards in front of her, towering over her, with a noose dangling between them. Then again came the image of her and Cassie running down a street, hand in hand. The sense of urgency from her unborn child was even stronger. But now the urgency was tinged with fear.

Sepherin took a breath to calm down against the force of the child's insistence. This had been happening more and more, bits of words, emotions, fears, happiness, all emanating from the one in her womb. It confused her. Only Shovitics were telepathic. The Hobonol weren't and the Falwasz certainly weren't. Perhaps the blending of Hobonol and Falwasz was responsible for it. She had stopped wondering about it many ten-sleeps ago; it was something far beyond her understanding.

She finished putting the broken mug bits in the garbage and turned to the cupboard for a new cup. "But what were they doing?" she asked as nonchalantly as possible.

"Nothing, really. They were sitting in their car at the light. They had the windows down. I think they were hungry, there was a sausage cart on the corner and they were both sniffing the air."

A memory flashed in Sepherin's mind, at only five seasons of age, begging her mother for another briska cookie. "Please, mommy, please!" she heard the image of her younger self say. She wanted to be sick at the thought of her unborn child begging her in such a dramatic way.

Cassie and Sepherin looked at each other. Sepherin finished pouring more coffee for Carlota, added a bit of cream, and then handed it to her while sitting down at the table.

"If they were uptown, then we're okay here, aren't we?" Cassie asked.

"Carlota, did they follow you at all? Even for a minute or two?"

"No, dear, I came out of the office and ducked right into the subway. I only saw them for a few seconds. I don't think they saw me at all. Why?" she turned to Cassie, "Do you think it might have been your ex's people?"

Cassie saw Sepherin nodding out of the corner of her eye, "Yes, I do. It sounds like them."

"Well," Carlota looked at Sepherin, "pity the fool who comes after Ramb-ette the knife-girl over there."

No one laughed.

That had been two months ago. This early December evening, having seen no sign of the Imperite Guards since Carlota's brief sighting, the women were enjoying a peaceful and relaxing evening.

"Well, you girls, since you're here and have no plans, how's about you help me put up the Christmas tree and decorate it."

Cassie's face lit up and she clapped her hands together. She had been in tears a few days ago, thinking about her mom and dad, knowing this would be the first Christmas she didn't spend with them. She had only been able to contact them once since fleeing Kincardine, using an internet phone service which wouldn't reveal her location. One of the nerds who worked with her had set it up, not asking any questions, just being happy to stick it to the telephone company. She missed her parents, and the fear and worry in their voices was still eating away at her. With Christmas approaching, she had a few crying jags, trying to hide them from Sepherin. The Earther and the alien had grown extremely close in the last few months, to the point that Cassie knew they would be together, in some way, forever.

Sepherin had a couple of lectures about 'Christmas' on the way to Earth, and had seen lots of photos. She still didn't understand why the spirit of an old man wanted to give things to people.

As the tree was put up and the decorations applied, Cassie took great joy in recounting the Christmas story to the two women. It made her feel almost — normal — for this one evening. After they were finished decorating the tree and Carlota plugged in the lights, Sepherin was spell bound by how beautiful it was. Carlotta brought out some homemade egg nog she had made that afternoon.

"To my new friends, may the wind be always at your back, and the sun shine always on your face."

The girls drank their toast, with Sepherin's eyes going wide. Never, had she ever tasted nectar as delicious or satisfying as this *magical concoction* as she referred to it.

Then Sepherin offered her own toast, a traditional toast of the House of Tekin. "The sun is born every morn', and the moon is new in its due; so cheer with me what never leaves, the love of friends like you."

The women finished their egg nog while listening to Harry Connick Jr.'s Christmas album.

A week before Christmas, Cassie finished her shift at Starbucks on Danforth Avenue in the early afternoon. She bundled up in her winter gear and headed out the door. Two steps onto the sidewalk, she stopped dead in her tracks. Waiting at the lights was a black sedan, with two men in black suits and black fedoras, with perfectly trimmed crew-cut hair, very square jaws, and wearing Ray-Ban sunglasses.

One of them looked right at her and sniffed the air.

Cassie turned and ran back into the coffee shop. She looked over her shoulder and saw both men had exited the car, leaving it in the live traffic lane. They were moving towards the store.

"Cas, what's wrong?" asked Ben, her slender bookworm co-worker.

"Those men …" she rasped in fear and then ran for the back of the store.

The front door burst open just after she disappeared into the store room, heading for the rear delivery door.

"Where is the little black girl?" asked Salo, in his sibilant manner of speech.

"What black girl?" asked Ben, giving them a weak smile.

Salo's partner, Kevit, both on loan from China, reached over the counter and grabbed Ben by the collar. "Do not play games with us, where is she?"

"Hey!" Mick Harrington, on break from the construction site around the corner, was sitting at the back table. He thought Ben was a little poofter, but he liked the kid regardless. The guy always smiled and had a joke to tell. Mick did not appreciate these funny looking *sons-a-bitches* roughing him up.

Mick stood, making sure they saw the full size of his beefy, muscular, 190 cm tall body.

Kevit let go of Ben and reached inside his jacket. Salo pushed past him, not wanting his partner to draw the weapon in such a public setting. He grabbed Mick, trying to push him aside. It didn't work.

Mick smiled as Salo had rushed towards him, muttering, "This is gonna be fun."

Kevit never had a chance to draw his gun. Mick took out Salo with one punch, knocking him unconscious and knocking his sunglasses off his head. As Mick grabbed Kevit, pulling his empty hand out of his overcoat, a woman who went to check on the unconscious man started screaming, and then a man started screaming. As Mick beat Kevit senseless, another man knelt down by Salo's unconscious form and exclaimed, "Holy fuck! What the hell is he?"

By this time, Kevit's sunglasses had also come off, and Mick had seen the mostly empty eye sockets and the eyeworms around them. A fan of everything sci-fi, especially the UFO conspiracy videos on YouTube, Mick had realized he was beating a Man in Black. With this realization, he beat him harder. He figured it was his duty, as a human, to defend another human from this un-Godly abomination. In his mind he was simply offering a little payback for all the people who had been abducted. He had no idea Kevit and Salo were here to protect Earthers, not that it would have mattered. They had attacked Ben.

By the time Kevit succumbed to the assault, and collapsed, the store had emptied of everyone except Ben. The poor guy stood behind the counter, quivering with fear, with a look of sheer horror on his face.

As Mick dropped Kevit to the floor in a bloody heap, he saw that the MIB had an impressive looking handgun in a shoulder holster. Grabbing a napkin from the counter, he reached inside the jacket, and unsnapped the retention strap. He pulled the gun out and tossed it on the floor by the kick plate for the counter. Looking up at Ben, Mick asked, "You saw him pull the gun, right? *Right?*"

Ben nodded, too terrified to speak.

They heard sirens in the distance.

"I'm going to wait outside. You comin'?"

Ben nodded and came around the counter. He latched onto Mick's muscular arm and followed him outside, whimpering as they stepped over the two bodies. He didn't let go of him for a long time.

When the police arrived, with the ambulance right behind them, the first two officers went in, and then came right back out. Both had turned pale. As they went out the door, they didn't see that Salo had started to move, regaining consciousness. Less than a minute later the paramedics went in with the police right behind them.

There was no one there.

The floor had blood on it, and they found the handgun right where the big construction worker said it would be. They also found one of the men's sunglasses. But the two bodies that had been there only a moment before were gone. One of the officers ran to the back of the store, into the store room, and out into the alley. But there was nothing. There was no sign of them, no trail of blood, nothing.

Going back out front, having a hurried discussion with his partner and the Sergeant who had just arrived on scene, they decided that the two men *had indeed* made good their escape out the back *before* the officers arrived. They decided that when the officers first went in, there was nothing there except some blood on the floor. It was the only way this would play out, without everyone involved getting a first class ticket to the funny farm.

Ben was looking at the cars, at the drivers getting out of their cars, astonished looks on their faces. He turned to the police officers, "Did you just see that black car disappear?"

Cassie was halfway home before the shakes started. She had run like hell down the back alley to the subway station. With so many people around her she still didn't feel safe; she still kept swivelling her head back and forth, watching the stairs at both ends of the subway platform. She got off the train two stops early, and grabbed the first bus, not wanting to go straight home in case they were still following her. She rode south bound for ten minutes, then got off the bus and hustled along Gerrard Street, winding up in a small Punjabi restaurant.

The proprietor, a beautiful South Asian woman named Jayanti, saw the woman was both pregnant and in distress. She took her back to her office, but the young woman wouldn't say anything other than someone was chasing her. Jayanti made a phone call, and ten minutes later her two sons arrived at the restaurant. They drove Cassie home to her place in the Village. Having grown up watching too many Bollywood movies, they took pleasure in following a meandering and circuitous route, keeping an eye out to ensure they weren't being followed — and ready to raise hell if they were.

Chapter 49

The Tekin's butler walked down the driveway, wondering what in the Holy One's name was going on. The Tekins had given the house staff the evening off for the *third time* this past ten-sleep. In fact, they had insisted they take the evening off and spend it on the town. Mater Tekin had gone so far this evening as to give him a bundle of notes to pay for their merriment. *Something odd is going on in the House of Tekin*, the butler thought, *something odd indeed*.

After the house staff left, Alabast lit the burner under the big water boiler on the counter so the water would be ready to prepare tea and kimsa for those arriving.

Michalz was still working in his study while she prepared for the arrival of the senior Cabal members. When she heard a light rapping on the kitchen door, Alabast opened it to find Roguk Fozretson standing on the steps. He was twisting his workman's cap in his hands, looking like he had been chastened and cowed.

"Roguk," Alabast smiled, sensing he needed a friendly tone at the moment, "please, come inside."

He bobbed his head and thanked her. He stood just inside the door, looking, it seemed, at every individual tile on the floor.

Alabast pulled a stool out from the counter where the staff ate their meals. "Have a seat. I think the water is hot enough, would you care for some tea?"

"Please, Mater Tekin, that would be so kind."

As she prepared the cup, testing the water with her pinkie and being satisfied it was hot enough, she spoke, "Roguk, you look deeply troubled. I take it that you and Eleniak have spoken?"

As a husband and wife frequently speak, he knew the older woman had honed in on the source of his discomfort. She could only be referring to one conversation, made necessary by her revelation to him that he was to be the father of a child on a planet far, far away. Had Sepherin not been under the threat of return to Umitia for execution, he would have said nothing. However …

"Yes, we have, this very day. She is incensed, and feels betrayed in the most egregious of ways, as I knew she would." He took a deep breath and then sipped his tea.

"And?"

"And I will spend a great deal of time and effort, in regaining her trust."

Alabast was silent, waiting for more.

Roguk looked up, his handsome face distorted with the stress and shame which had been brought to the surface with the information that Sepherin was pregnant, and might be returning to Umitia to be executed.

Roguk continued after another sip of tea. "Eleniak will not disavow me. She knows it was the only time, I keep too good of an accounting of my days, what with business as robust as it is. I have given her a blood-vow that my fidelity will be with her, and her only."

Tears welled in his eyes as he continued, "She said that during Sepherin's wilding, she suspected, but chose not to ask. Had I not said anything, she never would have asked. She knew how close Sepherin and I have been since childhood and with Sepherin leaving, without it being thrown in her face, she had made her peace with it. But with Sepherin returning — and the discontent that will result with the …" he couldn't bring himself to say 'execution', "… with her coming back with a child, even though our night together must remain secret, the betrayal will nevertheless be on display, in Eleniak's eyes."

316

Alabast was surprised. She sipped at her tea before responding. "Roguk, it would seem that Eleniak is much stronger a woman than I had surmised, more than you had surmised, apparently."

He just nodded.

She sighed and then went on, after glancing over her shoulder to make sure Michalz was not approaching. "Roguk, I will confess that I am not pleased about this situation, but I, too, can appreciate the moment and the timing, and how much you two meant to each other. That it took place, and worse, that there is a child, in a society where such a cross-clan union means a short drop at the end of a rope, the two of you were ridiculously …" she trailed off, remembering her own sin — feeling the hypocrisy of her own words.

She went on, "I will not judge you in this matter, Roguk. What is done is done. If they capture Sepherin after the baby is born, they will most likely leave it behind. If she is still pregnant when she is taken, she knows better than to give the name of the father, especially in this circumstance. With luck, the child's dominant features will be of the Falwasz clan, and no questions will be asked."

Roguk was nodding. "Has there been any word? Has she been captured?"

"Our source has not indicated as such." Only the highest members of the Cabal knew that Cobus was the source. It was a most guarded secret.

The front door chime sounded. Alabast stood, as did Roguk, but she heard Michalz hurrying from his study to answer it.

"You must leave now, Roguk, you cannot be here with our guests arriving."

He stood and reached out, taking Alabast's hand, "Anything that I can do, I will do. You know that Mater Tekin. When she is brought home, I will sacrifice my life to save hers, if that is what it takes."

His words irritated Alabast. In one breath he was vowing his fidelity to his wife, and in the next breath he was offering his life for his illicit lover, who happened to be her own daughter. She said nothing though, resisting the urge to slap the young man. Alabast knew the urge was bred by her own stress, and that Roguk, while he and Sepherin had been foolish, was still a good man at heart.

"I will let you know if there is anything you can do. Now, I must insist, it is time to leave, and do so discretely. If Michalz were to find you here …"

Roguk nodded, and without any further words he departed, dashing out the door, through the garden at the back of the house, across the lawn, and into the woods.

Alabast joined her husband, and greeted Frederik Oguustson, the mayor of Kilkestand City and third member of the Cabal. Within a few minutes, the other two members arrived: the elderly Miras and almost as elderly, Pilip. Both were the heads of extensive Houses of Falwasz, and industry leaders, as much as one could be on Umitia. Finally, Themedit came down from his room to complete the Cabal. They gathered in Michalz' study. Alabast had prepared the tea and kimsa for the guests and served them.

An Imperite Guard from the Palace's legal council's office had called upon the Tekinsons that morning. The councillor's duty was to inform them that Sepherin Tekin was going to be returned to Umitia when she was apprehended, to be tried as an oath-breaker. Alabast and Michalz had reacted appropriately, making the councillor glad he had brought several Imperite Guardsmen with him. After their histrionics had settled down, not that much acting was involved on their part for they were still shocked and maddened by the whole situation, the Shovitic legal councillor imparted to them the necessary information for the moment. He then made himself available to answer their questions about the due process and the trial which would take place when she was captured and returned.

The councillor departed, still feeling uneasy about the whole situation. He had more facts than he had revealed to the Tekinsons. Something about the whole situation didn't add up. He kept his thoughts to himself, however, lest those thoughts find their way back to Kalabot.

Now, with the guests who were the leaders of the Cabal of the clans finally settled, Frederik Oguustson was the first to address the group. "Friends, I believe we've all had time to decide what our response will be if Sepherin is returned, alive, to Umitia. I'll say my piece and then ask for your decisions."

Everyone nodded, saying nothing at this point.

"It has been over forty seasons since an oath-breaker was returned and executed. At the time, the populace was living with little oppression from the Palace. There was no public outcry about that event. Now, after the implementation of Kalabot's many edicts and oppressive laws, the mood of the people is different. I have spoken with many people, as have all of you. I know there are many, in all the clans, who are nearing their breaking point."

"They are *at* the breaking point, you mean," said the dowager Miras, crinkling her nose.

The others murmured their agreement.

Frederik continued, "While I am a peaceful man by nature, and though I am not of the Falwasz clan, I cannot conscience a young woman being executed for defending her kin according to Clan Law, even if it was the most curious of circumstances. I also don't believe that the good people of Umitia will stand by for this, if they are properly roused."

"I believe," interrupted Themedit, the eldest member of the group, "that we will have difficulty doing that. Unfortunate as it is, if the Palace gets wind of dissenting voices, the Manager will act swiftly and decisively against those who speak out."

"Yes, agreed, old friend," Frederik responded with a nod, "however, I am not suggesting we stand on roof tops and street corners. We all know those who believe as we do. We must get them talking, finding out who is of a like mind, and spread the word this way."

Michalz was getting frustrated, and it showed. Finally he spoke out rather brusquely, "Frederik, it's all well and good that the people should be incensed, but what are we going to do about Sepherin? What if she is already on the way back here? What if ..."

He was interrupted by the doorbell. Michalz stood and said, "Pardon me."

As the Tekinsons had dismissed the house staff while the Cabal gathered, it was his responsibility to respond. He opened the front door, and much to his surprise he found Kimla standing there, in her black suit, black-brimmed hat, and dark glasses. He had a moment of panic, glancing around outside to see if there were others, but there were none.

Seeing the look on his face, she asked, "Is there a problem, Master Tekinson?"

"No," he said gruffly, "I'm very busy and expecting guests. What do you want?"

With no expression or emotion, Kimla simply said, "I have a selection notification."

Peering from the door to the study, and seeing that it was Kimla at the front entrance, Alabast hurried to join her husband, wondering which of her remaining children was going to be taken from them. Granted, the training period was a full season, but they would still be taken at the end of the training.

"Who is it for?" she heard Michalz asked.

Kimla looked at Alabast as she stood beside her husband. Kimla knew this particular notification was not going to go over well, but she had spent time with the Tekinsons, and believed she could handle any negative response.

To Alabast, Kimla gravely stated, "I'm sorry, Mater Tekinson, this notification is for you."

Alabast sat quietly in the study, reading the notification again. She was to complete her training and be deployed to *Kofrem alpha*, a system over 1,150 light years from Umitia. It would take almost two seasons of deep space folding just to reach the system. With the year of training on top of the travel time, she would be 65 seasons old by the time she arrived — if she arrived.

The group was quiet while Michalz expended his rage in vitriolic. He had exploded in front of Kimla, rushing forward and taking a swing at her. Kimla had deftly sidestepped the assault and used Michalz own momentum to send him crashing to his hands and knees. She pulled her pain stick and waited to see what he would do. Technically, the attempted assault was a death sentence. However, Kimla knew the Tekinsons well, and was willing to overlook it. Even she thought this selection was strange and had expected Michalz, a proud man, to respond as he had.

Now, all that Michalz had left was his scathing and acerbic recitation of everything wrong with Umitia and the Shovitics in particular. His rage finally focussed on the computing system that selected the candidates, a process which was completely automated. No one person was allowed to select a candidate as the selection was based on a myriad of complicated factors. This was how it had been for hundreds of seasons. No one in the room could remember any time when a selected Imperite had been over the age of twenty-five seasons.

Alabast folded the notification as Miras sat beside her, patting her arm, but remaining silent. Alabast looked up at her husband, seeing his rage, his concern, his fear, and his love. The others in the room were equally as shocked and angry.

Alabast wasn't.

She had expected *something* — but not this.

"Themedit," she said loudly as she stood, interrupting her husband's rant, "there are sandwiches and cakes in the cold unit. Would you please serve our guests? I need to speak with Michalz in private."

Themedit stood and headed for the kitchen. Alabast took her husband's hand and led him from the room, up the stairs, and to their bedroom.

When she turned to look at her husband, her face was awash with tears.

"My dearest," he said warmly, stepping forward to embrace her.

She stepped back from him. "Please, Michalz, sit with me." She led him to the edge of the bed, and then took his big, beefy hand in her slender fingers, gripping him tightly.

"Almost twenty-four seasons ago, when there was the explosion at the foundry, we were on the verge of losing everything."

Michalz remembered all too well. He had lost many good people that day, and had mourned for them beside their families. He had also been approached by a group of Hobonol workers who demanded large payments to keep quiet about what they knew. Michalz had saved costs by not performing all of the inspections his equipment needed, although the money was still recorded as spent. They claimed, rightly so, that his actions had endangered the lives of all the workers. They knew the inspections had not been completed, though the company had still been invoiced for them, according to a pecuniary accomplice in the administration office.

Were this to become known, the ramifications would destroy his entire House. He paid the workers for their silence.

But one of them decided that he truly was incensed, beyond the desire for financial punishment. He was a Hobonol brother of one of the eleven people killed in the explosion. He had gone to the Imperite Guards and informed them of Michalz' deception, which led to the deaths.

The assets of the House of Tekin, including every family within the House, not just Michalz' family, were frozen for the duration of the investigation. It lasted a full season All the households within the House of Tekin lived on the money which they had on hand, as they were no longer able to access their holdings at the financial institutions. Eventually, those funds ran out, and the many Tekin families had to resort to living on handouts and loans, a few of them having to sell possessions to put food on the table. As the investigation progressed, and the investigators tried to unwind the complex paper trails, it became evident that they would indeed soon come to the truth.

Michalz had confided in Alabast at the time, that if the Tekin Foundry was found guilty, if he was found guilty, then the entire House of Tekin would be ordered to dissolve. The families' land holdings would be appropriated by the Palace and sold to the highest bidders. The homes, equipment, and personal possessions of every member of the House, no matter where they lived on Umitia, would be confiscated, and the family members would be turned out with only one suitcase per person. He had been terrified, sick with worry that this was going to come to pass, as were all the household heads under the House of Tekin's charter.

"And do you remember," Alabast continued, "how surprised you were when the Guards arrived to inform you that the investigation had been concluded, and that the House of Tekin was without any fault in the accident?"

"Why, of course," he smiled, remembering too clearly the joy and elation he had felt at such an unexpected turn of direction.

"There were over 1,600 households under the charter of the House of Tekin," Alabast continued, "and they would all have been turned out, without a single note to their names."

Michalz nodded, "Yes, my dear, but we were lucky. They couldn't follow the trail in depth enough. We lucked out." He squeezed her hand.

"No, we didn't luck out, Michalz." She looked at him, tears rimming her eyes, a sob catching her by surprise. "The day before you were informed of the conclusion of the investigation, was the day when the real decision was delivered."

Michalz' brow furrowed, "What do you mean the *real* decision? And the day before? What are you talking about, woman?"

She looked up into her husband's eyes, steeling herself for what was to come. "On the day before you were informed of the conclusion of the investigation the lead investigator arrived while you were out. He came with a dozen Guards. I knew it could mean only one thing. I asked the investigator directly and he conceded that, yes, the House was found to be at fault. He said they had found the deception in the administration of the foundry's finances and inspections, and that the House charter was going to be revoked."

"Alabast, what on Umitia are you talking about? We were cleared!"

"No, my wonderful husband, we were not."

Alabast stood and went to the window as Michalz looked at her in confusion.

"Michalz," she said with a quavering voice as she turned to face him, "I told the investigator there was one more piece of evidence that could clear our names, which had not been examined. I refused to divulge it to him, though. I told him it was so sensitive that I would only reveal it directly to the Manager."

"Kalabot? You spoke with Kalabot?"

She nodded, looking down at her fingers folded together in front of her. "I told the investigator to arrange an appointment for me. He did so, and told me Kalabot would see me right away. I changed and freshened myself, and then the investigator took me to the Palace himself, to await the results of the — interview."

She sobbed out loud, the tears falling down her cheeks freely. She put a hand to her forehead and took a great stuttering breath, trying to calm her nerves. Michalz rose from the bed and stepped to her, putting his arms around her and drawing her close to him. She didn't resist. She put her arms around him and lay her head on the shoulder, terrified it would be the last time she felt his embrace.

"What did you say to him?" Michalz asked, his mind confused, yet filled with fear.

Between sobs, she replied, "It's not what I *said* to him, my husband."

And then Michalz understood.

It wasn't her words that had saved them, for she knew nothing that could save them. She could only have offered Kalabot something, and it wasn't rocket science to figure out what it was.

Now Michalz sobbed with his wife, tightening his grip around her, holding her tight, pressing his head against hers.

Alabast heard her husband's voice; hoarse, strained, and quiet as he whispered one word: "No."

She nodded her head against his shoulder. "I'm so sorry, my husband, but I saw no other way. They had found us guilty and the entire House was to lose everything. So many thousands of us were to be cast into the street and ... and ..."

"Shhhh," he said quietly, "be still, my wife, be still."

They stood in their embrace for several minutes. Michalz needed time to process. His wife had committed an act that would, if revealed, mean her death. Yet she had managed to save the livelihood and life of thousands of people under the charter of the House of Tekin.

He thought of his wife, of her embrace, of her devotion, of her love, of her dedication. He had never doubted her fidelity, ever. There had never been cause to. Michalz had never dallied with anyone from the moment he first set eyes on Alabast, when she was a slender waif only fifteen seasons old. From that moment on, his eyes had only been for her. As her body had grown and filled out in true Falwasz form, his love had only deepened and grown. He knew as well, that from the moment they met, her eyes had only been for him.

Now, standing with his arms around her, he felt her grip tighten. She expressed her grief in sobs, and tears, and stuttering breath. He knew what she had done was not an act of defiance, not an act of outrage, not an act of revenge, and most definitely not an act of passion.

Michalz knew that what his wife had just revealed to him was merely an act of commerce.

It was a trade; it was an exchange. She had bartered her beautiful body for the future of the House of Tekin, and for all those under its charter. She had forfeited her dignity, her pride, and her self-respect to ensure that her family and the rest of the House continued to flourish and thrive. In the face of what future they *could* have come to, he could not bring himself to fault her for what she had done, for what she had …

As he stood with his wife, holding her and comforting her, his thoughts turned in another direction.

He did the math.

It added up.

His heart shattered.

The man's tears flowed in torrents, his sobs louder than hers, his grief greater than any he had ever felt.

He thought of how different, how oddly un-Falwasz his favoured daughter was.

"Sephy — she is not mine, is she?" he whispered.

Alabast's wails of grief exploded — loud and unchecked. As she nodded her head, she collapsed against her husband, her matronly weight dragging them both to their knees.

Finally catching enough breath to speak, Alabast pressed her lips against her husband's ear, "She is your daughter in so many, many ways, except for one."

The images rapidly flashed through Michalz' mind: he saw himself holding the newborn baby; he saw a two-year-old Sepherin sitting in his lap as she at briska cookies, getting crumbs all over his desk; he saw the five-year-old holding out a bouquet of wild flowers she had picked, and then suffering many ten-sleeps of rash because some of what she had collected were poisonous; he saw her at age ten, putting on a play that she and her brothers had written, producing it for a home full of guests, who were all enthralled and cheering for them by the time they were done; he saw the fourteen-year-old swimming in the warm waters of Lake Otoput, during a family vacation; he saw the graceful young woman of seventeen seasons, dressed in her first fancy ball gown for the annual clan celebrations; he saw the beautiful, proud, and fierce young woman, standing at the spaceport, as she knocked that Hobonol bastard on his ass.

Michalz knew in his heart, that no matter what truths had been revealed, Sephy had been, was, and always would be his daughter, in every sense of the word.

His daughter.

And he was going to be damned, if she was going to die at Kalabot's hand. And he was going to be doubly damned, if Kalabot was going to take his wife of forty-three seasons away from him with the ridiculous notification.

He held Alabast at arm's length and looked into her fearful eyes.

"My love," he began slowly, "every morning, when I wake beside you, I am grateful to the Holy One to do so. Every day, when I come home from the foundry, I can imagine coming home to no one other than you. When my heart beats, when I take a breath: I do so, much easier, because you are part of my life. What you did — was a transaction, it was a necessity. Without your — sacrifice — we would most likely not even be alive today. And you are correct: Sephy is my daughter, in every way that matters."

Alabast's breath was coming in gulps as she listened to him, she clutched at the front of his shirt. "Then, you forgive me, my husband?"

Michalz smiled as he cupped her face with both of his hands, "It is I that you should be forgiving, my wife. Were it not for the stupid, stupid actions which I took, to save only a few coins here and there, you would not have been placed in the position to make such a sacrifice. The shame is mine, not yours. It is you who must forgive me."

They stayed in the room for another ten minutes, composing themselves. They both washed their faces at the bathroom sink, and then went back down stairs. They had decided what they must do. They had decided they must trust the Cabal's discretion.

"My friends," Michalz addressed them. "We know why it is that Alabast has been selected for the Imperative."

Chapter 50

Kalabot had not slept well since he had spoken with Cobus, and since deciding that the Imperte, *his daughter*, had to die, and quickly. Such a grave decision weighed heavily, even on the cold-hearted Manager of Umitia. He knew the public perception of him was not favourable. Kalabot understood that the clans saw him as a heartless automaton without concern for them.

However, he knew it was the opposite which was true. Kalabot cared so much for Umitia and all Umites that he knew it was his duty, his obligation, to rule with a return to the iron glove of the old days. Otherwise the people of Umitia would risk turning into one of the blended, hodgepodge societies that were overtaken by greed, avarice, lawlessness, and immorality. Too many worlds had fallen into the same trap, with few of them extricating themselves back to a progressive and pure society which would evolve, rather than decay. It was not lost on him that the planet which Sepherin Tekin had been sent to, teetered on that point in its own development.

Of course, Kalabot understood that to rule so effectively within such rigid structure, meant that sometimes someone, *someone who was responsible*, had to go around the rules.

The selection of Imperites was a straightforward, yet complex process. All members of the Falwasz clan were tracked, throughout their lives. The process had a centuries' old algorithm which looked at schooling scores, personal interest, intelligence scores, hobbies, family associations, ratio of selection in a home, ratio of selection within a House, and then it would select the candidates most likely to succeed in the Imperative without unfairly burdening any single House. It was well known amongst the higher echelon Shovitics that fully 99% of Imperites lived to ripe old ages on their selected destination worlds, never having the chance to do what they were trained to do. That fact was not known to the clans Umitia. In fact, Umitians had no information on what became of the Imperites once they departed. For all intents and purposes, they were considered dead as soon as they departed. Hence the funeral ceremony for Imperites three days before their departure, a tradition honoured by all the Houses of the Falwasz clan.

The exception to the 1% rule was the planet known as Earth. On that Humanesh planet, almost 6% of all Imperites encountered the opportunity to complete their imperative. In all of recorded history since the beginning of the Imperite program, the only Earth placed Imperite that failed to complete the Imperative had been Tameht Tekin. Kalabot thought this astounding, since even the Earth-born Falwasz' own mother, Jakula Tekin, *had* completed the Imperative.

Kalabot had received a copy of the report that the Earther girl made to her authorities. In it, she said Tameht had been tricked by the Master of the ship he had been on, that he had intended on completing the Imperative However, if wishes were flowers, Umitia's desert would be one big garden. Kalabot, like all Shovitics, knew it was actions that spoke a person's true nature, not their professed intentions.

Kalabot was counting on Sepherin Tekin dying during the process of her apprehension. He knew that anger was high throughout the Imperite Guards regarding the death of two of their own at the hands of an Imperite. The mood had only worsened after learning that an Earther had critically injured a Guard during his pursuit of the witness to Sepherin's crimes.

The Watch Commander of the duty frigate, responding to the emergency extraction request, found the two Guards in a severe state. He had reported that Kevit Folir had a serious skull fracture, and was unsure if he was going to recover. This angered Kalabot, but his anger was tempered by the knowledge that the injuries meant Sepherin had eluded capture again. It both pleased him, and frustrated him. He was not happy at his own lack of equivocality on the matter.

The thought that had bothered him of late was that if Sepherin did indeed return to Umitia, then Alabast Tekin would risk her life to play the trump card which Kalabot could not afford to have played. He considered simply having Alabast executed, but such an order, even from him, would have caused problems amongst the Guards. The execution of Umitians was a rare, but occasional necessity to ensure societal stability. The execution of the mother of the Imperite proclaimed an oath-breaker would generate too many questions, especially if it came from his office, totalitarian or not. Umitia was a complex world.

That was the reason why, on the morning of the day that Kimla delivered the notice to Alabast, Kalabot went to the Imperite administration office. He knew the current batch of selections was being processed and his timing was crucial. As the Manager, he could get away with many things, but overtly tampering with the selection process was not one of them. Doing things that were not over, however, was something he was no stranger to in his pursuit of a progressive Umitia.

Kalabot found a Shovitic operator sitting at the terminal for the system that processed the data on the Falwasz. Kalabot ordered him to leave the office for a surprise inspection. The Guard thought nothing of it, such an inspection happened, rarely.

Shuffling through the stack of current notices that had been printed, Kalabot picked one at random, and then replaced it with the notification for Alabast Tekinson that he had already prepared. It took him only a few minutes to alter the computer records to show that she had been selected, instead of the young man who he had removed from the list. The system, thankfully, only recorded who was selected; it never recorded why the algorithm had selected them. When Kalabot was satisfied, he rose and opened the door. To the operator standing outside waiting patiently, Kalabot nodded once and said, "Your efforts are exemplary."

The day following Alabast's selection was a busy one. Word had spread like wildfire. The result of her selection had a surprising reaction. In an oppressive society that was masked by beauty and surface freedoms, the growing dissent with the Shovitic rule was churning beneath the façade. From shortly after the crack of dawn, representatives of many Houses from all of the clans (except the Ashvelyn clerics and the Shovitics) began arriving at the home of Themedit Teminson, head of the House of Tekin. They each expressed the outrage and dismay of their house at Alabast's selection. Then, surprisingly, they each pledged to support, assist, and defend the House of Tekin in any action it took to protest this selection. Each representative stressed the word: *defend*.

Those representatives all hung around the grounds of the manor as others arrived. Many brought food and drinks with them, using the opportunity to discuss matters both light and heavy with those from Houses they rarely got to see. The Tekinson's butler sent hastily scrawled notes to nearby Falwasz homes to borrow the services of servants to assist them in offering hospitality to all those who had gathered. Not a single home refused the request.

By the time Kimla arrived to follow up with Mater Tekin after her selection, arriving after the midday meal, there was quite a crowd. When the butler opened the door, Kimla stood with her back towards him, facing the crowd which had grown quiet. She held a pain-stick, concealed in her hand within the sleeve of her jacket. She had, as usual, come alone. She refused to give the gathered clansmen the satisfaction of calling for backup. She was, after all, an Imperite Guard.

"Yes?" asked the butler, not suppressing the hostility in his voice.

Kimla turned her head to look at him, holding his gaze for a moment to express her own hostility. "I will speak with Alabast Tekinson," she finally stated.

Alabast was close by and came to the door quickly.

"I have a need to speak with you, in private."

That was, indeed, a surprise. The Imperite Guards rarely asked for such an audience, especially with a selected Imperite. The butler made as though he was going to speak, but Alabast held up her hand.

"Join me in the parlour," Alabast said, stepping aside for the tall woman to enter. She excused the butler, asking him to gather the house staff in the kitchen until the guest departed. She didn't want any of the walls to have ears.

"Well, Kimla, what do you have to say to me?" she asked once the parlour door was closed.

"There is much … we are …" she paused, taking off her darkened glasses. Alabast could see now, from the wild gesticulations of her eyeworms, that Kimla was extremely agitated. "I am here to inform you that your training …" she trailed off with a sigh.

"Yes?" Alabast was growing tense. It was rare for training to commence so quickly, but this was what the notification had said. Usually the training did not commence for at least three or four ten-sleeps.

"The training coordinator is unable to find a placement for you in the class that starts in two sleeps' time. He has deferred your training to the next program."

"When will that be?" Alabast asked tightly. Kimla was being evasive, something she had never encountered before with her. For many seasons, this Shovitic woman had been responsible for the selected Imperites from the household, including Sepherin.

Kimla's eyeworms stopped moving and came to attention, sticking straight out towards Alabast. "I find it extremely odd that a Falwasz of your — age — is being selected as an Imperite. Do you not find this odd?"

Alabast didn't know what to say. Yes, it was damn odd. It was unheard of. Yet, she knew full well why she had been selected. Kalabot wanted to get her out of the way before Sepherin returned, so that she could not reveal any of the history which would cost them their lives.

"Yes, it is strange, isn't it. However, as a Falwasz, I serve at the pleasure of the Palace."

Kimla said nothing, she just nodded.

"Do you know when my deferment will be?" Alabast asked again.

Walking over to the window and peering out from behind the curtain at the crowd outside, Kimla spoke distractedly. "My section leader, who also finds this extremely odd, has decided to undertake a review of our training procedures and protocols. All are designed for the strength and reflexes of a much younger person. He is — concerned — that you should have the opportunity to receive the best possible training that you can tolerate. He wants to ensure your chances of success, should the opportunity arise for you to complete the Imperative."

Alabast said nothing. The words Kimla had spoken had given her a reprieve, a lengthy reprieve. Though not many people liked the Shovitics, the people knew that they simply operated under the edicts of the Manager. Unfortunately, the Shovitics were fiercely proud and loyal creatures, having sworn an oath of their own upon acceptance into the Imperite Guards. Still, what Kimla had told her, was another surprise in a ten-sleep of surprises.

Kimla finally turned from the window, continuing to speak in the sibilant manner of the Shovitics, "My section leader told me that once the proper reviews and procedures have been put in place, then he shall, of course, require you to complete a medical examination."

Alabast nodded.

"And a fitness test for entry into the Imperite program."

Alabast was beyond shocked, and her face showed it.

No Imperite had ever had to pass a fitness test. Their physical fitness was part of the selection algorithms. Then it dawned on her what Kimla was saying. She had just told Alabast that she would never have to enter the program; that she would never have to leave Umitia, regardless of what machinations the Manager had taken to put such suffering into play.

Alabast's look of shock turned into a contemplative smile. "I fear my days of sports and sparring are long behind me, Kimla, though I promise to give such examination and testing my fullest attention and efforts."

Kimla nodded once and put her darkened glasses on. "Our business here is concluded."

Alabast held her hand out towards the parlour door and led the way. As she opened it, waiting for Kimla to pass, the Shovitic stopped next to her. Without looking at Alabast, she adjusting her necktie and jacket while speaking to Alabast telepathically.

Sepherin has been apprehended. She is shortly on her way to Umitia.

Chapter 51

It had been a quiet evening at home for the women. While reading her book on the couch, Cassie stopped and looked up at Sepherin. Her roommate was standing in the archway to the living room, holding two cans of Diet Pepsi in her hands, a look of surprise and shock on her face. She was slowly bending forward at the waist, and bending at the knees.

"Stephy? What's wrong?"

The response was a long, intense, *"Owwwwwwwwwww!"* Sepherin's exclamation of pain at the sudden contraction was accompanied by her mind seeing the image of her mother hugging her too tightly.

"Oh, shit. *Lota!*" Cassie pushed her almost eight-month pregnant body up off the couch.

Sepherin looked up at her as she waddled over. Sepherin's voice was stressed *"Cas …"*

"I know, I know, sweetie. Don't worry, let's go sit down in the kitchen." Cassie then yelled, *"Lota! It's time!"*

As she led Sepherin to the kitchen to sit down, she heard Carlota coming up the stairs, on the double. She didn't knock, she just used her key to open the door. Stepping into the kitchen, glancing at both the women and seeing the look on Sepherin's face, Carlota's mother-hen instinct went into high gear.

"Oh, sweetie, you're going to be fine, just fine." Carlota stepped over to Sepherin and pulled her head against her chest. She could see Sepherin was nervous, and scared. "You have your bag all packed for the hospital, luv?"

"For a whole month now," Cassie chided.

Sepherin just looked at her, and finally burst into tears.

"Cassie, behave, look what you've done," Lota admonished gently.

Sepherin looked up at Carlota and tried to smile while the tears flowed, but was overtaken by another contraction.

Carlota's mouth dropped open. She looked at Cassie, "When was the last one?"

Cassie looked at the clock, "Three minutes ago." She was shocked as well.

"Owwwwwwwwwwww!" Again, her mind saw the image of her mother hugging her too tightly. The image would return with every contraction.

Cassie grimaced as Sepherin grabbed her hand and squeezed, hard.

As the contraction passed, she spoke quietly, "I want my mom." Then she held out her other hand and Carlota grabbed it, holding it tightly.

"You'll be okay, sweetie," Carlota murmured as she slowly stroked Sepherin's long brown hair. "Of course you want your mother, that's only natural. But you're mom isn't here, so you'll have to make do with Cassie and me. Now, where's your bag? I'll go get it."

"Bedroom closet, on the blanket box. The white one." Sepherin sniffed, and dabbed at her eyes with a tissue Cassie handed her. Carlota let go of Sepherin and darted up the narrow stairs at the back of the kitchen.

"You're going to be okay, you know that, right?" Cassie said earnestly.

Sepherin looked at the stairs to see Carlota was out of earshot, then whispered to Cassie, "I'm an alien with a baby in my belly, what if the doctors — what if there's — what if …"

338

"Shhh! None of that, now," Cassie smiled at her, "you're going to be just fine. You've told me lots of your people have come to Earth pregnant. Don't make something out of nothing, girl."

The room was silent, for too long.

Cassie and Sepherin looked up at the staircase to see Carlota standing on the third step, the overnight bag in her hand, and a shocked look on her face.

Femi drove down Parliament Street slowly, the front windows down, both Imperite Guards ignoring the cold.

"There," Corvu pointed, "that place. *Jet Fuel Coffee Shop.* It's fitting."

Femi nodded, smiling at the name of the establishment. He pulled the black sedan over to the side of the road, stopping in front of some yellow-green and aubergine painted residences. As they got out of the car, Femi looked up at them, crinkling his nose, and slowly shaking his head. *Whoever coloured those places should be ...*

He had to move quickly as a passing car blatted its horn, almost clipping him.

Corvu followed behind him and crossed the street carefully; enough Guards had been injured lately. He used his communicator to let Kippa's team and Dorsee's team know where they were. The two teams started heading their way to regroup and plan the next day's patrols. The three teams had been focussing in the Cabbagetown area of the city because they had been catching so many traces of Falwasz scent over the last couple of months. It wasn't every day, but it was enough that they knew the Imperite was living in the area, or visiting the area. They

339

staggered their shifts so that at least one of the teams was always out and searching.

Carlota stared at the two women from the stairs, pursing her lips. When she had still been in the Navy, and still been Karl, Carlota had seen enough odd things to know that there were more things in heaven and Earth, than are dreamt of.

Everyone was silent, until Sepherin leaned forward, one hand on the table, one hand holding Cassie's in a death grip again, moaning with another contraction.

Wincing from the pain, Cassie looked up at Carlota, worried at what her reaction was going to be. "Do you think we're crazy?" she asked.

"No."

"Are you mad?"

"We'll talk about it later. We need to focus on Stephy right now." Carlota's voice was sounding gruff, with an edge.

Cassie remained silent. With the contraction passing and able to extract her hand from Sepherin's grip, she went to get their winter coats.

The contraction finally passed, and Sepherin looked up at Carlota. "You don't seem surprised."

Carlota looked into Sepherin's eyes, and finally gave a brief smile. "For many years now, people have looked at me, judged me, and called me crazy — and worse things. Yet from the day you two girls moved in here, you have accepted me, and treated me with respect. You've given me your trust, and your friendship. So I'll ask you: which is crazier, a woman born in a man's body, or a woman from another planet?"

Sepherin just looked at her, unsure of what to say.

Carlotta leaned forward and kissed Sepherin on the forehead. "Come on, luv. We have to ..."

Carlota stood straight up, a look of surprise on her face, her mouth going round as she sucked in a deep breath of air.

"What is it?" Sepherin asked, anxious.

The after-image was still in Carlota's mind. *She had seen a flash of Sepherin, standing in some kind of airport terminal, hugging both of her parents. With the image came the overpowering feeling of a fierce, consuming love.*

Carlota told Sepherin.

"That was the baby. It's — communicative."

"You're a telepath?"

"No," Sepherin shook her head, "my people are not. Only the Shovitics, the people chasing us. I have no idea why the baby can do this. I'm guessing human babies don't do it, either?"

"Not that I've heard of, luv."

Cassie returned with the jackets and helped Sepherin put hers on. She looked at their friend and landlady, "We good, Lota?"

"We're good. Can you help Stephy down the stairs while I go bring the car to the front?"

Five minutes and two more contractions later, the women were in the car and Carlota headed down the short dogleg of Aberdeen Avenue towards Parliament Street. As soon as the car started moving, Stephy wretched, but didn't puke.

"Roll the window down, hurry, I think I'm going to be sick."

Cassie reached over her friend and pressed on the button, lowering the back window all the way. It was cold, but it wasn't as cold as it usually got at this time of year. Sepherin sucked in a few breaths of fresh air. Then her body stiffened, her face screwed up with the pain, and she screamed with another big contraction.

Stepping out on the sidewalk, sipping his Americano, Corvu noticed Femi looked disappointed. "Is the coffee not good?" he asked in his sibilant, native dialect.

Femi looked up at the decorative rocket ship on the front of the premise. "I was expecting something more interesting inside."

Corvu turned back to the busy street. He saw a sedan parked behind theirs, and another one just passing them, headed northbound. The other two teams had just arrived. He realized they should have just waited inside, regardless of the stench of the humans packed so tightly in the establishment.

Both Guards felt the hair on the nape of their neck stand up. They both sniffed the air, inhaling deeply through their sensitive noses.

They both smelled Falwasz, and it wasn't just a trace. Corvu saw Dorsee and Polu sniffing the air as well.

Then they heard a woman scream, loudly. Corvu whipped his head to the left. Only thirty feet away, he saw a red car emerging from a small side street. It was turning south, away from them. The rear-door window of the car was down. The oath-breaker, Sepherin Tekin, was sitting there in full view and she was screaming in agony.

They both dropped their Styrofoam cups and ran across the street to their car, traffic screeching to a halt from both directions. Corvu saw Dorsee and Polu, who had been coming towards them, rushing back to their sedan. He heard a screech of tires a little ways north of them, and figured it was Kippa and Garun turning around.

As they jumped into the sedan, Corvu looked up and saw the little black women looking right at him from the back window of the red car. Femi started the car and pulled out into traffic, his big American steel bumper tore the front fender of a passing Honda Civic as he did so.

Corvu lifted his communicator, but already heard Polu calling the east end team and the west end team.

"Faster, Carlota, faster! It's them! It's them!"

"What? Who?"

"The men chasing us, they're right behind us, they were parked up the street!"

Carlota looked up in the review mirror and saw the big, square headlights of a car pulling out on the road, smashing into a small compact, and not stopping. *Oh, mercy, just what we need right now.*

She stepped on the accelerator and kept an eye on the rear-view mirror. "What will happen if they follow us to the hospital?"

The contraction had passed, and Sepherin was panting. "If you stop the car, for any reason, they can have it transported aboard their ship."

"What? If I stop? Even at a light?"

"Yes," she grunted. "Oh no, *here it comes again* ... don't stop Lota, please, don't stop for anything ... *owwwwwwwwwww!*"

Cassie was freaking out. She was almost hyperventilating, looking from Sepherin to the car behind them. "Don't go to the hospital Lota, *lose them!*"

"If I slow down for a corner, can they beam us up?"

343

"NO!" Sepherin screamed through gritted teeth, *"Owww, it hurts, it hurts so much!"* The contraction started to pass. "Anything they TransMat retains its kinetic energy."

"Gotcha," Carlota said. "So if they transport us when we're doing sixty, we appear in their spaceship doing sixty, right?"

Sepherin just nodded, gritting her teeth as another contraction came over her.

"Lota, she's having another contraction. We don't have much time."

Carlota glanced over her shoulder at them, and then focussed on the road again. "How fast do your people give birth?"

"Not this fast!" Sepherin almost screamed through the pain of the contraction. *"Something's wrong!"*

"No," Cassie whimpered. She closed her eyes and began praying, feeling Sepherin crushing grip on her hand. She flung her other arm out to brace herself as Carlota made a left turn, her foot barely touching the brake pedal

"Oh, grosse," Sepherin said through the pain. Her hand was between her legs and came up wet. Her water had broken.

"I know it's moving! Just tag it and take it when it stops!"

The Watch Commander's voice came over the air, without the level of stress Corvu had. "We have tagged it, but we keep losing lock. We need line of sight for a moving object, and it has to be moving slowly. We're moving the frigate now, but it will be at least two minutes for us to get into position ... there, it just changed direction again and we lost the lock. Do what you can to force them to a more open area. 802, out."

"Call the others, if we can herd it down to the highway, then we can box it in and stop it, and then they can take it."

By the time the next contraction came, Carlota's tires screeched almost as loud as the woman in labour, taking another left-hand turn onto Front Street. She had doubled back, heading west instead of east, then turned south, and was heading east again. As she turned, she saw the headlights of two sedans turning south only a block behind her. Then behind her on Front Street, a block away, she saw a police car light her up and she heard the distant siren.

"Shit, girls, it's the fuzz."

"Don't stop, please. They'll kill her." Cassie said, quietly, seeming to be coming to terms with the fate of the words.

Carlota was headed back towards Parliament Street. She wanted to get to the highway and take it over to University Avenue, where she could quickly get to the hospital.

She accelerated, fishtailing the car, but kept control of it. Then she had a brilliant idea. If the cops were coming after her, why not go right to them?

Carlota said over her shoulder, "There's a police station up ahead, let's go there, it's only two blocks away."

"NO!" both Sepherin and Cassie screamed.

"Why not?"

"BECAUSE!" they both screamed.

"Lota, you have to find someplace for us to hide, *now*! Her contractions are less than a minute apart." Cassie's face was covered with tears as well; she was back in a full-blown panic.

Carlota just grunted, moving the car into the right-hand lane. She only had one option that she could think of. She looked in her rear-view mirror and saw the first black car turning the corner. It plowed right into the back side of the police car, spinning both of them in the intersection. The second sedan came right through the wreckage, taking the corner hard, stopping only a moment as the Guards from the first car, unhurt, ran to join them.

It was just enough to give her a chance. She jerked the wheel to the right and headed onto the Front Street extension, where it diverged from the curve onto Eastern Avenue. The condominium construction site loomed ahead of them. The six towers, in various stages of construction, would give them lots of places to hide. She knew that if she got on the highway, she'd be too exposed and they might try to ram her, to stop her. With the amount of traffic still on the roads, this was the only option. It was only blind luck that had allowed her to keep moving without stopping, without having an accident.

She begged God silently for there to be no oncoming traffic, and pressed the accelerator. It was just after 10 p.m., and the construction site would be empty. She rocketed across Cherry Street without hitting any cars or pedestrians. Her car smashed through the tall construction gate, with the sound of metal on metal. She slammed on the brakes while turning the wheel, causing the car to skid sideways on the gravel. Then Carlota stomped on the accelerator and sped down the first construction road inside the compound.

Femi and Corvu were breathing heavily in the backseat. Femi had banged his head hard enough in the collision to draw some blood, but he was more pissed off than in pain. Corvu considered the ramifications of having the car TransMat from the accident scene, with the cops and onlookers standing right there. He knew, though, it was a stupid thought. They had risked this once already when Salo and Kevit's car was TransMat from the intersection outside of the place they were attacked. There was nothing in the car that he could think of that would be a problem. It was registered to the U.S. Air Force, but government agents, Earther agents, would quickly make any questions go away.

As they came around the curve in the road, Dorsee slowed down the car. He had been distracted when Carlota took the Front Street extension, and didn't see where she had driven. Now, looking down the road ahead of them, he couldn't see the car anymore.

Then he saw the east end team, Fitid and Senji, blowing southbound through the intersection up ahead. He sped up and took the corner hard, after only a cursory glance to see if any traffic was coming. As they rounded the corner, the tail lights of Fitid's car were disappearing to the left, into a construction site.

Dorsee followed them as he heard Dorsee's partner, Polu, calling the other two teams over the communicator.

It was a massive construction site. There were eight condominium towers in various stages of construction. In addition to the towers, the place was a complicated warren of trailers, commercial spaces under construction, parking structures, building equipment, and enclosed materials yards.

Carlota made a series of quick turns, with Sepherin screaming through another contraction. The car was on rough ground and had to slow down.

"Faster," Sepherin panted through the scream.

Carlota was getting to the end of her rope. She had to get them out of the car. A condo structure loomed in front of her which only had the first ten floors poured. There was plywood hoarding around the ground level of it, obviously to keep people out. She gunned the engine and headed for a part of it that didn't look too strong.

The car exploded through the barrier with a spray of wood and all three women screaming. The car came to a stop inside the building. Carlota got out of the car and tried to open Sepherin's door, but it wouldn't budge. The side of the car was dented in. As she scrambled around to the other side, Cassie had her shoulder on the other door and was pushing. It was moving, but only barely.

Sepherin screamed again, *"The baby's coming!"*

Carlota grabbed Cassie's door and with a powerful pull, got it open. Cassie tumbled out; Carlota reached inside, grabbed Sepherin's hand and pulled, yanking her out of the car with no regard for her condition or screaming. Picking her up in her arms, Carlota carried Sepherin deeper into the building with Cassie right behind them.

There was a flash of dim blue light.

Carlota and Cassie turned to see that the car was no longer sitting there.

They ran. When they reached the other side of the construction site for this building, they saw headlights approaching. They ducked down behind a stack of lumber. Carlota looked at Sepherin as her face was screwing up for another scream. She reached up with one hand and pressed it hard over her mouth, letting Sepherin scream into her palm, muffling the sound.

The car moved past the building, slowly.

When it was out of sight, and Sepherin's contraction passed, Carlota picked Sepherin up again and they dashed across the rough road into another building. There was a small gap in the hoarding. Hoisting her pregnant charge higher in her arms, Carlota lashed out with her foot and made the opening big enough for them to get through.

The inside of this building was a lot further along in construction. They moved past stacks of supplies, equipment, and through a few half-finished rooms and corridors.

Sepherin started flailing her arms, "Holy One! Holy One! Please! Not yet … *owwwwwwwwww!*"

The four Guards were swivelling their heads, looking at everything they could, as the car moved slowly along the uneven gravel roads.

Corvu raised his communicator, "Where is the vehicle?"

The communications officer replied they had lost the tracking of it in the cement structures, but that the Watch Commander was overseeing the search for it.

No sooner had that been said, the duty frigate called them again.

They had found the car and had TransMat it aboard. A few moments later the Watch Commander informed them it was empty.

"Where did you take it from?" Corvu asked.

"The building ahead of you, on the left."

Dorsee gunned the engine.

They were in a big room filled with boxes and piles of cinder blocks. There was a single light bulb weakly illuminating the room.

"Here! Over here!" Cassie said. She was grabbing some tarpaulins bundled up on the floor to spread them out. As she yanked on the tarps, she was greeted with three teenagers yelling in surprise, pushing away from her and their makeshift sleeping bags.

Cassie only hesitated with surprise for a moment, then she finished spreading them out and Carlota set Sepherin down.

"Dude! She's pregnant!" one of the boys exclaimed to his friends.

"What did you bring her here for?" the young girl asked, "Why aren't you at a hospital?"

They all shut up and took a step back when they saw the stocky older woman pick up a pipe and go stand by the entrance to the makeshift room, obviously waiting for someone to come through the door.

The younger boy nudged the older one, thrusting his chin towards Carlota and whispered, "Dude. She's a dude."

"No way," his friend looked closer at Carlota.

"Way!"

Carlota looked at the three of them and held a single finger up to her lips, shushing them silently, then winked at them.

Sepherin screamed in pain again as she shed her jacket, and reached up under her housecoat to pull off her underwear. Cassie helped her.

"What do we do?" Cassie asked, quietly, breathlessly. "I don't know shit about giving birth except going to the hospital and panting."

Cassie looked up at the three street kids, "Help us, please."

They looked at each other, dumbly. Finally, the oldest boy, about fifteen years old, came over and knelt down by Sepherin. "What do you want me to do?"

"Here, help me get on my knees," Sepherin panted, holding out her hand, the contraction passing, but another one looming. "The baby's coming, it's coming now."

"Are you sure?" Cassie asked, "Shouldn't you be on your back?"

"I've watched my mother give birth three times, all at home, I know what to do. Just …" she grunted with a spasm of pain, pleading, "… just don't leave me alone."

As the boy helped Sepherin get onto her hands and knees, he looked over at his friends, no more than eleven or twelve years old. "Come on, help us."

The boy and girl looked at each other and bolted, running out the door past Carlota.

"Jerks," he muttered, turning back to the woman in labour.

"What's your name?" Cassie asked the boy.

"Jake."

"Jake, is there any water here?"

Sepherin screamed again, her legs started to straighten, lifting her body slightly.

"Yeah, but nothing to boil it." The kid sounded like he was in shock, but at least he wasn't freaking out.

"We just need it to clean up the baby when it's born. Can you get some?"

"Yeah, be right back," he stood up, "I promise." Then he went deeper into the room, disappearing through a doorway they hadn't noticed.

351

Polu pointed at the fence, "There, that is where the car was taken."

Dorsee stopped the car and all four Imperite Guards got out. They all drew their weapons and moved into the building as they heard the Imperite screaming in the distance. Two went left, two went right. She could be anywhere in the stacks of equipment and building materials.

They were moving slowly, methodically. She was obviously in the throes of giving birth, or imminently ready to do so. She wouldn't be moving anywhere fast.

Femi grabbed Corvu's arm, and pointed to the far side of the structure they were in when Sepherin screamed again. "That way."

As they moved closer to the far side of the building, they saw Dorsee and Polu heading in the same direction. All four of them stopped and raised their guns as they saw two kids explode through the fence from the taller building across the road. The kids were running like the Devil himself was on their heels.

As soon as the small humans were out of sight, the four Guards advanced on the next building, weapons drawn.

They moved into the structure and waited. They heard the Imperite scream again, this time much closer.

Corvu led the move forward again, moving through rooms of supplies and equipment, connected by hallways which would someday be, ironically, a medical centre.

The four of them moved cautiously. Movement caught Polu's attention and he rushed forward, scrambling over a pallet of floor levelling compound. The others looked where he was headed.

They all saw the dark- haired kid running from him, dropping a half-full water cooler bottle.

Polu had the lead, only a few feet behind him, but then he slipped on a box of nails. The kid had knocked it over onto the floor as he went by the makeshift bench it had been stacked on.

They all heard another scream from the Imperite, it was coming from the room where the boy dashed into.

Jake burst into the room through the door he had departed from.

"There's men here! They have guns!" he said, panting with the adrenalin pumping through his system, pointing at the door he just came through.

Carlota moved quickly, taking up the same position beside the opening. "How many?" she asked quietly.

"I saw four."

They all heard two car doors closing in the distance.

"Make it six," Carlotta muttered.

Jake moved away from the door.

"Did you get the water?" Cassie asked, beyond caring about being quiet.

His face was flushed, his breathing rapid, his hands were shaking. "I dropped it when they started chasing me. *They have guns.*"

They all heard the running in the long corridor outside the door.

Sepherin screamed again.

There was a wet smashing sound as Carlota grunted and swung the pipe. It hit Polu right in the middle of the face, clotheslining his body, flipping the Shovitic in the air. Unfortunately for Polu, he landed hard enough on his head to break his neck.

There was a gunshot, loud and echoing in the relatively small space.

Cassie screamed with fear.

On her hands and knees, Sepherin was screaming for another reason, her legs extending, her body arching up in the air. "IT'S COMING!"

Cassie turned away from the door, she got close to Sepherin and held her hands out, her lips moving in silent prayer.

Jake rushed over to her, taking off his jacket, and taking off his T-shirt. "Here, for the baby." Then he picked up a piece of wood and ran to join Carlota.

He didn't make it.

There was another gunshot.

Jake fell to the floor in a bloody heap. He was dead.

Carlota screamed in rage.

A gun appeared around the corner, turning to aim right at her. She grabbed the arm and smashed it against the corner of the door frame. She heard the sickening crack of the bone, the hand reflexively letting go of the weapon. Carlota took it, stepped into the open door and fired twice into Corvu's chest, killing him instantly.

There was another roar of a different gun.

Carlota's head rocketed back with a small spray of blood. The bullet had cut a deep gash in her cheek and her ear. She staggered out of the way and put her back to the wall. As she did so, an Imperite Guard appeared in the original door they had come through across the room. Carlota raised her gun and fired. She missed, but it caused him to back away from the opening.

This time she sensed, rather than heard, the movement beside her. She put the gun up, pointing at the door as she heard Cassie screaming, "Push! Push! I can see it!"

The two Guards rushed through the door backwards, one pointing their gun to each side. Dorsee was pointing the gun in Carlota's direction, but Carlota had crept back from the opening slowly so the gun wasn't pointed at the right spot.

There was another mighty scream from Sepherin.

Carlota got her gun on target first. Dorsee's head disappeared.

"OH GOD, NO!" Cassie screamed.

Carlota rushed forward, afraid to fire as the girls were behind the other man in black. She charged Femi, growling loudly in a surprisingly masculine voice. Femi still hadn't had enough time to get his gun around. The retired Navy Petty Officer hit him high.

Outweighed by a hundred pounds, Femi went flying through the air, but had enough wits about him not to wind up with the Humanesh on top of him. Unfortunately his gun went flying out of his hand. As he regained his feet, he saw Fitid and Senji rushing through the other door, with Kippa and Garun coming in behind them.

"IT HAS NO EYES!" Cassie screamed, and then so did Sepherin.

Time stopped, it seemed.

Carlota got to her knees and then stood up. She looked at the men and the woman who had been pursuing them. They were all staring at Sepherin and Cassie.

They were all walking slowly towards her.

They had all lowered their guns.

The formed a semi-circle around the women.

Carlota didn't know what to do. She had lost the gun she had taken from the Guard she killed. She stood there wondering what Cassie meant by saying the child had no eyes.

She moved closer to them as well.

Sepherin had collapsed onto her hip after the baby came out, she was panting, she was exhausted, and she was terrified.

She rolled over slowly, being careful not to kick Cassie or the baby as she did so.

She saw Cassie, kneeling, holding the baby in the dirty T-shirt the dead kid had given her. *What did he say his name was?*

She pushed herself up on her arms, and then tried to get Cassie's attention. Cassie wasn't looking at her; she was looking at the baby.

"Show me," Sepherin said breathlessly.

Cassie finally looked up. She had wrapped the baby in the T-shirt, but it wasn't warm enough. She looked around and saw the jacket Jake had taken off. Looking up at one of the aliens standing around her, Cassie pointed to the jacket. Surprisingly, the guard fetched it for her. They were all staring at the baby.

Wrapping the jacket around the newborn, she finally handed it to Sepherin.

Sepherin felt Carlota kneel behind her and helped to prop her up.

Holding the baby close, wrapped haphazardly in the dirty, but warm, jacket, Sepherin moved the T-shirt to look at the baby's face. She saw that the baby didn't have any eyelids.

It had eyeworms.

The eyeworms were closed until she pulled the baby closer. Then the eyeworms slowly unfolded outwards, and in the dim light of the one light bulb in the room, Sepherin saw the ocular stump deep in the mostly empty eye sockets.

Her breath came in a gasp. She didn't understand. Sepherin looked around in bewilderment. She had no words. The baby she had carried inside her had the eyes and facial structure of a Shovitic child. The high forehead, the long nose, the pointed jaw, even the skin looked far paler than Falwasz skin. It was even paler than Sepherin's own skin.

At least it explained how the baby communicated with her; how it had disabled the Guards she had wound up killing.

One of the Imperite Guards knelt down on one knee, looking closely at the child. He looked up at the Imperite. "The father ..." Fitid asked, "... is Shovitic?"

Sepherin shook her head, "No, he's — Hobonol."

Carlota had been silent until then. With her hands on Sepherin's shoulders she quietly spoke, "What's wrong with the child's eyes? Why are they like that?"

Carlota looked up as Fitid removed his sunglasses.

Carlota pressed her lips together and said nothing more.

Fitid stood and stepped back, gathering in a small group with the other Guards. They began a hurried telepathic conversation.

I believe her, Senji began, *in what she says about the father being Hobonol.*

The child is from a Shovitic, that is as plain as day. It cannot be a Falwasz and Hobonol union, Femi was adamant in his telepathic tone.

I say we kill them all, Garun stated simply.

Our orders were to return the oath-breaker and the witness, and I for one … Kippa turned to look at the baby again, *… will not bear the curse of killing a child.*

Why? The ever-practical Garun folded his arms. *How many more of us have to die? We've lost Taffi, Minino, Corvu and Polu. There's a good chance Kevit won't survive. All because of this oath-breaker and her host. I say we end all of them and just take back the bodies. We can tell the Manager it was an unfortunate outcome of the apprehension.*

No, Senji said, the only woman in the group of Shovitics. *Many season ago, when this one was born,* she gestured to the Imperite, *my eldest brother was given an assignment to watch the mother of the Imperite before she gave birth. He was then ordered to acquire blood samples. He told me because he had a bad feeling about why Kalabot had him do this.*

They all knew that Senji's brother had been executed by Kalabot, but no one ever knew why — and no one ever dared ask.

This … she continued, pausing to find the words, *… situation, is one which could have significant consequences.* She finished with a loaded statement, to say the least.

Femi was looking at Sepherin. She was holding the child to her exposed breast, getting it to suckle.

Have any of you considered that this is the child of the prophecy? He asked them.

They looked at him with a stunned expression on their faces. Then they all turned to look at the child again.

Sepherin was looking at the Imperite Guards, adjusting the jacket the baby was in, and trying to keep him from their view. Carlota had helped her check: the infant was a boy. The look on Sepherin's face was one of defiance. She had accepted her fate. She was captured. Her only concern at this moment was to keep her son alive, regardless of what he looked like. She had no comprehension as to why he looked like a Shovitic, but such a question was something that could be addressed after he was safe.

Carlota still knelt behind her, holding Sepherin upright. Cassie was sitting cross-legged beside her. The three of them were silent, listening to the baby suckle as they waited for fate to make a decision.

Cassie was over her initial shock. She had been living with an alien, on the run from more aliens, and the most important person in their life was a woman in a man's body. She figured that the way the child looked was just par for the course.

Cassie followed Sepherin's gaze, looking up at the Men (and Woman) in Black staring at them. "What do you think they're going to do?" she asked quietly.

"I think they're deciding whether they're going to take me back home, or if they're just going to kill me."

"You mean *kill us*," Cassie added with a resigned whisper.

The prophecy of Alita Kiut? Senji asked. *Are you serious?*

I believe he may be on to something, Kippa thought-spoke to them.

The nonsense of that prophecy is thousands of years old, Garun managed to convey his derisive tone with this telepathy.

Femi repeated the prophecy from memory, *The Shovitic hybrid shall raise the six clans, and Umitia shall forever change. Once again, the Shovitics will find a new home. For the good of all that is dear, do so with gladness, dignity, and sanctity for the hybrid's life.*

Garun grunted with impatience, *I don't believe it. I mean … it can't be from an oath-breaker, can it?*

Perhaps we should seek guidance from the Manager, Senji turned back to them.

Garun shook his head, *We already know what he wants us to do.*

There was a dim flash of blue light in the open space by the rear door in the room. They looked up to see the Watch Commander from the frigate, with four more Imperite Guards, all armed with weapons.

The older Shovitic looked around at the bodies on the floor, at the Imperite Guards, and then at the Humanesh huddled together.

"You have captured the oath-breaker and the witness." It was a statement, not a question.

"I am no *oath-breaker,*" Sepherin spat at the Commander, her face darkening with anger.

He stepped over to the women on the tarpaulin. Those who came with him, followed closely. "How many Guards have you killed, Imperite? It is clear that you …"

She cut him off, "I claim the Third Law for my actions."

The Commander hesitated. He removed his darkened glasses and they saw his eyeworms twitching in indecision. Finally he replied, "No, the Third Law does not apply. The Guards were attempting the honourable justice prescribed in the Oath. You have in fact, violated the Third Law, Tekin."

"And your Guards were trying to kill him for something that was out of his control, they …"

"SILENCE!" the Commander waved his hand in the air, impatience in his voice. "The matter will be decided by the Manger when you appear before the Tribunal of the Guards." He turned to those behind him, "Are we ready to TransMat the oath-breaker and witness to the ship?"

Yes, Sir, we are. But there is a complication. Senji, the woman, responded.

And what would that be? The Watch Commander responded telepathically.

The senior Guard followed Senji's gaze at the Imperite and at the baby suckling at her breast.

Then he looked closer.

Then he knelt down and took a good look at the baby's face. The baby's eyesworms opened so the iris on the end of the ocular stump could look right at him.

The Watch Commander stood up rapidly. He stared at the woman and child. Finally, turning to the Guards, he asked, *Do you have an explanation for this?*

Senji and Femi both shook their heads.

The Watch Commander looked back down at the woman and child, thinking to himself, *A Shovitic hybrid. Could the prophecy true?*

Sepherin pulled the baby off her breast and handed him to Cassie. Her face screwed up with pain and she started moaning loudly.

"What's happening? What's wrong?" Fitid asked, kneeling down again.

One of the Guards who had come down with the Watch Commander stepped forward, holstering his weapon. He was also a medic. "She must pass the placenta." He looked at Sepherin, "I must cut the umbilical cord before you do so."

Ten minutes later, umbilical cut and placenta passed, the new mother and infant could be moved. During that process the Watch Commander had returned to the ship, with three of the four that had accompanied him. He had Corvu and Polu's corpses TransMat on board.

Sepherin waited, wanting to cry, wanting to scream, but too exhausted to do either. Carlota held her, and Cassie cried openly, but quietly. The baby was sleeping peacefully, wrapped tightly in the T-shirt and jacket, held tightly to his mother's chest.

One of the Imperite Guards motioned for them to stand.

Carlota helped Sepherin to her feet, but Cassie remained on the floor, just staring straight ahead.

Fitid stepped over to her, "Stand, human."

"Go to hell."

Fitid reached down and grabbed Cassie's arm, forcing her up off the ground.

She turned on him and slapped him across the face. He was so shocked at the little one's vehemence, he just looked at her. Then she slapped him again, and then she started pummeling his chest with her fists. Grabbing both of her hands, he quickly spun her around and pulled her back against him.

Carlota moved fast, but Fitid was ready for her. He let go of Cassie with one hand and landed a punch right in the middle of Carlota's face. But Carlota was a lot tougher than she looked. She kept right on moving, reaching out and grabbing Fitid by the throat.

Before she had a chance to do any serious injury to him, however, Senji and Kippa had her by the arms, pulling her backwards. Carlota's feet tangled together and she went down hard. Looking up from the floor, she heard Sepherin scream "NO!" as the two Guards pulled their handguns, both pointing them at Carlota's head.

They did not pull the triggers.

Carlota took a breath — a million years later she took another breath — another million years later, it seemed, she took another breath. They were still pointing the guns at her, but seemed to be having another one of their telepathic conversations.

"Please, no. Enough have died," Sepherin said, looking over at the young boy whose name she still couldn't remember.

Kippa kept his gun pointed at Carlota as Senji put hers away. Senji looked at Sepherin and spoke out loud, "This Earther is not involved in this matter, but she knows too much."

"Then erase her memory," Sepherin said, an edge to her voice, then looked down at Cassie. "Erase hers too."

Senji looked at Cassie then back at Sepherin, "No, she is the witness. We need her testimony, given the volatile response your trial and execution could generate."

"Me?" Cassie said, looking at the female Imperite Guard, "I don't remember anything. I was drinking that night. I made it all up." She struggled against Fitid, and then stomped on his foot. He let her go, but stayed within arm's reach of her.

"Then just erase hers," Sepherin tossed her head towards Carlota. Then she looked down at Carlota, her eyes filling with tears at the surprise of how much she truly loved and cared for the older woman.

She watched as the Imperite Guards had another hurried telepathic conversation. Finally, Senji turned back to look at Sepherin as she raised her communicator.

The three Humanesh and the baby felt a tingling in the base of their spine.

Then there was a dim flash of blue light.

Chapter 52

With the oath-breaker on board, the duty frigate was under instructions to depart immediately for Umitia. Immediately, in terms of interstellar travel, is relative. For a journey of seven ten-sleeps, only seven because they didn't have to make any stops on the way, they needed to provision first. The Watch Commander, the ship's captain, left the executive officer in charge of those arrangements.

All that the XO had to do was place the order through the 88th Air Base Wing at Wright-Patterson AFB, and then wait for one of the five Imperite Guard's patrol craft assigned to Earth to deliver the supplies to the frigate. Total time for this would be about two hours.

Unfortunately, being in such a hurry, a live internet feed from the International Space Station happened to catch the silver disk, the patrol craft, departing Earth's atmosphere at considerable speed. Before the patrol craft even docked with the duty frigate, videos of this were appearing on YouTube. The conspiracy guys had a heyday of commenting, analyzing, blogging, and doomsaying.

Leaving orbit with such short notice was going to affect the Imperite Guards' operations on the planet. Fortunately, Didic Valeni, the Watch Commander had time to arrange a temporary solution to their absence. Frigate 734 was on the way to a nearby (again, relatively speaking) star system. It was rerouted to Earth, but was nine sleeps away. The Watch Commander made an executive decision, not wanting to leave the remaining teams on Earth without support for so long. He contacted the Eben at their base on Mars and got them to agree to dispatch one of their battle cruisers to high Earth orbit to fulfill the frigate's role until the replacement arrived. Their TransMat was much better than the Umite's anyways, it didn't have the electrical compression problem and thus no flash of blue light associated with the process.

After his ship's arrangements had been made, Valeni lifted the ERB handset once more. Pressing the three- digit code, the device connected to the handset in Kalabot's office. The internal workings of the equipment routinely and reliably, established a microns wide stable wormhole between the communications stations.

The device was opened on the other end, but Valeni heard nothing.

"Sir, I am reporting the capture of the Imperite oath-breaker."

Silence.

"Two Guards were killed in the apprehension."

This time he heard a deep sigh of displeasure, but nothing more.

"I also have to inform you that after many ten-sleeps, Kevit has finally succumbed to his injuries."

The connection was broken.

The Watch Commander hung up the handset and turned to leave his office.

Kalabot was standing in front of him.

Valeni was startled, but didn't show it. This wasn't the first time he had seen the old man appear out of thin air.

"Take me to the Imperite."

The younger Shovitic was happy to do so. If the Manager killed her here, there would be no need for the unplanned return to Umitia. *But,* he asked himself, *what if the child was the one spoken of?* The fate that may befall the child in the Manager's legendary wrath made Valeni uneasy. He led Kalabot through the corridors and down two decks to the medical area of the ship. He brought the leader of the Imperite Guards, and all of Umitia, into the room where the initial examination of the Imperite and the mystery from her womb were being performed.

The senior medic looked up from his computer terminal as the Watch Commander entered the examination room without announcing his intention to do so. Seeing who was with him, the medic stood with his surprise evident on his face.

The Imperite sat in a chair, holding the infant who was wrapped in a clean pillow case. She looked up at the Watch Commander, then saw Kalabot step around him. She clutched the child tightly and tried to push the chair back with her feet, but the chair was already against the wall. She recognized her fear; then feeling her heart pounding in her chest, she recognized her anger — and savoured it. She kept her eyes locked on the old man.

"You are finished?" Valeni asked.

Nodding, the medic said, "Yes, both are healthy. The Imperite requires some food, liquids, and rest. The child appears to be healthy, but there are odd readings in its bloodwork. I'm not sure," he paused, looking at Sepherin and the child, "if this might be because of the nature of the child's biology. However, I see nothing to concern me for its health."

"Transmit the bloodwork to my office, and then delete the records from your system," Kalabot said to the medic.

The Shovitic hesitated only a moment, looking from Kalabot to the Watch Commander, "As you desire, Sir."

Taking a few steps forward, Kalabot bent at the waist and looked closely at the sleeping child. He stood there for a long time, looking first at the child's face, then at Sepherin's face, then back to the child. Finally he turned and walked out of the room.

Find out who the father is, Kalabot said telepathically as he departed.

Didic Valeni turned to Sepherin, "Who is the father of the child?"

She looked up at him, angry, but tired, "He's from Umitia." She had visibly relaxed once Kalabot left the room. But the question created a new distress for her. If she answered the question, then

Roguk would swing from a rope beside her after her brief, laughable, trial.

"Yes, I surmised this, given the timing of your arrival on Earth and the birth of the — child. I want to know *who* the father is."

Sepherin sighed, closing her eyes and snugging the baby close to her chin. "He's a Hobonol."

"Who?" Didic asked with an edge, getting irritated. He was not an Umite used to repeating his orders.

Sepherin remained silent.

"Aside from the fact that you have killed or been responsible for the deaths of five Imperite Guards ..."

"Five?" her eyes opened.

"Yes, the one who tried to apprehend your little friend passed away from his injuries a short time ago. His name was Kevit. You bare responsibility for his death as well as the others."

"The only good Guard is a dead Guard," Sepherin said without emotion. She closed her eyes and leaned her head back against the wall, resigning herself to whatever fate may hold for her and her child. With Kalabot on board the ship, she was just happy to still be drawing breath.

The medic watched his Commander's pale face darkening. The older Shovitic's bony hands clenched into fists, his lips were pressed hard together, and his eyeworms were pointing straight out at the oath-breaker.

Finally, after forcing himself to calm down and relax, Valeni spoke again. "You are aware that aside from your other crimes, mating with someone from another clan is a forbidden act, punishable by death?"

Sepherin's eyes opened for a moment, and then closed again. "Shovitic law is not clan law, and I claim the priory of clan law in all I have done. Besides, how many times can you kill me, *Guard*?

By my reckoning it's only once."

"I want to know," his voice was coming through gritted teeth, strained again by her insolence, "who the father of the child is. *Tell me, now!*"

After a moment, still without opening her eyes, Sepherin responded. "Commander, do you know how an Earther would respond to the ridiculous demand you are making of me?"

"No. How would an Earther respond?" he practically sneered at her.

She raised the back of her hand to him, and extended the middle finger.

Commander Didic strode into his office and found the Manger sitting in front of his desk, drinking a bottle of water.

Well? Kalabot asked silently.

"The father is a Hobonol. She refuses to divulge his name."

Kalabot stood and adjust his tie, and his jacket.

"Sir, she is responsible for the death of five Guards. She has mated with one from another clan. She has disrespected us with her refusal to follow orders. Why do we not just execute her and be done with this?"

"No."

"But, Sir, executing her ..." The Watch Commander tried to take a step back, but the shorter Manager was standing right in front of him, his hand around Didic's throat, squeezing.

"Nothing is to befall the Imperite." Kalabot's eyeworms were sticking straight out at the Watch Commander, the tips of them gyrating wildly. Kalabot wasn't sure why he did that, he knew that Valeni had a valid point. But this was — instinct? Perhaps it was something else? Kalabot didn't over analyze it; he had plenty of time for that before she arrived on Umitia. If only he had the ability to move someone else through space and time with him, this would be over a lot faster.

Didic Valeni stared into the old man's mostly empty eye sockets. He smelled the hint of decay on the old man's breath. For the first time in his life, he was afraid.

The Manager leaned even closer to Didic's face, "And nothing will befall the child."

"No, Sir, nothing will happen to either of them. I will ensure their safe delivery on the honour of my household." Shovitics did not have the House system of the other clans.

Kalabot let go of the Umite's throat and took a step back, adjusting his jacket once more.

"What of the humans with her?"

Kalabot thought for a moment, and then said, "I still want the witness."

"And the other one?"

"Too much has been seen and known, even for a memory wipe. Dispose of the human."

With that said, Kalabot put his hands down by his sides, closed his eyes, and moved through time and space.

The Watch Commander stared at the empty room, resisting the urge to shiver with relief. A few moments later he came out of his temporary fugue to the sound of the communications device on his desk. He picked up the receiver and listened to the communications officer.

"Sir, I have a secure transmission for you from Lieutenant General Rosewood on Earth."

Sepherin leaned against Carlota, sitting in the hastily repurposed holding cell.

Carlota was holding the baby in her arms, smiling down at the sleeping child. She was over the revulsion of the eyes. For Carlota, it was a child, and the child of a friend. That was all she cared about, regardless of what the child looked like. Besides, she had found his ticklish spot and she had worn him out with his newborn sputtering and squirming equivalent of laughter. Lapsing back into slumber, as infants do so quickly, the child slept peacefully in Carlota's strong arms.

When Sepherin had been brought back to the room, Cassie had been taken to the medics. She'd been afraid to leave Carlota, but Sepherin assured her it would be okay, they just wanted to make sure she was healthy enough for the trip. Thirty minutes after leaving, Bobov, one of the Imperite Guards stationed outside the room, opened the hatch for Cassie to return.

"I'm fine," she said right away. She sat down beside Sepherin. Cassie was emotionally exhausted from the last hour of insanity before being taken aboard the ship. She was beyond crying, beyond fear, beyond caring. She knew she had seventy days to deal with all that shit. Right now, she just wanted to sleep.

Turning to look at Sepherin, Cassie asked, "Why do they all look at me so funny? Don't you have any black people on your planet?"

Sepherin shook her head, "Nope."

"Not even one?"

"Nope."

"Guess I'm going to be quite the spectacle."

"You'll stand out, that's for sure."

"Guess who's coming to dinner?" Carlota said with a smile.

It started as a chuckle, then became a snort, then turned into rib-shaking laughter. The stress and the fear fuelled the emotional and physical release that the laughter brought them. In this case, it certainly was the best medicine. They settled down when the baby woke, fussed a bit, and then went back to sleep under Carlota's smiling gaze.

A few minutes later, Bobov opened the door again and pointed at Carlota, "You, come now."

Carlota handed the baby to Sepherin and leaned in close, whispering in her ear, "The medic is about to get the surprise of his life."

Sepherin smiled as Carlota kissed her on the forehead. The older woman stood after leaning forward and kissing Cassie on the forehead too. "You: get some sleep. That baby in your belly needs you to rest."

As she headed out of the room, Carlota stopped and turned back to the two women, looking at them for a moment. "You two, you know how much I love you, right? Like you were my own sisters?"

They both smiled and nodded. "We love you too, Lota," Cassie replied for both of them.

With a final look at the baby in Sepherin's arms, a single tear rolling down the older woman's cheek, Carlota left the room.

"So, any names picked out yet, new mom?"

Sepherin shook her head, "I haven't even thought about it yet."

Cassie leaned over and kissed the baby on the forehead. She, too, had quickly made peace with what the baby looked like. She had a hell of a lot more to worry about.

"Maybe after Lota gets back, we can talk about it then," Sepherin said, tiredly.

Both of the women dozed off quickly, leaning against each other.

Sepherin awoke when the baby started fussing and making hungry noises. Adjusting her filthy robe, Sepherin offered the baby her nipple and the little boy suckled heartily. The reading on the time piece on the wall worried her: she realized that Carlota had been gone for the equivalent of two hours. Sepherin and the baby had been with the medic for half an hour; so had Cassie.

Tillim, Bobov's partner, opened the door and looked in at the baby feeding. "We have departed Earth orbit, we will not perform the first fold until after the next meal. Your food will be brought to you, along with some clothing."

He started to shut the door, but Sepherin called out to him, "Wait."

He looked back in at her.

"Where is our friend?" Sepherin asked, as Cassie stretched and opened her eyes.

"Your friend has left the ship."

"You transported her home?" Cassie was surprised and relieved.

The Guard had no expression on his face and no emotion in his voice. "Your friend has left the ship."

He shut the door as Sepherin's breath caught, and the tears started flowing. She started sobbing, a strangled sound of despair coming with them.

"What? What's wrong?" Cassie asked, afraid again.

Sepherin understood the Guard perfectly well. She looked at Cassie, and told her what had happened between sobs.

"They put her out the airlock."

Part II
The Umites

Clan Law

In the mists of eons past, far before our recorded time, the name of Umitia was despised amongst all of the known worlds. With blood, and loss, and suffering have we shed this past.

By word, by deed, by oath, or by law: do no thing that returns us to those days.

The First Law: Your first consideration shall always be the welfare of the clans and the clansmen of Umitia, be they known or unknown: kinsmen are they all.

The Second Law: The oath of a clansman is binding upon their household, and their house, but not their clan; the punishment of honourable justice, likewise, is shared by a clansman's household and House, save unto death.

The Third Law: Save the pursuit of honourable justice and then the preservation of life, through action or hesitation, let no clansman be killed by your hand or another's.

The Fourth Law: Let no clansman be hungry, be thirsty, be naked, be without succour, or be without a place to lay their head.

The Fifth Law: The clansman's foundation is the strength of the Houses of Umitia. Devoted are all clansmen to the honour, and then the strength, and then the health of their House.

The Sixth Law: Our joy of life comes from our blood-kin and our love-kin. Let no thing be in your mind and your heart ahead of them: to this, all the laws are blind save none.

The Seventh Law: Humbled are we to the guidance of the clan Shovitic. They have brought us from the turpitude of the past to the contentment of today. Save the sixth law, follow the clan Shovitic humbly and with gratitude, for their ways are the clans' path to peace.

Chapter 53

Michalz ran his beefy Falwasz hand through his thinning hair. He turned from the window and put his arm around Alabast, pulling her close, pressing his head against hers.

"I wished she would not be captured."

Alabast nodded, "As did I, but we knew it was inevitable."

"So," he said after gently squeezing his wife, holding her at arm's length, "we must act. We cannot allow *our* daughter to end with a rope around her neck."

"I will call the others."

"No," Michalz shook his head, "why don't we take a stroll through town this evening. We can meander, and go places randomly. It will be safer than using the communications equipment."

It was not above the Shovitics to examine the communications of someone under suspicion, especially for crimes relating to the relationship with Shovitics. While they were not under suspicion themselves, now, more than ever, was a time for paranoia.

Alabast informed the butler that she and her husband would take dinner in town, at one of the popular Treanda clan restaurants. The self-envisioned majordomo of the house offered to prepare the ground car, but Alabast and Michalz insisted they would walk.

As they slowly sauntered down the main boulevard of Kilkestand City, they said little, but smiled often at those who passed them. Seeing the Tekins out strolling in town was a rarity, but not unknown to happen.

As they stopped in front of the restaurant they had chosen, they had a small exchange of inconsequential matters while watching the street. Seeing no Imperite Guards in the area, they entered the restaurant. The maître d' came and welcomed them, offering a table by the window. Alabast asked if a table near the back would be available, she claimed to have had the sniffles and wanted to avoid a draft. She also knew that was where Miras Lidian often dined.

To their luck, the dowager Miras was dining with her two eldest daughters.

"Alabast, Michalz, how nice to see you this evening," Miras said with a smile.

"Yes, so nice to see you again, Miras, it has been far too long," Michalz responded.

Miras caught the signal loud and clear, she had seen them only two days ago. She gestured with her hand, "Would you two care to join us? We have only just ordered."

"Oh, thank you, Miras, we couldn't possibly. Besides, we are having our own little celebration," Alabast said politely.

"Oh? And what are you celebrating?"

"Our daughter, Fedina, is on her way for a visit." Alabast held Miras gaze as she spoke.

Miras knew full well that Fedina lived on the outskirts of Kilkestand, only a few minutes away by ground car.

"I see," Miras responded without hesitation. "How lovely. Will Themedit be joining you in your celebration this evening?"

"No, I'm afraid not," Michalz shook his head, "he has gone hunting with his old friend Pilip."

Ending their exchange with a polite parting, Alabast and Michalz went on to their table and enjoyed a fine meal. They chose not to linger over dessert and left before Miras. Her daughters had, oddly, chosen to cut the evening with their mother short.

Standing on a street corner, Michalz asked Alabast, "Is it time to head home my dearest?"

"Yes, I believe it is. However, could we walk down by the public gardens? I heard the Palace gardener lives near there, and his property is not to be missed this season."

It was a long walk, but they enjoyed it. They amiably passed the time discussing matters that would never be revealed for their true intent, were they to be overheard by any of the many passing them on the streets.

Arriving at the public gardens before sunset, they easily found the house of the Palace gardener, as many people would pass by in the evening to see the rare and exotic plants he had on display. The Tekins lingered at the gate: Michalz admiring the display, Alabast looking around at the crowd for any sign of Guards who may be watching.

Instead, she saw the familiar figure of her half-brother walking up the street. As was his custom, he would stop for a few minutes and answer questions from the onlookers around his gate. He greeted each person with a nod and a smile.

Pausing at the gate, he looked at Michalz, "Master Tekin, I am honoured by your visit."

"Thank you, Master Scheepers, I have looked forward to this for a long time," he responded with a smile and a nod of his own.

"Really," Cobus said after a pause, moving his gaze to Alabast.

"There are many gardens we would like to see in the city," Alabast continued the conversation. "Many of them seem so far away though, to walk to, that is. But a journey of a thousand steps — you know the saying."

"Indeed, I do." Cobus nodded.

"So we decided that today would be the first day of that journey we have decided to take."

"And a beautiful day for it, you have chosen," Cobus smiled. "If you folks will excuse me, though, I must attend my evening meal or my wife will be vexed with me. I'm late enough already."

Themedit, Pilip, and Maris were the driving force behind the preparations. Being old and retired, the Imperite Guards paid little attention to them as they were known to wander about town looking for activities to stimulate their minds. They were also well known to visit relations, and friends, often. It was only slightly remarked how these Falwasz seemed to have friends across all of the clans.

Speaking only with those they trusted, and admonishing those to do the same, they called for *perfect citizenry*. The first step in their plan was to lull the Imperite Guards with a false sense of security.

Within days the Imperite Guards' local protective forces noticed the number of confrontations with disrespectful and obstinate Umitians had dropped to almost nothing. They also noted that they were no longer getting calls for trade disputes, domestic disputes, or petty thievery amongst the Hobonols.

Even their contacts within the Houses, the larger industries, and the crime syndicate of a Treanda clan House had no explanation. The only word they had was that Gorque Serin, the leader of the only crime syndicate on the planet, had ordered his people to take it easy and do nothing without his express permission.

Designed to put them at ease, these actions made the Imperite Guards more nervous than before. However, they chose to keep their thoughts to themselves, less the Palace be angry with them for acting like a bunch of old Hobonol women.

The day after their evening meal and stroll, Alabast went out shortly after breakfast. She carried some plans and swatches for decorating Fedina Tekin's new house. Her destination was the residence of the builder, Roguk Fozretson.

"Madam Tekin," Eleniak said, surprised, but tight lipped, as she opened the door.

"Good morning, Madam Fozretson," Alabast smiled. "I have brought the samples your husband asked for. I wanted to drop them off so he could get to work with them right away."

"I'm sorry, Madam Tekin," Eleniak said, without much warmth in her voice, "my husband left early."

"Yes," Alabast continued to smile, holding Eleniak's gaze, "perhaps I could come in for a few minutes, and have some tea with you?"

That took Eleniak by surprise. She was seething inside at having the mother of the whore who had gotten pregnant by her husband standing at the door. Eleniak surmised that Alabast had to know what the situation was, and what she was feeling. Yet the older woman still nonchalantly asked to be invited into her home, and continued to hold her gaze without wavering.

Eleniak's seething hatred was bettered by her curiosity. She opened the door wider.

"Please, come in, I'll put on the water for the tea."

Chapter 54

"Good morning, Karl." Sepherin smiled at the infant as his eyeworms slowly turned outwards and spread apart, stretching much like a person stretches their arms after a nap. She could see the pupils on his ocular stump adjusting to the light.

The baby made a throaty gurgle, curled his fingers into fists, and prepare to let loose one of the throaty wales which would announce to those on this level of the ship that he was awake, and that he was hungry. Before he could blat his displeasure, Sepherin tucked him under her arm and led his hungry lips to her nipple.

She smiled and touched his nose as he hungrily gulped his breakfast. Sepherin took a breath to stop the tear that she felt burning behind her eyes. She thought that Carlota would be tickled that the child had been named for her. Sepherin sighed again and put further thoughts of Lota out of her mind for now.

She looked around the slightly more spacious and comfortable room. The Guard in charge of the communications team on the frigate had, surprisingly, offered his quarters to the Imperite and her human companion. When he informed her, he only asked if he could touch the child in return for the use of his room. The Imperite Guard had gently placed his hand on the infant's head, smiling the hideous Shovitic smile as he did so. Then he left the room and ordered the two Guards on duty in the hallway to move the prisoner and witness to his quarters.

The quartermaster found a second mattress to put in the room. It took up most of the space, but allowed the women to have their own sleeping platforms. Cassie was thankful for this as her belly full of baby made her splay her arms and legs to find comfort when she slept — and she had started snoring.

As baby Karl enjoyed his breakfast, there was a knock at the door. The knocking was something new. The Guards in the hallway, regardless of who was on duty, no longer just opened the door and entered.

"Come in," Cassie said groggily, having just woken.

The door opened, revealing the frigate's quartermaster standing at the threshold. Seeing the baby feeding, he quickly turned his head. He held out his hand with a package in it.

"I have found what you have asked for, Earther. Please forgive my intrusion during the child's meal time."

Cassie took the package, seeing that he had indeed found a needle and spools of black thread.

"Thank you," was all she said, and shut the door. She sat on her bed and rubbed her eyes, yawning, then leaned back and rubbed her belly. Carlota's death was distressing, for both of the women. But they knew they were going to be cooped up on the ship with the Shovitics for almost two more months, so they had to make the best of the situation. Cassie and Sepherin both knew that Lota would not want them to do anything to make the situation even more difficult for them. They knew that if Lota could, she would have told them, "Toughen up sisters, life's shit; make a margarita out of it."

Still rubbing her belly, Cassie looked up at the timepiece on the wall, "Is it breakfast time yet? Baby's hungry."

The ship's galley had finally figured out how to prepare food that the Earther could eat. The standard Shovitic fare made her so sick during the first three days, she had been at risk of dehydration. The Watch Commander had almost turned the frigate around to get a supply of Earther food. You would think it odd he had such concern for a prisoner, even if the prisoner was a witness. However, she was a pregnant prisoner, or witness, however you want to look at it. Such a fact changed things considerably in the mind of a Shovitic.

She was doing fine now with what they served her. 'Doing fine' meant she didn't throw it up. It still tasted like boiled cardboard. Sepherin, on the other hand, had no problem with it. She had eaten it extensively on her journey to Earth, not so long ago, in between the meals that introduced her to Earth foods.

"Yes, they'll be taking us soon. Is that the needle and thread?"

Cassie nodded. She was glad she would be able make alterations to the clothing that had been given to them. She only had to alter hers, as she was so short compared to the Shovitics who had provided from their own wardrobes. Sepherin was so tall, the two shirts given to her barely fit, and left her midriff exposed every time she moved.

A few minutes later, Sepherin had the baby leaning against her shoulder as she slowly rocked back and forth, rubbing his back. Finally, the explosive belch announced his satisfaction, and he went back to sleep.

"Has he communicated at all, yet?"

"No," Sepherin closed the makeshift swaddling blanket around him, "not since he was born."

"Maybe he's just got nothing to say," Cassie mused without expression. She had been having a hard time lately accepting what was happening to her. She had kept up a dialogue with Sepherin, to pass the days, but Sepherin could tell Cassie was on edge.

She still thinks they're going to take her home after the trial. The Imperite knew better. She knew what Cassie's fate would be, but kept if from her. The young woman was under enough stress as it was.

The Guards soon collected them, and led them to the crewman's galley on the deck below. Both of the Imperite Guards found themselves holding Cassie by the arm and helping her as she waddled along. Cassie had gotten over her revulsion at the sight of the eyeworms. No one assigned to duty on the frigate wore darkened glasses or hats. She also found the Imperite Guards to be, though initially terrifying, quite polite and accommodating. When they were first brought on board, there had been much-to-do made about the fact that Sepherin was responsible for so many deaths of their kind. Over the few days they had been under way, it seemed like everyone had forgotten about the deaths, and had been hypnotized by the baby.

The frigate had a crew of seventy-three, but only a dozen or so Imperite Guards had arrived in the galley for the morning meal. As the women sat, the two Guards from the hallway sat with them for their meal as well. The steward brought over a plate of fresh bread, something the Shovitics could actually cook quite well, which had been toasted. He knew it was the only thing they prepared that the Earther liked and given how pregnant she was, he would do all he could for her comfort. The Shovitics' complex attitude toward killing has absolutely no explanation considering their attitude towards the sanctity of life for a child, a young child's mother, and pregnant women.

As Cassie bit into a piece of toast, wishing for some butter, or even some margarine, a Shovitic stopped by the table.

"I am Christo, a junior weapons officer," he introduced himself politely. "May I ... see the child?"

Such an impromptu visit was nothing new to them. Most of the crew had stopped by to see the child. That was how they had received the gifts of clothing, makeshift swaddling blankets, and a comb for the women's hair. Sepherin turned slightly on the bench and pulled back the cloth so he could see the baby. He smiled his hideous smile and reached out tentatively, looking at Sepherin.

She nodded.

The Shovitic placed his hand gently on the forehead of the infant, brushing the child's hair once, and then withdrew his hand. He reached into a bulging pocket on his uniform jacket and pulled out a short glass jar.

"If you will permit me, Sepherin Tekin, to present to you a small gift. It is something I have had with me since leaving home. It is my last bottle, and I wish for you and ..." he looked at Cassie, "your friend, to share it."

Sepherin took the bottle from his hand and looked closely at it, then smiled. She looked up at him, "Christo, thank you, I know this must be a sacrifice. It is appreciated." She looked at Cassie, then back at him, "I'm sure my friend will find it a delight."

Sepherin, like Cassie, had become confused in the two ten-sleeps aboard the frigate. The Imperite Guards on board had initially been insanely angry with her, but that had started to change. Now, such a short time later, they were treating her with a respect and kindness she had never encountered in a Shovitic before. Even Kimla had never been this nice to her.

With a nod, the man left them to their breakfast fare.

"What is it?" Cassie asked as the steward began bringing bowls of the tasteless boiled cardboard.

"Put some on your bread. It's a delicacy from home," Sepherin said, meaning Umitia. "We can't grow these berries on our planet, so we have to import them from the Eben's homeworld."

"The who?"

"Another race."

"Great, more aliens," Cassie muttered as she opened the jar and sniffed. She dipped the tip of her finger in it and tasted. "*Oh-Em-Gee*. This is delicious!" She spooned a small drop on a piece of bread and spread it around. Her face lit up with a smile as she enjoyed the Molyak berry preserves.

Sepherin touched the tip of her finger into the preserves and then touched her finger to the sleeping baby's lips. His tongue came out, still asleep, and when he tasted the sweetness his eyeworms opened, dancing excitedly. After licking his lips clean, he fussed and fidgeted. Sepherin spent the rest of the meal time alternating between eating the tasteless porridge, and treating her child to a fingertip dipped in the succulent nectar of flavour.

"Good morning, Sepherin Tekin. Good morning, Cassie Scott."

They looked up to see Fitid standing there. As he was an Earth-based operative, he still wore his sunglasses and hat. He had become a frequent and curious visitor at the women's makeshift prison cell.

Unfortunately, he tended to smile a lot. Having sharpened, shark-like teeth to begin with, the gums of the Shovitic clan emitted small amounts of two different gases. When combined, they caused a swirling, and colourful kaleidoscope effect which was not beautiful, but accented and magnified the hideousness of their dentition.

"I see you've been gifted with Molyak preserves."

"Christo was kind enough to share his last bottle with us," Cassie replied, without hostility.

Fitid had asked many questions of Sepherin, and of Cassie, concerning their lives. He had shown a real interest, and had always been polite and respectful, once they were on board.

Sepherin thought that he always seemed to be skirting around something, never directly coming out and asking what he truly wanted to know. *Perhaps it's time to be a little more direct with him. Maybe I can find out why everyone is being so — weird.*

"It appears the little one has a sweet tooth." He bobbed his head once as he said, 'little one.'

"Fitid, perhaps you could join us after the morning meal?" Sepherin looked at Bobov and Tillim who were still sitting with them, staring at her. "There is a matter of some delicacy, concerning my friend's pregnancy which I would like to ask for your assistance with — discretely."

Both Guards looked back at their bowl at the mention of Cassie's pregnancy.

Cassie looked up at Sepherin, wondering what the hell her friend was talking about, but kept her face neutral.

There was a soft knock at the door shortly after returning to the room. Cassie opened it, and stepped carefully to the side, allowing Fitid to enter.

The infant was sound asleep in a mound of towels forming a berm around him on Sepherin's bed. Fitid looked at the child for a moment, and then turned to the women.

"How may I be of assistance," he asked Cassie.

The Shovitic's sibilant speech pattern was still something Cassie was having a hard time adjusting to.

"I'm afraid," Sepherin spoke, drawing his attention, "that I wasn't completely honest with you."

Fitid looked at her, standing a bit taller, his slowly gyrating eyeworms slowed and pointed towards the woman.

"Please," Sepherin said, patting the bed next to her, "sit with us, and let us talk plainly with one another."

She couldn't see his eyeworms behind his sunglasses, but she could tell he was running an evaluation matrix in his mind, as only a Shovitic could. Finally he sat, removing his hat and putting it on the bed beside him.

He looked at Sepherin and asked, "What shall we speak of — plainly?"

"As one Umite to another, I would like to talk with you without there being any secrets, or any lies. This is the First Law, no?"

"As you wish."

"Would you please remove your sunglasses?"

Cassie realized that Sepherin was exaggerating her politeness, sounding more like a lady of the manor than a single mother on the way to her execution. She wondered if she would get to meet Sepherin's mother.

Fitid hesitated only a moment. but then complied. While there was a limited amount of control over eyeworms, they had an autonomic response to a Shovitic's emotions and mental state. Their position and movement could often reveal what words concealed.

Sepherin looked past the eyeworms, looking directly into the pupils on his ocular stumps. "On many occasions we have spoken."

He nodded.

"During many of these conversations, you have asked Cassie and me about our lives before these recent events transpired."

He nodded.

"It has seemed, to both my friend and me, that you have been very interested in my life before my departure from Umitia."

He just starred at her.

"I have often had the sense that there is an unasked question, a question you have been skirting."

There was a pause before he nodded, and a longer pause before she proceeded.

"Has the ship's Commander asked you to find out who the child's father is?"

Fitid shook his head slowly. He wanted to know for himself. He wanted to know how the child had come to look as it had. Was it merely a fluke? Was it an age-old recessive genetic anomaly? Was it a divine joke? Was the child, perhaps, truly a hybrid between Falwasz and Shovitic, the first hybrid?

"I want to know for my own reasons."

"I have told you the father is a clansman, of the Hobonol clan. I have also told you that I will take his name to the grave, for to reveal his name, would send him to the grave as well."

"It is not for this reason that I wish to know."

"Then why do you wish to know?"

"Because of the way your child looks."

"And what is wrong with the way he looks?"

Fitid's eyeworms were getting agitated. "Sepherin Tekin, look at your child," he nodded towards the sleeping infant. "There is nothing Falwasz or Hobonol about him. He is Shovitic in his appearance."

"He is *not* Shovitic, Fetid. You were present when he was born, holding a gun on me. You saw him come from me, from my body. How could he be Shovitic when I am not?"

"Then how do you explain the eyes? How do you explain the bone structure? How do you explain ..."

"He is not Shovitic, Fitid, he is my child, and I am a Falwasz! My son is a clansman, of the Falwasz and Hobonol bloodlines!"

"He cannot be. The child is Shovitic. Or he is, at least, partially Shovitic. He must be. *His father could not be Hobonol!"* Fitid's voice was rising; his eyeworms were swelling slightly as they pointed directly at Sepherin.

Cassie sat silently, biting her lip, wondering if their brief respite of kindness from the Imperite Guards was about to end. She wanted to tell Sepherin to stop, to make nice, to keep an even keel, but she didn't. She was on an alien ship, locked in a room with two aliens who were arguing, and the argument was heating up. She exhaled and inhaled sharply, realizing she had been holding her breath.

Sepherin ploughed on, "It was not a Shovitic between my legs, Fitid, of this I would have been very much aware — unless one of your kind raped me in my sleep "

Fitid looked like he had been slapped in the face.

"How dare you imply that we would …"

"I will imply as I might when you imply that I am lying to you, Shovitic!"

"You do not realize what …"

"Realize what? Realize that I am your prisoner?"

"You are not — you are — but . ."

"Well what are you trying to say? Am I not your prisoner or am I?"

"Of course you are not my — you are my — you …" Fitid found he was angry, confused, and being backed into a corner. He was so close to the line of so many Codex of Crime laws that his mind was reeling with what to say, and what not to say.

"How do you say that when you take me to Umitia against my will?"

"You are going to Umitia because …"

"Because why, Fitid? Because I'm going to be executed."

"Yes, because …"

Parry and thrust, Sepherin knew exactly what she was doing with her words, and it was working.

"Because this infant's mother is going to swing from a short rope when you get me there!"

"No!" he leapt to his feet.

"Yes!" Sepherin stood as well, looking down at the shorter man. "*You are taking me to Umitia for execution!*"

"Yes — no — we cannot — we will not — his mother ..."

She interrupted him again. "Will not what, *Shovitic*? What will you not do, *Guard*?"

"We will not — we will ..."

She took half a step closer with rapid-fire each question, "Why do you say you will not kill me when you know I am going to be killed? Why do you say you will not execute me? Do you deny I'm going to my execution?"

He tried to back up, but could not get further away from her, "Because you ..."

She cut him off again.

"*Why,*" she pointed at the infant, "*do you say you will not kill his mother when ...*"

"I did not say ..."

"YOU DID!"

"NO!"

"WHY?"

Fitid reached out and grabbed Sepherin by the arms, shaking her, "*Because we will not kill the mother of the prophecy!*"

The room was dead silent.

Fitid let go of Sepherin, his shoulders slumping. His arms hung limply.

After a moment, the door opened. Everyone looked at the two Imperite Guards in the hallway. They stood there, a confused look on their faces, not knowing what to do. One of the hard and fast rules in Shovitic culture was to never reveal to a clansman the prophecies of Alita Kiut.

Fitid, what have you said? You cannot discuss this! One of them exclaimed telepathically.

He looked at the Guard in the doorway, responding out loud, "Have you not looked at the child? Do you not think we are beyond such secrecies, regardless of how ancient the tradition?"

The two Guards looked at each other, obviously in conversation. Finally they turned back to him, "We have heard nothing. We are going to the galley for some hot kimsa. Do not leave them alone until we return."

The door closed, leaving Sepherin starring down at Fitid, her hands on her hips, her brow furled in confusion.

"What *prophecy* are you talking about?" she asked.

Fitid ran his hand through his dark hair. He sat on the edge of the bed again. "Please, Sepherin Tekin, sit with me, and I will explain."

Cassie was wide eyed, no longer scared or worried. This was turning out better than *Days of our Lives*.

Fitid spoke slowly, making sure his sibilant speech didn't confuse them.

"A thousand seasons after the great war with the Eben, there was a Shovitic who adopted a monastic life. After his coming of age, he went to the mountains of Sestaland, where he dwelt alone for all of the remaining seasons of his life. From time to time, during recreational days, our people would encounter him. They found him to be interesting, and to be strangely clear sighted about life. Soon, he became a figure of renown, who our people sought out for matters of spirit and conscience."

"I've never heard of this person."

"And you never would, normally. The prophecies and person of Alita Kiut are a closely guarded secret of the Shovitic clan. We revere his words, and when we are taught of him, we must vow to never reveal him to the clansmen."

"Why is that?"

"Because of the Great Prophecy."

Fitid looked around the room nervously. His fingers were interlaced, his arms resting on his legs, his thumbs rubbing together. He looked at Sepherin again. His eyeworms were crisscrossing in a moving lattice over his mostly empty eye sockets, indicating the level of fear he was feeling at the present moment.

"Tell me of this *Great Prophecy,* and why you're all so scared of it."

Fitid looked intently at Sepherin, then at Cassie, and then back down at his hands. "Alita Kiut, in his later years, began speaking words of the future. These words he spoke, they all came to pass. It was a strange time, and a time of confusion. The clans were still redefining their relationships, and the Shovitics were accelerating the presence in the galaxy as keepers of the peace. Many of the challenges he foretold, we encountered. All of them we overcame with success, because the Manager of the day listened with an open mind to what Kiut said. In fact, the idea for the Imperite program comes from his teachings."

"So there's more than one prophecy?"

Fitid shook his head, "All of that is just history, it is just background so you will understand better why this is such — why this is so important. Why your child is so important."

Sepherin held her tongue. She could still see how agitated Fitid was, how afraid he was. She reached out and put her hand on his arm.

"Please," she said softly, "tell me."

"One day, the Manger at the time went to visit Kiut himself. He was living in such a place that you could not fly in, nor could he move in the manner that Managers sometimes do. The Manager had to climb the hills himself to reach him. Spending a night and a

397

day and a night with the old man, the Manager sat and listened to many things, and learned many things. At the end of his visit, the Manager said to Kiut, 'Tell me, wise one, what is the greatest of all the prophecies that you have given?' To which the old man replied, 'The Great Prophecy for the Shovitic clan will be the prophecy that I shall give with my final breath.' "

Fitid was sweating; Cassie could see that his lips were dry. She drew a cup of water from the small sink and handed it to him. He drank quickly, licking his parched lips to make them soft again, and then he continued.

"The Manager, after returning to the Palace, not the same Palace we have today, a different one, became concerned. He was afraid that Alita Kiut may pass away, all alone, with no one to hear the Great Prophecy that he had said would come. As a result of his concern for this, the Manger established a small order of Shovitics who were considered to be spiritual men."

"Shovitic clerics?" Sepherin whispered in surprise.

"Indeed," Fitid smiled, the irony not lost on him.

"But I thought that only the Ashvelyn communed with the Holy One?"

"Indeed," Fitid said again, "the Shovitic clerics were not an order concerned with the clansmen's deity; they were merely formed to ensure that Alita Kiut would not be alone when he died. They were serious men, they were committed, and they were open minded. Much more than the Shovitics you know today."

"You seem to be open minded," Cassie interjected quietly.

Fitid looked up, and unfortunately for Cassie's queasiness, smiled at her. "I am a direct descendant of one of the order of Shovitic clerics. It is why in today's Imperite Guards, I can never rise above the level I currently hold. There has been much, shall we say, distrust of those who descend from those twenty."

Sepherin put her hand on his arm again, squeezing it gently. "Please, Fitid, tell us of the Great Prophecy."

"Many seasons after the establishment of the order, after the Manager retired and was replaced, came the day of Alita Kiut's passing. Knowing his time was near, and knowing there was something important to be shared, Kiut gathered the Shovitic clerics from their nearby monastery, for want of a better word.

"As they gathered around the large, flat stone that he had slept on for most of his life, with only a thin blanket, he smiled at them and said his time was at a close. They asked him, 'Kiut, what is the Great Prophecy?'

"He took two deep breaths, and then he spoke. 'There will come a day when is born unto the Falwasz clan, a child of the Shovitic loins. Much will be made to do about this child, when the child is discovered to be what the child is.' Kiut then looked at each of the twenty Shovitics with him and gave what we call, 'The Great Prophecy'. His words are memorized by every Shovitic on the day of their coming of age. This is what he said:

'The Shovitic hybrid shall raise the six clans, and Umitia shall forever change. Once again, the Shovitics will find a new home. For the good of all that is dear, do so with gladness, dignity, and sanctity for the hybrid's life.'"

The room was silent for a long time. Cassie watched her friend's face. She could see that Sepherin was digesting the words, digesting the story. Cassie understood this was all something new to Sepherin, something that the Shovitic clan had never shared with any of the other clans. The Earther had to suppress a smile, thinking this sounded like when Ritchie used to prattle on about the Vatican having secrets about UFOs deep in their archives. *If only he could see me now,* she thought, without any emotion towards the memory of her child's father.

Finally, Sepherin spoke. To both Cassie and Fitid's surprise, she didn't ask about the hybrid that had been spoken of.

"This prophet said, 'Once again you will find a new home.' What did he mean by this?"

Fitid said nothing, but his crisscrossing eyeworms swelled so much he could barely see: shock, surprise, and fear.

"Fitid, the Umites have always lived on Umitia. Why would he say the Shovitics had to find a *new* home?" Sepherin asked again.

Then it struck her. She recoiled from Fitid, pushing away from him, scrambling back to the far corner of her bed. Her eyes were wide and her mouth was open in shock.

Cassie sat up, holding her belly, looking from one to the other. She was alarmed, but didn't know why. She just saw how Sepherin was reacting to Fitid, and if Sepherin was reacting that way, it couldn't be good.

Fitid stood. "We have spoken enough, I must leave."

Before his hand touched the door, Sepherin was off the bed, had grabbed him around the neck and thrown him to the floor. She dropped down with one knee beside him, and one knee in the middle of his back. He grunted and protested with a hiss as she grabbed his hair and yanked his head back.

Now Cassie was pushing herself back on the bed. "Sepherin, *no* ..." she whimpered.

Sepherin spun her head to glare at Cassie, the look on her face causing the Earther to clamp her mouth shut and her eyes to flow tears of fear.

Turning back to the Imperite Guard on the floor, yet again committing an act that warranted her death, she spit at him, "What are you, Shovitic? Where do you come from, that you would have to leave, *again*?"

"We are clansmen, just like ..."

"LIE!" Sepherin roared, smashing his face down on the floor then yanking his head back. *"Do not lie to me anymore! Are you of Umitia or are you not?"*

He said nothing. He moaned with the pain of her knee in his back, and her hand pulling his hair. He grunted as his arms flailed around trying to get a purchase on her legs, to pull her off of him; but she had positioned herself so that he couldn't get enough leverage to do so.

"Answer me!" The unbridled rage in her voice clearly revealed the danger he was in, how close she was to killing him.

He struggled harder, his breath hissing through his teeth. His hands kept grabbing at her, but his arms were too long, and she was too close to his shoulders.

He couldn't get a grip with enough leverage to pull her off.

He knew he had said too much, far too much.

There was more than one reason the Great Prophecy was never revealed to a clansman — and it had not escaped Sepherin's notice.

Sepherin reached down with her other hand, and got a good grip on Fitid's neck. "Tell me now. What are you? What are the Shovitics? *Are you from Umitia?"*

Finally, with his breath coming hard, with his vision getting fuzzy from the lack of oxygen caused by her grip around his neck, he relented.

"No!"

Sepherin let go of him and stood up quickly. She looked at Cassie and then back at Fitid, who was rolling over and just starring up at her. He was rubbing his neck, his eyeworms sticking straight out and pointing at Sepherin.

Cassie watched as a heartbeat slowly passed.

She was waiting for one of them to kill the other. She could see the handgun in Fitid's shoulder holster, but he had not drawn it, and Sepherin had not disarmed him, though she had almost killed him.

Finally, the Imperite reached out her long arm, bending slightly.

Hesitating, the look on his face showing resolve and acceptance, he reached up and took her hand. Once standing, they looked at each other for a moment longer. Then Sepherin sat, and Fitid sat as well.

Cassie finally inched forward to the edge of her bed. "I'm lost. What the hell just happened here?"

"The Shovitics are not clansmen of Umitia," Sepherin said slowly.

"Wait, what? You said there were seven clans, including the Shovitics, right?"

"It would appear there are only six," Sepherin said quietly, to which Fitid nodded, hesitantly.

"You're confusing me. You said there were seven clans, now you're saying there are only six. If the Shovitics aren't a clan then what are they? Where are they from?"

Sepherin looked up at Cassie and saw the realization dawn on her friend's face.

The Sovitics were actually aliens, they weren't really from Umitia.

Cassie wondered if she was going insane. She was sitting in an alien spaceship; on the way to an alien planet; with an alien best friend; who just found out that her planet, her world, was controlled and ruled by — aliens.

The hysterical laughter exploded from Cassie. The irony and surrealism of the situation had hit her like an electric shock. She held her belly, the bulge shaking, her breasts shaking, her head rocking back as her mouth flew open with every burst of almost hysterical laughter.

Sepherin and Fitid both stared at her, unsure how to react, confused about why she found this situation funny.

Fitid had, in the space of a few minutes, revealed two of the most closely guarded secrets of the Shovitics.

Sepherin had learned that everything she knew about her world's order and rule, about those in charge, about those who charted and controlled the destiny of the six other clans, were a race of beings that were not of her own world.

The baby awoke at the sound of Cassie's mind briefly coming unhinged. The infant fussed and kicked at its blankets.

Sepherin was still stunned. She just looked at the child, her mind still a million leagues away.

Cassie's laughter quickly dried up, and she got control of herself again.

Fitid tentatively reached out to the child. He paused and looked at Sepherin, who did not react. He pulled the berm of towels aside and carefully picked up the child. Cradling it in his arms, the Shovitic looked down at the infant, gently stroking the forehead and hair with his bony hand. Fitid smiled, helpless not to. A child was so precious to the Shovitic people, in a way that the clansmen would not understand.

He looked up at Sepherin. She seemed to be back from wherever her thoughts had gone. She held out her hands and Fitid carefully passed the baby to her.

Looking at the mother and child, his mind slowly eased at the turmoil he had caused by what he had said. It was a peaceful vignette in a setting of revelation, deception, and impending death. He looked from the child to the mother, marvelling at how the hybrid child had so many of his mother's features.

His skin was light coloured as was hers, not the usual olive tone of the Falwasz. His face was long and narrow like hers, not the usual square shape of the Falwasz. Unlike his mother, he had

403

eyeworms, but the irises of his ocular stocks were the same golden brown hue as his mother's, not the dark browns and blues of the Falwasz. He even had the beginning of a long, patrician nose like his mother's, similar to that of …

Fitid actually squealed with surprise as he rocketed off the bed, moving so fast that he actually hopped in the air. His eyeworms were gyrating so fast and wildly you could barely see them. His mouth was wide open in shock, as Sepherin's had been a few minutes before. He broke out in another cold sweat all over his body, as he realized that it was not the infant who was so important.

It was Sepherin Tekin.

It was the only thing that could explain how the infant looked as it did.

Was *she* the child of the prophecy?

Fitid rushed from the room without another word.

Chapter 55

Kimla knocked on the Manager's office door and heard his voice in her head.

Enter.

She passed through the tall double door and strode across the large room to his desk. Then she waited for three minutes until he acknowledged her again.

After closing the book he was reading from, he glanced up at her. "You have delivered the notice to Alabast Tekin?"

"A few days ago, Sir."

"What did she say?"

Kimla only had to pause a moment, clearly recalling the things that Alabast had said. "She intends to give it her fullest attention and efforts, Sir."

"Good, good."

"Is there some cause for concern, Sir?"

Kalabot snapped his head up to look at Kimla, his eyeworms becoming still and pointing at her. She could see his ocular stump moving slightly, directing his pupils to scan her face, and body language. She was too old of a hand, though, to let something like an emotion give herself away.

Finally he asked, "And if there was a concern?"

Kimla smiled only slightly, "Then I would be honoured to make the concern — go away."

Kalabot nodded once, "Thank you, Kimla Pilu, your service is valued. You are dismissed."

With a single nod in response, she spun on her heel and headed for the door. Kimla knew she would never harm Alabast Tekin, but the words had seemed to assuage the Manager, the one person who truly terrified her. Before she was halfway to the door, Kalabot spoke again.

"Stop!"

She halted, her stomach clenching, but her face remaining neutral. She turned to look at him.

"Sir?"

Kalabot held out a piece of paper. "This is a copy of a document from Earth. Please have it translated and then delivered to the Palace Council."

"Yes, Sir." She strode forward and took the paper from him.

As she was about to turn, Kalabot spoke again.

"Pilu, please stay with the document and the translation, until it is in the hands of the council. It is sensitive."

"As you wish, Sir."

Kimla left the office and went up one floor to the offices of the planetary coordinators. She found the one responsible for Earth and had him do the translation. Kalabot loved paper, where everyone else used computers. Kalabot had said often that a hacker cannot hack a piece of paper. Therefore, the coordinator translated the document onto paper.

A ground car was ordered for the trip of several leagues to the Palace Council's office. Curiosity getting the better of her, Kimla pulled the paper out of the envelope and read the translation. She was thankful for her darkened glasses so that the driver of the car would not see her eyeworms. The paper was returned to the envelope without comment, as she contemplated what she had read.

Taffi and Minino had overreacted, they had not listened. For that, they had died, and rightly so in her estimation. Tameht Tekin had upheld the Oath by trying to get the Humanesh off the Eridani ship. That the Eridani had tricked him, while it was embarrassing,

406

it was not his fault. Everything that had transpired was because the two Guards had overreacted. She thought Taffi always was a hothead, just like his brother, Zekra.

In this situation, all the Imperite had done was to protect her host. Kimla found it odd that Sepherin would go to such a length to protect a host, though. Risking death for killing a Guard was extreme. Regardless of the young woman's reasons, killing the Guard was still a capital offense.

Kimla got out of the car at the offices where the Palace Council was located. She went up the steps, but stopped midway. The question was still nagging at her. From what she knew of Sepherin Tekin, she was wholly dedicated to her family, but aside from that she did not seem to have any political or activist affinity, otherwise she would not have been selected. She was just — a Falwasz girl. An odd looking one, but she was nothing special. So the question remained in the forefront of Kimla's mind. *Why did she risk killing the Guards over a host? We would have assigned her a new one, right away.*

After delivering the envelope to the council, Kimla dismissed the car and driver, preferring to walk back to the Palace. She told the driver she was going to stop for some refreshment along the way. She had in fact copied the document before handing it over, and she needed to think about what she had read some more.

She was greeted with a nod of the head or wave of the hand by many people who she passed on the sidewalk. Having been in her position as a program facilitator for many years, she had dealt with many families in the capital city. She realized soon into her walk that of those who didn't greet her in a familiar way, no one had averted their eyes, and no one had sneered at her. In fact, many more people than usual simply nodded a polite acknowledgement in passing.

These were strange times. Hostilities towards the Shovitics had been growing, slowly, for years. But all of a sudden, everyone was being — indifferent — at worst.

She put the observation out of her mind, choosing to spend her thought processes on the more important matter at hand. *How has this situation with the Imperite gotten so out of hand, so fast? And why? And why is the Earther being brought with her?*

When she got back to the Palace, she went to the communications room in the basement.

"Corla, I require communication with Earth."

The on-duty technician, Corla Havinta, led Kimla to a booth which offered privacy.

"Whom are you contacting?"

"Station twelve."

A moment later the handset was at her ear, and she could hear the connection being made.

"Station twelve."

"This is Kimla Pilu, calling from the Palace. I need to speak with Zekra or Shivinin."

"They are on remote assignment."

Kimla's brow pinched together. *Remote assignment? What does he mean by that?*

"Are they not accessible?"

"We can contact them, but they do not have a wormhole connection."

She hesitated only a moment. "I need to speak with them, it is a matter of some urgency. Can you have the duty frigate send them to your office, and call me back?"

"It is that important?"

"Yes."

"Very well, it will be done."

"I'm waiting in the communications office at the Palace."

The Imperite Guard at the other end signed off. This wasn't the first time that Kimla wished Shovitic telepathy had a range greater than half a league.

Ten minutes after breaking the connection, Kimla heard Corla's voice. "I'm transferring a call to you, from Earth, line three."

"Kimla Pilu," she said.

"This is Zekra Kortic."

"I offer my heartfelt sadness for your loss, Zekra. I knew Taffi in the academy."

"I'm sure this is not why you called, but I accept your sadness with gratitude."

"I wanted to ask you about Sepherin Tekin …"

His snort of disgust cut her off, "Is the bitch dead yet?"

"No, but she is on her way to Umitia right now."

"Send me images when she swings from the rope."

There was an uncomfortable pause; Kimla didn't really know how to proceed given the venom in his voice. She decided straightforward would be the best way. Zekra would lose patience if she tried to be circuitous.

"I need to ask about Sepherin and her host. Was there anything special about them?"

"Which host?"

"Sepherin Tekin's."

"Yes, and I ask again, which one?"

Now Kimla was stumped. How could an Imperite have more than one host?

"I'm not sure I follow you, Zekra," she said slowly, "are you saying she had more than one?"

"Yes, the first ones were killed when …"

Kimla heard another voice, muffled, and it sounded like a tussle for the handset. Finally she heard Zekra again, speaking to someone else, probably his partner.

"... matter now. At least someone is asking questions."

She heard the handset being held up to his mouth again.

"Are you still there?"

"Yes," she replied.

"The oath-breaker's first host was retired, as was her Earther spouse and her two hereditaries."

Kimla took a sharp breath. *Her original host and her family were murdered?*

"By who? Who did this?"

"Taffi and Minino."

"*What?* By our own Guards?"

"They were *retired*," Zekra said slowly.

Kimla's eyeworms exploded open in dismay. She took another sharp breath. The hairs all over her body stood on end. She could feel the goose bumps on her arms and legs. Her head swam. There was a brief buzzing sound in her ears.

Only one person could order an Imperite to be retired. As if that wasn't bad enough, her hereditaries, her children, had been retired as well. *That* could only have happened under a direct and personal order from the Manager.

The fact that those children still lived was taken to the grave with Taffi and Minino when they were killed. Even Zekra did not know this.

"Did you faint?" she heard Zekra on the handset.

"No," she said, her voice unsteady.

"It gets more interesting."

"Proceed."

"Her new host was an Earth-born Falwasz."

"And this is interesting, why?" Kimla felt a sense of dread crawling up her spine.

"His name was Tameht Tekin."

"Tekin? Who was his mother?"

"Jakula." Zekra didn't say anything else, he let her work it out for herself.

As she had worked with the House of Tekin and Michalz Tekin's family so often, she knew quite a bit about them and their relations. She knew that Michalz' own mother was selected for the program a long time ago. Her name was Jakula.

If the new host, the Earth-born was Jakula Tekin's child, this meant he was Michalz Tekin's brother. Which meant he was …

"The new host was her blood-kin?"

That answered some of Kimla's questions, but created a whole bunch of other ones.

For the first time in a long time, Kimla felt afraid.

As Kimla strode out of the communications centre without a word, Corla watched the tall Shovitic, a woman who could have been her twin, with guarded eyes. It had indeed been a strange phone call. Corla was required to routinely listen in on phone calls off-planet, on a random basis. As the day had been slow, she had listened to Kimla's call to Station 12. With her curiosity piqued, she had listened to the incoming call from the remotely posted guardsman.

What she had heard troubled her greatly. After a few moments' deliberation, she decided that perhaps she had not listened to the call after all. She didn't want to get Kimla killed when she didn't have the full context of the conversation.

As Corla went on with her duties, Kimla wasn't the only one feeling afraid.

Chapter 56

With the half-lie that his research was part of the investigation into the oath-breaker, Fitid easily gained access to the medical results from the Imperite and the infant's checkup when they boarded the ship. He wasn't a medical professional, but as an Imperite Guard there were certain things he had been trained in concerning both Falwasz and Earther body chemistry.

The initial test results looked normal for both the mother and the child. They were so normal in fact, the results could have been Falwasz, Shovitic, or even an Earther. Next, he looked for the in-depth histology results, but the medic had not felt the need to go that far in his examination. Fitid also noted that the basic bloodwork profile of the infant was missing. Looking in the refrigeration unit, he found the blood samples that had been extracted from Sepherin and Karl.

The proper examination took only a few seconds in the analyzer. Loading Sepherin's blood sample, the first thing he looked for was the blood protein called *transferrin*. The analyzer extracted a sample of the protein and shunted it to the molecular analyzer. The readout was what he expected: 679 amino acids and three carbohydrate chains. She was definitely an Umite, not an Earther, who have only two carbohydrate chains in the protein. Next, he examined the blood sample for the child, with the same results.

Fitid knew that this only proved the two were descendants from Falwasz, but it was the essential first step. He needed to prove they were both descendants from a Shovitic as well, or at least the child, if his surprising hypothesis was incorrect. He keyed in a different analysis program for little Karl's blood. Two minutes later, after shunting the extracted sample to the molecular analyzer, the results were back. The child had 4.8 mg/mL of *mannan-binding lectin* (MBL) in his blood. The child definitely had Shovitic blood in him.

Fitid put Sepherin's blood sample back in the machine and ran the same test. This time, he turned away from the machine, folded his arms, and starred at the wall. Two minutes later, there was a beep, the test was done.

Fitid continued to stare at the wall.

He wanted to look, but he had to work up the courage to do so.

If the results came back the same, then things were going to drastically change. If Sepherin Tekin had elevated MBL readings … then she was also of Shovitic blood, and therefore, things would get interesting once they arrived on the homeworld.

The Humanesh average reading for *mannan-binding lectin* in the blood was 1.49 +/- 2.12 mg/mL. The Shovitic average level was 4.7 +/- 1.12 mg/mL, a level which would slowly kill a Humanesh. The Shovitic level of MBL was also one of the reasons why they never got the common cold. Their blood disrupted the viral pathogen before it had a chance to make them sick.

Fitid took a deep breath and slowly turned on the stool to face the screen, his arms still folded.

He looked at the readout on the screen.

5.1 mg/mL.

Sepherin Tekin was a Falwasz-Shovitic hybrid.

Sepherin Tekin was the child of the Great Prophecy, not her son.

The only question that remained was: who is her father?

With her patrician nose, and Kalabot's interest in her — Fitid had a terrible feeling.

Sepherin held the door for the two Shovitics from the

414

engineering department as they departed. After visiting the night before, to see the child, they had returned this morning bearing a solution to a problem.

It only took about twenty minutes for them to install two sets of brackets on the end wall of the room. From the brackets on the wall hung two functional, but ugly, bassinettes. They had been cobbled together from storage locker panels, water duct insulation, and the fabric of two chairs. They were, as said, ugly, but they were safer than anything you could buy, anywhere.

Karl loved the rocking motion, he eyeworms dancing with joy every time Sepherin put him in it. When they started the install, she had the engineers position them so that as she lay in the bed, she could simply reach out with her foot to rock the baby. It saved a lot of up and down the first night, and each subsequent night of the journey. It would be the same for Cassie, who was almost at her due date.

You're mad, Senji said, learning close for no reason other than the conspiratorial nature of their telepathic conversation, something they could block from others.

It makes sense. You've read the history of the Imperite and her family. We were both in training when the accident happened at the foundry. You have to remember the rumours and accusations that were talked about. Then all of a sudden, the investigation is closed and the Tekins were cleared of any wrong doing.

Maybe they were innocent? She raised an eyebrow.

Kalabot ordered the investigation closed, I'm sure of it.

But how can you prove it? She asked. *No, let me rephrase the question, how can you prove it without Kalabot knowing?*

There was a pause, then Senji's eyes widened in understanding.

Fitid, no, you can't expose her to that danger.

But if it's true, think of what it means, what could come of it.

Senji was silent, her eyeworms dancing in disarray.

The Imperite was born exactly nine months after the investigation was so mysteriously terminated. Exactly nine months. There is only one person who could have ordered an investigation to be terminated. I already have the proof that the Imperite is the hybrid, and she's the first hybrid ever known of. That makes her the child of the prophecy, not the infant. This means we may have a civil war on our hands if our people refuse to leave. If the father is who I think it is, then there is a way out, a way back from the brink of war.

If he gets wind of this, he will kill you, kill your mate, and most likely kill me for being your partner. Her words were sound, but the telepathic current held doubt.

They were silent again for a moment. Fitid watched Senji's face, watched her eyeworms, she was deep in thought. Finally, the stocky Shovitic woman leaned back in her chair.

Do what you must, my friend, but do it carefully. And keep my name out of it.

I shall. He stood and left her quarters.

"What are you thinking about?" Sepherin asked.

Cassie had been starring at the wall above Sepherin's head for hours it seemed. She was just sitting there, rubbing her belly, saying nothing.

"I want to go home."

"I know."

"No, Sepherin, really. I want to go home. I want to be with my mom right now. I wanted her to be there when the baby's born."

Sepherin was silent.

"These — *bastards* — I wish they'd stop being so damn nice to me. It's making it hard for me to hate them."

"They're going to kill me. Hate them for that."

Now Cassie looked at her friend, the alien. Then Cassie snorted as she realized that on this ship, *she* was the alien.

"What about what Fitid said. He said they wouldn't kill the mother of the child of the — *whatever.*"

"He's only one voice. There are millions of Shovitics. Besides, the Manager could kill me from his office just by wishing it to be so."

"Is he a god?"

"No, certainly not him. He's a sour, scary, sallow old ..."

"I get the picture. But if your child is this prophecy child, and he's a Shovitic, why would he kill you?"

"Because I'm an oath-breaker and that's what the law says must happen."

"Yes, but ..."

"And my child is the product of two people from different clans, which is also punishable by death."

"Was that what you meant by the Third Law? What you said when they found us?"

"No, that's — the Clan Law is different, it's above all. The laws about breeding are part of the Codex of Crimes."

"And you die for breeding with someone from a different — clan?"

"Yes, and my House will be dissolved and all of its blood-kin and love-kin cast into the street with only the clothes on their backs and what they can carry in their hands."

"Your whole family?" Cassie was shocked.

"No, my whole House. I'm of the House of Tekin. It is made up of hundreds of households. My punishment will be shared by everyone with the name Tekinson or Tekindottir. Only they can't kill them, they can only kill me. So they take everything from them and leave them with nothing."

"But your name is Tekin, not — those other two names."

"When we pledge the Oath of the Imperite, we drop the genderific from our names. It's tradition."

Cassie closed her eyes and shook her head, not understanding. She went on, "So the punishment for crime is — *shared*? Is that the same with all of your laws or just the one about breeding?"

"All of them."

Cassie was silent for a few minutes. Finally she said, "You don't seem so upset about it, anymore."

Sepherin grimaced and shrugged, "It is what it is. I've resigned myself to my fate, and theirs."

"What about Karl? What happens to him?"

Sepherin smiled. "My mom will raise him, as well as she's able to." She knew that the fourth Clan Law meant her own family would quickly be invited into the home of another Falwasz House.

"They'll let her?"

"You don't understand Shovitics and children. They may execute me by the pursuit of honourable justice, but a child, they would protect with their lives to the last one of them — and it doesn't matter what clan the child is from."

Cassie was silent again for a few minutes before speaking.

"I really want to go home."

"Even if we turned around right now, your child would be born long before we got back to Earth."

Without responding to Sepherin, Cassie stood and opened the door.

Bobov looked down at her, his lips curling slightly in a smile, "Time for another walk?"

Cassie nodded and they left, the door closing behind her. It was about the only exercise she could get. Her walks with Bobov or Tillim had become a common sight. The frigate was large enough to allow for lots of different destinations, however, her favourite was the two landing bays for the two patrol craft the frigate carried. She got a kick out of the fact that she was in an alien spaceship that carried, round, classic UFOs.

Back in the cabin-slash-prison cell, the Imperite was troubled. Sepherin wanted to comfort Cassie, but she couldn't. She had no clue what to say to her friend. Sepherin wasn't only thinking about her own demise; she was also dealing with the knowledge that Cassie was also going to be killed at the end of the sham trial. It was how Kalabot did things. She comforted herself with the knowledge that her mother would look after the Earther child as well. Perhaps her mother could appeal to Kimla to have the child returned to Earth, to Cassie's blood-kin — *maybe*.

The only thing which gave her hope for herself was what Fitid had said about not killing the mother of the child of the Great Prophecy, *if* Karl was that child.

For the millionth time, she wondered how the hell her family or Roguk's family, had wound up with recessive Shovitic genes in them. It was the only explanation for the way Karl looked. *Who in the hell in our families mated with a Shovitic, and why? What would be worth risking the penalty of death for such an act?*

Chapter 57

Cobus knocked lightly on the door, wondering if Kalabot would be upset that he had not arranged an appointment ahead of time.

Enter.

Responding to the voice in his head, Cobus opened the door and went into the office which always reminded him of a ballroom.

"Good afternoon, Sir. I was hoping you could spare a few moments for me. I apologize for not making an appointment, but, well, I have an exciting proposal and I thought you should see this right away."

"Cobus, I'm sorry. I have many things to deal with at present. As you are aware of some of those things, and now the clock ticks faster as — the oath-breaker is on her way to Umitia."

"You're still concerned about the people's reaction?"

"Yes, of course, and other things."

"Of course. Then perhaps I have come at the most opportune time then."

Kalabot sighed and sat back in his chair. He looked at Cobus who stood there in his workman's clothes, with rolls of paper under one arm. There was the sheen of perspiration on his high forehead, his white mustache was practically twitching with excitement as he adjusted his glasses that were sliding down his nose. He had an odd smile on his face, and his free hand was flicking his fingers against his thumb.

"Fine, Cobus, what is it that is so exciting for you to share?"

Cobus rushed to the desk, pulling the rolls of paper from under his arm.

"You are worried about how people will react to the news of the oath-breaker? Then give them something else to think about, and to take pleasure in."

Kalabot reached out and held down one end of the roll of paper, looking at the plan-view drawing of an oddly shaped structure.

"What is this?"

"In the evenings, old friend, many people in Kilkestand City take to walking the residential avenues to look at the gardens of others. My own house has many people out front of it each evening when I return to my wife. There has been many unofficial competitions between neighbours, and sometimes between whole streets, as to who will have the most varied and beautiful gardens."

"I have heard of this, Cobus. It is something that I have discretely viewed on occasion myself."

Cobus nodded, "I'm sure you have, Sir, I'm sure you have. But without a doubt, the most beautiful gardens on our entire planet are right here at the Palace. They even surpass the Hyperion Gardens."

"A testament to your fine skill, Master Gardener."

"Sir, do you know what lament I hear most often, at the unofficial judging of the unofficial competitions?"

"I'm sure you are about to tell me."

"That the ordinary folk cannot compete with the Palace, when the Palace is the only place that grows the hundreds of varieties we import from other worlds."

Kalabot was silent. It dawned on him what the drawing was.

"Then this is more than just a greenhouse plan you have lain before me. Correct?"

"Yes, old friend. This is a plan for a cultivation centre. It is a place where we can take the flora of dozens of worlds, and take the

422

seeds and clippings to produce large amounts of those plants. Then in this section," he pulled a new sheet to the front, unfurling it with Kalabot's help, "is the visitor centre. Here our citizens can purchase the starters for a modest fee, as well as obtain the necessary knowledge for growing the alien beauties in our soil. In this corner here," Cobus pointed, "is a small lecture area where I can deliver information sessions for those who wish to learn more about gardening, garden design, and how to produce their own cultivars."

"This is a large structure, Cobus."

"Yes, it is, but it is mostly air. It is the outer walls, the ceilings, the floors. There are few internal walls; there are only three mechanical rooms, and there is this one large storeroom. The open concept will make its construction go very quickly."

Kalabot looked at the plans carefully. Umitians loved things that were beautiful, and beautiful gardens were a decadence which was common to all six clans. The amount of homes without gardens in the capital city could be counted, literally, on one hand. Kalabot had mused to himself, more than once, it was a shame that only the Palace had the beautiful flora from other worlds.

"Cost projections?" he asked Cobus.

"Here, Sir, I'm sure you will find the final price tag acceptable."

He did indeed found it acceptable, shockingly low even.

"Timeline?"

"How long until the — until her return, Sir?"

"Roughly four more ten-sleeps."

Cobus scratched his head, then folded his arms and stroked his chin. After giving it some thought he said, "If we convert a part of the existing green house, we can begin the cultivations within a few days. We can then begin construction on the public section right away. We could finish it within five ten-sleeps. Sooner, if we budget for more labourers. We could then continue construction on the working areas of the cultivation centre, and take our time with it as the current greenhouse would already be doing the work."

Kalabot nodded slowly as he looked at the plans and thought about what they would be offering to the populace for the first time. It would not make people forget that a Falwasz was to be executed; it would not make Kalabot forget that his own daughter was going to be executed, but it would indeed be something to help the wounds heal quicker.

Kalabot looked up at Cobus and smiled his hideous Shovitic smile. "Old friend, you have truly come through for me in a time when I am afraid to trust others." He reached out and put his bony hand on Cobus shoulder. "I beg you, begin as quickly as possible. I will have the construction contractors …"

"Sir, if I may, I know a Hobonol who has done much work in the form that this structure will take. I believe the results would be superior if we bring in someone new, someone with experience working with these types of wood in this manner."

Kalabot nodded and patted him on the shoulder again, "As you wish Cobus. I am placing you completely in charge of this project. Hire who you wish, your budget is approved, in fact, I will increase it by fifty percent. Please ensure construction moves along smoothly so we can open this prior to the …" He trailed off, lost in thought for a moment, his eyeworms betraying his inner state. Then he looked back up at Cobus, "Please have this open as soon as possible."

Thanking him, Cobus gathered up his papers and practically ran from the office. His first stop was to make a phone call to his wife, who was going to take a walk, and perhaps meet a certain someone on the street and have a seemingly innocuous conversation with them.

As the office door closed, looking at the summary sheet that the head gardener had left behind, Kalabot called the communications centre. "Please have the Commander of Information Services come to my office."

Chapter 58

"And why does the transmission need to be secure?" The communications officer looked warily at Fitid.

"I have been deployed for almost fifty ten-sleeps, my mate and I have not seen each other in a long time. I would like to have," he looked around, an embarrassed smile on his thin face, "a private conversation with her."

Finally the Imperite Guard in charge of the communications equipment smiled as well. "I understand. She is on duty now, at the Palace?"

"Yes, she should be accepting the inbound connections."

A few minutes later, Fitid was alone in the room, speaking with his mate over an encrypted circuit which was transmitted through the ERB device.

"Corla, it is so good to hear your voice."

Her business-like tone had softened when he came on the line. He could hear the happiness in her voice, "Fitid, it is good for me as well to hear you. It has been so long, and I have missed you." She lowered the volume of her voice, "But why are you on an encrypted circuit?"

"I would like to spend this time talking of ourselves, my mate, but I am afraid we must discuss another matter."

Corla was surprised. "What would that be?"

"There is much I need to tell you, but I cannot do so, even on an encrypted circuit. I promise I will explain everything in person."

"You are coming home?" her voice quickly changed to one of evident delight.

"Yes, I accompany the — the oath-breaker."

There was silence on the line.

"Are you still there?" he asked.

She took a deep, slow breath. She was feeling a bit like an emotional yo-yo. Corla responded, "Yes, I am. Do you need to discuss her?"

It wasn't much of a leap, Fitid knew his wife was not stupid. "Yes."

Corla knew her mate well. If he was calling her concerning the Tekin Imperite, then something was troubling him. Whatever was bothering him, she knew it was more than just her duty as his spouse to assist him; it was a duty of her passion to aid him. She knew he was a thoughtful man, and not a man to jump to conclusions without solid evidence. But she found the coincidence of him calling about this, so soon after Kimla's strange call to Station 12, disconcerting.

"Tell me what you need."

He did. She was shocked, so evidenced by the silence on the other end of the device. He let it linger for a few moments.

"Corla? Are you there?"

"You know what will happen if I get caught digging in closed investigation files, do you not?"

"You do not need to, Corla. Your uncle was the lead investigator into the foundry accident. You can ask him."

He could hear her breathing over the device, thinking about what he said. Finally she spoke, "Perhaps I could invite some relatives for dinner tomorrow evening."

"That would be lovely," he let some relief into his voice. Then he steeled himself, "There is one other thing I need, something your uncle will not able to help with."

He heard her quietly chuckle, in the gravely Shovitic way. "Of course, it was too easy. What else do you need? A copy of the key to Kalabot's office?"

"I need a copy of the Palace visitor logs for the week the investigation was terminated."

"You know," Corla said sarcastically, after a brief hesitation, "you could just disavow me, rather than plan such an elaborate suicide for me."

"Please, Corla, I would not ask if this were not so important. I know it is a dangerous request, but I know you will be careful."

"You're lucky I love you."

"Yes, I am indeed very lucky," he said softly.

Silence hung between them again. He wasn't sure what else to say, his mind was so preoccupied with his own thoughts, and with concern for the untenable position he was putting his mate in.

Corla was thinking about the conversation she had so recently listened to. Wondering if she should relate its contents or if that would be pushing luck's fortune. She decided to say nothing, but did not dismiss from her mind the thought that Kimla and her husband should speak.

Without saying anything else, Corla broke the connection, leaving her husband holding his handset and wishing he had been assigned to a different planet.

Chapter 59

Kimla's gaze didn't waver from the insolent butler's. To make her point, she removed her darkened glasses and let the eyeworms show him how pissed she was.

"Fine," he said, "I will wake her."

After a night of difficulty sleeping, Kimla had risen early and done three iterations of the forty-seven positions of the *kun'pah*, the full-body and slow-moving physical meditation for combat which all Shovitics practiced daily.

She had then gone to the Palace, to the office where the Imperite program support teams worked from. Finding nothing to help quell the turmoil in her mind, she made an early morning visit to the Tekin household.

Shortly after the butler left her standing in the foyer, he returned. "Mater Tekin has been awoken and will join you shortly. She has ordered me to offer you refreshment."

Kimla could hear the ire in the man's voice, though he kept his face neutral. She wasn't the least bit thirsty or hungry, but the chance to get under the snooty servant's skin was too good to pass up.

"Some hot kimsa would be appreciated."

She watched him turn towards the kitchen and stalk off, waiting till he was halfway there, and then called to him. He turned and stiffly walked back to her with the irritation obvious on his face.

"What?"

"A pastry would go nicely with the kimsa."

She saw his face growing redder, but then he took a deep breath and acidly responded. "It is my pleasure to serve."

She waited until he was again halfway across the foyer.

"Wait."

After a slight pause, he turned and all but stomped back to the Imperite Guard standing inside the front door.

"Yes?" he at least tried to be a bit more controlled, if not polite.

"Should I seat myself anywhere I like while I wait for the Mater of the house? Or perhaps it is a new Falwasz custom to leave their guests standing in the reception hall of their homes?"

"I didn't realize you were a guest. I thought you were the Palace's hired help, merely delivering a message."

She had to give him credit: she had walked into that one. She was able to not smile, barely. Without the chance to make a comeback, the butler led her to the parlour where Alabast had received her selection notification.

Kimla looked out the window, enjoying the beauty of the Tekin gardens and expansive lawn, now that there were no people camped out there. Only a few minutes passed before the downstairs maid came in with a gold tray bearing a hot pot of kimsa, and a plate of pastries which were still warm. Kimla stirred some cream and three spoons of sweet cane into her cup. She sat on the couch, enjoying her second breakfast of the day. She wasn't hungry, she just wasn't going to give the butler the satisfaction of knowing she had only tried to rile him.

The door opened and Alabast came in. To Kimla's surprise, the mater of the household greeted her with a smile as she sat across from her.

"Alabast, I apologize for the early meeting."

Alabast covered a yawn with the back of her hand, politely, yet still making a statement about what she thought of the early hour. "It is not a problem, Kimla, what did you wish to discuss."

"As we approach the date for your physical," Kimla stood and quietly stepped towards the parlour door, "I thought it best if I come and make you aware of the itinerary for the day." Kimla grabbed the door handle and opened the door quickly. She looked around the reception hall and found no one listening.

She closed the door and turned to Alabast. As Kimla returned to her seat, she paused to look at the wall joining the parlour to Michalz' office.

"The office is locked," Alabast said, "and my husband still slumbers. The walls will have no ears."

Kimla sat, her back straight, with her hands flat on her thighs; a common Shovitic pose. "Alabast, on your honour, are you recording anything that is said in this room?"

The question cleared away any lingering cobwebs of sleep for Alabast. The question was surprising, and worrying.

"No, Kimla. Nothing is being recorded." Alabast didn't have to ask why she wanted to know, she was obviously about to reveal it.

Kimla patted the divan beside her, "Please, Alabast, join me here that we may speak quietly."

Wanted or not, the Shovitic was a guest in the house. It was beyond all protocol of decorum and common decency for a guest who was not a blood-kin, or a love-kin, to be so familiar with a hostess. In fact, such a request would normally be considered downright rude.

Alabast knew, however, Kimla was well aware of all of this. Alabast understood that by making this request, Kimla was going to discuss something sensitive with her, and that Kimla looked nervous, if not scared.

Alabast moved around the low table between them to sit on the paisley divan.

Kimla took off her fedora, and ran her hand through her short dark hair. She took off her dark glasses, and set them on the low table with her hat.

"Alabast, I must share something with you. It is something that would mean the execution of me and my whole family, were it to be known. I fully expect you to share this with Michalz, but it must go *no further* than he. Will you make an oath to this, an oath binding you and him?"

"Is this about Sepherin?" Alabast asked.

Kimla just nodded.

"Consider my oath given, that I and my husband will be bound to what you have asked."

"Thank you, Alabast." Kimla reached into her jacket pocket and pulled out a piece of paper. She unfolded it and began speaking slowly.

"Alabast, this is a translation of a document created on Earth, where Sepherin was sent. This is an official's report of information given to them concerning matters that occurred prior to the death of Tameht, her host." Kimla looked up at Alabast, her eyeworms were still and slightly drooping, revealing a deep sadness in her spirit.

Alabast was confused and nervous because she had no idea what was going to be revealed. She was worried it would make things worse for Sepherin, not that there could be much worse than a death sentence. She was sensible enough, however, to remain quiet and let the Imperite Guard proceed in her own time.

Finally, Kimla continued, "According to the statement of an eyewitness, the eyewitness who accompanies your daughter as we speak, Tameht was about to complete his Imperative."

There was a sharp intake of breath from Alabast, "*About* to?"

Kimla nodded. "He was abducted by the Eridani in the normal way. However, he had a young Earther woman with him, a woman who shared employment with him. According to her statement, Tameht killed many Vesna, Trigla, and drones. The witness stated that she participated in this, and was responsible for some of the deaths herself."

"In truth? A true-blood Earther did this?"

Kimla nodded again, "She did so at Tameht's side. They killed all aboard, save the Eridani Master in charge of the vessel."

Alabast kept her tongue still. She knew this would go faster if she didn't keep interrupting.

"Tameht was upset that the Earther would perish if he completed his Imperative with her on board. Therefore, through coercion, he manipulated the Eridani Master into returning the Earther to where they came from. However," Kimla snorted in disgust, "the Eridani pulled some trickery and transported Tameht to the surface as well, thus escaping the Imperative, escaping death."

She sat silent for a moment, allowing Alabast to take it all in.

"So, the host was about to complete the Imperative, but stopped to first save the Earther, and the Voiya tricked him?"

Kimla nodded.

Most of what Alabast knew was through the word of Cobus, something that she could not reveal. The palace's council who visited had, in fact, given little information about what transpired where Sepherin was posted.

Kimla held up the paper and began summarizing the events as they had been recorded by the Earther officials. As she concluded, she looked at Alabast and awaited a response.

The older woman looked away from Kimla, then stood and went to the window, drawing the curtains wide open. She looked out on the garden and the manicured lawn. *Tameht was not an oath-breaker. He was completing his Imperative, but he hesitated in order to save the Earther. Is that not the whole purpose of the Imperative?* It confused her that he had been called an oath-breaker, when this information revealed he had been duped by the treachery of the little Voiya, the Eridani Master. Alabast turned to Kimla, "So why did the two Guards declare him an oath-breaker? Why did they want to execute him?"

"All Imperite guards have a standing order that if an Imperite has been found to have failed their Imperative, they are to be executed on the spot. So, if they find an Imperite who has been on an Eridani ship, yet lived, they are to be executed. The two Imperite guardsmen would have easily smelled the Eridani Master and the blood of his retinue of Vesna, Trigla, and drones on Tameht, so soon after his encounter. They would have known he had been on the ship."

"But what about the Earther woman? He didn't break his Oath, he tried to save the Earther. He was duped, he was not a coward."

Kimla just nodded.

"So why would they try and kill him?"

Now Kimla shook her head, "I do not know. I think, in my own mind, they overreacted. It's that simple. Should they have asked more questions? Yes, I think they should have. However, I have known one of those guardsmen for a long time. He has always been hot-headed, and rash. His partner was not much better. But, such a personality is often beneficial for those on planetary assignment. In this situation ..."

The silence hung between them for a few moments after Kimla's words trailed off.

"So, because my daughter was trying to save her uncle, her *blood-kin*, from the unwarranted attack by the — Guards — she is to die?"

Kimla could say nothing, Alabast's reasoning was sound. It took a few seconds, but it finally sunk in for Kimla. *How did Alabast know* ...

"Alabast, how do you know her host was her blood-kin? I have not yet revealed this to you."

This mess, in Kimla's mind, was getting crazier and crazier. Now the Tekin woman knew things that only a select few Guards were aware of. Right now, there had to be trust between Kimla and Alabast. If Alabast answered the question, then she would have to lie. Kimla made the instant decision that how the woman knew what she did was not important; there was something going on here that Kimla needed to get to the bottom of, but didn't know how to do it. She decided that the answer to the question was not important. As the older woman was about to respond, Kimla put up her hands to stop her, "No, wait, nevermind. I don't want to know how you know this."

After a moment of silence had passed, Alabast took a deep breath, drawing herself up to her full height. "My daughter was acting to save her blood-kin. On her behalf, I claim the priory of the Third Law."

Looking up at her host, Kimla said, "Third Law begins with 'Save the pursuit of honourable justice'. You cannot claim Third Law in this case, for it merely condemns her, it does not reprieve her. Taffi and Minino, the guardsmen who died, would have believed they were honourably in pursuit of justice according to the Codex of Crimes."

"Then I claim priory of the Sixth Law."

Kimla looked up at Alabast, her eyeworms slowing, closing slightly, a squint for want of a better word.

Alabast spoke quietly, but firmly, "Our joy of life comes from our blood-kin and our love-kin. Let no thing be in your mind and your heart ahead of them: to this, all the laws are blind save none."

Her words gave Kimla some pause. The situation at hand, an Imperite, a clansman, had never been tried for killing an Imperite Guard. It had simply never happened. While the Third of the clan laws was clear, the Sixth Law did obfuscate that certainty. Such matters, however, were the realm of the Palace Council's office, not the realm of a mere Imperite program facilitator.

"That is a matter which you should take up with the Palace's Council. I believe one of them has visited with you?"

"He has, though he offered far less than you have."

"As is their nature."

Silence hung between the two women for several more moments.

"Is there something else?" Alabast asked, strain evident in her voice.

Kimla looked up at Alabast, and then looked at the door. She patted the divan next to her, "Join me again, please."

Alabast sighed deeply, and did as asked, wondering what in the name of the Unholy One was still to be revealed.

"Why is it," Kimla began, her eyeworms straight out, as she looked at the older woman, "that the Manager has such peculiar interest in your daughter?"

Alabast felt a shock jump through her whole body. She saw Kimla looking oddly at her, as Alabast felt her face drain of blood. Droplets of perspiration emerged on her forehead. She looked away, taking a tissue from her sleeve and using it to wipe her brow.

"Whatever do you mean, Kimla? What interest has he taken in her, beyond the interest in executing her?"

The Imperite Guard didn't miss a thing. She was as surprised by Alabast's reaction, as Alabast was surprised by the question.

"The Manager took steps to ensure that Sepherin was placed with Tameht Tekin."

"How so?"

"The original host family, the one which you and your husband helped select for Sepherin, was retired."

"Retired?" Alabast looked at Kimla, "Is this possible? I thought that an Imperite, once selected, was posted for life?"

Kimla let the silence hang, watching the honest confusion passing across Alabast's face. Finally, she continued, "I mean they were *retired*, in a most — *final* way."

The older woman's face held no understanding of what Kimla was saying.

It was Kimla's turn to sigh, frustrated, "Alabast, the original host, her husband and her children, were killed. This was done on the orders of the Manager."

Alabast recoiled from Kimla, her hands flying to her mouth to stifle the cry of alarm. "That cannot be *true!*" Alabast finally exclaimed, "He ordered them killed, for no reason?"

"There was a reason," Kimla continued, "it was to have your daughter placed with her blood-kin."

"Could he not just have ordered it to be so?"

"It would have looked peculiar, were he to do so. Such interference in the program is something that just isn't done.

Alabast was at a loss for words. That the original host and her family had been killed, on the orders of Kalabot, was unthinkable.

Kimla continued, "So why is it, Madam Tekin, that the Manger has such a *personal* interest in your daughter?"

Alabast knew full well why, but she could certainly not reveal the truth to an Imperite Guard.

Getting no answer, Kimla went on with the next question, "There is something else which troubles me."

Numbly, her mind still reeling, Alabast could only ask, "What is it?"

"The Imperites are selected randomly by a computer program. It evaluates many factors. There is, in my understanding and my supervisor's understanding, no possible way the program could have selected you for the Imperative. And yet, I delivered the notification myself. It could only have happened if the program was interfered with, and there is only one person who could have done that. Again, the Manager."

Alabast said nothing.

"Why would he go to such lengths to tamper with a proven and fair process, to have the mother of the oath-breaker — sent away?"

Alabast stared at her hands, trying to control her breathing, feeling the terror of how close Kimla was coming to asking a question that she dared not hear, let alone respond to. She was grateful that the Shovitics could only broadcast their thoughts, and not read minds.

"I am afraid I have no answers for these questions, Kimla. I think, that perhaps …" she looked up at the woman, resolve settling over her features, "… that perhaps, you should consider not asking these questions of anyone else."

Kimla pursed her lips, knowing the older woman's words were a caution, not a threat. She also knew that Alabast was correct. Kimla didn't know, however, if she was going to be able to let them go. Something smelled funny about this whole situation, which is an understatement given the sensitivity of the Shovitic sense of smell.

"I guess I cannot expect you to know the thoughts of the Manager." Kimla rose, putting on her hat and dark glasses as she did so. "I have disturbed you enough this early morning. I will leave you now, and urge you to remember the oath you gave me."

"I am not an oath-breaker," Alabast said absently, her mind still whirling.

As Kimla reached the parlour door, unescorted, she turned to look at Alabast. "You know, there is something else that I have often found curious."

Will this morning not end? The Mater of the house let out a breath she hadn't realized she had been holding. "Yes? What would that be?"

"I've often wondered at how — Shovitic — your daughter looks."

At that moment, both women's blood almost froze; both women felt bolts of alarm rushing through them — for different reasons.

For Kimla, it was her own words which made her swoon, something she had mused on, but never considered in the light of recent considerations. She let go of the doorknob and leaned back against the wall. She had stopped breathing with the sudden revelation that hit her. She gasped for air once, and then gasped once more as it all came together in her mind. *Sepherin does look Shovitic, and Kalabot has an incredible personal interest in her.* She looked up at Alabast, who was looking back at her with mortal fear written across her face.

The terrifying words came quickly to Kimla, her mind finally forming the words: *Kalabot is Sepherin's father.*

As the thought ricocheted around her mind, the even more stunning, and possibly disastrous thought emerged.

Sepherin Tekin is the child of the Great Prophecy.

"No — It cannot be," Kimla muttered to herself, staring at the carpet, not seeing it.

Sepherin was the herald of the next phase of the Shovitic race.

Kimla knew, from the oral history of their people, Umitia was the third world that the Shovitics had integrated themselves with over the last hundred thousand seasons. Each time, a significant event had occurred which heralded a drastic change for their clan. Each time, their entire clan, their entire race, had pulled up stakes and found a new world to move to. Each time it occurred because the world they had become part of had reached a point where it no longer needed the Shovitics.

This history, at the present time for Umitia, actually made sense to her. Society had grown in size and intelligence since the great wars. Even Kimla thought the laws enacted by Kalabot since he took power so long ago, were oppressive. She had thought more than once that if he left the people of Umitia alone, they would govern themselves adequately.

Her next thought was of her own family. Her widowed mother, her uncles, aunts, cousins, nephews, nieces, her brother and his wife — they would all be uprooted from everything they had known. The way of life was pleasant on Umitia. It was rich in nature, art, and beauty. They would be hard pressed to find a world like this to move to. *How quickly would it happen? Would it take days? Cycles? Seasons?*

Then she felt a chill shiver through her body. What would happen to the Imperite program? It was only a few hundred seasons old, and it began only because of the clan hatred of the Eridani. Where else would they find a world where the Imperite program could continue? What other world would have the hatred, the commitment? What would it mean for the three known galaxies if the Eridani learned they were going to be unchecked? This alone, could mean the end of the Shovitic race. They would have to launch an all-out war against the Eridani. As powerful as the sizeable Shovitic fleet of patrol crafts, frigates, and destroyers was, it was still no match for the total might of the Eridani and their allies. While the Eben participated in peacekeeping duties, she had no doubt they would refuse to join an all-out war, given the state of their own people. With the Eridani so recently aligning with the Kuabatay, they had an even more formidable war machine at their disposal. If the Shovitics went to all-out war with the Eridani, it could easily mean the end of the Shovitic race.

But would they even survive that long? Shovitics had been part of the Umitian world since before history was recorded on this planet, how would the clans react when they learned the Shovitics were not truly Umitian? When they found out that those who

442

controlled, policed, and administered them were not really of their world, what would they do?

The Shovitics might find themselves facing an untenable war right here on Umitia, before they even had a chance to leave. While the Imperite Guards had much more firepower and technology of weapons, the Umitians would be so incensed and in such large numbers, all the weaponry in the galaxy might not make the difference. And if the Umitian clans turned on the Shovitics, would her people even put up a fight?

One-on-one pursuit of honourable justice was perfectly acceptable. Being faced with the prospect of committing genocide against those whose world they inhabited, Kimla had a hard time believing her people would not just lay down arms and surrender. In a Shovitic mind, mass surrender would be preferable to a genocide of those who they shared so much with.

After taking a moment for all of this to sink in, Kimla looked up to see Alabast staring at her. *Kalabot, is the father of her daughter.* Kimla knew Alabast's fear was that Kimla had put together the truth about Sepherin's parentage. The corner of Kimla's mouth turned up in a sardonic grin. With so much at stake, she couldn't, at present, care less about Kalabot being the father, if indeed he truly was.

Returning to sit on the divan, Kimla removed her hat and dark glasses and turned to face Alabast.

Alabast's breath was deep and shaky, and tears had welled up in her eyes. She knew, deep inside, that Kimla had just worked out who Sepherin's father was, but she had no idea yet what the broader implications were. She only knew that such a revelation came with a death sentence. She waited in terror for what was going to be said as the younger woman sat next to her.

"Is Kalabot the blood-father of Sepherin?" Kimla asked, her voice faint. Her tone was curious, not predatory.

The older woman didn't look away. She had been asked a direct question and were she to lie, a blood test would prove it as such. Lying to an Imperite Guard was not a capital offense, but it was enough on its own to dissolve the charter of a House in such a circumstance. Alabast knew that to answer yes, would mean her own life was forfeit, but also, so was Kalabot's, according to the law.

Then a new thought occurred to Alabast, *Perhaps if he is dead, there will be leniency for Sepherin upon her return.*

The word practically leapt from her mouth, "Yes."

What came next, however, was not what Alabast was expecting.

After a deep, slow breath, Kimla nodded once, and then began speaking.

"A long time ago, lived a great Shovitic. His name was Alita Kiut ..."

Chapter 60

The word spread quietly, at first, and then it picked up speed. The word brought to life a seething resentment that had long been held close to the chest of those growing weary of the Shovitics. Now the resentment spilled out to their mouths, and to the ears near those mouths.

An Imperite was going to be killed. Worse, an Imperite who was the mother of an infant was going to be killed. Worse, she was going to be killed for killing two Imperite *Guards*, the word 'guard' being spoken with disgust.

A lot of people did not believe it. Not that she was going to be killed, but that she had killed two Guards. The Shovitics, slender and tall, were not physically daunting; but their combat abilities and utter ruthlessness were legendary amongst the races who encountered them. Even the Eben approached Shovitics with wariness. The thought that an Imperite had been able to kill not one *Guard*, but two, was difficult to accept.

Those same people were at a complete loss, however, to fathom another reason for the Imperite's return to Umitia and her execution. Even the oldest amongst the clans could only remember one Imperite who had ever been executed as an oath-breaker, and that was for *refusing* to complete the Imperative when taken by the Eridani.

There were a lot of people, as well, who *did* believe she had killed the two Imperite *Guards*. A lot of people were of the mind that it was about time someone showed those damn Shovitics *what-was-what* and gave them some *what-for*.

Questions were asked, comments were made, discussions were held, and rumours started while long held hatreds and distrusts boiled to the surface. On both continents, in the households of all six clans, in parks, in drink parlours, at picnics, at schools, at places of work: voices grew louder, tongues grew sharper, and dissent took on the language of demand — on both sides of the table.

In the quiet mountain town of Allaroo, the six local Imperite Guards — three husband and wife teams — were roused from sleep in the early hours one morning to the sound of fire alarms in their own homes. All three houses were burned to the ground, but luckily, neither the Guards nor their children were injured.

Several thousand leagues away, in the small city of Halveris, several Guards were targeted with the same kind of attack the following night. Unfortunately, fate was not so kind. An Imperite Guard's daughter, only eight seasons old, died in one of the five fires that night.

In the small city of Halveris, the detachment of thirty Imperite Guards was bolstered overnight by a task force of nine hundred more Guards. The man who was responsible for organizing the arsons, a man of the Treanda clan, was quickly identified and captured. By decree of the Manager, his chartered House was dissolved, a House of over 5,000 clansmen spread across dozens of cities and towns.

The next day, under the most intriguing of torture methods, the eight men who had lit the fires were identified. A public gallows was hastily constructed and they were condemned to be hung for their crime, a crime which had resulted in the death of a child.

It *was* a heinous act, all would normally have agreed.

However, these were not normal times. The clansmen were of a mind that it was merely an accident. No one would kill a child on purpose, and therefore it should not be treated as a capital crime. There was also a vocal crowd who considered it prescient justice considering that the Shovitics were going to execute Sepherin Tekin, and though she was an adult, she was still someone's child. That she was the mother of a child was not yet common knowledge, else things may have turned out far worse in the normally peaceful down of Halveris.

The eight men who were arrested were from three different Houses. The charter of each of those Houses was revoked, turning nearly eighteen thousand more clansmen, from both continents, into the streets. As it was in the Codex of Crimes, they were turned out with only the clothes on their backs, and a single suitcase in their hands.

The day of execution for the arsonists arrived quickly. All agreed it was unfair that all eight were held equally responsible, though only two of them had started the fire where the child died. The public square of Halveris City hosted the hastily constructed gallows. From early morning, it was surrounded by hundreds of Imperite Guards. Approaching the noon hour, the prisoners were led, heads held high and showing no remorse, to their doom.

Before those clansmen could mount the gallows, the streets quickly filled with the roaring voices of factory workers, labourers, farmers, retirees, homemakers, and office workers. Both men and women rushed to the public square, armed with whatever they could arm themselves with: shovels, axes, metal pipes, chains, and even one old woman who came in a rage of screaming fury armed only with two knitting needles.

Thirty-six Imperite Guards died in the resulting melee.

One thousand, four hundred and thirteen clansmen perished: more than half the small city's population.

To the guardsmen's credit, not a single child under the age of adulthood was killed.

That the Shovitic guardsmen were merely in the honourable pursuit of justice was not lost on anyone. Tensions had been twisted so high, though, that no one cared. All that the populace of Umitia chose to hear of this event was that half a city of clansmen had been executed by the Imperite *Guards*.

After the Halveris Massacre, as it became known, the temper of all clansmen flared and more violence broke out. People took to the streets in protest. Guards' facilities were surrounded with

447

violent demonstrators; ground cars were overturned, some set ablaze; Shovitic homes were pelted with rocks, and other disgusting biological matter. Patrolling guardsmen were also randomly and savagely attacked, as well as many Shovitics who were not guardsmen.

To the clansmen's credit, no more Shovitic children under the age of adulthood were harmed.

Unfortunately, Halveris was the site of the first riot, but not the last. Within a few days, Imperite Guards dealt with riots in every large city on the planet, and several smaller ones. Even rural towns had those who took to the streets in violence, and with a lust and cry for Shovitic blood.

The world of Umitia had, in less than a ten-sleep, reached a boiling point. Kalabot was, to use an Earther idiom, madder than a Baptist in a brothel.

Within a few days of the Halveris Massacre, using article 43 of the Codex of Crimes, the Manager declared a state of 'Clan Rebellion.' Following this declaration, the Imperite Guards were authorized to pursue honourable justice with the administration of lethal judgement, without due process. The Imperite Guards moved against the perpetrators of capital crimes swiftly (remember, attacking an Imperite Guard is punishable by death).

As all this was taking place, the Palace issued a general recall to all Imperite Guards on patrol duties, in all but the most criminally unstable systems. Off-world guardsmen were left without the resource of orbiting duty frigates as they, too, were recalled. Within four sleeps, the Imperite Guards presence had been quadrupled on Umitia. The many Shovitics who were not part of the Imperite Guards, because not all were, quickly found themselves being conscripted if they were healthy enough to carry a weapon and shoot it. In a short time, the standing force of forty thousand Imperite Guards on Umitia became a presence of two hundred and ten thousand, both proper guards and conscript guards. This massive show of power was on a world with a population of less than ten million, including the Shovitics.

Initially, on average, for every Imperite Guard that was attacked in the streets, three or four clansmen wound up paying with their lives, not one of them seeing a councillor or a magistrate. Luckily for the clansmen's families and Houses, the seizure and dissolution of their House was no longer to be pursued in these matters, as the relevant section of the Codex of Crimes was suspended once a state of 'Clan Rebellion' was declared.

The random street attacks turned into gang attacks, and then into full blown riots. Within a ten-sleep of the Halveris Massacre, the Manager took more extraordinary steps.

First, Kalabot declared a planet-wide curfew for every clansman, not of the Shovitic clan. Anyone found on the street after the standard dinner hour, could be shot on sight without question or explanation.

Next, he ordered all commerce and trade to be suspended. All businesses were forced to shut down; all agricultural concerns were ordered to stop tending to their crops; all stores and suppliers were ordered to shut their doors; all those employed by others were ordered to stay at home, including domestic help.

Finally, he had the power grids turned off in every city and town, except for the power grids that supplied the Palace, the spaceport, and the military bases.

With the resulting uproar, Kalabot had the growing number of Imperite Guards redistributed to the higher density population areas, leaving smaller rural and seaside towns unattended. Most of those smaller towns and villages effectively returned to life as normal, ignoring the edicts, until the power was turned off. Even then, the ingenuity of the Hobonol and Silthit clans quickly brought online alternate forms of power generation.

In the larger cities, families began rationing food, and sharing food amongst neighbours. Clansmen are great hoarders, with root cellars and supply rooms in every house that would see them through difficult times. It had been this way for thousands of seasons amongst the clans. The closing of supply centres was an annoyance, not an end to life. This was something Kalabot knew when he made the decision. But he also knew it would help keep people at home.

With these edicts in place, armed patrols of the streets increased. At first, anyone found violating the curfew or engaging in commerce was shot. Within a couple of days, the Imperite Guards themselves decided that there had been enough killing. Those violating the Manager's edicts were then simply beaten, rather than killed. As the administration of honourable justice took the turn towards a non-lethal response, surprisingly, the guardsmen found the instances of attack decreasing, instead of increasing as they feared they would. As the instances of attack decreased, so did the severity of the non-lethal response. By the time a ten-sleep had passed after the Halveris Massacre, violation of the edicts resulted in not much more than a half-hearted slapping around.

Soon, the Imperite Guards began talking to clansmen, and the clansmen began talking back.

After a few more days, the Imperite Guards found no one violating the edicts. After the imposition of the edicts, there were only two more riots, in places far from Kilkestand City, and then the riots stopped all together.

Within two ten-sleeps of the first fire in Allaroo, the planet had settled into a quiet state of — waiting.

In total, over seven thousand, four hundred and twelve Imperite Guards were killed in the attacks and the riots. Tragically, over two hundred and thirty thousand clansmen perished, almost a full twentieth of the planet's population.

The history books would simply refer to these days as: *The Second Clan Rebellion.*

Eventually, being satisfied with the reports from the field that the populace had come to its senses, Kalabot lifted the second and third edicts, but not the curfew; though he imposed detainment as the punishment, it was no longer a lethal offence. Life returned to a semblance of normality.

There was one thing, fortunately or unfortunately, that Kalabot had completely failed to pay attention to during the Second Clan Rebellion. That was the words, fears, and attitudes of the Imperite Guards. While they followed the letter of their oath, the guardsmen's oath had been horribly strained and tested in the preceding days.

The Shovitics mourned the losses of their own clansmen, but they also mourned the losses of their planetary brothers and sisters in the other six clans.

Kalabot was not aware of the many stories of succour and aid provided by the Shovitics to the other clansmen. He was not aware of the countryside Shovitic families who fed, hid, and protected many of the other six clans, keeping those people safe from the patrolling Guards. Kalabot was not aware that on three different occasions, facing angry mobs in some smaller towns, those Imperite Guards had simply turned and departed, leaving the clansmen standing in bewilderment. They simply refused to fire on those who had been their neighbours for all of their lives.

It had totally escaped Kalabot's notice, and the notice of his internal security operatives, that a fifth column was forming within the ranks of the Imperite Guards. Well, there was *one* Guard that raised the concern, but his compatriots generally agreed he read too many novels of fiction.

Obliviously, Kalabot enacted the machinations to return society to a vestige of its former self, until such a time when the curfew edict would be lifted. In the meantime, businesses re-opened, enabling commerce and trade to resume.

The heavy presence of Imperite Guards on the streets remained in place for a time, but slowly those numbers dwindled to something slightly more than normal. While it would be wrong to say that peace had been restored, in the larger cities a state of détente between the guardsmen and the other clans had been achieved.

And then Sepherin Tekin arrived home.

Part III
Homecoming

Chapter 61

Meanwhile, back on duty frigate 803, life went on as normal. While reports of the events transpiring on Umitia reached the ship, the guardsmen of the ship were not affected by it, other than having concern for their own family and friends.

By the time of the Halveris Massacre, there were still several ten-sleeps of travel ahead of them. They were certain that the steps the Palace was taking would return things to normal long before they arrived. They hoped.

After Fitid departed a daily security briefing, something new since the eruption of hostilities on the homeworld, he returned to his cabin to check his messages. Transmissions from Umitia took a while, as they did not go through the ERB. After several days of waiting, he finally had a message from his spouse, with an attachment.

Before opening the attachment, he read his spouse's message. It began with her relating that some of the family had come for dinner, before the hostilities started. The only mention of her uncle was that when she had asked for his thoughts on other career options, he was at a loss as to why anyone would change direction so suddenly. Fetid knew exactly what it meant. Her uncle, the investigator in the Tekin Foundry accident, had no idea why the investigation was terminated and the verdict changed.

Fitid turned to the item attached to the electronic message. The attachment was a scanned copy of the handwritten visitor logs for the Palace, for the week the investigation into the Tekinson foundry ended. He turned to the page covering the day that the end of the investigation was announced, and quickly scanned the two dozen names printed, then signed, on the page. There were some names he recognized, but not the name he was looking for.

He scrolled back through the log's display to look at the previous day.

And just like that, the other shoe dropped.

The last visitor of the day, at the bottom of the log, was Alabast Tekin.

Fitid sat back and did the math in his head one more time. Sepherin Tekin was born nine cycles to the day, after Alabast Tekin's visit to the Palace — after her late-night visit to Kalabot.

Sepherin Tekin is the child of the Great Prophecy.

Before deleting the entire thing, he went back and read the message from his spouse again. It did contain certain words of comfort between a husband and wife. It was oddly formatted though. *She must have been distracted when she typed this,* Fitid thought.

Then he realized that she was as careful in personal communications as she was in business communications. If she was typing the message, no matter how distracted she was, Corla would not have sent it until it was grammatically perfect, and perfectly formatted.

This message was anything but that.

Fitid read the message several times, extracted what was intended, but found no reason for the manner in which she had written it. He turned away from the monitor for a few minutes, thinking about what his next steps were going to be, then turned back to the monitor.

It jumped out at him right away.

Somewhere in the recesses of his mind, the desire to make sense of the message found something to make sense of. It was the last letter on each line. Each line had been ended in a specific place, allowing those last letters to spell out a message. He had looked at the left edge of the message which was perfectly aligned; however, this message would have been too obvious there. The last letter of each line spelled out: tellkimlapilutrustretekin.

Fitid saw a couple words jump out at him:

'Tell kimlapilutrustre tekin'.

After staring at it for a minute, he could see 'trust', but didn't know if that was the word intended. He didn't recognize 'trustre', 'lutrust', or 'lutrustre'. Then he realized it was 're tekin' at the end. This left 'kimlapilutrust'.

Something was nagging at him, and then he realized what it was. Kimla Pilu was the Guard who had been Sepherin Tekin's handler when she was selected for the Imperite program. That was what he needed to decode his mate's message:

'Tell kimla pilu trust re tekin.'

It was too obvious to be coincidence.

Fitid didn't know that Kimla had been in touch with Zekrin, and Kimla didn't know that Corla had listened to her conversation.

Fitid returned to the communications section. He requested a secure connection to the Palace, to speak with the Imperite Guard Kimla Pilu. He was truthfully able to state the reason for the secure connection was Guard's business, which was Guards' vernacular for, 'shut up and do what you're told.'

Chapter 62

Not long after the Halveris Massacre, Cassie went into labour. No one had ever given birth aboard a duty frigate before. The ship's three medics had, therefore, been reviewing all of the medical texts for Falwasz birthing, as both Falwasz and the Earther were Humanesh, with no distinction between them in regards to gestation and delivery.

Their efforts did nothing to allay the fear that settled upon Cassie as the contractions grew closer and more intense. The medic placed in charge of the delivery had never had any exposure to delivering a child, Humanesh or Shovitic.

We can make this distinction now, because Sepherin and Cassie had learned that the Shovitics were not really from Umitia. It would eventually be revealed to Sepherin that they weren't even Humanesh.

Where Earthers and the five Humanesh clans of Umitia were of the class *Mammalia*, the order *Primates*, the family *Hominidae*, the genus *Homo*, and the species *sapiens*; the Shovitics were of the class *Mammalia*, the order *Creodonta*, the family *Oxyaena*, the genus *Homo*, and the species *sapiens*. Fortunately for Earthers, the *Creodanta* order did not survive the early Eocene epoch — on Earth. Earther taxonomy can be applied to most Humanesh aliens as Earth, though it's a fact known to very few, is the seed planet for sentient Humanesh life, cosmologically speaking. Therefore, because of this taxonomy, where Humanesh descend from primates, Shovitics descend from a form of prehistoric — *cat*.

Aside from the lead medic's lack of experience in matters pertaining to childbirth, his bedside manner was also a little rusty. He made the mistake of attempting to check Cassie's dilation in the middle of a contraction. He awoke fifteen minutes later to find himself in another medical bay of the ship, having his broken jaw attended to by a snickering colleague. When the lead medic had shoved his fingers up Cassie's hoo-ha in the middle of a contraction, her left leg had piston pumped, connecting squarely with his now-broken jaw.

The ship's second medic became the lead medic for the delivery. His bedside manner was far more cautious and conciliatory than his colleague's had been.

Seventeen hours after the first contraction, with Sepherin on one side and Fitid on the other side, both holding Cassie's hands, amongst much screaming from all three (because Cassie almost broke Sepherin and Fitid's fingers from squeezing so hard), the ship was able to claim status as the only duty frigate ever to have a Humanesh give birth on board.

After the newborn's airway was cleared, and a robust slap on the ass, the arrival of Richard Tameht Scott was heralded by a deep, resonant wail that was heard throughout the whole deck of the ship. While the baby was cleaned up by the medic, with Sepherin's supervision, the Watch Commander arrived to extend his good wishes to the Earther, and to confirm for her the date and time of the child's birth, according to where she came from. There was, however, no birth certificate to be issued.

It was a difficult message for the Watch Commander to deliver, knowing what the young woman's fate would be. He just hoped that a suitable House would be found to raise the child, and that someone more callous than he would inform the young Earther that she would also be executed after the trial.

While Sepherin had to return to her quarters several times during Cassie's labour to feed little Karl, by the time Cassie and Richard were settled after the birth, she realized she had not been back to her quarters in almost six Earth hours. Rushing back to her room, her prison guards, who were now more or less companions, were hot on her heels and barely able to keep up. She opened the door to a find she need not have worried.

Fitid had strong-armed Senji, the only female Shovitic in off-world service, to look after little Karl during Cassie's labour and birth. Not having a maternal instinct in her body, Senji was at first frustrated, then scared, and then curious. At some point in the last six hours, her maternal instincts surfaced. When Sepherin returned to the room, Senji was propped up on the back corner of the bed, fast asleep. She had removed her jacket and shirt, and then wrapped a blanket around herself with little Karl sound asleep against her warm, pale skin. When she woke to find Sepherin smiling at them, she explained it was the only thing she could think of to stop his crying, and it had worked.

A few hours after the birth, Cassie and Richard, Rick for short, were returned to their prison cell/cabin. While Rick was certainly not the child of the prophecy, the Shovitics, as has been explained, absolutely love children. Within two days, the entire crew had stopped by in the cafeteria, at meal times, to give the new addition a hideous, but loving smile, and a brief touch on the forehead.

Chapter 63

It had been several days since Kimla had the most revealing conversation with Alabast. Not really knowing what to do afterwards, Kimla had taken a personal day from her duties. She spent most of that day at the archives on the far side of Kilkestand City. She read numerous sections from the manuscripts studying all the prophecies of Alita Kiut, particularly those dealing with the Great Prophecy. She then spent the rest of the day looking up interpretations of the prophecy, including information she had never seen where it had been believed the prophecy was fulfilled. In both cases, simple blood tests ruled it out.

She did find an interesting article on the interpretation of the relevant sections of the Codex of Crimes regarding the fulfillment of the prophecy. It had been written several hundred seasons ago by a Shovitic scholar of the law. The bottom line was that prophecy or not, the Codex still stood firm on the punishment for both the mother and the father of the child. It was still a death sentence for breeding between clans.

Kimla wondered where on Umitia they would find an Imperite Guard willing to kill the mother, *or the father*, of the child of the Great Prophecy.

She spent the next few days tending to her other selected Imperites, immersing herself in her duties, while attentively following the news of the horrible fire which claimed the life of a child in Halveris City.

One morning in the Imperite program office, while planning her days' visits, she was surprised to be summoned to the communications centre. She was even more surprised at the conversation that took place with Corla's husband.

The riots had not broken out in Kilkestand City yet. The day of the call from Fitid, Kimla joined her brother, Talin Pilu, for lunch at a Shovitic-owned restaurant in the Olde Towne district.

It didn't take him long to realize how distracted she was, but she kept putting off his brotherly concern. The restaurant wasn't busy, and they lingered over their meal, talking of inconsequential matters in between her dodging his more prying questions. Finally, when dessert was served, with only two other patrons in the restaurant, she started talking. She felt that if she didn't tell him, and get his perspective, she was going to explode. Of all the people in the clan Shovitic, he was the one she was most certain she could trust.

"*The child of the prophecy*?" he whispered, shock in his voice.

After a few moments of silence, "You are going to have to arrange a blood test when she returns."

She told him about the call from Fitid and that the blood test had been done.

"Kimla, you cannot allow her to be executed — *we* cannot allow her to be executed."

Kimla sighed deeply, crossing her arms under her small breasts. She started chewing on the corner of her lip, mimicking Sepherin Tekin's mannerism.

"Kimla," he leaned forward, speaking quietly and earnestly, "think of what this means. If this is so, if she is the one, then this entire world is about to change. Think of us, our lives. Our people have lived on Umitia for tens of thousands of seasons, and this is all going to change. We are going to have to redefine our entire race, as it *must be*. If the child of the prophecy were allowed to pass unremarked, then the implications — everything we stand for — *our entire race's purpose must not be put in jeopardy*."

Kimla was silent, staring at her bowl of fruit and fresh cream.

"Kimla, if we are to have a new purpose, a new future, a new destiny — then she cannot be executed."

"Brother, I'm not sure that others will see it in the way you do."

He sat back and let a small smile play across his face, "I think you would be surprised."

Talin looked at the other two diners who were about to leave, "Parski, Lumin, come over here for a moment."

Kimla sat forward fast, grabbing her brother's arm, "No! Talin, what are you doing?"

He smiled at her as the two Shovitic men came over to the table, "Proving you wrong."

Chapter 64

Kalabot went out through the basement door and up the long earthen ramp to the lawn. He stopped and watched the workmen who were digging the foundation for the new greenhouse, showroom, and sales centre. He watched them without paying attention, his thoughts focussed on the troubles brewing in the cities and towns across both continents of Umitia.

The Halveris Massacre was foremost in his mind, the images of the burned child mingled with the images of over a thousand dead clansmen. There was a small, rarely visited place in his heart that grieved for those clansmen, but he firmly believed they had brought that wrath upon themselves. Anyone who could *not* see that was blind, in his estimation. Regardless of what was driving this nonsense from the clansmen, whoever killed the Guard's little girl should have swung from a rope, end of argument. As the two men who started the fire were spirited away from the gallows by the mob, they failed to be punished for the death of the child. Kalabot decided that later in the evening he would pay a visit to those two men and dispense some honourable justice of his own.

He came out of his reverie as he realized Cobus and a tall young man were walking towards him. The man looked like a Hobonol labourer, but his eyes seemed much more intelligent than average.

"Fair morning to you, Kalabot."

"And to you, Master Gardener."

"I'd like to introduce the contractor that we have hired for this project. This is Roguk Fozretson."

"I'm honoured, Sir," the tall, muscular clansman said.

"Cobus has informed me that you have considerable experience working with these types of wood for the construction."

"All of my life, Sir. I trained first with my family and am now a master carver. I also have a lifetime of experience as a home builder."

"Very well," Kalabot said. "This project is important. Please ensure only the finest hands you have apply their efforts to it."

"Would you care to see our progress?" Cobus asked with a smile.

Kalabot looked at him, but said nothing.

Cobus smile faltered, "I suppose there is not much more to see than a large hole in the ground and some cement foundation work."

"Keep me informed of the progress, Cobus." Kalabot stepped to the side and then walked, glided is more accurate a term, around to the front of the Palace.

Cobus and Roguk looked at each other. Cobus nodded once and the two men headed towards the basement entrance. With the troubles brewing, there were two Imperite Guards stationed at the door instead of only one. The Guards just looked at the two men as they stopped in front of them.

"If you will excuse us, we need to enter the utilities room just inside the entrance." Cobus spoke evenly, no tremor or fear in his voice.

"For what reason?" asked the arger of the two Imperite Guards.

"This is the general contractor for the project. I need to take him into the larger utilities room to show him the water distribution network for the grounds and the existing greenhouses." Cobus smiled and waited.

The two guardsmen were silent, but from the look on their faces it was obvious they were having a telepathic conversation.

"You have only begun the foundation, Master Gardener. You are not ready to connect the plumbing."

Cobus was about to reply when Roguk spoke up, "Which of you is the plumber?"

Cobus felt a chill run up his spine, *No, Roguk, no. Do not raise their ire. Not now, not with what's going on in the world.*

The smaller guardsman took a step forward. "I think your mouth is in danger of running away from you," he said with his annoying sibilant speech pattern.

"You misunderstand, Guard. I do not insult you, but simply inquire if you know something about the construction of the water supply system that will address my immediate needs without us entering the Palace?"

Neither man was smiling.

"You would imply," the Guard said, with an ugly tone, as he took a step closer to Roguk, "that I am here for your benefit? That I am here to work for *you*?"

Roguk looked over his shoulder and pointed at the construction site. "Do you see the earth mover, standing ready, but doing nothing?"

The Guards gaze did not waver.

"That earth mover is ready to dig where we will install the inlet station for the new project. Because your people would not allow the Palace blueprints to be viewed by anyone, but Shovitic engineers, we were not able to establish the final location of the sub-structure. We were told this would be established when we were ready to begin construction. We have, as you can see by the big hole in the ground, commenced construction. I need to see precisely where the mains are, and where the sub-junctions are, so that we can place the inlet station sub-structure for the most efficient lay of water lines. So unless you are a plumber, or a mechanical engineer, we need to see the room inside."

The Guard's jaw was working, his eyeworms showed hesitation. But still, Cobus knew that Roguk was pushing the line with his insolence.

"Of course," Roguk continued, taking a step back and smiling slightly, "you could always explain to the Manager why his newest project has been delayed."

Cobus worked hard not to smile at the young man's final jab. He relaxed, knowing it was going to work.

The two Guards finally stepped aside.

Once in the basement corridor, Cobus unlocked the first door on the left and they entered a dark, damp, smelly, but spacious room. It contained the primary water distribution matrix of pipes, with the requisite dozens of valves. Everything in this room distributed water to the greenhouses, the Palace, and the gardens. It was one of the few rooms which had survived the destruction of the previous palace almost 150 seasons past. Of course, some reconstruction had been done to permit the newer (relatively speaking) water distribution system.

It was Cobus' knowledge of this that had allowed him to come up with a most complicated, yet logical plan to spirit Sepherin and her child from the clutches of the Palace.

The Guard who followed them into the room quickly grew bored, and returned to his station outside. As he did so, the door to the room slowly closed behind him. Cobus led Roguk behind some pipework to stop in front of a square cover in the wall. With a ratchet wrench from his tool belt, Cobus deftly undid the covers retaining bolts and set it aside. Roguk pulled a torch from his own belt and shined it inside.

The wall he was peering through was a false wall which covered piping and conduits long in disuse. It also revealed a narrow tunnel that seemed to run the length of the Palace, at the edge of the basement foundation. Three minutes later they were squatting by what were obviously toilet fittings. Cobus showed the restraint mechanism that held the plumbing fixtures in place. After spraying some lubricating oil on the joints of the restraints, they quickly came undone with only a minimum of effort and little noise.

The modular design of the one-piece toilet and sink, something common in prisons on many planets, swung inward with a slight squeak. Cobus quickly applied some more graphite in a liquid carrier to eradicate the noise. Without entering the room, as the hole was too small for Roguk, he peered inside. It was the Palace holding cell. It was the only holding cell in the building.

They put the one-piece fixture back in place, securing the restraint mechanisms, and quickly returned to the main mechanical room. Roguk took a few quick measurements with Cobus' help. He then measured a second time, just to be sure. Measure twice, cut once — or dig once, in this case. The two men returned to the construction site without acknowledgement from the Imperite Guards outside the basement. The digging machine began its work.

Cobus stood to the side of the new hole, leaning on a shovel. He watched Kalabot in the distance. The old Shovitic was still gliding slowly around the many garden beds. Cobus sighed deeply and wondered what was going to happen when Kalabot found out about his treachery. Cobus wondered if he would be the only one to feel the Manager's wrath, or if Kalabot would kill his wife as well?

Chapter 65

After his contemplative stroll in the gardens, Kalabot returned to his office to find the senior planetary coordinator waiting for him.

As Kalabot seated himself, Gouhn stood opposite the desk and waited.

"Well? What are we to discuss?" Kalabot asked as he folded his long bony fingers together in front of him.

"With recent events, Manager, we are concerned there may be more violence when the oath-breaker is returned to the planet." He didn't say child of the prophecy, he was afraid Kalabot would kill him on the spot. But he was friends with people who were friends with Kimla and her brother. He had heard the whispers. However, as most, he was hesitant to believe it fully until she returned and it could be confirmed. Until then, play the game.

"It would appear that she need not return for the violence to occur. But, yes, when she arrives there may be more troubles."

"We will need to bolster the presence of Guards, here, in the city."

"Of course, did you need to *ask* me for permission?" Kalabot asked testily.

"Sir, no, of course not. But this will leave the provinces under protected."

Kalabot sighed, "Gouhn, there will be a few more riots, some more people will die, but this will die down in time, before she arrives. I am going to enact a few special provisions which will assist in quelling this nonsense."

"A curfew?" the Guard asked.

Kalabot nodded, "Yes, and if that does not suffice, I will enact the provision to stop all commerce."

Gouhn nodded, "Yes, there is precedent for that. It was done once in the past as I recall, with effectiveness."

Kalabot looked up at the Guard, "Is there anything else?"

"Yes, Sir." Gouhn hesitated. He knew he needed clarification on the next matter, but hated that things might get so far as for the clarification to be important.

"Well?" Kalabot leaned forward, staring intently at Gouhn.

"Sir, what will be the orders for quelling insurrection if it occurs when she is returned? If the people truly do revolt, if the measures you take do not have the desired effect, how far are we going to go?"

"When it comes time for the trial," Kalabot responded quickly, too quickly, "there will be no tolerance for interference. If anyone attempts to stop the proceedings, or disrupt the proceedings, kill them. Kill anyone who so much as raises a fist."

Gouhn felt numb. He felt the need to urinate. He had expected suppression and incarceration. He thought he was being stupid worrying about an order for executions. Yet that was what Kalabot had just given him: an order to execute Umitians, *en masse*, if necessary. Gouhn knew that he was responsible for security on Umitia, and Kalabot was making a decision which flew in the face of everything the Shovitics stood for. He could not allow this.

"Sir, I must respectfully disagree with you. To take such an action would only incite a volatile populace to …"

Kalabot cut him off, "Are you refusing to do as I say? *Have you not seen this nonsense in Halveris city?* I have already received reports of other riots breaking out. *Do you suppose we should tolerate this? These — peasants — they* will obey us *or they will fear us!*"

Kalabot was practically bouncing with rage as he spoke. His fist was pounding on the desk to emphasize his words, spittle flew from his lips and his eyeworms had splayed wide open, revealing his rage.

"But, Sir! To kill protesters in large numbers would …"

"I DON'T CARE WHAT IT WOULD DO." Kalabot screamed at the Imperite Guard. "THE OATH-BREAKER WILL SWING FROM THE GALLOWS AND NOTHING WILL STOP IT FROM HAPPENING!"

Gouhn had enough. What Kimla and her brother had said was obviously true. Nothing else could cause the Manager to respond this way. He decided that he would not be part of this horror, this travesty, this — dishonour. He looked Kalabot squarely in the eye sockets and said, "No."

With no indication he was moving, Kalabot appeared in front of the desk, only centimetres from Gouhn's face. He spoke quietly to the planetary coordinator, "What did you say to me?"

Gouhn smelled the stench of the old man's breath; he felt the waves of rage coming off of him; he could see every muscle in the old man's body was tightened and tensed, like clock springs.

"I will not be part of this, Kalabot. I will not be part of a massacre when they are only defending — *the child of the prophecy.*"

Kalabot flew backwards, like he had been slapped. His eyeworms pointed straight outwards at Gouhn, his lower lip started quivering.

"You …"

Gouhn nodded his head, "Yes, I know that Sepherin Tekin is the child of the prophecy. I know she's your daughter, Manager. I will not be part of …"

Gouhn's words were choked off. His hands instinctively went to his neck, but Kalabot was using the power of the Manager to strangle the words from the man, and strangle his life from him.

Kalabot's worst fear had been realized. Someone other than Alabast knew he was the father of the child. *Cobus? Was it him?*

Did he say something? Kalabot shook his head. He knew that Cobus would keep the secret, for to reveal it would have meant Kalabot's rage against him, his wife, his children, and his house.

The Manager watched as life fled from Gouhn, and then he let the body fall to the floor in front of his desk. He stared at it. Leaning back against his desk, Kalabot folded his hands in front of his face and shut his eyes. *What am I becoming?*

Kalabot had no problem ending a life, but for a reason. Gouhn had done nothing deserving of death. He had taken a stance, a moral stance, which was what a Guard should have done in this circumstance. Kalabot knew he had overreacted.

Sepherin was his daughter: fact.

Sepherin was the child of the prophecy: fact.

Sepherin only killed those foolish Guards to defend her blood-kin: fact.

The Manager had the power to overturn any decision reached after the pursuit of honourable justice: fact.

When Sepherin returned to Umitia, the entire Shovitic race would be uprooted and forced to find a new home amongst the stars: fact.

Kalabot didn't want to have to leave Umitia. He didn't want to leave the beauty of the world and the peacefulness of the world. It was a Garden of Eden compared to worlds like Eridani Prime, Pikaya, Earth, or Feloram. But Kalabot knew that even the adventure of their race moving out through the stars again would be denied him. Instead, he and Alabast would swing from a rope for their crime of cross-clan union.

No.

He didn't want to die, and he didn't want to leave Umitia.

Kalabot looked down at Gouhn's body. He had not overreacted, he had preserved the Shovitics' homeworld, and he had preserved his own life. He was, after all, the Manager. He was above the Codex of Crimes in regards to terminating individuals who posed a threat to Umitia. *And an Umitia without Shovitic rule is a world destined for peril, isn't it?*

He knew that more would have to die, but this was for a greater good. When it became known that he had acted for the best interests of the entire planet, he would be understood, so he wanted to believe. But leaning against the desk, his hands folded in front of him, looking down at Gouhn's cooling corpse, there was a part of Kalabot's *koum* that knew this was not true. He was simply acting to save his own life.

Kalabot paced around the office as he continued to reassure himself that he was acting honourably. Finally he lifted the phone and spoke brusquely to the person on the other end. A few moments later, there was a knock on the door.

"Come," Kalabot called out, sitting behind his desk again.

Kervin, the assistant planetary coordinator, opened the door and entered the large office. He stopped short as he saw his superior crumpled on the floor, his face a mask of agony in death.

Recovering quickly, he approached the Manager's desk, keeping his eyes on Kalabot and avoided looking at the body of his superior, his friend.

There was a lengthy silence as Kalabot stared at Kervin, looking for some sign of — he wasn't sure what. Finally he spoke to the man.

"Congratulations on your promotion, Kervin. We must discuss the details of security for the trial and execution of the oath-breaker." Kalabot leaned forward slightly, "Or do you have the same — *reservations* — that your predecessor had?"

Chapter 66

Weapons on Umitia were the sole purview of the Shovitics, ever since the last war. That is, guns were the sole purview of the Shovitics, be they chemical, electrical, or laser.

A pitchfork, shovel club, bow and arrow, table leg, etc., were anyone's domain. As we saw in Halveris, even knitting needles can be a weapon.

The Shovitic directorate that monitors business activities, to ensure compliance with the directives in place, noticed there was a seven percent increase in the manufacture of farm implements. As the new growing season was approaching, this went unremarked.

The three principal manufacturers of farm implements, all of them Falwasz industries, were located around Kilkestand City. Due to the efficiency of the Umitian commerce system, those manufacturers all used the same transportation hub on the north side of town. Computerized and manual records all showed farm implements being delivered to the hub, and boxes of implements distributed to various merchants in all of the provinces on both continents. It was an efficient system. The Shovitics needed only to sit at the desk and monitor the movements of quantities of merchandise. They didn't actually inspect those outbound shipments to see if the boxes were empty, or if they existed at all.

They didn't, however, monitor shipments within the city. For example, suppose a hotel ordered a dozen new conference tables. The Shovitics monitoring the economic systems would not bother with those crates, or inspect them to see if they actually contained tables, or perhaps, farm implements — implements which could be lethal if they struck a person hard enough, or struck a Shovitic hard enough.

This may have been noticed by Shovitics who were not part of the Imperite Guards, but most Shovitics working in the city, those who worked for businesses owned by the other six clans, found themselves without employment. Most were told that this was a temporary measure, until the nonsense with the oath-breaker was concluded. Their employers simply, and rightly, stated they were concerned for the Shovitics' safety at this time. Therefore, they were ordered to stay at home, without loss of pay. That particular aspect of coming events had been argued for, and won, by Themedit Tekin. His son thought he was a doddering old fart sometimes, but Themedit had connections and a respect from his years in commerce which still pervaded Kilkestand City business associations to this day.

Another efficiency of the Umitian world is its transportation system. Small personnel shuttles and the more popular ground trains moved people from town to town, city to city, province to province, and continent to continent. The Shovitics at the commerce directorate thought it was odd that there had been a 12% increase in riders since the lifting of the order that had shut down commerce. They didn't do anything about it though, the income was good for the transportation companies and was spread almost evenly across all the transportation industries.

The one thing which did make them ask some questions though, was that within a fortnight, there wasn't a single commercial accommodation available anywhere in the capital, in Kilkestand City. They couldn't understand what the draw was.

Then it dawned on them.

The directorate of information had been announcing the new plant distribution and sales centre on the Palace grounds. Knowing how avid Umitians are about gardens and beauty, this *had* to be the explanation. It also explained the explosive growth in Palace gardens tours which were being conducted, to the point that more attendants had been assigned to conduct the daily tours.

It never dawned on the Imperite Guards, of Kilkestand City, that there was a massive peasant army building around them.

Chapter 67

Cobus leaned on the shovel, taking a breather as he watched the large group of visitors being led through the garden. For many years he had been responsible for the tours. Given the explosive increase in visitors, and that his attention needed to be focussed on the new facility being built, he handed this responsibility off to one of his assistants.

As the group stopped in front of the construction area, Cobus heard the tour guide excitedly describing the new facility and what it would offer. Cobus allowed a small smile. A high percentage of the group were men, a much higher percentage than usual. By their dress and appearance, a lot of them seemed to be from out of town. He had been noticing a lot of out-of-towners in the last few days. *I wonder if the cabal knows how effective they have been?* He wiped his brow and looked down as the workman finished the wooden form that would hold the cement which was too be poured that afternoon.

"Hey."

Cobus looked down at Roguk, who had stuck his head out from under the overhang in the hole that would become the water control room for the new building. Cobus touched his broad brim hat and made his way down into the hole to join Roguk. As he did so, he passed his shovel to the older wood carver from Roguk's company who, when wearing similar clothes and similar hat, looked remarkably like Cobus — from a distance.

The previous day the work crew had cut a strip of sod from the construction project to the Palace. They excavated a trench, laid the pre-fabricated tunnel, then filled it in and replaced the sod, all before the end of the day. The extra soil had been carefully removed to the construction site proper so as not to mar the beautiful lawns. They had done such a good job, leaving two small lines in the grass that would soon fill in on their own, that Kalabot himself had come out to congratulate Cobus and the new contractor on the job.

This morning's crew had cut through the Palace basement wall, and the false wall, to gain access to the fittings room. Roguk's team was installing the pipework that would carry the water, and protect the power cables.

Hunched over, both men shuffled to the end of the tunnel and through the outer wall of the Palace. There was about three feet of space to the false wall, and this is what occupied their attention. The Shovitics had overseen the installation of the barriers that closed off the dead space between the two walls. Roguk's team had just finished modifying the dead space barriers so one of them could be opened.

With an 'all clear' hand signal from the foreman at the construction end of the tunnel, Roguk and Cobus opened the false wall and began the first dry run.

It was one minute and forty seconds to get to the bathroom fixture that led to the prisoner cell. With both of them working, it was twenty seconds to remove the securing clasps. They didn't bother opening it, they didn't want to risk doing it again to potentially alert anyone to what was happening. Securing the fixture took thirty seconds. They moved slower on the way back, as there would be three people and a baby (they didn't know there was a witness with Sepherin), so they called it two minutes and ten seconds on the way back to the false wall. Out through the dead space barrier, they didn't bother counting the time to close it, because they wouldn't be. They counted thirty seconds back through the tunnel for a group of three plus a child. In total, extraction from the go signal would take about six minutes.

After Cobus went back to the dirt pile and took over backfilling the cement forms from his look-a-like, Roguk ran it again. He figured that without the old man slowing him down, he could do it in just over four minutes, if Sepherin was mobile and not injured — and not in a mood to argue with him.

"Which restaurant is that?" Michalz asked, his forehead pinching in the middle as he tried to think of how he knew the name.

Alabast was long practiced at not rolling her eyes at having to remind Michalz of the names of people and places, something he was horrible at remembering. "It's the restaurant we strolled to when we found out *Fedina* was coming for her visit — the night we saw Miras and her two daughters."

Michalz smiled, "Oh, yes, I remember. I didn't know my father was friends with the owner."

"I'm not," the old man spoke up from the corner, his nose still stuck in his book, a passion he unknowingly shared with Kalabot. "I'm friends with his father. We were chums in school."

"You can remember back that far?" Michalz chided.

Themedit looked up over the top of the book, squinting one eye, "You want me to turn you over my knee and make some memories come back to you, *young man?*"

Michalz smiled, urgently, but playfully, waving his hands in defeat, "No, no, Father, no need for that at all."

"Boys, if you're done, perhaps we can get back to the plans for Fedina's visit," she said, glancing up at the maid who was passing by the door to the office.

Michalz straightened his cravat, and then took a sip of his tea. "Yes, well, we won't be able to leave her there long. As soon as they realize she is gone, they will start a door-to-door search for her."

"That's why I think we should use the river," Alabast said quietly.

483

Her husband and her father-in-law both looked up at her, slack jawed.

"The river?" Michalz finally asked.

Alabast nodded, "Yes, it makes sense. The rear of the restaurant is only across the road from the water. We can get her there in only ..."

Themedit harrumphed and sat up in his chair, laying the book on the end table beside him. "Alabast, you know that with the curfew there is also a ban on all river travel. Any boat will be stopped, or sunk!"

Alabast was quiet, she hadn't considered the curfew. If Sepherin arrived after curfew, the whole plan would have to be delayed until the following sunrise.

"I admit, the river is most convenient," Michalz spoke up in defence of his wife's idea, "but Father has a valid point."

"But still ..."

Themedit sighed deeply, "What would you have her do, Alabast, swim to the cottage country?"

Alabast pursed her lips and bit back the reply on the tip of her tongue.

"The river is ideal," Michalz mused quietly, more to himself than anyone else, "if only there was a way to get her down the river unnoticed. But even the traders are not allowed on the waterways after dark."

Themedit picked up his book, "The only thing allowed on the river after dark is those damn two-man patrol craft those infernal Shovitic bastards use."

Alabast looked up at Themedit, "Two-man patrol craft? They don't have those larger patrol boats?"

He shook his head as he turned a page in this book, "No, those are too large for the river, even the traders have to use smaller skiffs and boats. The wake is too disruptive from the larger propellers. They use the smaller boats with two-man crews."

"How many can they hold? Those boats they use?"

"They use them for pleasure boat rescue; I think they can hold up to ten or so."

"But there are only two of the Imperite Guards on them?"

"Mm-hmm."

Alabast stood, but waved her husband back to his seat as he started to stand.

"Where are you going?" he asked, only to watch her exit the room without saying anything.

The following morning Kimla strode up the walkway, still curious as to why the Tekins wanted to see her. Her program supervisor had received a request from Alabast Tekin to discuss the matter of the physical that would be required for her entrance to the Imperite program. It was something which Kimla knew Alabast would never be required to take, and she knew that Alabast knew this as well.

As she approached the front door, wondering if she was going to have the chance to annoy the butler, she heard a voice call to her.

"Kimla! Over here."

The Guard stopped and turned to look at the corner of the house. Alabast was standing there in a summer dress, with a parasol to keep the hot sun off her dark, but sensitive, skin. Kimla strode over and greeted her politely.

"I am told you have some questions, about the — physical?"

"Yes, I do," Alabast said as she hooked her arm around Kimla's, startling the Shovitic with such an uncommon and intimate gesture. "Walk with me while we talk."

"I'm afraid I'm confused, Madam Tekin. Are you still under the belief that …"

Alabast threw her head back and laughed just as the grounds keeper sauntered around the corner of the house. "Why Kimla Pilu, I never knew you had such a wicked sense of humour. Come, let's stroll to the natural spring on our property while you tell me some more."

The grounds keeper eyed them, shaking his head, and then turned back to his work.

In a quieter voice Alabast said, "The house staff are busy doing a thorough cleaning. They are in and out of every room. We will have no privacy in the house, but other than the grounds keeper, whom I gave a lengthy list of chores this morning, there will be no one outside to hear us."

Twenty minutes later, sitting on the rough bench by the natural water spring, Kimla felt like she wanted to vomit. She couldn't believe that Alabast had just asked her to do what she had just asked her to do. Kimla's eyeworms were gyrating frantically as she ran over the plan in her mind, seeing a dozen ways it could go sideways, and imagining a dozen ways Kalabot could kill her for even thinking of it.

But thinking of it she was.

So far her brother and the growing cadre of fifth column thinkers in the ranks of the Shovitics had been unable to come up with a way to save the hybrid. The only real plan they could think of was outright mutiny, a treason which would fail without sufficient numbers. What Alabast told her was indeed the only way Sepherin would get out of Kilkestand City, if her escape was found before they got past the city proper. But what Alabast was asking of her, was — terrifying — in how boldly she asked of it. Kimla could have her executed for voicing such treason, without a trial. She would be within the law to execute her right now, on the spot.

Kimla sighed deeply and stood, not noticing the old man hidden by the foliage of the trees. He watched her, and heard her, as she simply said, "I must speak with my — I must speak with ..."

Kimla took a handkerchief from her pocket, lifted her hat, and dabbed the perspiration from her forehead and neck. Finally she just said, "I will be in touch."

Then she spun on her heal and strode back towards the Tekin's manor, and to her waiting ground car.

Alabast stood, slowly twirling the parasol resting on her shoulder. After Kimla went around the bend in the path and was out of sight, Alabast turned towards the trees. Knowing where to look, it only took a moment for her to see her half-brother. She nodded to him and headed to the house.

Cobus put on his hat, and turned to walk deeper into the woods, back towards the public park only two leagues distant. A moment later, unbeknownst to Alabast, Roguk stood and joined him.

Two days later a courier dropped off a message for Alabast Tekin. It was from the Imperite program's office:

```
Kimla Pilu to Alabast Tekin
Local Delivery
Program Selection Correspondence:
I have spoken with my brother. He has
agreed to assist you with the questions
you posed, in regards to your upcoming
physical. He added that it would be his
honour to assist the Mater of the House
```

```
of Tekin in such a worthwhile endeavour.
He suggests that you meet in two days.
```

Alabast folded the note, and went into Michalz' study. She struck a match, set the paper to the flame, and then tossed it in the hearth of his small fireplace. She stood with her hands folded as she watched the paper turn to ash. *So, my daughter will be home in two days. I must let Cobus know.*

Instead of going to Cobus' home, which would risk unwanted scrutiny, as she was sure that agents of the Palace, of Kalabot, were watching her family, she instead went to visit Eleniak Fozretson, someone whom she had started visiting occasionally. To those who asked, Alabast had found the woman's skills at design and planning to be incredibly useful in the construction of her eldest daughter's cottage, and now she was consulting her on other changes she was planning for her own home. It was a lie made up only of truths.

On her way there, she stopped at the Message Service and sent a 'gram to her two youngest sons, both close to Sepherin's age. The message simply said:

```
Alabast Tekindottir To Tekin Cottage
Wamkalus Laketown
Personal Correspondence:
Boys, be home in two days.
```

With Sepherin's imminent arrival, it would not be a suspect message. It would also give Danik and Piotr the chance to send several preplanned messages from the Message Office at Wamkalus Laketown.

Eleniak passed the brush through her hair and put on her wide-brim sunhat. She stood in the hallway, looking in the mirror. She was still unsettled inside. She despised and hated Sepherin for what she had done, but she had chosen to forgive her husband. So how could she not forgive Sepherin?

Easy, she's a tramp.

Picking up her shopping satchel, she put Sepherin out of her mind and reminded herself that Madam Tekin wasn't Sepherin, and she was doing this for Madam Tekin, someone who brought Roguk a lot of work.

Switching her thoughts to what she needed at the market, Eleniak headed out to the waiting ground car. She went to the market every afternoon at this time, and had been doing so for the last three ten-sleeps. She loved preparing meals with fresh ingredients, so her daily excursions had become more than subterfuge; they were something she looked forward to.

She invariable ran across Doris Scheepers in one of the market's aisles. Being of some renown for her husband's gardens, Doris was often politely greeted by strangers.

Today, Eleniak found her handling the melon fruits, tapping on them to see if they were ripe.

"Fair morning, Madam Scheepers," Eleniak said with a smile.

"And to you, Madam Fozretson. I heard from Cobus that you and Roguk are expecting your first child. I offer my congratulations."

Eleniak gave a small smile, while touching her stomach. They had only found out two ten-sleeps ago, but hadn't told anyone, at least she hadn't. She figured that Roguk would be too excited to say nothing at all.

"Indeed, we are. I've not said anything though, until we are at least past the first trimester."

"An understandable choice, my dear," Doris was already on

guard. She had seen Eleniak many times, but this was the first time the young woman had engaged her in conversation in the marketplace.

Doris asked the obtuse question, "You and Roguk should get some time away; my husband works him far too hard. Perhaps you could do that now, before the baby arrives?"

Eleniak expected such a question about timeliness, but the thought of Sepherin arriving back on Umitia with her bastard child still stung. "Yes, that would be lovely. I decided this morning that I was going to speak to him about it."

"Truly?" Doris felt a tremor of fear, or perhaps it was excitement. She knew what was at stake, and that their lives were at stake if a conspiracy of treason was found out.

"Yes, I thought that perhaps your husband could give him two days away from the Palace project. My husband has a good crew working for him. They would be fine on their own."

Doris smiled, "Perhaps he will. I see the market has a new shipment of Molyak juice in from Sapro. Perhaps I'll get a bottle and take it to him right now, so I can put in a good word for you."

As the end of the work day approached, Cobus walked up the front steps of the Palace and pulled the door open. He took off his hat and held the door as a few of the Imperite Guards exited. His politeness was in his nature. He glanced only briefly at Kimla Pilu, part of the group, but she gave no sign of recognition. Alabast had told her much, but she had not told Kimla who Cobus was, or what his involvement was. Cobus went up the grand staircase to the main floor in the atrium, and then slowly sauntered down the hall towards the large office of the Manager.

After knocking and being bid enter, Cobus stood before the Manager's desk, waiting patiently while the Shovitic finished the document he was working on.

Finally looking up, Kalabot was a bit brusque, "What is it Cobus? I am busy today."

Not wanting to upset Kalabot by dilly-dallying, Cobus got right to the point, "Sir, there was a delay in some of the special fittings for the water distribution network control system."

Kalabot looked up at Cobus, his eyeworms slowing and pointing right at him, "How much of a delay?"

Cobus gave a small smile, "Not long enough to worry about. However, to make sure we stay on schedule, the contractor would like to have a night crew of fitters and system installers to catch everything up. It will be a small crew, there will be no additional cost, and Mr. Fozretson will personally supervise the work."

"Only one night?"

"No, Sir. Two nights for the installation, and one more night to do the testing while the day crew is not about to be inconvenienced. It would require that the crew violate the curfew."

Kalabot leaned back in his chair, drumming the fingers of one hand on the desk, as he watched Cobus' face. Finally, he sighed and responded, "I will submit the authorization to the Palace Guards. However, I wish for you to be on site with them. They may need access to the Palace and I wish you to oversee this personally."

Cobus smile broadened pleasantly as he nodded in acknowledgement and said, "I would have it no other way."

Chapter 68

That the child of the prophecy was on board the ship was no longer a secret to the crew. That the child of the prophecy was Sepherin, and not the infant, had turned a surreal situation into something which was deadly real.

It had started with one of the medics having a quiet word with Fitid. Then Senji told him someone else had asked her some pointed questions. Then the ship's Watch Commander had stopped by Fitid's quarters late one evening for an informal 'chat'.

Before the final fold into the system of Umitia, the Commander called a special "all hands" meeting in the mess hall. The small space was packed almost shoulder to shoulder as the crew of Imperite Guards gathered, minus the two Guards on the prisoners' door and the bridge crew.

Senji sat beside Fitid, her arms crossed, her right hand close to the weapon under her jacket. When Fitid had told her what the Commander wanted him to do, she had a shit-fit. Eventually, however, Fitid won her over. Senji admitted to him that the thought of uprooting their entire way of life to move someplace else was indeed overwhelming, to the point she was almost willing to overlook the prophecy. However, duty was duty, and it was this trait which allowed her to be an off-world operative, just like Fitid. She finally realized that her duty to something greater for her people, was greater than her duty to her oath made before Kalabot when she was sworn in. This was a truth which many Shovitics, on board and on planet, were coming to realise.

It was no surprise the crew was not shocked by the announcement that Fitid had irrefutable proof that the child of the prophecy was on board. Almost to a one, their jaws dropped when he announced it was Sepherin, and not the infant. He presented his evidence as to her hybrid nature, but kept quiet the association he had made to the Manager. This had only been shared with Senji — and the Watch Commander.

With his superior's agreement, he had to talk to Sepherin about this before it was revealed to the rest of the crew. There was a process here, something the Watch Commander needed done step by step, by the numbers, and he needed all of the little boxes ticked off. What the elder guardsman was about to have his crew do was treason, and would result in the death penalty for all of them if it went sideways.

The Commander's plan was a simple one. Armed with the knowledge acquired by Fitid, he would attend the trial of the oath-breaker — a term which gave him pause to consider the juxtaposition of Sepherin's roles in this mess. An oath-breaker goes against all that is important to Umitians, including the Shovitics. However, were she not the oath-breaker, it would not have been discovered that she was the child of the prophecy, the one responsible for fulfilling the greatest prophecy of Alita Kiut — and the one responsible for sending the Shovitics into a new future.

However, it was what it was, and the truth was the truth. He, the Watch Commander, would present the evidence at her trial. He and Fitid both agreed that once the trial panel heard the truth of who she was, they would never order her execution. They simply couldn't. Could they?

But if they did, that's where the rest of the crew came in — and the acts that would be treasonous.

Fitid knocked on the prisoners' door, entering when he heard Cassie respond. Sepherin was bathing Karl and Cassie was gently rocking little Richard in her arms. Fitid couldn't help but smile. He touched both children lovingly on the forehead.

Sepherin was trying to be pleasant, but the weight upon her was obvious. It was only one more fold and then a day's travel to Umitia. She would then be home, and to her knowledge, would shortly thereafter be swinging by the neck from a rope, with Cassie soon to follow her. At least Cassie's death would be quick and painless: a gunshot to the back of the head — in the basement of the Palace. This was still eating at her as well, whether or not to tell Cassie what her fate would be.

"There is something I must speak with you about, Sepherin. Perhaps, though," Fitid glanced at Cassie, "we could have this conversation in private?"

Cassie looked at Sepherin and raised her eyebrows, silently asking the question.

Sepherin shook her head, "No, I'd prefer Cassie stay."

Fitid nodded, it was as he had expected, but given the subject he was about to broach, he had asked to soothe his own conscience.

Taking a breath, he asked her outright, having already discussed the approach with Senji. "Sepherin, do you know who your father is?"

She gave him an, 'are you shitting me?' look. "Of course I do, Fitid."

"Who is it?" he asked.

Sepherin looked at Cassie, and then back at Fitid. It slowly dawned on her what he was asking.

"You're a bastard."

"Sepherin, please, I am not trying to impugn the reputation of ..."

"*My mother!*"

Fitid pursed his lips for a moment, then continued on, "Sepherin, think about it. The only reason Karl locks as he does is that there has to be recessive Shovitic DNA in you. And look at you, Sepherin, you do not look like a Falwasz, you look like ..."

"Enough!" she said with tears forming in her eyes.

"No!" he replied back just as quickly. "Sepherin, we asked why Kalabot had such an interest in you, but you had no reason for it."

"That doesn't mean ..."

"And ..." Fitid talked right over her, "look at you, look at your skin colour, the shape of your face, how tall you are ..."

Sepherin stood, passing the baby to Cassie, then she spun on him, "Are you calling my mother a *whore*? Someone who risked her *life* to sleep with one of *your* kind?"

"Not just any of us, Sepherin, but one in particular, one who ..."

He was faster than her only because he was ready for her. She lunged and swung at the same time, but he dodged the punch and lashed out his foot. Hooking it behind her calf, he pulled her off balance and then flung her face first down on the bed, spinning around to sit on top of her.

"Get off of me!"

Holding both babies, Cassie had jumped up and was standing in the corner, as far from them as she could.

"GUARDS! GUARDS!" Cassie yelled.

The door opened slowly; Bobov and Tillim looked at Fitid wrestling with Sepherin on the bed. They had been listening to everything. The first in the door turned and took Cassie by the shoulders, propelling her out into the hallway. Then to Cassie and Sepherin's horror, they followed her out and shut the door behind them.

"What do you think you're doing you son of a bitch?"

"Sepherin, calm down, please! I have no wish to harm you, in fact, my desire is the opposite!"

"You have a funny way of showing it," she said through gritted teeth. It was at that moment her hand found purchase which would give her leverage. With a massive contraction and expansion of her abdominal, back and thigh muscles, she bucked once — twice — and on the third try she unseated Fitid and sent him crashing to the floor.

Instead of turning on him, she stood and backed away from him, trying to process what he was saying, what she didn't want to hear. She knew he had no wish to harm her, but she had no wish to hear what he was saying either.

He was saying the man she adored and admired from the age she could adore and admire was not the man she thought he was. Fitid was saying that the embraces, the butterfly kisses, and the tears of the man who raised her were those of — *of a stranger*. He was saying her father was not her father.

Fitid got up off the floor. He watched her carefully as he straightened his jacket and tie, waiting for her to launch a second attack, but it didn't come.

"My father..." she began with an edgy voice, but was interrupted.

"Your father," Fitid spoke over her, "is your father in so many important, wonderful, and memorable ways — except for one. One single way that you would have no knowledge of. It does not make anything that followed less mportant. It does not lessen his love for you, nor your love for him. In fact, it makes it more important — to both of you. But that one single way that should have so little meaning for you — will change things for *every* Umitian."

Her breath was coming in heavy rasps as Fitid finished speaking. The tears flowed freely and she started to slump against the wall. Fitid stepped closer and grabbed her arms to keep her from falling. Sepherin looked into his eyes, her breath hitched, and the cries of anguish came in earnest. She slumped forward, putting her arms around his shoulders and buried her face in his neck as she cried.

When the tears slowed, whispering, Fitid told Sepherin about the blood tests, and what they confirmed.

Her scream came suddenly, a scream of loss discovered, a scream of betrayal revealed.

Oath-breaker, Falwasz, Imperite, mother, young woman — at this moment Fitid didn't care what she was. He felt her anguish, her fear, her suffering. He just held her and let her cry. He held her tight, as she held him. When her crying diminished to a series of chugging gasps, he had her sit on the edge of the bunk. Fitid wet a face cloth and then wiped her face while she sat there. It was at this moment that Fitid came to understand parental instinct, and fully realized what it was his words had done to her. It made him want to protect her even more.

"Thank you," she said meekly.

Fitid rinsed the cloth and hung it up by the sink. He could hear the Earther in the corridor raising a fuss so he stepped towards the door, no longer keeping a weather eye on the emotional Falwasz woman who could easily hand his ass to him if she wanted to.

He pulled the door open and Cassie stopped yelling at the two Guards. The only sound was Rick's crying at the noise and upset of his mother. Fitid was a little more than disconcerted by the fact that the infant hybrid, Karl, was staring directly at him, not making a sound.

Fitid beckoned to Cassie, "Come back inside, it's okay."

Cassie marched back into the room, the two Guards in the hallway holding the babies. "*Are* you okay?" she asked her friend.

Sepherin nodded.

"You don't look okay." Cassie turned her head to glare at Fitid. Then she took a step towards him, stuck a finger in his face, and unleashed a torrent of abuse which would have made all three Shovitics blush, were they able to blush.

Several minutes later, a timid Fitid sat on the edge of one of the beds. He had to promise to sit still, not stand up, not speak until spoken to, and he had to hand his gun over to the Guards in the hallway. The three Shovitics had a brand new respect for Earther woman.

With the babies settled and back in their makeshift bassinettes hanging from the wall, Cassie sat down beside Sepherin, opposite Fitid. Sepherin had been distracted by Cassie's tirade. The distraction gave her time for a few questions to pop into her mind — as well as some less pleasant thoughts.

"Fitid," Sepherin spoke almost in a whisper, "I admit that I have had some questions of my own since my son was born. I have wondered whether the recessive genes were in my family or in ..." she almost said Roguk's name. "... or in the family of my son's father."

Fitid didn't say anything. He wanted to see if she was going to make the connection, if she even knew enough to make the connection.

"Also, my appearance has often been commented on, and the kids I grew up with were not so polite about it. I was often called the *Shovite.*"

Fitid clenched his fists for a moment, but nodded in understanding. *Shovite* was a pejorative term that infuriated all Shovitics; much like Cassie would have been enraged had one of them called her a *kaffir*.

"But now," Sepherin continued, looking Fitid in the eye as she did so, "I think you know more than you've said."

There was a pause as both women watched Fitid, watched his eyeworms reflecting his inner state. Finally, he nodded.

Cassie could see Sepherin was trying to hold back more tears. She could also see that Fitid was not there to harm Sepherin, nor did he appear to take any pleasure in her friend's discomfort.

499

"There is a phrase on Earth that I think would apply to this situation," Cassie said as she looked from one to the other. Both the Shovitic and the Falwasz looked at her, waiting. Cassie tried to give a smile, "It's time for you two to put all of your cards on the table."

Didic Valeni stood behind the table, the small room again filled by an all-hands meeting.

"So, it is agreed then. Should my words fail to hold sway at her trial, then ..." he paused to take a breath, but didn't need to continue.

Vriklin, a second engineering mate, spoke for all of them, "Then we will protect the child of the prophecy with our lives."

Chapter 69

Danik Tekinson sat at the outdoor café table with his girlfriend. They ordered yet another cup of kimsa and more pastries. Perela quietly complained that all of this pastry was going to go straight to her hips. Danik teased that she loved the excuse to indulge. They had been sitting there most of the morning, enjoyed lunch, and were still sitting there long into the afternoon.

While this may have caused some question under normal circumstances, the circumstances were not normal. As well, the Falwasz server was friends with Danik, and the café owner was friends with his grandfather. No one bothered them about being there all day.

Perela started a new conversation with her beau, this time talking about how she was would have loved to study medicine, were she of the Silthit clan and not of the Falwasz clan. Danik was about to respond when they both turned their heads at the sound of a heavy engine. They watched as a large ground car, filled with Imperite Guards, drove up the main boulevard and through the Palace gates. No sooner had the gates started to close, they heard another heavy engine approaching, this large ground car was also filled with guardsmen. Conversation, pastry, and kimsa forgotten, they watched three more large ground cars full of Imperite Guards go through the Palace gates.

Danik arose and excused himself. This was what they had been waiting for. Perela knew it meant that Danik's sister would be arriving soon. She looked around at the people on the boulevard, going about their day. She looked over at the Palace gardens entrance, and saw the lineup of those wishing a tour of the grounds were protesting the rest of the day's tours being cancelled. They were being turned away until after the trial, due to take place the day after Sepherin arrived.

Perela looked over her shoulder at the café window. She could see Danik's friend putting up a yellow piece of paper announcing a 25% discount on all merchandise. As she turned back to her cup of kimsa, she saw the office across the street putting up a yellow sheet of paper with a similar announcement. As she swallowed a mouthful of the hot, rich beverage, she could see an identical notice going up in many windows along the boulevard. She wasn't the only one who noticed. As those on the street saw the fantastic offer of savings, their paces slowed down as though they had nowhere else to go. By the time Perela had finished her cup of kimsa, she could see that the amount of people out on the streets had tripled — and the number was still growing. A disproportionate number of them carried shovels and hoes, with new-purchase tags hanging from the handles — yet no one carried any other shopping bags.

Perela looked at her time piece; it was still several hours until curfew.

Valeni stood, and looked down at Sepherin. He tried to smile, but then remembered how her Earther friend hated when he did so.

"As I said, Sepherin, I don't believe my words at the trial will fall on deaf ears. The panel that will be convened will be intelligent and thoughtful, and the Manager does not sit on the tribunal."

Sepherin nodded. "Thank you, Commander Valeni."

"No, Sepherin, it is we who thank you. You have fulfilled the prophecy; it is time for us to take the next step in our destiny." Valeni looked over at Cassie, "And I guess this means your life will be saved as well."

Sepherin bit her lip and looked at Cassie. The small black woman said nothing. She just sat there, looking at Valeni as he turned and left the cabin. When the door was shut, she looked at Sepherin. A single tear rolled down her left cheek.

Finally, Cassie asked, "When were you going to tell me?"

Sepherin was at a loss for words. She stood and turned, sitting down beside Cassie on her bunk. She reached out and took Cassie's hand, Cassie held her tight.

"I figured it out on my own," Cassie spoke quietly.

Sepherin looked up in surprise.

Cassie smiled, "After what they did to Lota, I knew the life of an Earther wouldn't have much meaning. You said once that Lota knew too much, that she had seen too much for one of the memory-thing-a-ma-bobs. So, the math wasn't hard. Either they keep me on Umitia, or they kill me. In all our conversations you've only talked about the clans, you've never said anything about aliens living on Umitia."

"Cassie, I …" Sepherin started to talk, but was overtaken by a sob and a look of shame.

"Shhh," Cassie said and pulled her taller friend closer. She turned a bit and leaned back against Sepherin, draping the Falwasz woman's long arm over her shoulder and chest, holding her hand.

"If the Commander is successful, then you won't be hung. I'm guessing that if you're this all-mighty-child-of-the-prophecy, you'll have some sway afterwards, and you can save me."

"I hope," Sepherin said quietly.

"Do you think the ship's crew would step up for me, if this Manager guy still wants me to die?"

"Not for an Earther, no. But for the mother of an infant, maybe."

They sat quietly for a while. Every once in a while Sepherin would reach out with her long leg and give the bassinettes a gentle nudge. Cassie sat against her, holding her arm, with tears silently rolling down her cheeks. They heard the final fold being

503

announced over the PA system. As the countdown concluded, both women exhaled, felt the brief disorientation, and then both inhaled deeply.

Cassie sat up and turned to look at Sepherin. Getting on her knees she cupped Sepherin's face with both of her hands and smiled at her. Then she kissed her alien friend on the forehead.

"If they kill me, I want you to raise my son."

Roguk finished the temporary wiring that Cobus had specified as he heard the argument start. He stood up and looked at the old man who was standing almost toe to toe with the taller Imperite Guard.

"… twenty-two years! And every single day I have spent devoted to the Palace, the training facility, and the spaceport. Kalabot himself has placed me in charge of this project and no mere *guard* is going to tell *me* that I have to *leave* the Palace grounds!" Cobus leaned even further forward, his upturned face only a finger's breadth from the Guard's chin.

The Guard took a step back. "But Master Gardener, we have orders that the grounds are to be cleared of all visitors. That includes …"

"That does not include workers!"

"But these men are not employed by the …"

"And they are not tourists here to smell the flowers! These men are employed by the contractor hired to build this facility. The Manager himself authorized an overnight presence by these men to perform critical installation and testing."

"But it is not night!"

"Do you challenge the spirit of the Manager's direction? Should we ask him? Would *you* like to go to him with such a juvenile question? Would *you* like to ask him?"

The Guard hesitated.

Cobus pressed his advantage by stepping around the Guard and beckoning for him to follow. "Come! Right now! We will go and see *my friend* Kalabot in person and straighten this nonsense out once and for all. You can tell him yourself how his desires are not good enough for you."

"Master Gardener ..." the Shovitic hadn't moved.

Cobus stopped and turned again, "Well? Are you coming? He is in his office now, or do you plan to make him schedule his day at your own personal behest as well?"

"I don't think ..." the Imperite Guard started, but was cut off.

"And that is the problem with your damn automatons. You *don't* think. Do you not realize how important this project is to the Manger? To all of Kilkestand? To all of Umitia? Do you not think that ..."

"Enough!" the Guard relented, holding up both hands. "I'm sorry Master Scheepers. You are correct in all you have said. Continue your work." The Guard and the two with him left the construction site and headed off into the gardens to see if there were any more tourists who had not yet been removed from the Palace grounds.

Cobus turned at the sound of Roguk and another man snickering. He smiled at them and winked. Walking over to Roguk as they all watched the Guards moving off into the flower beds, Cobus whispered, "Have you finished wiring the explosives?"

The butler was confused. Most of the household staff had left that morning for the cottage on the shores of Wamkalus Lake. Only he and the eldest maid remained at the family residence. The master and mater's daughter was due to arrive any day, and be tried for a capital crime. Yet they were planning a vacation? He understood they would need time to grieve in private once their Oath-breaking daughter was executed, but this was a bit like putting a burden-beast before the cart.

Hobonol himself, he was used to the eccentricities of the household family. However, that they were displaying so little grief and remorse at what was to come troubled him. Though he would not discuss such a matter with the family, his own blood boiled, as did the rest of the household staff, at what was to take place. None of them understood how the Falwasz so willingly participated in the Imperite program, the only clan to be selected as Imperites. Nonetheless, he knew all of his family and friends were enraged that an Imperite was to be executed. He knew this had less to do with clan loyalty and more to do with people being fed up with the current administration, to wit, the Manager.

Now, with the arrival so close, Master Tekinson and his wife had decided to dine in town. The old man, Themedit, had joined them. The butler closed the front door after watching the ground car depart. Sitting on a stool in the kitchen, he graciously accepted the mug of hot tea from the maid who was only a year his senior. They said nothing about it. It was not their place.

Chapter 70

Because the Palace itself was shielded from TransMat beams, the reception party of Imperite Guards formed a circle at the rear of the Palace, out of the view of the main gates and public view from the boulevard along the eastern perimeter of the Palace grounds. Even those on the river had no view of where they stood.

They didn't wait long for the first TransMat to occur. Six Imperite Guards from the ship, including Didic Valeni, appeared with a dim flash of blue light. With the proper greeting out of the way and ensuring the safety of the area, the Watch Commander of the ship raised his hand and spoke quietly into his communicator. His eyes scanned the construction project and could see some workers were watching. They were far enough away to be of no concern.

The Guards present knew the oath-breaker and her child were arriving, and they knew a witness was arriving. They didn't know the witness also had a child, and no one had a clue that her skin was so strangely coloured.

The Imperite and the witness, holding their infants, appeared with four more Imperite Guards with another flash of dim blue light. Fitid and Senji flanked Sepherin; Bobov and Tillim flanked Cassie.

Cassie's appearance surprised the assembled Guards, but no one said anything. There were a few brief smiles as they looked at the two infants. The assembled Guards moved in closer around the party and walked in silence towards the side entrance to the Palace basement. No one noticed that there were two less faces watching them from the construction site.

Sepherin noticed Kimla in the group of Guards surrounding them, but Kimla gave no acknowledgement so neither did Sepherin. Of all the things which had disheartened her lately, being ignored by Kimla had a profound effect on her. But no tears came. Sepherin had found her strength again and was no longer going to be swayed and controlled by emotions. She held her head high, with Karl clutched tightly to her chest, and she swore she would not give one more Shovitic the chance to see tears in her eyes.

Sepherin didn't know what was about to happen, Fitid had not told her. He knew a dozen things could go wrong, and he didn't want to build false hope. He also didn't want her or the Earther to accidentally reveal it to anyone else on the ship, again, as he didn't know how far he could push their agreement to defend the Imperite. The Guards from the ship had agreed to assemble additional patrols close to the Palace, in case some Guard was of a mind to pursue honourable justice against the Imperite before the trial.

As they stepped in through the basement entrance, the corridor which ran the length of the Palace was empty except for two people. Kalabot and Kervin, the newly promoted planetary coordinator, awaited them outside the single prison cell. Given that the prison cell was in the basement of the Palace, the most heavily fortified and protected structure in Kilkestand City, Cassie thought it was odd that there were no more Guards present.

The group stopped in front of Kalabot.

"Sir," Valeni spoke to the Manager, "I present to you the Imperite Sepherin Tekin, and the Earther witness, Cassie Scott."

Kalabot stared at Sepherin momentarily, his eyeworms betraying nothing. He then turned his attention to the smaller Earther woman. He stepped closer and looked into her eyes, then at her skin. He reached out and touched her face, even though she tried to recoil. Then he looked at his finger tips and rubbed them together. As he looked up at Cassie, she spit in his face and lashed out with her foot, kicking him in the shin.

With a roar of rage, Kalabot reached out with both hands for her. The bedlam quickly settled as D dic Valeni grabbed Kalabot, pulled him back, and then stepped in front of him.

"Sir! You will not harm the witness until the trial is concluded."

Didic was tensed up, everyone was tensed up. Sepherin had grabbed Cassie with one arm and pulled her closer, stepping back from Kalabot and Valeni. Valeni was waiting for Kalabot to kill him for grabbing him.

Kalabot was vibrating with rage. His venomous scowl of unbridled anger was directed at Valeni. The other Guards were exchanging glances, but doing nothing other than stand at the ready; but for what, they weren't sure.

"I am sure, Manager," Valeni finally went on, "that given the young ladies' predicament, that she has been brought across the galaxy, that she has recently given birth, and that she is soon to be executed, you can forgive her for being angry and needing to lash out. Can you not? Can you not give this understanding to a Humanesh who has recently given birth to a beautiful, healthy child?"

Those words seemed to have the desired effect. Kalabot got himself under control. After a few moments, he said, "She is forgiven. Put them *both* in the cell. The trial will commence after tomorrow's breakfast."

Once they saw Sepherin being TransMat to the lawn, Cobus and Roguk were on the move. The original plan had been to remove her from the cell in the still of the night. Plans change, however. They had made the decision that the longer she was in the cell, the more likely someone would come to check on them and possibly catch them in the act. They had decided to be in place when Sepherin was put in the cell. Besides, the sun was approaching the horizon so night wasn't that far away.

Roguk forgot about Cobus slowing things down. After seeing the TransMat, his thoughts were focussed on the bundle in Sepherin's arms: his son.

As Kalabot and Kervin headed towards the stairs, Kimla turned to the Guards around Sepherin and Cassie, pulling a piece of paper from her pocket.

"I have a schedule prepared for Guard duty through the night and the trial. Most of you will be reeded in the morning, so tonight I will stand guard. I ask that Bobov and Tillim take first watch, since you are most familiar with the oath-breaker and the witness."

Kimla made the word oath-breaker sound like she was spitting it out. She knew some of the Guards brought in were sympathetic, but there were many faces she did not recognize. The Guards from the frigate were also an unknown quantity to her. She was sure of Fitid and Senji, but had not spoken with Fitid since the call five sleeps ago.

One of the Palace regulars spoke up, "Kalabot will want there to be more of a presence than this. Will he not?"

Kimla nodded absentmindedly, "Yes, I have stationed four Guards outside each entrance to the Palace. You," she looked up at the one who spoke, "will be outside the entrance we just came through." She then gave the names of three more in the group to take the post with him, as well as two more to another entrance. She directed the rest to the temporary barracks on the first floor of the Palace, in the ballroom. The Guards who had been brought into the Palace earlier in the day would be housed there until after the trial.

"Kimla Pilu," Fitid spoke up, "perhaps you can schedule the cell guards from our ship's crew? We have many who are familiar with the routines and the needs of the two women, and their children."

Kimla nodded and took out a writing stylus to cross out some names, and make notes. "Very well, this will be done. I'll get the names from you before you leave." She looked up at him, hesitating only a second, "Fitid, will you and your partner assist me in settling the oath-breaker and the witness?"

"You're going to put her in the prison cell with me?" Sepherin asked irritably.

"Where would you have me put her," Kimla asked loudly, for the benefit of those Guards still departing, "in Kalabot's bed chamber?"

They heard some snickers from those still in earshot. Sepherin was about to retort to "Kimla the betrayer" as she thought of her at that moment, but she was silenced when Kimla gave a little smile and gave the eyeworms' equivalent of a wink.

Cassie saw the brief look of shock on her friend's face, and the lingering tension in her shoulders started to ease. The quick exchange between the two women filled her with hope.

Fitid was looking down the long hall, towards the communication room. He smiled briefly as he saw Corla stick her head out, and nod towards him. They would reunite later, if he survived the evening.

Kimla took a heavy key from her pocket and unlocked the cell door. As she opened the door she looked down both ends of the hallway to ensure no one was in hearing distance. She turned to Fitid and looked at him, then looked at Bobov and Tillim.

Before departing the frigate, Fitid and Senji had a gunpoint discussion with Bobov and Tillim regarding Sepherin and what was going to happen on Earth. They had expected some resistance, but instead found both of the Guards smiling and nodding their heads at the plan.

Fitid had received a call from Kimla only a few sleeps before, but he had only shared what he learned with Senji, until he told

Bobov and Tillim. He did not share Kimla's revelation with anyone else, as he thought it would be pushing things too close to the breaking point with the Watch Commander and, perhaps, others.

"They are with us," Fitid said quietly.

Kimla nodded once, and looked at Sepherin, "Please, step into the cell."

Both Sepherin and Cassie had realized that something was afoot, so they both quietly did as they were told.

Kimla handed the heavy key to Bobov, "Lock us in and do everything you can to keep this door closed as long as possible."

With the five inside the small cell, Bobov looked at Sepherin. "Now as then," he said, holding his one hand palm up.

Sepherin replied quickly, more from habit, holding one hand palm down, "Then as now."

Cassie looked up at Bobov and was about to mimic the departure words, but was completely flabbergasted when Bobov leaned down and kissed her on the cheek.

"With our life, we will protect you and your child," he whispered in her ear, and then kissed her on the cheek again.

Cassie didn't know what to say. She didn't have time either. Bobov stepped back and he shut the heavy cell door shut. They all heard the lock sliding into place.

"Okay, what the *hell* is going on here?" Cassie spoke first.

Kimla said nothing, she just reached out with her foot and tapped on the toilet fixture twice. To the surprise of everyone, the toilet fixture swung inwards.

"Uncle Cobus!" Sepherin exclaimed, realizing that the secrecy of his lineage was no longer a priority. Her smile soon froze as she saw the other person stick his face in the small opening. Roguk smiled at Sepherin, and then he turned to the shorter woman beside her, his face showing the same odd expression as Cobus' face held.

"Guess who's coming to dinner?" Cassie muttered for the second time in as many months.

The plan for three adults and a child became an operation for seven adults and two children. It still only took a few minutes to get through the dead space between the walls and back to the construction site. As they emerged into the light, they saw Cassie was breast feeding her son as she moved. Little Rick had started to fuss, and rather than have him wail and raise the alarm, she gave him what all young men want most — food.

When they reached the construction site, Roguk stopped to hug Sepherin. She let him do so, but did not hug back. She was confused, scared, surprised, angry, and felt more surreal than she had since leaving Umitia less than a season ago.

Roguk finally asked to see the baby. All eyes were on him as she undid the blanket and let Roguk finally see his son. As he saw the paleness of the skin, the shape of the face — and the eyeworms, his face froze. He looked up at Sepherin and then back at the child. He took a step back.

"This — this is ..."

"*Your son,*" Sepherin said firmly, but quietly. Holding the baby forward slightly, she asked, "Do you not want to hold what you sired?"

Fitid grabbed him by the arm, "There will be time for questions later. We must move, now! How are we to get her out of the Palace grounds?"

Also taking Roguk by the arm, Cobus ushered them forward, hidden from the view of the Guards outside the Palace by strategically-placed stacks of supplies. The back of the delivery ground car, the flatbed with canvas sides and boxes still onboard, did not have room for all of them, but that worked to their favour. Fitid and Senji jumped up into the cab beside Roguk in the driver's seat. It would hopefully make their exit from the grounds uncomplicated, and perhaps the explosives would not need to be used to distract the Guards. It would also give Fitid a few minutes to dial in Roguk to the concept of recessive DNA, without going into details about the lineage of the child's mother.

Kimla and Cobus held the children while the two women got on the flatbed of the ground car. They handed the children up, and then joined them.

They were concealed on three sides by the cab, boxes, and canvas. Hidden under tarps, Karl began to fuss. Sepherin tried to settle him, tried to offer him her nipple to feed, and tried to hold him closer and tighter. None of it settled him. Finally, she saw a distinct image in her mind of Karl, as an infant, standing high atop a mountain. The vision didn't alarm her: it was accompanied by a sense of peace which flooded through her body.

Sepherin sat up, and held Karl up close to her face, so he could see out the back of the flatbed. Cobus uncovered his head to see what the movement was. When he saw them sitting up, he reached out to pull Sepherin back down, but his mind was flooded with the vision of his first child on the day of her graduation. Only it wasn't her that was graduating, it was Sepherin who he saw in his daughter's ornamental graduation gown. Cobus didn't understand what he was seeing, or why he was seeing it, but he dropped his hand and just watched.

As the large ground car lurched out of the construction area, the engine growling with subdued power, Sepherin was afraid that at any moment a Guard would appear behind the truck and see them. As the truck began moving, however, she saw snow falling around the truck. It was snow, just like in the high mountains of Sestaland, and just like back on Earth. It got heavier and heavier until she could see nothing beyond the ground car. Sepherin finally realized there was no snow; this was just another vision. She glanced at Karl who was no longer fussing. Wrapped in his swaddling blanket, Sepherin realized that Karl was making them invisible — no, he was making them *unseeable* to anyone outside the ground car.

If only you could make us truly disappear, my son.

As the thought flitted across her mind, she felt Karl's head turn slightly towards her. She looked down into his sweet face, and her mind was flooded with more images.

Shortly after locking the door, Bobov turned his head to the sound of the footsteps on the stairs. Kevit, the planetary coordinator, who was also responsible for homeworld security, turned the corner and came striding towards them.

"I need to see the prisoners," he said as he stopped in front of them.

"I'm afraid that is not possible," Bobov replied.

"It is an order."

Tillim stepped up beside his partner, "He said it is not possible."

"I demand to see the prisoners, *now!*"

"Your statement is not valid," Bobov said, no hint of sneer on his face.

"What?"

"You said prisoners, plural. There is only one prisoner. The other is a witness."

Kevit looked like he was going to lose his mind. "I don't care if they are figments of my imagination, open the door!"

"They have had a long journey, and a long day, so they must rest. These are Kimla's orders and we do not take orders from you," Bobov punctuated his words by shoving Kevit backwards, causing him to bump into the smiling Tillim.

Kevit glared at them both for a moment, then spun on his heels and stormed off towards the communication office.

As they watched him enter the room, Tillim turned to his friend and partner. Putting a hand on Bobov's shoulder, he quietly said, "It has been a pleasure serving with you my friend."

"And so with you," Bobov said without smiling. "At least our deaths will have meaning."

They turned as they heard Kevit's scream of rage. He had found Corla sitting at her desk with her phone disassembled, performing a minor repair. Unfortunately, it was the only phone in the office which could call out, as the ERB had just gone into a maintenance cycle.

Once again, they watched Kevit storm off towards the staircase.

A short time later, the Manager was standing in front of the Guards.

"Open the cell door, now."

Bobov didn't flinch. He looked right into Kalabot's eyes. "I'm sorry, Sir, but I have orders not to allow the prisoner and the witness to be disturbed."

"Then I am giving you new orders, open the door," Kalabot spoke quietly, his voice all the more menacing for it.

Tillim spoke up, "Sir, we do not have the key. Kimla took it. She is to relieve us soon, so there was no need for us to have it, as the prisoner and witness were not to be disturbed."

Kalabot reached out with his mind, scanning the Palace and grounds, going to the limit of his ability to detect another, but could not find Kimla.

"Where has she gone?" he asked, his voice and eyeworms betraying his growing rage.

"I do not know, she has not …" Bobov stopped talking as the Manager simply vanished from in front of him.

Only a moment later they heard him scream inside the cell.

Kalabot moved himself through the cell door, appearing in the middle of the empty cell. He looked around, but saw nothing out of place. The two beds did not even look like they had been sat upon. He inhaled deeply, and he definitely smelled them. He smelled something else, something musty, damp. He couldn't place it, but he didn't really put much thought to it. Sepherin was gone. She had disappeared from right under his nose. It was too much. Kalabot screamed with rage as he had never screamed before.

Kalabot appeared in the hallway again. *"Where are they?"* he demanded loudly.

Silence was the only response from the two Imperite Guards from the frigate.

With a gurgling squeal, Bobov clutched his chest and then fell to the floor, dead. At that moment, Kevit came down the stairs and around the corner. He hurried forward as he saw Bobov fall. Kevit wasn't stupid, he could see that this was going from bad to worse far too fast.

Kalabot turned to Tillim, "Answer me and I'll spare your life. *Where are they?*"

Tillim looked at his partner, then back up at Kalabot. He took one step forward and shoved the old man hard, sending him sprawling. "You should be ashamed of yourself, Kalabot."

"No!" Kevit screamed, *"What do you think you're doing?"*

Kevit was helping Kalabot to his feet as Tillim replied, "Offering my life to save the child of the prophecy brings me no shame."

With a growl of anger from Kalabot, Tillim joined his partner on the floor, dead.

"Child of the … ?" Kevit began, but stopped as Kalabot turned on him.

"The oath-breaker is gone. The cell is empty. Sound the alarm."

Kalabot reached in his pocket and pulled out a piece of paper as Kevit scurried back towards the staircase. He unfolded the copy of the schedule that Kimla had prepared for the prisoner detail. The first line on it was her name, and hand written beside it was "Fitid/Senji to assist".

The paper fluttered as the furor overtook him again. Once more he closed his eyeworms and cast his mind out through the Palace and grounds, but again, could not sense any of them. In fact, he found he could not sense anyone. His eyeworms flew open in surprise. He was the only one that could block a Shovitic's telepathy, only he could …

No, Sepherin can do this?

He recognized Fitid's name. He knew that his mate was …

Kalabot stepped into the communications room and looked at Corla sitting at her desk, a neutral expression on her face.

"Where is he?" Kalabot asked, his face darkened with his growing rage.

Corla said nothing, she just folded her hands and stared back at Kalabot.

"TELL ME!" Kalabot screamed.

Corla slowly stood, and straightened her uniform. Then she looked at Kalabot and said, "He is doing what you should have done. He is saving the child of the prophecy."

Kalabot spun and left the office as Corla's corpse flopped forward across the desk. He stood in the hallway, trying to decipher where they would have gone so quickly that he could not sense them. That was when the two-tone alarm klaxon started blaring.

Then, just for a brief moment, he sensed them. He sensed Fitid and Senji — and Sepherin. They were at the gate. Then once again, they were no longer in his senses.

The hallway shook with the force of the detonations.

Roguk slowed the large ground car as they approached the gate. He glanced at Senji beside him, but said nothing. There had to be at least twenty Guards at the main gate. Beyond it, they could see an incredible amount of people in the streets. The crowd was growing, and looked unsettled — and most of them were carrying shovels and hoes in their hands.

The Guards at the gate were focussed on the crowd, which was slowly moving onto the broad, slightly arched, bridge over the river on the public side of the gates. Roguk could see another Guard was passing out the larger weapons the Imperite Guards used in battles. He felt the bottom of his stomach drop and the urge to go to the bathroom.

Senji reached across Roguk and tooted the horn once. Some of the Guards looked at the vehicle, and at the occupants in the cab.

The Guard in charge nodded and moved towards the gate. He unlatched it and started to swing it open, but at that most inopportune moment, a loud two-tone klaxon started blaring from speakers around the Palace grounds. All the Guards on the gate turned towards the large ground car, raising their weapons.

As those Guards put their focus on the three in the cab, Fitid and Senji acted as one. They each drew their sidearm and pointed it at Roguk's head.

At the sound of the klaxon, Cobus got to his knees in the back of the ground car. Seeing the faces looking towards them from the construction site, he lifted his hat in the air and waved it at them. He watched the faces looking towards them, but none seemed to acknowledge him.

He turned to Sepherin, looked at the child, and then back at her.

She seemed to understand what he needed. She kissed Karl on the forehead, "Let him signal."

Cobus waved his hat in the air again, and seeing the expected response, he lay down.

Staring at the two large calibre handguns pointed at his face, Roguk flinched in surprise at the eight explosions, one right after the other. They were all centered in the gardens on the far side of the Palace, near the river.

The Guard in charge of the detail left four men behind, but ordered the others to follow him towards the river. The explosions had to be a diversion while the prisoners were escaping, that could be the only possible meaning of the klaxon, and the detonations. Given their location, the only logical point of escape could be the river. They certainly wouldn't just try and drive out the front gate with such a heavy presence of Guards.

He had only gone a hundred metres when he heard the ground car's engine roar to life, and realized how wrong he had been. With his men, they turned as one and saw the large ground car surging forward directly at the one who was standing in its way.

It was Kalabot.

Michalz and Alabast took each other by the hand and held tightly as they heard the not-so-distant explosions. They were waiting in the kitchen of the restaurant owned by Themedit's friend. Only a dozen metres away Alabast could see Talin and another Shovitic in the patrol craft tied to the small jetty on the river bank. They were both looking towards the Palace grounds.

Talin turned and looked back at the restaurant, he just nodded his head once to acknowledge Alabast and reassure her that this was planned. She knew it was, but she was still worried for her daughter and grandchild.

Being only three hundred metres from the Palace gate, they all heard the roar of the engine, the screams, and the clattering of iron as the truck burst though the more than ornamental gates.

As most of the Imperite Guards on the gate took off towards the river, Fitid and Senji both holstered their weapons.

"Go! Now!" Senji hissed at Roguk.

With a sigh of relief that they had not truly turned on him, he put the truck in gear, but as his foot moved towards the accelerator, Kalabot appeared in front of them, between the truck and the gate. Roguk and the two Guards could see he was infuriated.

Roguk glanced at the Guards beside him. There was fear on their faces. Then without warning, the image of a small Shovitic child appeared in his mind. The child was bouncing on his knee, laughing and giggling, and Roguk's heart was filled with love. He stomped on the accelerator just as Kalabot started moving towards the truck.

The look of surprise on the old man's face was priceless. Roguk kept his foot down on the accelerator; the engine protested the surge of power, but did what it was supposed to do.

Kalabot scrambled to get out of the way of the truck. It happened too fast for him to use his ability to move through time and space. He barely got out of the way of the front of the truck. As his mind started to form the intent for all in the truck to perish, he looked at the back of the truck. All he had time to take in was the vision of his old friend, Cobus, sticking his head up from the tarpaulin.

Cobus was looking Kalabot right in the eyes. The look on the master gardener's face, his grimace, his wide eyes, the animalistic scream — Kalabot was stunned that his old friend, the only person he truly trusted, was turning on him — and Cobus was swinging a shovel.

Kalabot threw up his arms, but Cobus' swing connected square on, sending Kalabot flying backwards. He landed hard. His head struck an ornamental stone at the edge of the driveway and the Manager was knocked unconscious.

The large ground car hit the gates with a massive amount of kinetic energy and tore them from their hinges. No sooner through the wreckage, everyone felt their stomach flip from passing over the low peak of the bridge at speed. Roguk stood on the brakes and turned a hard left. A dozen Falwasz who knew the plan were hurriedly getting people out of their way. The truck accelerated towards the back door of the restaurant he was fast approaching.

The main force of Guards returned to the gate just as the sea of people in the streets roared with satisfaction and moved back onto the bridge. There were thousands of them on the bridge and the broad boulevards beyond. They moved so fast that the Guards were not able to follow the truck on foot.

Thinking quickly, the Imperite Guard in charge of the detail ordered his men to lift up the gates by hand. The press of people had stopped just short of the wreckage. They knew that were they to actually enter the Palace grounds, the Guards might open fire. But if they remained at the line without crossing it, the Guards wouldn't. They hoped.

The Guards lifted the gates and set about shoring them up with whatever materials were available. The weapons they carried made short work of the smaller trees that were long enough and strong enough to hold up the heavy metal grills. It only took five frenzied minutes to put the makeshift fortification back in place. It only needed to last until reinforcements arrived from the river's edge, and from the city.

The medic in the group was attending to Kalabot as best he could, but the medic knew the Manager had to be treated in the medical centre in the Palace. With all the other Guards attending to the gate, he raised his communicator to call for help, but it would not work. All he got was static. He looked towards the Palace, but saw no one coming towards them. He could see several dozen Guards at the water's edge, but it didn't look like they had figured it out yet. They had gone towards the explosions; none had come to the main gate. He looked down again as Kalabot started to stir.

The Guard in charge of the gate detail looked out over the sea of angry Umite's, wondering who was blowing a whistle. He was also wondering just where in the name of the Unholy One the reinforcements from the city were.

Then he heard more explosions in the distance.

Moving into place after the trucks had driven a large contingent of Guards into the Palace earlier in the day, Danik was with his brother, Piotr. They, with others, were waiting in a large shop which was closed for the evening. They weren't alone.

The Imperite Guards had six hundred Shovitics in reserve in a nearby warehouse that had been unoccupied for two seasons. They had been there for several days, and had been under surveillance by the clansmen. When the signal went up for people to gather, back alleys, storm sewers, and courtyards began crawling with Falwasz, Hobonol, Sterin, Silthit and Treanda clansmen. There were even a few Ashvelyn clerics, though they were not armed with shovels, pick-axes, or any of the other farm implements that never made it through the distribution depot. In total, there were 1,500 clansmen around the warehouse, and not a single one of them had been seen by the Imperite Guards.

When the surveillance camera showed the Shovitics in charge of the reinforcements assembling their men for deployment, Danik stepped out onto the street, and crossed to the far side. He raised a whistle to his lips and blew it as hard as he could three times.

The Silthit on the detonator cranked the handle a few times and then pressed down on the plunger. Small, but powerful explosions planted around all the entrances to the warehouse went off, one after another. Before the sound of the explosions finished assaulting the ears of the Shovitics inside, the noise was replaced with the scream of Umites racing from their hiding places. They were all running into the cavernous space.

Some of the Imperite Guards raised their weapons and began to fire warning shots, but their own men stopped them. As the warehouse filled with the 1,500 Umites, the 600 Imperite Guards did nothing.

They had been gathered to stop an assault on the Palace. To a one, they were there to keep the peace and prevent anyone from being killed. None of them had forgotten the Halveris Massacre, nor the troubles in the outlying townships and cities. None of them had the stomach to see any more clansmen die. The Shovitics began laying down their weapons. A few at first, then a few more, and then all of them.

As the screaming voices of the clansmen died down, a surreal silence descended on the warehouse. The clansmen had expected a fight. They had not expected this. Danik made his way to the front of the crowd of clansmen. He looked at the Shovitics who were just standing there, looking back at him, no expression on any of their faces.

"So, there is to be no fight then?" he asked the Guards.

The Shovitics all looked around at each other. Then almost as one, they got down on one knee.

"Sepherin!" Alabast rushed from the back door of the restaurant.

The ground car had slowed and turned into the alleyway so it could not be seen from the Palace gates. All of the passengers hurriedly exited and then Roguk sped onwards, to give a false trail for any Guards who may be pursuing them.

Alabast ran up to her daughter, wrapping her and the baby in a tight embrace. Sepherin said nothing; she just pulled back and looked at her mother, her face neutral.

Then her father was there, wrapping his arms around her.

Sepherin smiled and a tear slipped from her eye. "Father," was all she said, kissing him on the forehead. As she embraced him, she turned to look at her mother again, her face again betraying no emotion.

Alabast had new tears in her eyes, but for another reason.

Cobus came up behind them with Cassie and Kimla beside him, "Come, we must hurry."

"Wait," Sepherin said. She pulled the blanket from over Karl's face and held him for her parents to see.

Alabast looked at him, reached out to touch his forehead, and cried harder.

Michalz, standing beside his wife, also looked closely at the child. But much to Sepherin's surprise, he smiled, leaned forward, and kissed the child on the cheek. Looking up at his daughter, Michalz asked, "The child, he is healthy?"

Sepherin nodded, confused.

"And his name, dear?" her mother asked with a jagged voice.

"His name is Karl, I'll explain later," Sepherin sounded as confused as she felt, looking from her mother to her father.

Michalz looked up at Sepherin and smiled the smile she had feared she would never see again. "My child — my heart, it is I that you must forgive, not your mother."

Cobus yelled at them, "Now! We must move!"

They heard a commotion coming from the restaurant. The owner flew out the back door, "Guards have entered the restaurant; they are searching."

Alabast, Michalz, and Sepherin ran towards the jetty and onto the boat. As the boat pulled away, Sepherin quickly introduced Cassie. Neither of her parents had anything to say about how different she looked. But they made just as much of a fuss over little Rick as they were making over Karl.

They hadn't gone far when as one they turned to the sound of the gunfire and the screams of people dying.

Chapter 71

Kalabot stood up, a little unsteady, but rapidly composing himself. He looked at the gates haphazardly held in place, and the Guards facing them crowd. He grabbed his head as a bolt of pain passed through it, but he shook it off, looking at the blood on his fingers.

He pushed the doting medic away and strode forward to the line of Guards. He stared out at the crowd that was yelling and jeering. They were calling out, "Shame", "Free the Imperite", "Leave her alone", and a few less than pleasant phrases. He turned on the Imperite Guard in charge of the gate detail and demanded to know where the truck had gone and why it hadn't been followed.

The man told Kalabot, "The crowd will not allow us to follow them. We are waiting for reinforcements."

Both of them turned towards the river and saw the dozens of Guards that had gone to the water, and were finally moving towards the front gates. Kalabot turned back on the crowd. A line of drool started descending from his lower lip, his breath was coming heavier, and his fists were clenched so tight he felt a knuckle pop.

"Kill them," he turned to the line of Guards, "open fire and kill them all."

The Imperite Guards all looked at one another, but did nothing. The one in charge spoke up, "Sir, I do not think that ..."

Kalabot pulled a new trick out of his hat, one that no Guard had ever seen before. He closed his eyes and operating as one body, all of the Guards raised their weapons and opened fire. It was much to the Guard's own dismay. They couldn't release their fingers from the triggers, they couldn't let go of the guns, and they couldn't point them away from the crowd. Kalabot had made puppets of them all.

What the Guards would remember most were the screams. The people at the front of the crowd turned to run, but the sea of bodies was too large, packed too tightly together. Nearly two hundred fell before Kalabot released his control of the Guards. As he did so, one of the Guards cried out in rage and turned his weapon on Kalabot. But the old Shovitic was ready for this. The Guard dropped to the ground dead before he could point his weapon.

The others stood there, the dismay on their faces, many sobbing with grief. The crowd had been large, and vocal; but they had been peaceful. They had done nothing more than save one of their own, and do so without violence. This horrific tragedy was all on Kalabot. The Guards watched the people crying, the wounded being tended to, people from all five clans wailing over the bodies of dead loved ones. One of the older Shovitic guards turned his weapon on himself.

The old man looked at the line of Guards. "Do I need to do this for you? Any man who does not raise his weapon right now and open fire will have his entire family ..."

"FATHER!"

Kalabot spun around as a collective gasp arose from the people who were watching. Sepherin stood on the other side of the gates.

As the gunfire continued, Talin sped up the boat. But Sepherin was staring at the distant sound of death and terror. She handed Karl to her mother and grabbed Talin's arm, "Turn around, go back!"

He shook his head, "No, I'm getting you as far from here as I can."

"Father," Sepherin turned to Mchalsz, "make him turn around."

"No, Sepherin, we must get you to safety, we must …" he was cut off by a tremendous wail from Karl, in his grandmother's arms. They all turned to look at him, but they saw that he was still sound asleep. When they all looked up again, Sepherin was no longer on the boat.

"WHAT HAVE YOU DONE?" Sepherin screamed at Kalabot.

"WHAT DID YOU SAY TO ME, OATH-BREAKER?"

Sepherin looked behind her, at the bodies on the ground, and then turned back to him.

"Make this right."

"The only thing that will make this right is when you swing from a rope!"

They both heard the child's voice from nearby, one of those unable to get away when the gunfire opened, but lucky enough not to be missed. "Did she call him *father*?"

Sepherin advanced towards the gate, her own hands in fists, her teeth clenched, her lips drawn back in a snarl, "You can make this right, *do it now!*"

"They have earned what was wrought, these …"

"They have earned nothing! It is YOU that have betrayed them!"

"I AM THE MANAGER OF ALL UMITIA!" he barked as the Guards from the river all came up behind them, weapons raised.

"YOU ARE BUT WHAT THE CLANSMEN ALLOW YOU TO BE!" she screamed back at him.

"Do you really believe that? DO ANY OF YOU REALLY BELIEVE THAT?"

Sepherin turned at the sound of more screams. She saw three people who had been tending to a wounded person had slumped over dead. As she watched, three more slumped to the ground, dead.

She spun back, marching towards the gates that were between them, "FATHER! STOP IT!"

"I AM THE MANGER, I WILL DO AS ..." he cut his words off as Sepherin was suddenly on the other side of the gates, standing right in front of him. The look of shock on his face was nothing compared to the shock on the faces of the Guards, who were all in a thorough state of confusion.

"If you won't make this right, then I will."

Sepherin took one more step forward, wrapped her long arms around Kalabot, and they disappeared into thin air.

Chapter 72

They appeared out of thin air, standing on a jagged surface. The uneven ground caused them to fall. Kalabot felt Sepherin's grip on him break. He saw her rolling away from him.

The heat was incredible.

They both started gasping and coughing. Kalabot looked around him: the sky was thick with smoke, and the light was orange from rivers of magma flowing all around him. Looking towards the greatest source of heat, he saw that he was standing only an arm's length from the edge of a volcano rim. The brilliant pit of boiling lava tossed and churned, threatening to spit fiery death on both of them.

Sepherin, coughing, got up on one knee, glaring at her progenitor.

In the back of the truck, Karl had imparted the nickel tour of what she could do as the child of the manager, with the powers she inherited. She only had time to gain a neophyte's understanding about moving through time and space. When she had grabbed Kalabot, she had desired to go back to the beginning, and that was where she had taken them through the mysterious mechanics of temporal causality. They were on the rim of the very volcano which was responsible for forming the ground that Kilkestand City would be built on, billions of years later.

"You — you need to die," he wheezed at her, then lapsed into a coughing fit of his own.

"So I have heard, old man," and she coughed some more.

"You will destroy Umitia," he said.

"I will — *free* — Umitia."

"No!" he wheezed hard, his lungs having a problem filtering breathable air from the magma's discharge of chemicals: carbon dioxide, sulphur dioxide, hydrogen sulfide, hydrogen chloride, hydrogen bromide. The pair of them would die if they remained there much longer.

Staggering dangerously close to the rim, trying to stay upright, Kalabot spit at her, "Stay here and die. Let the world be as it was."

"It will never be as it was," she coughed again, trying to pull herself to a standing position.

"Stay here and die, Sepherin. I will kill the Earther and then ..."

A strangled scream erupted from her labouring lungs as she launched herself at him. She grabbed him for the second time in as many minutes, holding him tightly. They flew off their feet, launched into the air by the power of her lunge, heading directly into the pit of boiling lava which promised an excruciating death.

They hit the ground hard and rolled to a stop in a grassy meadow, a fresh breeze cooling their skin, their noses filled with the sweet scent of blooming flowers, and the bright sun shining down on them.

Separating, they both lay there for a long time, breathing, coughing, and getting the toxins out of their lungs. Sepherin was the first to sit up; she looked around to make sure that Kalabot was still there. She crawled over to him, and saw that he was conscious and still breathing heavy of the fresh cool air.

Finally Kalabot sat up. He looked around for his wide-brim hat, but didn't see it. Then he remembered, he had lost it back at the rim of the volcano. He looked at Sepherin and asked, "When are we?"

"Later," was all she said. She stood and then held out a hand to him. He took it, and she helped him to his feet.

"Why do you hate me?" she asked, taking a couple steps back from him.

"I do not hate you, but you are ..."

"Inconvenient?"

Kalabot just looked at her. The momentary spell was broken as they both looked to the left, towards the roar of something vicious and hungry sounding beyond the tree line.

Kalabot turned back to his daughter, "You are an unfortunate mistake."

Sepherin had no love for Kalabot, and no real care for what he felt about her. But somewhere deep in the recesses of her psyche, a brief flare of pain was the response to his words.

"I am loved by my parents, by the ones who raised me. I don't think you could even understand the concept of that word: love."

Kalabot's thoughts inadvertently flashed to those of his wife, of her mute smile as she painted, of the look in her eyes when he came home to her, of the kiss of her sweet lips on the morning of the day she died. But try as he might, as he looked at Sepherin, knowing she was his, all he could feel was the grip of icy indifference.

"Do you know how you came about?" he asked with a sneer on his lips and a cruel, taunting tone in his voice.

Sepherin said nothing. She had heard supposition from Fitid, but not facts.

"Your entire house was to be dissolved, their charter revoked, and all cast out into the street. This was all because of your *father*, because of Michalz' greed."

Sepherin took a step closer to Kalabot, and he stepped back. He knew that look on her face; he had seen it in the mirror more than once.

Regardless of her physical presence, he pushed on, "And your *mother*, came to me, to plead for the House, to plead for her family's riches."

"That does not change the fact that I am here, the child of a Falwasz and a Shovitic, the child of your precious prophecy."

535

Kalabot laughed, tossing his head back, then spoke with a hideous smile on his face, "You are the child of a whore who couldn't keep her legs closed!"

With a roar of heartfelt rage, Sepherin charged him again, launching herself through the air and tackling him, bringing him to the rocky dusty ground.

The light had changed, it was colder.

He rolled away from her, glancing around at the small plateau in the mountains she had brought him to. He looked at the view of a small city, Kilkestand City, but from an earlier time than they had departed.

Kalabot looked at Sepherin, "The Mountains of Sestaland?"

She nodded.

"But I cannot move here, I cannot ..."

"I am not your, father. I am — more."

Kalabot had enough of this. He closed his eyes, knowing where he needed to return. But when he opened his eyeworms, she was still before him, and they were still on the plateau. He tried again, but nothing changed. This time she was smiling.

"You are doing this? You are preventing me from moving?"

Sepherin nodded, "It's something my son taught me, something that I inherited from you."

"Your — *son?*"

She nodded, her smile broadening.

Kalabot nodded once, running his hand through his dusty hair. It was his turn to smile, "If you inherited it from me, then the power you use ends with your death."

Kalabot reached into his jacket and pulled out his handgun. With one smooth motion he pointed and fired, but she wasn't there. Then he felt her arms around him from behind. Wrenching his arm back, she applied pressure in the right spot and started hammering the back of his forearm against her knee. With a spasm of pain, his fingers opened and the gun went flying out of reach.

Kalabot screamed with rage. He spun on her and pushed against her, but her long legs quickly moved her body out of the way, and she sent him tumbling forward. She followed through with a swift kick to his backside to send him sprawling.

Seething with anger and embarrassment, Kalabot turned around, not fully standing. He looked at her, looked at the gun on the ground and launched himself towards it. But Sepherin was faster. Her foot met his head, sending him sprawling again with a yelp of pain. She picked up the handgun before he reached it.

Kalabot looked up at her slowly, expecting the gun to be pointed at him. Instead, she held it up in the air and smiled, and then the gun simply wasn't in her hand any longer.

Kalabot pushed himself back against a rock, touched his head, and looked around for his hat, remembering again that he had lost it by the volcano.

"*Father*," Sepherin said with acid in her voice.

He looked up at her.

"Why must I die, father?"

Kalabot looked away from her, "Do not call me that."

"It is what you are."

"It does not matter what I am, child, you must die to restore order."

"If you had left me on Earth, there would be no disorder."

Kalabot had no response; he had already realized that himself, but too late to do anything about it. He stood, and faced the young woman who had become so much more trouble than he could ever have imagined. Had he simply gone back in time and

537

changed things on Earth, his earlier self would still have made the same mistakes which brought her here. Maybe. Perhaps he should have just gone there and killed her with his own hand. But had he done that ...

It was a temporal spider web of this doing that, and that resulting from this, which made his head spin. Killing her was the only way this madness would end, yet it wouldn't end, because the people in Kilkestand, outside the gates, were still dead. And they had all heard her call him, "Father." Kalabot had to smile with helplessness at the thought. Kill her or not, there would be a rope waiting for him as well.

"Why are you afraid of things changing for your people? Why does having the hybrid daughter of a Falwasz and a Shovitic scare you so much?"

"Because my people love this world, because I love this world. I do not want to leave it."

"But your people came here from somewhere else, and now it's merely time for your race of *gypsies* to move on to another world. Why does that scare you?"

"How do you know this?" Kalabot was shocked, but not totally surprised.

"I know many things, *Father*. I know that I am the child of the prophecy. I know that my arrival heralds the time your people must leave this world, and find a new world. I know that even though this is as it has been said, you and my mother are still to be put to death according to the Codex of Crimes."

"I do not want to ..." but his words failed him. Kalabot's shoulders slumped, and he sat down on a nearby rock. Once again, he lamented that Shovitics had no tear ducts, though it did not lessen his feelings.

"People know, *Father*."

He looked up at her.

"People know that I am the child of you and my mother. People know that I am an illegal cross-breed. They know that I am the hybrid that Alita Kiut spoke of."

Kalabot leapt to his feet at the mention of the old cleric's name, but then sat down again. Oddly, it didn't surprise him at all that she knew so much. It wasn't much of a stretch to figure out how she knew.

"Fitid, Valeni, they know? They have spoken with you about this?"

"Yes. Valeni was planning on arguing at my trial."

Kalabot looked up at her with his hands folded on his knees, there was no longer any malice on his face.

"He is going to argue that you are the child of the prophecy, and therefore, you deserve to live?"

She nodded, sitting on a rock near him.

"And therefore, the prophecy is fulfilled and the Shovitics must once again find a new home."

She nodded.

Kalabot looked up at her, and then held out his hand. She just looked at him, not taking it. He finally lowered his arm.

"There is one flaw with that," Kalabot said quietly.

Sepherin was on guard, she hadn't expected him to be able to argue with prophecy, "And what would the flaw be?"

"It is generally agreed that the appearance of the child of the prophecy means that the child will assume control of Umitia, while the Shovitics abandon it for a new home."

"As I understand it, yes."

Kalabot stood, slowly, and then turned to face her. "But none of this will take place if the child does not survive long enough to take power."

Kalabot launched himself at her yet again and bowled her over the rock. Tumbling to the ground beside her, Kalabot rolled over and grabbed a fist-sized stone. He spun around to strike, but Sepherin was already moving. She lashed out with her foot and connected with his ribs. She heard him scream as she heard the crunch of bones and saw him go down hard.

As he held his ribs and scuttled to the side, to get some room away from her, he yelled at her, "AND WHAT ABOUT THE SECOND PROPHECY?"

Sepherin had moved to advance on him, but stopped with his words. Fitid had said nothing about a second prophecy.

"There was a second prophecy, one that has been handed down from manager to manager, and never shared with anyone else."

"What is it?" she asked, with both anger and hesitation in her voice.

Kalabot pushed himself up, holding his side and sat down on a boulder again. She didn't see the rock concealed in his hand, held against his side. He smiled, and chugged a laugh, "I'm sure you're not going to enjoy hearing it."

She had stopped her advance, she folded her arms in front of her, but ready to move in case this was a ruse. "Go ahead, tell me."

Kalabot spit out a jagged tooth, and laughed as he lifted his old face to look at her, spit and blood dribbling down his chin. "The second prophecy is that the child born of Falwasz and Shovitic union will bear a son who will grow to conquer a galaxy, but …"

"Then why do you think this will make any difference, Kalabot? That my son will be a great leader who …"

Kalabot wasn't done, he raised his voice over hers, "… *but in so doing* will destroy Umitia forever!"

The silence was palpable. Kalabot stared at Sepherin. Sepherin stared back at Kalabot, chewing on the corner of her lip.

"You lie," Sepherin finally said as she moved towards him again.

No one had heard a splash when Sepherin disappeared, but the patrol boat did a few circles in the river, then started heading in its original direction.

When Sepherin disappeared, Michalz went right to Cassie, "Where has she gone?"

"Why're you asking me? I don't know!"

"Michalz," Alabast began tentatively, "I have seen Kalabot do that very thing, disappear into thin air."

"Yes," Kimla spoke up, "he has this ability. If she is his daughter, then perhaps the ability is within her as well."

The boat had slowly moved up the river, and around the great bend that would take them parallel to the shoreline of the Palace grounds. Talin slowed the craft and hugged the far shore, staying to as much shadow as he could in the twilight. As the Palace grounds came into view, his head whipped around at the sound of Alabast Tekindottir's scream.

She had been holding her grandson, but was now just holding an empty blanket. The child had been there one moment, and less than a heartbeat later, it wasn't.

Ignoring the pain in his side, Kalabot charged her again, screaming with rage. Anticipating her move, as she jumped out of his way, he turned and threw the rock right at her head. Sepherin went down hard, not unconscious, but dazed and bloodied.

Kalabot felt a change. He knew that she was no longer blocking him, but he could not leave this job half done. He had to finish this once and for all, daughter or not, too much rode on this for him to be maudlin about a child he had never raised.

As he approached, Sepherin started to get to her feet, but he lashed out and kicked her in the stomach as hard as he could. She screamed and flopped over onto her back. She wailed with the pain of his foot, and the jagged rock that she had landed on. Kalabot grabbed another stone and turned towards her as he raised it over his head, intent on dealing a lethal blow.

His eyeworms went wide and his mouth flew open in surprise.

A tall, handsome young man stood over Sepherin. He had blond hair, his naked body rippled with muscles, and his eyeworms undulated peacefully.

"Put the rock down, Grandfather."

Kalabot stared at him, frozen by the lad's words and the serene smile on his face.

The young man took a step towards Kalabot and one hand lashed out towards the side of Kalabot's head. But instead of attacking him, the young man gently held the old man's face.

Kalabot slowly lowered his arms; the rock that was in his hands wasn't in them anymore. He looked down and saw that Sepherin was still writhing in pain, but was facing away from him, trying to get to her feet.

The young man said nothing; he just looked at Kalabot, a Mona Lisa smile on his face, a gentleness and warmth in his touch. Kalabot's grandson leaned forward lightly kissed the old man on the cheek. Looking over his shoulder at his mother, the vision of an older Karl turned back to his grandfather, winked, and then he wasn't there anymore.

Sepherin regained her feet and backed away from Kalabot. She stumbled and for some unknown reason, Kalabot rushed forward to catch her. She screamed as she hit the ground and back pedaled away from him. She knew that she was in too much pain to focus, to use any of the rudimentary instruction her infant son had given her.

But Kalabot didn't attack. Instead, he sunk to his knees and sobbed. He loosened his tie, and then took it off. He unbuttoned the collar of his shirt and then sat there, hands slumped in his lap, as he sobbed without the ability to make tears.

With the pain in her stomach abating, and her breathing back under control, Sepherin managed to sit up.

"Why have you not killed me?" she asked, her voice husky with the tears and the throb and ache in her back.

They both heard the gurgle and splutter of an infant. They both looked towards the edge of the plateau. They both saw Karl, wrapped in his blanket, in the arms of an old man wrapped only in a blanket of his own. The man smiled at them and held the child up for them to see. Then the child was gone, and the man folded his hands in front of him and continued to smile.

"Forgive me, Daughter," Kalabot said, barely more than a whisper.

Sepherin rolled around the taste of blood in her mouth, and spat it out onto the ground. "Never," was all she said.

Kalabot nodded.

"You still need to make things right. The massacre at the gates — that cannot be allowed to have happened, not over me."

Kalabot allowed himself a small smile that she had nailed the temporal grammar correctly.

"I can do this, but so can you. I can instruct you if you would allow me."

She thought about it for a moment. "No, *you* need to do this."

He sighed and pushed himself up to a standing position. "Very well, I shall. In moving us through time, you have created a paradox, however. Once I return, as soon as my earlier self becomes aware of me, I shall cease to exist. When your earlier self becomes aware of you, you shall cease to exist."

Sepherin nodded.

"And that means you shall never hold your child again."

Sepherin looked up at him, wondering how he could be so acquiescent and cruel at the same time. She sighed heavily with the realization that it was just his nature.

"And my earlier self will never have suffered the horror of seeing the carnage you wrought."

Kalabot nodded to her, "Touché."

He started to close his eyeworms, but opened them again as she called his name.

Looking at him, no emotion on her face, she told him, "The clan Shovitic has a generation to find a new home, and then depart this world."

Kalabot hesitated only a moment; his shoulders slumped a bit more and then he nodded.

"And," she continued, "any Shovitic who wishes to remain on Umitia may, but as equals, not as controllers or rulers."

"That's very generous of you — Daughter."

"I have found many good hearts in your clan, in your race."

Kalabot nodded, "Anything else?"

"Yes, when I assume control, I will strike all laws from the Codex of Crimes that are isolationist to the clansmen."

Kalabot sighed, "That would be a mistake."

"Then let it be a mistake that clansmen make, and learn from, rather than have it decreed like we are children unable to care for ourselves."

"Very well, Daughter, is there anything else, or can I go and right my wrongs now?" The edge of sarcasm was obvious.

"Yes, one more thing. Effective this very day, the Imperite program is terminated."

Without saying anything else, Kalabot closed his eyes and disappeared. Sepherin stood up and looked around. She saw the older man dressed only in a blanket, and nodded to him once. Then she wasn't standing there anymore.

Wrapping the blanket tighter around him, Alita Kiut took small, thoughtful steps as he went back to his cave. His mind was preoccupied contemplating the vision and the words of prophecy that he had just been given.

Chapter 73

"Wait," Sepherin-the-earlier said. She pulled the blanket from over Karl's face and held him for her parents to see.

Alabast looked at him, reached out to touch his forehead, and cried harder.

Michalsz, standing beside his wife, also looked closely at the child. But much to Sepherin's surprise, he smiled, leaned forward, and kissed the child on the cheek. Looking up at his daughter, Michalz asked, "The child, he is healthy?"

She nodded, confused.

"And his name, dear?" her mother asked with a jagged voice.

"Karl. I'll explain later," Sepherin sounded as confused as she felt, looking from her mother to her father.

Michalz looked up at Sepherin and smiled the smile she had feared she would never see again. "My child — my heart, it is I who you must forgive, not your mother."

Cobus yelled at them, "Come! We must go!"

At that moment, they heard a commotion in the restaurant. The owner flew out the back door, "Guards have entered the restaurant, *they are searching!*"

Alabast, Michalz, and Sepherin ran towards the jetty and onto the boat. As the boat pulled away, Sepherin quickly introduced Cassie. Neither of her parents had anything to say about how different she looked. But they made just as much of a fuss over little Rick as they were making over Karl.

Alabast glanced at her daughter and noticed Sepherin's face seemed frozen, that she was looking beyond them, into a distance they would not be able to see. By the time the boat had gone less than a hundred of its own lengths, Sepherin stepped into the wheelhouse.

"Turn the boat around."

Talin looked over his shoulder at her, "What? No. We are heading ..."

"Turn the boat around, *now!* We are not going anywhere except to the Palace."

Kimla stepped into the small wheelhouse, "Sepherin, it is not safe there. Kalabot will be beside himself with rage. He'll kill you on sight."

"No," Sepherin said quietly. She looked down at Karl and the baby was looking right back at her. Sepherin looked up at Kimla and smiled, "Things have changed."

The Shovitic brother and sister, Talin and Kimla, stood there looking at each other, saying nothing.

Sepherin-the-earlier looked deep into Kimla's eyes, "Am I not the child of the prophecy?"

"Fine," Talin muttered behind her. He slowed the engine and turned the boat around, heading back up the river, towards the jetty near the Palace gates.

Kalabot-the-earlier stood up, a little unsteady, but rapidly composing himself. He looked at the gates haphazardly held in place, and the Guards facing the crowd.

Shaking off the medic, he strode forward to the line of Guards and pushed one aside. Kalabot stared out at the crowd that was yelling and jeering. They were calling, "Shame", "Free the Imperite", "Leave her alone", and a few less-than-pleasant phrases. He turned on the Imperite Guard in charge of the gate detail and demanded to know where the truck had gone and why it hadn't been followed.

The man told Kalabot, "The crowd will not allow us to follow them. We are waiting for reinforcements."

Both of them turned towards the river and saw the dozens of Guards near the water were finally moving towards the front gates. Kalabot turned back to the crowd. A line of drool started descending from his lower lip, his breath was coming heavier, and his fists were clenched so tight he felt a knuckle pop, his eyeworms were gesticulating like they were caught in a whirlwind.

"Kill them," he turned to the line of Guards. "Open fire and kill them all."

"NO!" a shockingly familiar sounding voice shouted from behind the Guards arriving from the lake edge. Kalabot knew the voice, it was his own. The Guards who had been rushing towards the gate all stopped, the Guards gathered behind Kalabot-the-earlier and were looking towards the voice, towards him and towards the voice again. Then the crowd of Guards all raised their weapons, but they weren't sure where to point them.

Slightly shorter than the younger guardsmen, Kalabot-the-earlier could not see right away, but he had a sickening feeling in his stomach.

"Put down your weapons!" the voice said, "The child of the great prophecy has arrived. Put down your weapons, and know that our time has come."

Kalabot-the-earlier growled and pushed through the guardsmen blocking his view. He stopped short as he came face to face with — himself, and Sepherin Tekin.

"What is ..." he started, but stopped. He already knew as he saw the two of them standing together. As soon as his eyes locked with Kalabot-the-later, the bedraggled version of himself flickered twice and then disappeared, leaving Sepherin Tekin standing on her own.

549

There were smears of blood on her forehead and face. Her clothes were torn, her arms and legs covered in scrapes, bruises, and dirt; there was a large blood stain on her back from the jagged rock she landed on. Sepherin-the-later smiled at Kalabot. "Father," she said, "it is done."

The guardsmen pointing their weapons at Sepherin-the-later were slowly lowering them as they looked towards Kalabot-the-earlier for instructions.

Kalabot and Sepherin-the-later stood there looking at each other, versions out of time, and out of synch, causing a paradox soon to be resolved.

"Lower your weapons, everyone, it is over." Kalabot said, looking around as he did so. He could see that the masses of people outside the gate were slowly pressing forward, to see what was going on.

Kalabot turned back to Sepherin-the-later, "So, what arrangement did you come to?"

Sepherin told him, as she had told the later version of him.

The Guards, hearing what was said, realizing what it all meant, all got down on one knee and waited for her first orders. Before she could speak, however, there was a gasp from the crowd. Sepherin-the-later and Kalabot, along with the Guards, turned to look at the gate, still standing upright. They watched the crowd part.

Sepherin-the-earlier strode up to the gate.

Everyone looked back at the Sepherin who had arrived with the second Kalabot, but she was no longer there.

Epilogue

The cabal quickly organized a small group of advisors, to assist Sepherin with her new mantle of leadership. She arrived at the Palace the morning after her return to Umitia, and the official ceremony took place to install her as the Manager of Umitia.

Her first order of business was to announce to the world that the Imperite program was terminated. The roar of approval and cheering could be heard for many leagues. She tasked Kimla Pilu with the job of assembling a team to contact all off-world Imperites to see if they wanted to return home. It was to be a question, not an order. Some did, but many did not. Those who did not return had all been gone a long time. They had built lives for themselves, lives which included family and children — and quite often, grand-children.

The Shovitics were ordered to maintain their presence in the galaxy as peacekeepers. Those assigned to off-world activities were given the option to remain in place, or return home to Umitia. Every single one of them chose to remain in place, except for Fitid.

On Cassie's behalf, Sepherin had a team of Imperite Guards, sorry, they were renamed *Shovitic Guards*. She had a team of them contact Cassie's parents to let them know she was alive and well, and that they were the grandparents of a handsome young boy with a healthy set of lungs.

Cassie stayed on Umitia for sixty more days because Sepherin asked her to. She was the normalcy and sanity that Sepherin desperately needed over the coming ten-sleeps, while she grappled with just what she had truly bitten off in becoming the Manager.

One of the first things Sepherin did, however, was change her title to Chief Administrator. The Manager was a title which would forever be associated with a Shovitic, not a Falwasz.

When it came time for Cassie to return home, Sepherin simply wrapped her and little Rick in her arms, and then moved them all through time and space.

This wasn't the end of their friendship, though. Many times in the coming years, Sepherin would spend a few days on Earth with Cassie, or bring Cassie and her family to Umitia for vacation. Their friendship had been tested by a forge no other friendship had ever been subjected to, and it came out all that much stronger because of it.

Roguk came to terms with the appearance of his son, but never became as close to him as he would have liked. It wasn't because of anything to do with the boy's appearance; it was because he had a family of his own to attend to. Eleniak gave birth, a girl, not that long after Sepherin returned home. In the following years she gave birth to seven more children for Roguk, all girls.

Roguk and Sepherin remained friendly, but there was a chasm between them which would never again be bridged. That suited Sepherin just fine. There was still a part of her that resented Roguk, and truth be told, herself as well, for their betrayal of his vows to Eleniak.

For Alabast and Michalz, it would be nice to say that life

returned to normal, but it didn't. Michalz found himself getting involved in many political matters and much to everyone's surprise, handling himself superbly.

When free elections were finally held to populate the new governing council that Sepherin wanted formed, he was elected by default, as no one in Kilkestard City would stand against him.

As the mother of the Chief Administrator, and the mother of the child of the prophecy, Alabast found herself busy entertaining dignitaries and such. She was eventually brought into the Palace, along with Eleniak, to convert the interior from a utilitarian office space, to a truly glamorous and enchanting palace, like in the story books of Earth. All of the windows that had been bricked over centuries ago were opened and replaced with glass. The gardens continued to flourish under Cobus' skillful ministrations. The Palace became a place for the people to gather during celebrations and holidays, without a single guardsman in sight.

For ten more years Cobus Scheepers remained the master gardener at the Palace, the spaceport, and the training academy. His project to make beautiful plants available to the people of Umitia was completed and became so popular, two more of the distribution centres were built and he was in charge of all of them.

After the changes Sepherin made to the Codex of Crimes, the first change of which was to make cross-clan breeding legal, it became known he was Sepherin's blood-kin. This raised his prestige even more and furthered his career as a garden consultant and horticulturalist.

As the end of his days came to a close, his final breaths were drawn with all whom he loved at his side. His smile on that day was of such peacefulness and contentment, that it became known as *The Scheepers' Grin*.

On the night of the return, Fitid found out his beloved Corla had been killed by Kalabot. His grief was incredible and those close to him feared he would never be consoled. By edict, all Imperite Guards had been forgiven for all deaths and other crimes committed on the night of her return. To extend Fitid's grief, this included Kalabot as he was, technically, an Imperite Guard.

Within a ten-sleep, Fitid had resigned from the new Shovitic Guards and then disappeared. He was gone for a full season before he showed up again. He had gone to the mountains of Sestaland, and spent the season in the old habitat of Alita Kiut. The Shovitic who returned was finally at peace.

Fitid Havinta soon found himself on the governing council as the second Shovitic with a seat. His clarity in purpose for all of Umitia, as well as his desire for the Shovitics to be absorbed by the new society rather than standing apart from it, served them all quite well. With his efforts and those of the council, old wounds were healed. For the Shovitics who remained after a new home was found for those who departed, they truly became clansmen of Umitia.

Following her return, Sepherin and her parents spent time talking about many things. She came to understand why what had happened, happened, and was able to let go of her own thoughts on the matter, reuniting properly with her mother. After Sepherin gave her forgiveness, the first thing the two women did was make briska cookies for Karl and Rick, with Cassie joining them and learning to cook her first alien dish.

The child of the prophecy found herself in multiple roles. First and foremost, Sepherin was mother to a healthy, inquisitive, and bubbly little boy. He never communicated with her again in the way that he had while he was in her belly. She found it odd, but never questioned it. Nor did she ever get an explanation for his appearance as a young man in the Sestaland Mountains.

As the Chief Administrator of the planet, she became grateful for the advisors the cabal had assembled. They were serious, intelligent, and well-spoken men. She had to put her foot down a few times, but they all played nicely together — for the most part.

Sepherin had an endless stream of potential suitors trying to get her attention, but she wanted none of it. She was just too busy and too tired to "court" or "spend time" with someone. Aside from that, she found, quite to her own surprise, that when her mind did drift to such things, there was only one person she could think about — which surprised her more than anyone — and it wasn't Roguk.

A season after returning to Umitia, she began allowing herself to grow closer to him, getting to know him better, allowing him to know her better. That love blossomed between them was a surprise to both of them, as it was to all who knew.

A lunar cycle before Karl turned five seasons old, Sepherin and Fitid Havinta were wed in a private ceremony at the cottage on Walkamus Lake. In the tradition of their world, she became known as Sepherin Havintadottir and in a display of Umitian pride, her Shovitic husband took the traditional last name of Havintason.

Twenty years after her return to Umitia, Kalabot found the Shovitics a new home. But not all of them went to it. Only 40% of the clan Shovitic chose to follow the destiny of the prophecy, the rest remained. However, they remained under the proviso that they were no longer a military force. They all were required to take up trades just like all of the other clansmen of Umitia.

By this time Kimla had married, and had three children of her own. While part of her did want to see what the new Shovitic life was going to be like, she was happy to remain on Umitia for the rest of her days. Raising her children, and then enjoying her grandchildren, filled her heart enough to make the curiosity a mere shadow to the joy that filled her life.

Kimla, her Hobonol husband Pevik, and their children were often guests of Sepherin and Fitid. They became lifelong friends.

Kalabot kept to himself after being relieved of his position as the one responsible for Umitia. Such solitude was nothing new for him. He took up residence at the training facility, and from there he managed the efforts of the Shovitic Guard to keep peace in the galaxy, where they were able to. Sepherin had placed him in charge of the newly formed Shovitic Guard, with the mandate that until they found a new world to inhabit, they would supply and train on Umitia, but never again police the planet.

The old Shovitic was unhappy about the end of the Imperite program; its necessity was something he truly believed in. However, it was out of his hands.

He spent a lot of time going off world with his troops, something the Watch Commanders of the many frigates came to dread. However, he did this because he was singularly responsible for finding the Shovitics a new home, and this he eventually did. By keeping up his contacts, continuing to barter information, adding to his vast storehouse of tidbits which could mean something, he was able to trade some of this for consideration to be allowed to establish a colony on a planet that was — austere — and nothing like Umitia.

Mars.

Don't laugh. It's because of the Shovitic interest and persistent efforts that five hundred years later, Mars came to have a breathable atmosphere.

Karl was a child just like every other child. Skinned knees, snotty nose, scolded for taking cookies before mealtime, crying that it was too early for bed, making his mother worry sick over his teenage antics — he was normal in every way.

One of his passions growing up was first astronomy and then xenosociology, when he had time between all the girls who always seemed to be trying to catch his eyeworms attention. His Shovitic features and full head of thick blond hair made him mysterious, and the girls couldn't get enough of him.

He did, however, seem to have an unnatural predilection for anything to do with Barnard's galaxy, the second of the three known inhabited galaxies. His mother grew increasingly worried as he took more and more interest in it.

Three days before Karl's fifteenth birthday, Sepherin send Fitid on a short trip to the other side of the planet, and then invited Kalabot to the house.

Father and daughter then sat with Karl and had a long talk with him about who they were, who the managers were, and the prophecies of Alita Kiut. Specifically, they told him about the second prophecy.

The next day Karl gave his telescope and star charts to a friend, and never mentioned Barnard's galaxy, or any other galaxy, ever again. Instead, he focused his interest on economics and politics. By the time Karl was thirty seasons old, he had replaced his mother as the Chief Administrator of Umitia, and they all lived happily ever after.

Mostly ...

~ ~ ~ The End ~ ~ ~

Cultural References

Samadhi - In the context used, it refers to a commercial perfume powder. I have a jar of this, have had it for years, and use it when I need to relax. Place a few grains on the back of your hand, rub the backs of your hands together, then rub the back of your hands on your face and chin. So very relaxing!

www.sensitiveplanet.com/scent-of-samadhi/

"You aren't being thrown into a sarlacc pit …" - A nod to my beloved *Star Wars, Return of the Jedi*.

"eggs and backey" - This quote, popularized in the movie *Kill Bill, Vol. 2*, was actually, "Wakey, waken, eggs and bakey." It originally comes from an old folk-song.

"… then three shakes of a lamb's tail later, she wasn't." - A *shake* is an informal unit of time equal to 10 nanoseconds (10 billionths of a second). It is used in nuclear physics. This is the average length of time that passes between two fission events in a nuclear chain reaction. I first encountered the expression "three shakes of a lamb's tail" in the Tom Clancy novel *The Sum of All Fears*.

"… with too much rouge and a Dolly Parton wig." - This is a mashup from two different lines in the song *Trashy Women*, by Confederate Railroad. I *love* this band.

"I think I need to make an appointment with Doctor Cottle" - A nod to *Battlestar Galactica*, the rebooted version. Sherman Cottle was the name of the character who was the Chief Medical

559

Officer onboard the battlestar.

"... Carlota had seen enough odd things to know that there were more things in heaven and Earth, than are dreamt of." - A modification of Shakespeare's lines:

There are more things in heaven and earth, Horatio,
Than are dreamt of in your philosophy.'
-*Hamlet (1.5.167-8), Hamlet to Horatio*

"Cassie was wide eyed, no longer scared or worried. This was turning out better than Days of our Lives." - I admit it, at one time in my life I was a soap opera junkie, and the one I loved most was DOOL. I mean really, is there anything funnier than Drake Hogestyn as a tough guy? Did you ever see him in *Seven Brides for Seven Brothers* (starring with Richard Dean Anderson)? Hogestyn is the brother that always wears the red puffy vest.

The taxonomy of Earthers and Shovitics - In one of the chapters of this book I digressed into a bit of taxonomy concerning the Humanesh and the Shovitics. I gave the Humanesh taxonomy, starting with 'class' as *Mammalia -> Primates -> Hominidae -> Homo -> sapiens*. This taxonomy is correct. The taxonomy I gave for the Shovitics is *Mammalia -> Creodonta -> Oxyaena -> Homo -> sapiens*. I made up part of this taxonomy. While *Mammalia -> Creodonta -> Oxyaena* is a valid taxonomical tree, the *Oxyaena* are extinct carnivorous mammals, superficially cat or wolverine-like. There is no genus *Homo* in the *Oxyaena* family. I made that up, too. Welcome to my world ☺

Other Worlds Referenced

Pi Mensae - A sun-like planet almost 60 light years from Earth. It has an Earth-type rock, *Pi Mensae b (HD 39091)*, orbiting in the habitable zone. However, a gas giant more than ten times the size of Jupiter, also orbits the planet. Because of the gas giants erratic orbit, it's highly unlikely that *Pi Mensae b* would be habitable.

www.solstation.com/stars2/pimensae.htm

Beta Hydri - It is an orange-yellow main sequence star (the same type as our own sun) that is only slightly larger than our own sun. It is 24.4 light years distant, and was one of the top 100 target stars for NASA's Terrestrial Planet Finder before the project was cancelled. For more information on Beta Hydri, visit :

www.solstation.com/stars/bethydri.htm

Umitia - This planet is a product of the author's imagination. As a point of reference for the planet, and its sun, the author chose HD 133600. This star is a solar twin, possessing a mass within 3% of our own sun. It resides in the constellation Virgo, and is 100 light years from Earth. There is limited information on this star, what I have comes from Wikipedia and Centauri Dreams:

www.centauri-dreams.org/?p=1571

en.wikipedia.org/wiki/HD_133600

Ousoon - This is a fictional star and a fictional race of Humanesh that were first mentioned in *On Mars: Pathfinder*, Volume 1 of *The Mike Lane Stories*. The Ousoon are a legalistic race, the galaxy's lawyers, as some call them. Their idea of haute cuisine is vegetables steamed to mush, with dried mealworms on top of them. *Blech!*

www.on-mars.ca

Jim Melanson

Poet, programmer, procrastinator, sci-fi geek, coffee snob, actor, writer.

A devoted Christian, Jim is a quiet and thoughtful man who tends to think deeply, and act slowly. Much of this inner reflection and self-assessment shows up in his writing. "Capturing what truly motivates us," is how Jim describes his approach to both fiction and non-fiction. This author has a direct, and sometimes *in-your-face*, way of writing. He tries to always use conversational language; and as one test reader of his first novel put it, "made the complexities of space flight seem almost understandable."

Jim read his first novel by Laura Ingalls Wilder at the age of eight, and this began his love affair with the written word. Jim's first foray into personal writing, as a child, was poetry. These and other poetic scribblings provided the content for his first book, *I Apologize for Nothing*, published in April 2014.

Life, a child, a career with the Police Service, and a part-time business authoring software all got in the way of pursuing his desire to write. In his 40's, Jim decided to turn his hand back to writing, mainly on topics surrounding self-development, spirituality, and Reiki. However, none of these really satisfied that craving for creativity. In 2013, Jim decided to pursue his creative yearnings, and he began writing for pleasure. Drawing on a solid work ethic from his experience authoring technical manuals and writing business proposals, Jim found writing for himself to be liberating and enjoyable. While working on his first fiction novel, he kept getting sidetracked by other ideas. He dusted off an old stage play he had written and published it under the title, *Mama's Slippers*, with the hopes of attracting production interest. He currently continues work on science fiction projects, including short stories and flash stories. You'll find many of these on Wattpad (wattpad.com/user/torontojim).

Originally hailing from the East Coast, Jim now lives just outside Cobourg, ON.

If you enjoyed this book, it would help me greatly if you posted a quick review. Just a few words, sharing your thoughts. Thank you!

www.jimmelanson.ca/write_a_review.shtml

www.ingramcontent.com/pod-product-compliance
Lightning Source LLC
Chambersburg PA
CBHW061505020726
47502CB00006B/1936